ISLAND OF FOG BOOK 4

Lake
of Spirits

D1513318

Lake of Spirits
by Keith Robinson

Printed in the United States of America
Published by Unearthly Tales on August 2011

Cover design by Keith Robinson

Visit https://www.unearthlytales.com

ISLAND OF FOG BOOK 4

Lake of Spirits

a novel by
KEITH ROBINSON

Meet the Shapeshifters

In this story there are nine twelve-year-old children, each able to transform into a creature of myth and legend . . .

Hal Franklin *(dragon)*—After a frightening first transformation, Hal now flies and breathes fire like other dragons. He can even belch flames while in human form, a talent he's just beginning to find useful.

Robbie Strickland *(ogre)*—At three times his normal height, and with long, powerful arms, Robbie is a mass of shaggy hair and muscle.

Abigail Porter *(faerie)*—She regularly sprouts insect-like wings and can shrink to the size of a real faerie, a mere six inches tall. Abigail owns a fascinating glass ball, a gift from her faerie kinfolk.

Dewey Morgan *(centaur)*—Although impressive in his half-equine form, this small, shy boy is ashamed of his roots after discovering what the centaur khan had done to humankind many years ago.

Lauren Hunter *(harpy)*—With enormous owl-like wings, yellow eyes, and powerful talons for feet, this beautiful white-feathered human-creature soars and swoops like a bird of prey.

Fenton Bridges *(rare lizard monster)*—Able to spit an endless stream of water that turns to glue, Fenton is black and reptilian with an impossibly long tail. Tentatively dubbed an 'ouroboros' by Miss Simone.

Darcy O'Tanner *(dryad)*—As a wood nymph, she has the ability to blend into the background like a chameleon, allowing her to sneak around unseen.

Emily Stanton *(naga)*—Part human, part serpent, Emily retains her arms while on land but has no use for them underwater.

Thomas Patten *(manticore)*—The redheaded boy spent six years in the form of a vicious, red-furred, blue-eyed lion creature with a scorpion's tail. Now he's struggling to adjust to human life.

There are other shapeshifters, including Miss Simone, the resident mermaid and esteemed leader of the village; her brother, Felipe, who resides in his dragon form within the Labyrinth of Fire; Orson, a winged horse who recently discovered how to fly; and many more . . .

Prologue

Simone stepped outside, banged the door shut behind her, and paused in the sweltering heat, grateful for her sleeveless dress. Part of her longed to return to the depths of the cool, dark cottage . . . but she was too excited and intrigued by the words of the messenger boy who'd stopped by minutes before: "Emergency at the lab. Old Bart needs you."

Her parents had been going on at her lately, telling her she needed to get out more, meet people, get a job—anything besides lurking in her room poring over dusty scientific journals. "You're *seventeen* now," her mom nagged constantly. "Old enough to earn a living. You might be an important shapeshifter, young lady, but you still have to pull your weight around here." And her dad always chimed in with, "Yeah. Time you got your nose out of those old books."

Simone joined the throng of slow-moving villagers that packed the dusty streets, weaving around them as fast as she could. It was even busier once she got around the corner, and it was hard to avoid being sucked into conversation. She darted past the market stalls with barely a nod and smile to dozens of familiar faces.

Her light, knee-length dress snagged on the handle of a wheelbarrow and brought her up short. As she pulled free, a couple of greasy-haired young men by the fruit stall leered openly at her. Flustered, she averted her gaze and hurried away, grimacing at the wolf whistle that followed.

Her mom often remarked that "a young woman of such beauty" had the world at her fingertips. Practically any man would give her a job if she asked; she tended to attract customers so was good for business even if she did nothing but sweep the floor. But Simone had only one career in mind, and that was working with Old Bart and his team of doctors and professors.

The science laboratory stood at the edge of the village. Carter's population was nearly four hundred strong, but the council that ran the place—a small group of bored men and women—still couldn't bring themselves to agree that the decrepit science lab was too close to noise and prying eyes, not to mention being too small. Things might be different if only Old Bart would show up at a meeting once in a while;

as the most senior and respected member, he could wield considerable clout if he wanted. But he despised politics.

Simone clicked her tongue with annoyance as she spotted a group of kids peering through a smeared side window, no doubt hoping for rare glimpses of new-fangled technology or 'ghastly' experiments. She strode past them, burst in through the front door, and nearly bumped into Dr. Kessler in the hallway.

She was a small, stern woman with brass-rimmed spectacles. "Young lady," she said with a frown, "one of these days you're going to knock me flying."

"Sorry," Simone said. She wiped her forehead with the back of her hand. "Professor Bart wanted to see me?"

Dr. Kessler nodded, looking troubled. She took Simone by the elbow and led her along the narrow hall, ignoring several doors that opened into cluttered laboratories. "You know," the doctor said softly, "the old codger doesn't have much time left."

Simone stopped dead, her mouth dropping open. "What?"

"He's been talking about it lately, saying he's feeling old, not got his wits about him anymore. He's tired, Simone, and I think he knows that he needs to pass the reins on to someone else."

More than a little shocked, Simone struggled for words.

"But that's not why you're here," Dr. Kessler said, urging Simone onward. "I'm just saying, that's all; warning you in case he starts moping." They came to a closed door at the end of the hall. "He's in here. Go on in."

Simone had been in this room many times. None of the doors in the science building were marked—something that irked her—but she knew this to be where a select few worked on the Shapeshifter Program. Being a shapeshifter herself, Simone had special privileges.

She turned the doorknob and pushed the door open. Dr. Kessler faded from her periphery as she moved into the dark, musty room. Professor Bartholomew, or Old Bart as he was known around the village, was standing by a sturdy oak bench against the far wall opposite the windows. On the bench stood a large glass tank about six feet long and three feet high. The professor's tall, lanky frame was hunched over as he peered through the glass into the murky water.

"You wanted me?" Simone said respectfully.

Professor Bart glanced over his shoulder and waved her closer. As usual he skipped any preamble. "Come and meet the new Jolie."

Simone drew in a sharp breath. "The *new* Jolie?"

She moved closer, absently noting how the tables in the cluttered room had barely an inch of space remaining on their surfaces. There were glass phials, books, papers, jars and boxes, numerous contraptions with clamps and rods and trailing wires, glowing energy rocks . . . and most of it covered with dust that blew in off the street whenever the windows were open.

Simone's eyes widened as she approached the glass tank. Inside was an infant humanoid figure with black, shiny eyes and luminescent scaly skin. Instead of legs, the one-year-old baby had a slender fishtail. She seemed happy enough, drifting from one end of the tank to the other, pressing her tiny fingers to the glass as she turned.

Even though Simone had never seen Jolie in this form before, the round face, button nose, and curly black hair were instantly recognizable. "Jolie," she mumbled, leaning closer. "So . . . she shifted, then."

"As we feared," Professor Bart said softly. He looked even more gaunt than normal, and his completely bald head seemed to have developed a few more liver spots in the last week. "The treatment failed."

He jerked a thumb over his shoulder, and Simone knew he was indicating a special adjacent room that, when the door was sealed and the machines working, reduced the amount of oxygen in the air. It was just a subtle difference, hardly noticeable, and nurses and nannies had been in and out of that room for the past year without any problems. But the reduced oxygen was important for Jolie.

"This is what I get for trying to outsmart nature," the professor mumbled.

"But you were doing so *well*," Simone assured him. "Normally they change within a month or two after birth. What you did was *working*."

"It wasn't enough." The professor turned to her and a smile wrinkled his face. "Shapeshifters have always been bred on the Other Side, in the alternate world with its lower concentration of oxygen. Centuries ago it was all witch doctors, barbaric ceremonies, mumbo-jumbo incantations, and a heap of good luck thrown in. There were far more failures than successes. I've made it my life's work to understand and refine the procedure, but the key factor in all this continues to elude me. How old are you now, Simone?"

"Seventeen."

The professor had been about to continue, but instead did a double take. His eyebrows shot up as he rounded on her. "Goodness me! Are you really? I thought you were just fifteen."

"I was," Simone said, smiling, "two years ago."

"And your twin?"

Simone frowned, sure that he was jesting. But he had returned his gaze to the tank and seemed perfectly serious. "He's seventeen, too," she confirmed. "We're all seventeen now, Professor. We've grown up."

"Time flies," the professor said, nodding sagely. "Well, anyway, how old were you when you first changed?"

"Eight."

"And your friends?"

"Eight," she said again.

The professor nodded. "Ten of you, Simone, born and raised in a secure location—well, twelve of you, actually, but ten that made it through the program." He scowled and waved his hand as if impatient with himself for digressing. "My point is, every one of you changed on schedule at age eight. It's the way of things, the way it's always been. But it's so blasted *inconvenient* raising shapeshifters in the other world, with all that running back and forth through portals, and the risk of discovery. So we can either go live high on a mountain where the air is thinner, or install a hypoxicator as I did in the room next door." He shook his head and gestured at the creature in the tank. "But neither alternative works. I'm beginning to suspect that thinner oxygen is not the only requirement for a successful shapeshifter program."

The fishtailed baby rose to the surface, peering directly upward as if fascinated by something on the ceiling of the room. "When did she change?" Simone asked.

"A few hours ago." He rapped his knuckles on the glass. "I had to dunk her in the emergency tank. I'm afraid the water wasn't particularly clean. I had to siphon it off, bit by bit." He spoke in a monotone, as if all the enthusiasm for his work had evaporated with Jolie's failure.

Simone turned up her nose at the thought of swimming in stagnant water. "Why the rush? She can breathe air, can't she? Like me?"

The professor closed his eyes and mumbled something under his breath. Then he turned and gripped one of Simone's bare shoulders with strong fingers, fixing her with a glare. "No, no, *no*. She's *not* like you. Mermaids breathe air like humans, whereas the miengu primarily use gills like fish. They *can* breathe air like humans, but it takes a special effort in this form; the miengu are more comfortable using gills. You and Jolie may look the same with your fishy tails, but there's a world of difference between you. Look at her skin, Simone. Is your skin scaly when you shift? Does it glow?"

"No," Simone admitted.

"Do your eyes turn completely black? Do your ears turn pointy?"

"No."

"Well, then."

The professor pointed into the tank, and Simone noted the slits on each side of the baby's neck. They looked like the razor-sharp gashes of a savage animal.

"The gills appeared the moment she shifted, so naturally she tried to use them—and suddenly she was gasping like a fish out of water. It's a good job her nurse was around. She came tearing in here like a lunatic, waving the baby around. That's what this tank was here for, you see, just in case."

He suddenly looked ashamed.

"I got complacent and let the water stagnate. But Jolie didn't seem to care. She was just glad to be submerged. She took her first underwater breath and looked positively surprised. Now look at her— happier than I've seen her in a year. She's one of the miengu now."

He rapped his knuckles on the glass again, harder this time, and Jolie turned toward him with black, expressionless eyes. Simone thought she saw the baby's pointed ears twitching like a cat's, but might have imagined it.

"So now what? What's going to happen to her?"

Professor Bart turned away from the tank, put his long arm around her shoulders, and ushered her toward the door. "This, my dear, is something you're going to have to help me with. You're just like her, you see, and I need—"

"You just told me I'm *not* like her," Simone complained.

The old man chuckled. "Well, you're more like her than I am. Simone, we can't keep her in this state. We have no idea how to raise a jengu. Even if we did, it's a simple matter of logistics. We can't keep her in a glass tank, and we certainly can't join her underwater. We don't know what kind of diet is good for her, or what makes her sick. We know nothing of use about these creatures, which is exactly why we wanted to raise a jengu shapeshifter in the first place."

His voice had risen, his familiar impatience bubbling to the surface. But he quickly sobered as they headed into the hallway.

"Simone, I hate to steal away your teenage years—"

"But you're going to anyway," Simone said, giving him a wry grin.

"The truth is, of the ten children that blossomed into shapeshifters on my watch, you're the one that shows the most promise as far as scientific research goes. You have a natural curiosity about you. That's why you've kept coming back to this dusty old building ever since that first visit when you were—what, nine?" He lifted his eyes to the ceiling, grinning suddenly. "Ah, I remember like it was yesterday: those big blue eyes of yours, peering into every corner, your lips in a permanent 'O' shape, the questions you asked. I could tell, even then, that you had a life of science ahead of you, whereas the others . . ."

He gave a grunt and said no more until he steered Simone forcibly into a brightly lit room where three men toiled over their desks. Not one of them looked up as they passed by.

The professor unexpectedly opened his inner floodgates and allowed his suppressed thoughts to pour out. "Did you know that Ellie ran away to be with the unicorns? What a waste of a shapeshifter *she* turned out to be! Riley is only now making headway with the goblins—after all these years. And your brother, Felipe; he's a good, strong dragon, don't get me wrong, but I do wish he'd stop moping around and get on with his job."

"He's trying," Simone protested. "It's not his fault the other dragons see him as an impostor."

"He needs to try harder," the professor grumped. "And Orson—well, I guess his handicap is my own stupid fault for bringing him into our world prematurely. Witch doctors knew the folly of that *centuries* ago, but I just had to find out for myself. I should have waited until he had taken to the air. Flapping wings vigorously is not the same as mastering flight, as I found out too late. Tell me, Simone—what exactly is the use of a winged horse that can't fly?"

She said nothing, allowing him to continue his tirade.

"Even you, Simone," he complained. "You won't go anywhere near your kind. The purpose of being a shapeshifter is to *learn*."

"Mermaids are silly and childish," Simone said under her breath.

The professor sighed. "Well, at least you're making yourself useful in other ways. Oh, and speaking of which . . . Did you know your friend Charlie Duggan is thinking of heading north to the town of Louis?"

They had arrived at a table by the window, but Simone ignored it and stared hard at the professor, her heart quickening. "Charlie's *leaving*? Are you sure? He never mentioned it."

"Ah, yes, well," he said mysteriously, "I suppose I should keep my mouth shut about that. But mark my words: he's leaving. There are no griffins around here, and there's no point him being a griffin if he can't interact with them and get to know them. There are plenty up near Louis. Dragons, too, for that matter. Maybe I should send Felipe with him!"

With thoughts of Charlie and Felipe dropping out of her life, Simone was only vaguely aware of what was rigged on the table: a foot-square section of silver fabric clamped securely between two metal rods.

Like Simone, the professor's mind was elsewhere. He remained motionless for half a minute, staring out the window at a group of boys that loitered there. Finally he sighed and nodded, as if he had just reached a decision. "Simone, I'm going to recommend to the council that you take my job."

Simone was dumbstruck. All thoughts of Charlie evaporated in an instant. She'd expected the professor to announce his retirement, but offering his job to her as well? She felt horribly underqualified.

"You have the aptitude for this line of work," he went on. "You were always planning to work here at the lab, yes? Especially since you can't stand to be around your mermaid folk. And I think the Shapeshifter Program needs a shapeshifter leading it. It's a no-brainer, really, when you think about it."

"But what about the others? Your *colleagues*?" Simone nodded toward the men seated nearby, who had surely heard the professor's announcement. If they had, they showed no sign of reaction.

The professor shrugged. "They all have jobs to do. Nothing will change that." He leaned closer and grinned. "Truth is, being in charge isn't all it's cracked up to be. You have to go to meetings, make decisions about useless stuff, listen to people complaining . . . It's really nothing to get excited about. But still, you need this job."

"Why?"

"Because, Simone, I want you to start thinking about the next generation of shapeshifters. There's no sense in waiting decades again. We *need* shapeshifters, and we need them now. We have a shortfall. We need to understand the other species that inhabit our land. We need to make peace with the naga in the woods, the same way that Riley is smoothing things over with the goblins. We also need a liaison for our snooty centaur neighbors, and one for the trolls, and one for the harpies. A manticore would be useful, too. And the dragons—if only Felipe could get through to them, become one of them . . . Can you imagine being buddies with *dragons*, Simone? Maybe we need another . . . In any case, shapeshifters are important. The *program* is important. And I want to keep the momentum going before all the portals to our breeding ground vanish without a trace one day in the future."

After this rushed, breathless speech, he shook his head and stared at the shiny fabric stretched before him. Grinning suddenly, he pressed the tip of his finger into the center of the sheet. He applied pressure, and the material yielded, stretching effortlessly.

"See that?" he said. "A normal reaction, yes?"

Simone shrugged, unable to find anything particularly interesting while her mind buzzed with news of her future job.

The professor released the pressure and the fabric sprang back. "Now press *your* finger into it."

Bewildered, Simone gave the experiment her full attention. She stuck out her index finger and mimicked the professor, pressing directly into the center of the silver fabric so that it yielded and stretched—but then it abruptly split apart and left a two-inch gap for her finger to pass through.

Assuming she'd torn it, Simone snatched her hand away and muttered an apology. But the words froze on her lips as the fabric shimmered and rippled, and repaired itself before her eyes.

"Marvelous, isn't it?" the professor said, delighted.

Miss Simone stared in amazement. The material was undamaged. She stuck out her finger again, and for a moment it yielded under her pressure. But then, as before, it split apart and allowed her finger to pass through.

As she stood back and watched it knit fluidly together, she blinked and shook her head. "I don't understand."

"It's enchanted," the professor said. He laughed. "Yes, I know, we scientists don't believe in magic. But there's no other way to explain it. Sometimes it's best to stop trying to explain every little thing in scientific terms and just accept it for what it is—a wonderful example of magic. And perhaps magic is why Jolie shifted early. I suppose it's possible that our world has an abundance of magic in the very air we breathe, whereas the other world does not. Perhaps it's not the lower oxygen but *the absence of magic* that enables a successful shapeshifter program—as those old witch doctors no doubt knew."

Abruptly, the professor took her by the elbow and ushered her from the room. Simone twisted around, not quite ready to move on. "Where did the material come from?" she asked. It seemed so innocuous at first glance, yet clearly full of mystery and wonder.

The old man spoke as they navigated the tables and headed for the hallway. "The miengu. Two years ago we negotiated with them. They seemed curious at the idea of a human-jengu shapeshifter and offered a subject: a female jengu, oddly alluring despite her black eyes and scaly skin. Never knew her name. Anyway, she came close to the grassy bank of the lake so that my colleagues could obtain a blood sample, and for the first time we saw miengu clothing half out of water. Fascinating stuff—just had to borrow a sample. Pure silk, you know. Where they get it is a mystery. It turns out that the material responds to the touch of certain types of people."

"Certain *types* of people?" Simone repeated.

The professor nodded. "The miengu, for one. They seem to enjoy the feel of it on their skin. It has a sort of magical warmth. Also, it doesn't need much work to shape and size it—they just make a very rough one-size-fits-all robe, and it adapts to fit snugly."

"Adapts?" Simone pressed, confused.

"Doesn't work for me, though," the professor remarked. "Nor anyone else in this place. But it works for shapeshifters. It *responds* to them."

"Meaning?"

The professor winked. "Another time, my dear." He tugged open the front door and stared out into the dazzling sunshine, watching villagers pass by in the street. An expression of sadness descended over his wrinkled face.

"So you're retiring," Simone said quietly.

He nodded. "Things are getting muddled. I'm becoming forgetful. I'm clear at the moment, but sometimes . . . well, I just don't want to be booted out of my lab because of some disastrous mistake caused by my dementia. I want to leave while my mind is mostly intact. You see?"

Simone swallowed hard, fighting to keep tears from welling up.

The professor apparently sensed her anguish and put an arm around her shoulders. "Now, now, no tears, please. Listen, I need you to take Jolie to the miengu. While you're there, see if you can get some more of that material. I have a hunch that you shapeshifter types might find it useful, no? When you get back, we'll go and see the council together. They'll be surprised to see my ugly old mug, let me tell you."

"I'm not sure I'm ready for all this," Simone said weakly.

"You will be. Look, I'm not going anywhere yet. If you don't waste any time getting started on the Shapeshifter Program, I can work with you, set you on the right track, peer over your shoulder, hold your hand, that sort of thing. Then, by the time I pop my clogs, well, you'll be—"

Simone rounded on him. "Don't you dare! You have at least another decade left in you. Please don't talk about . . . about *that* kind of thing. Not yet."

Professor Bart smiled and winked. "Go pack a bag, my dear. I'll have the nurses pack a few bags, too. You'll be going by boat up the river to the lake. Well, the nurses will; you'll be swimming alongside, cradling Jolie under the water. It's not far to the lake. When you get there, use your mermaid charms and see if the miengu will be kind enough to adopt the poor little thing."

"So that's it for her?" Simone said, unable to contain the wave of bitterness. "One of the lost?"

The professor shrugged. "So history has it. When they change this young, they *stay* changed and never figure out how to change back. Most don't even know they were once human. She's a jengu now, one of the water spirits."

The old man fell silent, chewing his bottom lip thoughtfully.

"But you never know," he said eventually. "Maybe one day, years from now, you'll figure out a way to bring her back into the world of humans."

Chapter One
Into the Labyrinth

The goblin brought the gigantic steam-driven vehicle to a halt at the edge of the labyrinth. He switched off the engine, and clouds of pure white steam hissed out from underneath, billowing up the sides. In the silence that followed, Blacknail leaned back in his creaky seat and said, "We're here." Hal had been awake for the last leg of the journey, but Abigail was still snoozing beside him, her head lolling on his shoulder. He hated to wake her so waited while Miss Simone, in one of the front seats, stretched and climbed to her feet. Fleck, her centaur colleague, was standing in the narrow center aisle, facing forward but sound asleep.

The vehicle had five rows of seats arranged in blocks of three on each side of the aisle, room for around thirty passengers in all. Hal and his friends called it a 'buggy' because of its six massive cast-iron wheels and the fact that it had been open-topped on their first journey, with just a small glass windshield in front of the driver. In truth, it was more like a bus, especially now that the goblin had finished adding a roof. With the welded steel framework overhead and the rough leathery fabric stretched across, it provided welcome relief from the unrelenting sun as well as the frequent downpours of rain over the last couple of days. Blacknail had promised to install glass in the window openings along the sides but hadn't gotten around to it yet, so Hal's seat was a little damp.

The goblin appeared to be settling in for a long nap. Miss Simone spoke to him for a moment, then patted him on the shoulder and headed up the aisle. She nudged Fleck as she squeezed past. He jolted out of his slumber and blinked rapidly, then stood up straight and promptly bumped his head on a steel bar.

A ladder was fixed to one side of the vehicle. Miss Simone hiked a leg over the side and began to climb down, her long, golden hair and silky green cloak whipping suddenly to one side as a vicious gust came out of nowhere. When she had dropped out of sight, Fleck peered down after her.

"Need help again?" Hal called.

"No, thanks," Fleck said, somewhat stiffly.

Hal chuckled to himself and nudged Abigail awake. She came to, her eyes open but not yet seeing. "Huh," she mumbled.

"We're here," Hal whispered, "and Fleck says he doesn't need my help getting down."

Abigail rubbed her eyes and turned to watch the show.

The centaur was making a play of securing a strange contraption on his broad horse back. It was like a small iron oven, complete with door, but it had a metal frame at the rear, attached to which was an assortment of crudely welded boxes and a few sacks hanging from hooks. Tubes ran all over and down into the oven. Most of its weight sat on Fleck's powerful withers, but he stopped it from sliding off by tying a strap around his human torso.

Being a scientist, Fleck was not the most formidable of centaurs. He had a gentle face and, usually, an inquisitive nature. However, right now he looked troubled and more than a little irritated as he prepared to jump down from the buggy. It was no easy task placing his forehoofs on the slippery metal side and then ducking his head to avoid the ceiling. He leaned out, his rear hoofs inching forward. Then, with a powerful bound, he scrabbled and leaped into the air.

And dropped like a stone.

Hal and Abigail hurried out of their seats when they heard a thud, an "oomph," and a clanging sound. Ten feet below, Fleck wriggled on the ground, limbs akimbo, trying to get up. Finally, the centaur scrambled onto unsteady legs like a newborn foal. His contraption lay on its side, the frame a little bent.

Behind them lay a barren, rocky landscape, flat all the way back to the distant horizon from whence they had come. Directly in front was the edge of a cliff, and beyond the cliff, towering high above, was an active volcano. The smell of sulfur was strong, and dust clouds danced in random places as the wind tore through. A gust picked up Abigail's ponytail and tickled Hal's face with it, and he brushed it away.

"Well, at least it's not hot this time," he said, swinging a leg over the side and feeling for the ladder.

"I prefer hot and calm to wind and rain," Abigail replied shortly. High on her back, the fabric of her light dress abruptly peeled apart and insect-like wings sprouted. She buzzed effortlessly into the air, her feet dangling. "*How* many times did it rain on the way here?"

Hal clambered over the side, hurried down the ladder, and dropped onto solid ground, mumbling as he went. "I don't know. Six? Seven?"

They had been traveling since dawn, eleven hours straight. Being a dragon shapeshifter, Hal could have flown and carried Miss Simone all the way. And if Abigail's faerie wings had tired, he could have carried her, too. But Fleck wasn't used to trotting such long distances and there was no way Hal could have managed a full-grown centaur and a heavy iron contraption, so a vehicle had been arranged. Blacknail had a rickety airship, but it had been torn apart by rocs and was still being repaired high on Whisper Mountain, so the goblin's trusty steam-powered vehicle had seemed the best bet.

"Let's get on with it," Miss Simone suggested quietly. She was looking up at the sky, where dragons had begun to circle. Fleck hurriedly hoisted his contraption onto his back, retied it, and trotted in a circle of his own, clearly agitated.

The four peered down into the chasm. Standing precariously on the crumbling cliff edge, they saw a river of slow-moving lava, some of it covered with a gray skin. Farther along, they saw a huge pool of bubbling red and yellow liquid, steaming and hissing. The last time Hal had been here, he'd felt the heat from where he stood at the top of the cliff. Today, though, the wind was strong and surprisingly cool.

Two hundred feet away, the opposite wall of the chasm was riddled with openings—caves and tunnels that marked the entrances to numerous lava tubes. Once, the landscape had been unbroken, but an earthquake had split the ground, forming a chasm, and the labyrinth of tunnels had effectively been cut into two. Most of the dragons that lived in the labyrinth had since migrated to the east side, and it was there that Hal had to visit.

"Let's hope the reception is a little friendlier this time," Abigail murmured, stepping up to Hal's side. Her wings became still and then retracted smoothly, almost fluidly, into the flesh of her back. A split second later, the eight-inch vertical slit in her dress repaired itself. Mesmerized, it took a moment for Hal to realize that Abigail was arching an eyebrow at him over her shoulder. "It's rude to stare, you know."

Hal snapped to attention and shook himself. "Okay, let's get this done. Just stand back and . . . well, let me do my thing."

He felt the burden of responsibility on his shoulders again. The last time he and his friends had been to the labyrinth, Abigail had been snatched by a dragon, and Hal had ended up badly burned and clawed. The mission had turned out all right in the end, but lives could have been lost. Hal was determined not to make the same mistake again.

As a trio of dragons circled closer, eyeing the group warily, Hal moved into a clear space away from Miss Simone, Fleck, and Abigail.

Then he transformed.

He hardly gave his shapeshifting ability a thought these days. Just a few short weeks ago, he had not even known he *was* a shapeshifter. Then, like his friends, he had begun to change. The first transformation had been slow, starting with an itch on his arm and then a scaly rash that came and went, coupled with occasional feelings of boldness and strength from deep within. Once, in class, he had belched up a sheet of flame, scorching the back of a chair. Then, in a forest, he had undergone the full shift to his alter-form in an instinctive act to protect himself from a vicious monster. It had been terrifying, but once he'd learned how to shift back into his familiar human form, the transformations had come more naturally thereafter, instantaneous and completely at will.

Too bad it had taken him much longer to learn how to fly.

As several thousand pounds of reptilian bulk suddenly filled the space, Hal turned and stamped, digging his claws into the ground and swinging his clubbed tail in an arc. Feeling a surge of energy, he straightened up and roared, sending a sheet of fire into the air. He felt as though he had suddenly been released from a compact prison, a wild animal that had flung off its restraints, clothes and all. His simple, flimsy shirt and pants, made of the same enchanted material as Abigail's, did more than just peel apart—they completely reshaped and formed into a sash that encircled the lower part of his neck, all in the blink of an eye.

He beat his wings, sending up huge clouds of dust, and launched into the sky. This time he would meet the dragons head on and stay out of reach as he negotiated.

"I'm here at the request of your leader," he yelled to the approaching dragons. This wasn't strictly true, but it would be a far more effective way of keeping these brutes at bay. "Go fetch him!"

The words left his lips in a series of grunts and roars. Hal had never understood the magic behind shapeshifter language; he had certainly never sat down in a classroom and learned to speak in a dragon tongue. Yet he did so fluently. The only thing he had to watch was using words and phrases that were too smart for dragons to understand or perhaps had no direct translation.

The three adults, each twice the size of Hal, soared around him in a spiral as he whipped straight upward. Their expressions were far easier to read now that Hal was one of their kind, and he saw scorn and distaste. *We know who you are*, one spat. *Our leader wants you dead.*

Hal had thought long and hard about this exchange throughout the entire journey to the labyrinth. He always knew that he would be held responsible for the ancient emperor losing his son. The ornery second-in-command, Lumphead, had chased Hal and Abigail through a 'hole,' a portal to the other world, and gotten himself blown to pieces by a military tank. The third-in-command, Burnflank, had thus stepped up in his place . . . only Burnflank was a whole lot nicer than the hotheaded Lumphead.

"I know your leader wants me dead," Hal roared, ducking and diving between the other dragons. The four of them were performing some kind of midair dance, with long bodies and tails flowing in and out as though they were an orchestration of streaming kites. "But that's for him to decide, not you. Go ahead—I dare you to harm a scale on my hide without his permission."

The resulting snarls and snaps reminded Hal of a pack of angry dogs. Still, they resisted the urge to attack, such was their respect for their leader. If Hal had learned anything about his alter-kind recently, it was that they rarely challenged the chain of command.

"Now quit delaying and take me to him," Hal demanded.

This parting shot was too much for one of the dragons. It whipped its head around and took a jab at him, its teeth closing around Hal's broad reptilian shoulder. Adrenaline surging, Hal brought up his tail and whacked the heavy club end across his attacker's jaw. It was akin to a light slap on the face, but Hal instantly followed up with a savage burst of fire that inflicted a great deal of pain. Even a dragon, with its tough armored hide, tended to recoil from the onslaught of another dragon's fire directly in the face.

With a screech, the creature fell away, trailing black smoke. It regained its flight immediately, limped and lurched through the air, and landed roughly on a clump of rocks sticking up out of the bubbling lava. There, it howled with a fury that made Hal shudder. *Another enemy*, he thought sagely.

His defiant, breathtakingly risky act surprised the other two dragons so much that they veered away and shot him cautious glances. Hal could almost hear their thoughts: *What kind of young whippersnapper dares to come here, to our home in the labyrinth, where the emperor wants him dead, and attacks a dragon twice his size?* The inevitable answer was no doubt just as troubling: *Either one who knows no fear and is extremely dangerous . . . or one who was truly invited by the emperor himself. Or perhaps both.*

In any event, the pair grunted and headed off, vying for the lead. Satisfied, Hal pumped his wings and sailed around in an extravagant arc, daring to sweep close to the numerous tunnel openings in the cliff face where dozens of dragons watched him silently. Hal felt empowered now. He was cautious enough not to feel invincible, but he knew that his act of boldness and aggression—and his bold-faced lie—had been the key to an audience with the embittered emperor.

He gave a wink to his friends as he swooped by but doubted they picked up on it. Abigail was white-faced, huddling up to Miss Simone, who stood with feet planted firmly apart and cloak billowing in the wind. Fleck seemed too nervous even to trot in a circle.

Hal didn't have long to wait. The two dragons emerged from a nondescript tunnel and launched off the ledge, spreading out as they approached. They looked angry.

You lied, one snarled. It flew right up to Hal, and their snouts touched as they both beat their wings furiously and hovered in place. *The emperor knows nothing of your visit. He nearly executed me for not killing you already.*

"So what's stopping you now?" Hal asked quietly.

For what seemed an age, Hal's life hung in the balance as the ugly adult monster pressed up against his face. Hot steam vented rhythmically from its nostrils while its wings beat steadily. In the background, Hal became aware of the curious howl of an approaching storm.

Because, the dragon grunted, *now he really does want to see you.*

With a hiss, the creature swept around, angled its gigantic leathery wings, and headed back to the tunnel. The other dragon waited, rising up and down with each beat, apparently trying with all its might to kill Hal with its glare.

Hal went after the leader, pleased that his audience with the emperor had been granted but dreading the danger he was putting himself in.

He landed deftly on the narrow ledge of the tunnel entrance, high up in the sheer face of the cliff. Below, lava churned slowly. It was more sluggish here, cooler, with dark gray and black skin trying to form on its surface. The molten rock flowed freely from the nearby volcano, splashing down a number of tunnels and exiting lower in the chasm. The dragons loved the year-round warmth of the labyrinth and had long ago learned their way around the tunnels and lava tubes. Hal, on the other hand, knew he could get hopelessly lost in no time at all, so he made sure to stick close to his lead.

The tunnel was pitch-black just a few yards in. But the bull dragon gave several bursts of flame to light the way, and Hal found that he had no need to do so himself as long as he kept up.

The tunnels wound and twisted, headed upward a short way, then down again and around some more random bends. They passed several forks and junctions, but the lead hurried on without pause, claws clicking on rock.

Abruptly, they arrived in a cavern. Hal recognized it immediately, partly because of its pungent smell. This was where the emperor spent his days and nights, perhaps unmoving due to his age. The enormous domed cavern had two vents in the ceiling through which poured rays of early evening light. Dozens of gnarled, twisted stalagmites grew upward, reaching for the ceiling. Two other tunnels led off, and Hal immediately got his bearings and recognized them both. He'd come through this cavern during his previous visit, sneaking from one tunnel to another right under the noses of the emperor and his dangerous son, Lumphead.

Hal's guide grumbled something, backed up, then clumsily turned and shouldered past, head lowered.

The ancient dragon's hide was dull and gray, its claws yellowed. Great folds of dry, scaly skin brought to mind some of the wrinkled old men back at the village, some of whom had to be over a hundred years old. How old was this dragon? Hal realized he had no idea how long his alter-kind lived.

Standing near the emperor was a much younger, far more vibrant bull, wings drawn up and tail curled serenely around its haunches. This one had seen a battle or two judging by the burns along its flank.

Hal tried to suppress an exclamation of delight and averted his gaze as Burnflank swung his head toward him. He forced himself to focus on the emperor, who had already fixed him with a steely glare.

You, the old one murmured. His throaty growls sounded wet and gurgling. *You have a lot of nerve, returning here. Give me one good reason why my faithfuls shouldn't rip out your guts where you stand.*

Hal sensed movement and glanced sideways. Out of the shadows, dragons appeared—mostly males but a few females as well, ten or eleven of them, all staring at him as they edged forward one paw at a time, hunkered low.

"Because I'm here to do you a favor," Hal said softly, aware that he was trembling. His dragon voice sounded pathetic and weak, a puppy in a room of snarling hounds. But something told him that was a good thing. There was no need for aggression now. In fact, aggression would get him killed in no time. Now was the time to bow and scrape, to be respectful. "I'm here to close the hole."

The old dragon tilted his head and narrowed his eyes. He said nothing, but the meaning was clear. He had no idea what Hal was talking about.

"The hole," Hal explained. "The portal."

This confused the old one even more. Perhaps there was no translation for the word 'portal' in dragon-tongue.

Hal tried again. "Deep in this labyrinth is a boiling pool. There's a hole there, a gateway leading to another world."

The emperor's eyes widened. *Where the humans came through breathing fire of their own.*

"Exactly," Hal said, relieved.

And where you murdered my son, the old dragon added.

Hal shook his head, an action that struck him as odd in his dragon form. It was okay nodding and shaking his head when trying to communicate with his friends, but with another dragon . . . it just seemed weird. "I didn't murder him. That's just it. I escaped through the hole to the other world and your son followed me through. He tried to find me . . . and that's when the men—the humans who breathe fire—murdered him."

He refrained from elaborating on the subject, hoping the simple explanation would be enough. Instead, he concentrated on the task at hand, which was beneficial to the dragons regardless of whether or not the emperor liked him.

"This other world," Hal said, "is full of humans who breathe fire. And they plan to return. I need to close the hole for all our sakes."

There was, in fact, no known way to 'close' holes, but Hal had no desire to get into technicalities. The old dragon stared at him for an eternity, then shifted his head a few inches, a tiny movement that prompted Burnflank to edge closer. Hal heard curious snuffles and grunts as the emperor whispered to his new second-in-command. Hal had never tried whispering in his dragon form before. The very idea that a creature his size could whisper seemed ludicrous to him.

He waited nervously, trying to ignore the hulking mass of dragons pressing in from both sides, blocking his escape. Burnflank was leaning close to the emperor, listening to the whispering and then returning grunts of his own. Hal suddenly noticed the piles of clothing on the floor behind the aging dragon and instantly wished he could forget about them again. He'd seen them before, of course, during his last visit . . . and, as before, he shuddered to think that these clothes—these sorry rags, torn and bloody—had once belonged to people snatched from the streets of their village.

But all that had changed. With the volatile Lumphead gone, Burnflank was the overriding influence in the labyrinth, the emperor's trusted second. And Burnflank was no ordinary dragon . . .

You will close the gateway, the old leader gurgled, finally returning his attention to Hal.

Hal felt a surge of relief. But he remained cautious. "And I have your word that I will not be harmed afterward? That my friends will not be harmed?"

The emperor scowled. *You alone will close the gateway this evening. But make haste and be far away by dawn. Our truce ends then.*

Bowing his head, Hal sensed a sigh of disappointment from the dragons crowding him at both sides. They began to turn and shamble away, bumping into each other as they went.

"I'll need a guide," Hal said. "And I'll need the centaur with me. Only he knows how to—"

You heard me, the emperor snapped, suddenly animated. For the first time since Hal had arrived, the old one heaved himself up onto front paws, belly sagging and tail flicking back and forth. The creature shook with the effort, and Hal knew without a shadow of doubt that this old leader wouldn't be around for very much longer. *You alone will close the gateway*, he finished with a grunt.

Hal bowed, knowing it was senseless to anger the monster further. "I'll need to fetch a machine from the centaur," he said, "and he'll need to show me how to use it. Then I'll be back." He cast a glance at Burnflank, who watched him through narrowed eyes. "Will you . . . escort me?"

Again, the emperor reacted. His body shook violently and a rumbling growl rose up from his throat. But before he could say anything, Burnflank placed a paw firmly on the old one's armored shoulder. *Still yourself, Old One. I would rather take care of this personally. Rest.*

Burnflank unfurled his tail and stretched. Behind him, the ancient dragon sank with a groan, his eyes burning fiercely.

Come, Burnflank said to Hal with a gruff barking sound. He strode toward the tunnel. Other dragons quickly moved aside and then stood and watched as Hal hurried past.

Burnflank said nothing as he led Hal through the dark, twisted labyrinth, occasionally lighting the way with blasts of fire. Nor did he say anything when they emerged into daylight at the cliff face. Burnflank launched from the ledge into the early evening sky. Dazzled for a moment, Hal blinked rapidly before following.

The sun was setting in the clear sky to the west. To the far east, ominous thunderclouds rolled in—yet another storm coming to dump on them.

Hal followed Burnflank across the chasm, then took the lead. He could see his friends clearly, huddled together near the six-wheeled iron buggy at the opposite side of the chasm. In the days of Lumphead, the dragons of the labyrinth would not have waited long before diving in to attack. But the new reign, helped along by Burnflank's wisdom and guidance, had steered the monsters away from picking on humans.

The two of them thumped down on the edge of the cliff, sending up more clouds of dust that the wind whipped away in a flurry. Hal felt a surge of excitement as Burnflank peered at the golden-haired woman with the billowing cloak. He stared for what seemed a long time while she stared quizzically back, occasionally shooting Hal a questioning glance. He nodded, trying to indicate that this was indeed Burnflank— her shapeshifter brother.

Tell her we will meet in private later this evening, Burnflank rumbled quietly. *Away from prying eyes.*

Hal glanced around, realizing that dragons were everywhere, flying in circles and peering out of the uppermost tunnels in the opposite cliff face. All were watching closely, curiosity getting the better of them.

He abruptly transformed and staggered for a moment as his center of gravity shifted. Routinely checking that his shirt and pants had reformed around him, and the light foot-shaped plastic soles remained correctly adhered to the bottoms of his feet, he approached his friends.

Abigail broke away from Miss Simone and ran to his side, gripping his arm firmly. Fleck nodded rapidly, murmuring to himself. Miss Simone continued to stare at Burnflank with her eyebrows raised.

"This is Felipe," Hal told her.

"But the burn . . ." she said, looking mortified as she gazed at the hideous scarring on the dragon's side.

"It's a battle wound," Hal said. "If he transformed back and forth a few times, it would probably heal. But that would give him away. He's better off staying in dragon form, showing off the scar."

Miss Simone moved toward the silent dragon, her hands beginning to rise in greeting. She hadn't seen her brother in a long time and had only recently found out he was still alive.

"Don't," Hal said sharply.

She stopped dead. "What? Why?"

"We're being watched. If these other dragons get the slightest whiff that he's a shapeshifter, then he'll be torn apart. We all will. He said he'll meet you tonight, away from prying eyes. In the meantime, just act scared."

"No problem," Abigail said, eyeing Burnflank with obvious awe.

Out in the daylight, he was certainly an impressive sight. Bigger than the three dragons that had approached them on arrival, and far bulkier, the emperor's new second-in-command radiated power and wisdom. The others were mere whelps in comparison. Burnflank would make a great leader once the old emperor fizzled out. That is, if the pretense could be maintained.

Hal explained that he had to go in alone with the machine. The centaur was both relieved and flustered. "But . . . I mean, that's fine, but you don't know how to use it . . . I mean, if you get it wrong, you could—"

"Then teach me," Hal said firmly. "How hard can it be?"

Chapter Two
The Hole

Under the watchful eye of a silent Burnflank and dozens of swooping dragons, Fleck showed Hal, Abigail and Miss Simone how the machine worked. In truth, the centaur didn't really *know* how it worked, only the process involved in setting it off. He went over it several times, pointing to the small dials on the top of the frame and the small sack that hung on the side. He opened the heavy iron door with a scrape and pointed at the glowing rock nestled inside, held in place by brackets. He made sure to point out the dangers of getting the temperature and the mixture of fluids wrong. Everything had to be just right, otherwise the procedure would fail with either a disappointing fizzle and pop or a deadly explosion.

Fleck was peering at a bundle of well-worn papers as he spoke. "The geo-rock's energy has to be released in a certain way for the desired effect. In the old days, people just bashed them open with hammers, and they exploded. Then, somewhere, a hole between our worlds opened." He glanced at Hal when he said this, then resumed his scrutiny. "At the right temperature, with the correct mixture of volatile liquids, and with a precisely timed impact, a hole can be created right in front of the oven."

"What are the liquids for?" Abigail asked, poking a finger into the side of a sack that Fleck had just been filling from a small tin container.

"Don't do that," the centaur said nervously. "That stuff alone is dangerous. Mix it with *this* stuff"—he pointed to one of the welded boxes—"and you get a flash that'll burn off your eyebrows. And mix both with the nasty-smelling stuff in here"—he tapped another of the welded boxes—"and you have a bomb on your hands."

"So it makes the geo-rock explode even more?" Abigail said, frowning. "And we do that because . . . ?"

"Because otherwise there's a delay before the energy coalesces," Fleck explained, waving his papers. "During that delay, in a form of stasis, Earth rotates on its axis at a thousand miles per hour and moves through space even faster, hence why some clumsily formed holes are miles away from their point of origin, with gateways that don't line up in the alternate terrains. Understand?"

"Well, I remember Dewey talking about all this back at Charlie's inn," Hal said carefully. "Not sure I really understood it, though."

Fleck sighed. "Let me try again." He spoke slowly and carefully. "If you throw a ball high in the air, and I mean *really* high, like miles and miles—straight upward into space—you can imagine that by the time the ball returns to earth, the earth has rotated on its axis a fraction. So even if you stand perfectly still and the ball goes absolutely straight up and back down, it will still come down some distance away—or miles, depending on how long it's up there."

"We should—" Miss Simone started to say.

But Fleck gripped Hal's shoulder tightly, leaning down so that his face was inches away, the bundle of papers in his other hand. "That's what happens when you crack open a geo-rock with a hammer, as they did in the old days. The energy slowly, lazily coalesces, forming a hole between worlds, but often far enough away that the person who cracked open the rock isn't even aware of it."

"Well, to be fair, the person who cracked open the rock is blown to smithereens in the explosion," Abigail reasoned.

Fleck ignored her. He waved the papers in Hal's face. "Imagine all those holes that ended up not just miles away across land but miles *in the sky*, perhaps floating in the vacuum of space . . . or holes buried deep under the ground . . ."

Miss Simone cleared her throat noisily.

"Well, anyway," Fleck said, his face reddening, "speeding up the explosion with volatile chemicals and intense pressure allows us to create holes very quickly, right in front of us, right where we want them—and safely. Since we don't know how to *close* holes, we have to improvise, and we do that by opening a new one right in front of the other, thereby creating a sort of loop that renders the first hole useless. You step through one and are immediately transported to the other world; then, before you know it, you've stepped through the second hole and are immediately transported back again. Call it a redirection, if you like. A *shunt*—"

"We should move on," Miss Simone interjected quietly. "The dragons are getting restless and Hal has work to do."

Burnflank, who had been listening intently, gave a grunt and strode to the edge of the cliff, looking back over his shoulder. Hal gave a wan smile and backed away from his friends, then transformed.

As his dragon bulk once more filled the space, he heard a number of barks from above, where dragons continued to circle. They sounded indignant, clearly infuriated by the shapeshifting act. Hal guessed they were disgusted by the idea of a *mere human* donning a dragon disguise.

Hal reached out with one of his front paws and gently grasped the metal contraption. Though fairly small, it was still heavy as he took to the sky and followed Burnflank across the two-hundred-foot gap to where lava bubbled and spat at the foot of the cliff on the opposite side of the chasm. Each tunnel entrance looked the same as the next, a black hole in the sheer rock face, yet Burnflank chose one without hesitation.

The dragon led the way into darkness. At first, there was no need to light the route with bursts of flame because several offshoot tunnels glowed bright orange from sources deep within—flowing lava and almost unbearable heat. Farther in, the tunnel grew pitch-black, and Burnflank gave a few huffs once in a while, providing flashes of light to see by.

Then he stopped. They had arrived.

Hal joined Burnflank at the edge of a drop. A few bursts of fire showed that he had arrived at the top end of the cavern containing the boiling pool of water. He could hear it bubbling, and the air was thick and clammy. Lower down, on the opposite side of the pool, the tunnel continued into darkness. This was where he and Abigail had ended up previously, their escape thwarted. With dragons pursuing and lying in wait ahead, and with no room to fly safely in such a confined space, the only chance for them both had been to jump into the pool—only the water was deadly, superheated by scorching plasma below the ground and bubbling up through gaps in the rock. It had taken a monumental effort for Abigail, in her buzzing faerie form, to keep Hal out of the water.

Yet there had been an escape route after all—a pulsing black hole, like a cloud of ink squirted from a squid that hovered just above the surface of the pool. A portal to Hal's old world.

To his surprise, Hal found that the pool was now lit with flickering torches. Soldiers had come through here and made their mark. Survivors of the deadly virus, wearing biosuits and carrying weapons, had tracked Hal's route and found a way through into this new world . . . but it was impassable without some form of structure over the steaming pool. And so they had built one.

It was simple but effective. A long, sturdy plank had been pushed through the hole from the other side and weighted down so that it protruded over the boiling water. If this were a pirate ship, the plank would be the ultimate walk of death. Cables had been attached to the bouncy end of the plank and secured to the surrounding rock walls. Then a makeshift platform had been nailed on and secured in a similar fashion. The entire rickety structure hung and wobbled a foot above the boiling pool. Four flickering torches lit the cavern and caused shadows to dance across the walls. There was an aluminum ladder, but it had been knocked down by a dragon and now protruded uselessly from the pool.

No doubt the soldiers had built the platform without interruption, but when they had begun exploring, traipsing around in the tunnels shining flashlights, they had come across a dragon or two—and rather than retreat, they had used their weapons to fight their way through. The emperor had spoken of humans that breathed fire, and that wasn't far from the truth, for these soldiers had used flamethrowers, effectively giving the dragons a taste of their own medicine. Hal had to admire their tenacity.

Do it, Burnflank rumbled, standing alongside and peering down at the platform.

"Why haven't you burned it all?" Hal wondered aloud. Even as he asked the question, he noticed that the planks of wood were badly scorched in places.

They fight too well, Burnflank answered. *They had this place guarded for a while, but then they vanished as if they had received an order to retreat. One of our dragons dropped down onto the platform and began to burn it, but the soldiers must have felt the disturbance under their feet. They came through and killed him, and he tumbled into the pool.* Burnflank turned to gaze at Hal. *Be careful, my young friend. I don't want to tell my sister that you burned or boiled to death in this cavern.*

Hal shuddered. He considered his options for a moment and sighed. No matter which way he thought about it, he would have to go down there and stand on that platform. To make this work, he had to be very close to the hole, no more than a foot or two away.

He took a breath and stepped off the safety of the ledge. He angled his wings in an effort to slow his descent but still landed heavily on the platform. Wood creaked and cables thrummed. He lowered the iron oven onto the platform and stood there a moment, bouncing gently, staring at the pulsing black cloud that floated before him. Then he reverted to his human form.

At that precise moment, two biosuited soldiers burst through, brandishing weapons.

Alarmed, Hal recoiled and almost fell off the platform into the bubbling water. He heard it hissing and boiling all around. Now that he was in his human form, the heat and humidity washed over him in an instant, drenching him in sweat. "Whoa!" he yelled, holding up both hands.

The soldiers stared at him down the long barrels of their flamethrowers, no doubt taken aback by the appearance of a young human boy.

"Don't shoot," Hal said, his voice sounding decidedly squeakier than he would have liked. "I just need to—"

Without a word, the soldiers rushed forward and grabbed him. Looking around with urgency, they backed up and dragged Hal straight through the pulsing hole. His feet never even touched the floor, and his protests were ignored. He had time to glance up at the tunnel above to see Burnflank's hulking silhouette, then down at the metal contraption standing on the deck . . . and then he experienced a moment of total blackness.

After that, the light in the basement was blinding. Dimly, he heard the sound of a motor outside the room and saw a bunch of cables trailing down from the door above, leading to the four enormous bright lamps that shone in his face. He blinked rapidly, seeing that the room had been cleared out and a new staircase installed; the previous one had been demolished by Lumphead. The basement now seemed to be a hive of activity. In addition to the two biosuited soldiers that had dragged him from the cavern, another four soldiers waited with long-barreled guns pointing his way, and a fifth suited figure lurked in the shadows near the stairs.

"Who are you?" a voice barked.

"I—well, my—" Hal stuttered.

"*What's your name, boy?*"

"Hal Franklin," he shouted.

"He's one of them," the lone figure said quietly. "One of the shapeshifters." It was a woman. Hal couldn't see her face through the biosuit mask because the light reflected off it as she approached. "You're the dragon."

Hal nodded, uncertain whether it was a good thing that this person knew who he was. "And who are you?"

"A scientist," she said. "I came straight here from the island."

She moved closer and Hal squinted, trying to see her face. He thought he recognized her, although he didn't know her name. She had been one of those in the cottage ravaged by giant ants; Hal remembered her suggesting they save the biosuits from the critters. Although he knew nothing about her, he thought she had seemed fairly level-headed.

"What are you doing here?" she demanded. "I assume you got through the labyrinth unscathed because you're one of them? A dragon?"

Hal nodded.

"So why are you here?"

While he was trying to think of something to say, one of the soldiers that had dragged him through the hole muttered something and stepped away. He sank back into the pulsing cloud and disappeared from view.

"I was just curious," Hal said, stalling. He had to think of something plausible. He couldn't tell these people why he was really here.

Unfortunately, the soldier returned within seconds, hoisting the heavy metal contraption. He clanged it down on the stone floor and Hal's heart sank.

"He brought this," the soldier said.

The woman bent to study the device. Even through her visor, Hal could see that her eyes were wide. "This is . . . this is what you people used to—"

She shot upright and advanced on Hal.

"You're here to close the gateway, aren't you? I saw that *centaur* carrying this thing right before the other gateway was closed back on the island. Only she didn't have it afterward when she took off into the woods."

"It wasn't hers anymore," Hal muttered.

"We all felt something in the air, a ripple of energy," the woman said. "And when we tried to cross back through the gateway, it didn't work."

Hal nodded, knowing it was pointless to lie. "We had to stop you coming through again."

"And so you planned to close this gateway, too?"

"Actually, we can't close them," Hal admitted. "We can only create new ones. I was going to use this machine to make another hole—another gateway—that would act like a loop."

The woman thought about that for a long time, during which Hal nervously looked around. These soldiers meant business. He felt that if he so much as breathed funny, they'd gun him down. He pondered the idea of backing into the hole and transforming. He was so close, no more than a few feet away. But two soldiers stood by his sides, a step or two behind him, and he feared they would grab him the moment he tried anything. Besides, he would never have time to get hold of the machine.

He could transform right here and now. It would startle them, and he could use the element of shock to grab the machine and duck through the hole. But he was afraid they would start shooting with their trigger-happy fingers.

"I see," the woman said after a while. "So we step through the gateway to the other world . . . and immediately step through a second gateway that leads back here. A loop, as you say."

"It's not ideal, but . . ." Hal trailed off and shrugged.

"All right," the woman said. She started to turn away. "Bring him outside. But bind him first, with chains. We don't want him turning into a dragon. And bring the machine outside, too. Let's take a good look at what—"

Hal acted on the spur of the moment. He'd remembered, suddenly, that he had developed an ability recently—breathing fire while in his human form. He hadn't experimented with it at all, but now seemed like a perfect time to see what he could do. Still, he didn't want to burn anyone so aimed his fire at the four dazzling spotlights, turning his head in a slow arc as the flames shot forth.

He was acutely aware of the danger he was in, blowing fire at the trigger-happy soldiers behind the lamps. But, perhaps because he was in his human form, and because he was just a twelve-year-old boy with two other soldiers standing right at his shoulders, they refrained from shooting and instead ducked and started yelling. Their guns were waving dangerously as Hal superheated first one lamp, then the second, then the third . . .

One by one, they burst into flame and popped. As the fourth light went out, Hal ignored the screamed warnings and struggled against the soldiers that had clamped their strong fingers around his arms. In total blackness, he heard scrambling sounds, someone tripping, and a number of curses. But the soldiers held him grimly. Flashlights would be shone around the place in a matter of seconds and he'd be a prisoner again.

Hal felt the butt of something hard strike him behind the ear. He went limp immediately, his thoughts scattering. Confused and in pain, he struggled to stay conscious, heard more shouts, saw the beam of a flashlight piercing the darkness, felt a kick in his ribs . . .

Unable to prevent the transformation, he reared up and roared, throwing off his attackers with anger. He swung his tail around, knocking all manner of obstacles aside. Some of them were soft and yelled, while others were hard and clattered across the floor.

A gun started firing. There were bright flashes and sharp, deafening reports. A nasty stinging sensation spread across his chest. A man behind him yelled in pain, and the woman screamed from across the room.

Hal breathed fire, and this time the flames were enormous, lighting up the room and enveloping the biosuited soldiers that crouched behind the spotlights, which were now a mass of twisted metal. Behind the men were wooden crates and Hal ignited those, too, along with a table and four chairs. Now that he had regained control, he took care not to burn anyone too badly if he could help it. Their anguished yells hurt his ears as it was.

Despite the chaos, he allowed them to scramble for the staircase, although one of the soldiers, whose legs were on fire, was too busy rolling across the floor to care about escaping. Hal left the soldier alone until the poor man had smothered the flames and staggered to his feet; then he encouraged him up the stairs with a well-aimed fireball.

The stairs caught alight and, as the last of the biosuited soldiers disappeared up them, Hal finished the job by burning the supports. When the stairs and crates were roaring and belching smoke, and his eyes were beginning to sting in the acrid fumes, he knew it was time to go. He grabbed the iron oven, turned, and ducked through the pulsing cloud.

The air was much clearer back in the cavern. Relieved, Hal turned around on the wooden platform. The flimsy structure bounced, bent, and creaked under his weight. The chains were still holding it up at the corners, but they wouldn't help if the whole thing snapped in half. The idea of being dunked in boiling water hastened his shift back into human form.

He took a moment to check himself over. He remembered he'd been shot at, had actually felt the bullets spraying across his broad dragon chest . . . and, with a shock, he realized that blood was soaking through his shirt. When he pulled the shirt up, he saw three tiny holes across his chest, each trickling blood. They were probably half-repaired already, though still leaking.

A wave of dizziness overtook him and he swayed. He knew he could transform several more times to fully heal himself; he'd done so before. Still, he had a job to do. The sooner he got it done, the sooner he could get out of this place. He glanced upward and found Burnflank watching him quizzically.

Hal knelt before Fleck's metal contraption, recalling the instructions. The first thing was to check the geo-rock. He pulled open the iron door and looked inside. The rock was locked in place, glowing bright orange, a source of energy that would keep a home powered for months. He closed the door with a bang.

Next, he checked the dials. One showed the internal temperature of the oven. He knew it had to reach two hundred and sixty degrees, or thereabouts. And it would only begin heating when he allowed two of the volatile fluids to flow and mix.

He twisted a small lever on the bottom of one of the welded boxes. He could hear nothing over the noisy bubbling of the pool but could feel the short hose thrumming as the liquid flowed through it. He moved on to the other metal box and released that fluid, too. This time, he saw the connecting hose kick and twist. Both liquids were now splashing down over the geo-rock and mixing. In seconds, they would react and begin to heat. Hal watched the temperature gauge as, gradually, the tiny needle began to creep up.

Fleck had already preset a couple of the other dials. One had to do with the duration of the burn, whatever *that* meant. A precise amount of liquids had been injected, and Hal had been given specific instructions to release the final sack of juice once the temperature hit two hundred and sixty. It was simple, really, he thought as a stab of pain shot through his chest.

The pulsing gateway before him bulged outward suddenly and a great black cloud of smoke—*real* smoke—billowed all over him, making him choke. In that moment, he could feel and taste the heat of the fire in the basement not four feet from where he knelt. He feared an explosion. If something blew up within that basement, it would sent fiery chunks of debris all over, and some of it would come flying through the portal. Although he couldn't see or hear it, the raging fire beyond was still deadly.

"Come on, come on," he whispered, watching the dial. It had just reached two hundred degrees. He assumed it was measured in Fahrenheit but honestly had no idea. For all he knew, it was Celsius or something entirely foreign to his world. In any case, two hundred and sixty was the target, and he had a little over fifty degrees to go.

He winced again, wondering if the bullets were still lodged in his chest. He found one shell on the wooden platform just a couple of feet away. He looked for the others but found none. They might have fallen in the pool, or they might still be lodged inside his flesh. He shuddered at the thought.

As the dial crept up to two hundred and thirty, his thoughts wandered. What if the bullets had found his heart? He could be dead right now. What damage had they done to his organs, and how much had been repaired when he'd changed back into his human form? He was still on his feet—well, his knees at the moment—so clearly he was not at Death's door . . . but how close had he come to being killed by a stray bullet?

Two hundred and forty . . . two hundred and forty-five . . .

It was then Hal noticed something that chilled him to the bone. The sack that hung from the side—full of liquid that needed to be dumped into the oven at the precise moment the dial reached two hundred and sixty degrees—had a bullet hole in it. The precious liquid was dribbling out, and as Hal peered closer he saw that it had been dribbling for some time. It pooled underneath the machine and ran through the cracks between the boards of the platform.

Hal ran his finger up the backside of the oven, finding it slippery and wet. The sack was perhaps half empty.

Panic set in. Did it matter if half had been wasted? He knew it did. Fleck had measured all the liquids carefully, studying the papers as he did so. Everything had to be precise. With half the stuff missing . . . what would happen?

Hal watched the dial. It was now up to two hundred and fifty-five. He had to make a decision: dump the remaining half and hope for the best, or abort and come back later. The idea of aborting mortified him. He couldn't come back here! He'd have to fly back to the other side of the chasm, get Fleck to repair the bag, replenish the liquids, and then fly back—most likely in total darkness by that time. Would the emperor be that patient with him?

But if he dumped the remainder of the liquid, would it be enough to do the job? It was supposed to—what? He heard the centaur's words in his mind: *It instantly reacts with the heated liquid and creates an internal burst of pressure that pulverizes the rock and releases its pent up energy, thus—*

Hal shook his head. Fleck would know what to do. The centaur would make an instant decision and everything would be all right. But right now, right here, it was all up to Hal. He couldn't fail. As far as he remembered, if the oven didn't get hot enough, or if there wasn't enough pressure, the geo-rock would implode and he'd have to start over—which was not an option.

"What do I do?" he asked himself out loud.

With his fingers hovering over the release valve at the base of the sack, Hal finally made up his mind. The dial was already at two hundred and seventy. He'd missed the boat, so to speak. But he knew what he had to do.

He climbed shakily to his feet and stepped back as another billow of black smoke puffed out of the gateway. Choking, he shifted to his dragon form, almost toppling off the platform as he did so. He fought for a foothold, his wings beating. Then he launched upward, his wing tips scraping the smooth walls on either side. It took only a few strong beats to rise to the tunnel above, and once his clawed feet scrabbled onto the solid rock, he found himself facing Burnflank.

Is it done? the dragon asked.

"We need to leave," Hal said. "It's gonna blow."

They hurried up the tunnel, leaving the cavern behind. At a safe distance, Hal stopped and turned to wait.

He didn't have to wait long. A tremendous boom rocked the labyrinth, and the floor beneath his feet shook. Seconds later, heat blasted out of the tunnel. Hal heard cracks and splinters somewhere, and the trickling of dust and small bits of rock. The rumbles continued for half a minute afterward, gradually fading into silence.

When he returned to the cavern, it no longer existed. The tunnel ended in a wall of fallen rock, completely blocking the way. Hal couldn't be absolutely certain but imagined that the cavern ceiling had fallen in along with thousands of tons of rubble from above. The strange little iron oven had done its job and the hole was blocked forever. But as it had turned out, Hal mused, a few boxes of dynamite would have done the job just as well . . .

* * *

Later that night, in the pouring rain, Hal waited with Abigail and Blacknail in the gigantic steam buggy. Fleck, furious at the loss of his precious machine, had already started heading back home despite the weather. "I'll go on ahead," he had said stiffly. "I'm sure you'll catch up."

The centaur wasn't angry with Hal, Miss Simone assured him, but with the situation. Still, he griped continuously about it just before he left. "If I'd known you were going to blow everything up," he muttered, "you could have used dynamite and saved me a long journey. Now I'm going to have to build another machine."

Hal rolled his eyes as Fleck took off into the night.

"So what happened?" Abigail asked again, staring at the spots of blood on the front of Hal's shirt. Now that the two of them were seated together in the buggy, waiting for Miss Simone to return, Abigail had resumed her fussing.

"It's nothing," Hal told her. "Seriously, I'm all healed up now."

"But *what happened*? Did you get clawed, or what?"

Hal mumbled something.

"Sorry?" Abigail persisted, a frown lining her forehead. "I didn't catch that. It's almost as if you were trying not to be heard."

"They shot me," Hal repeated loudly.

Blacknail twisted in his seat and stared at him with small black eyes, his face shrouded in shadows.

Abigail couldn't take her eyes off the three crimson spots. "They shot you," she said quietly. "In the chest."

"They were just stray bullets. I was a dragon at the time." He looked over her shoulder, squinting into the moonlight. "What's *taking* so long?"

Together, they peered into the distance. Two figures stood in the rain, holding hands and facing each other. Blacknail had parked well away from the labyrinth so that Burnflank, otherwise known as Felipe, could reunite with his twin sister in secret. He was wrapped in Miss Simone's cloak, hunched over as he swayed on two human legs for the first time in years. Hal couldn't help fearing that the transformation would heal those telltale battle scars and give him away as a shapeshifter . . . but the wound was old and deep and would still be there when Felipe returned to the labyrinth in an hour or so.

"It's quite sweet, really," Abigail said softly. "All this time she thought he was dead, a failure, when he was here in the labyrinth doing the work of a hero."

"He *is* a hero," Hal agreed. "He's second only to the big chief, and that old thing's on his last legs. When he's gone, Felipe will be in charge."

Abigail sighed. "An entire labyrinth of dragons led by a shapeshifter. Now *that's* an achievement."

Chapter Three
Back at School

The test was almost over and Hal knew he'd blown it. He hated math with a vengeance. The smudged paper on his desk might as well have been filled with scientific equations written in the language of centaurs for all the difference it made to him. He sighed and hung his head, defeated.

After checking to make sure Mrs. Hunter was fully absorbed in her book, he glanced around to see how the others were doing. In an effort to ground the children in some semblance of normality, Mrs. Hunter had installed the desks exactly as they had been arranged in their old school building back on the island—nine small wooden units, equally spaced in three rows of three. Hal sat dead center, as he always had. On the first day back at school in the new world, everyone had claimed their familiar positions almost without thinking.

Lauren sat directly in front of Hal so all he saw was the back of her head, but from her posture he guessed she was feeling deflated. She sat between Emily and Darcy. As usual, Emily had finished the test early and looked annoyingly satisfied with herself. Meanwhile, Darcy was sound asleep with her blond hair spread across her desk.

Hal looked to his left. Robbie sat there looking shell-shocked, his pencil broken in two. To the right, Fenton was staring at the ceiling, his test paper scrunched into a ball and his pencil jammed through the middle.

Mrs. Hunter chose that moment to look up at her students, catching Hal as he returned his gaze to the front. She narrowed her eyes at him, then continued her routine scan of the class before going back to her book.

With extravagant movements to give the impression he was stretching the kinks out of tired neck muscles, Hal sneaked a look over his left shoulder and caught Abigail's eye. She sat in the back behind Robbie and was busy chewing her pencil. When she saw him, she grinned and rolled her eyes. Hal feigned the look of someone who had just had his brain sucked out by a hideous monster, leaving a glassy-eyed, drooling shell. This made her grin even more.

Dewey sat right behind Hal, and a quick, awkward glance showed that the diminutive boy was still working through a sum, his tongue sticking out.

Hal faced front and checked on Mrs. Hunter again. She turned the page, oblivious. Hal slowly twisted around to where the ninth desk stood at the back behind Fenton.

Many things in the classroom were the same, or at least familiar. The room was larger but the windows smaller. There was only one door into the room, whereas the old school building had two. Mrs. Hunter's desk was much grander, not that she cared. Behind her, the clock on the wall above the whiteboard read 9:50 AM. School started at eight and ended at noon, with a recess at ten. Everything was back to normal . . . except for the ninth desk in the back corner. For years that desk had stood empty, a reminder of Thomas's supposed death when he fell off the cliff on the edge of Black Woods. Now, in this new classroom, in this new world, the desk was occupied once again—by Thomas himself, red-haired and wiry.

"Face front, Hal," Mrs. Hunter said quietly but firmly.

Hal jerked his head around. "Sorry."

The clock crawled the final few minutes. Then the test was over and chairs started scraping as Mrs. Hunter called for recess. "Turn your papers in as you leave," she said, remaining seated. Hal deposited his test paper and hurried outside with everyone else.

"Your mom's turning into a monster," Abigail whispered to Lauren when they were all standing on the small grass lawn. The irony was obvious to all, and there were a few titters.

"She's stressed," Lauren said, shrugging. "She said we have a lot of catching up to do. Just because we're all important shapeshifters doesn't mean we get to skip school. That's what she tells me, anyway."

"I'd hate it if *my* mom were teaching us," Darcy said, running her hands through her hair. She still looked sleepy. "I'd turn invisible with shame."

The sky was darkening. It looked like rain was imminent.

"So who did well on their test?" Emily said brightly, linking her arms with Lauren and Darcy. "I might have got a couple wrong, but otherwise—"

"Oh, I thought it was really easy," Hal interrupted, ignoring the surprised looks he received. "I thought Mrs. Hunter said she was going to work us over this time? I finished in half an hour, wishing there was more."

"Me, too," Abigail agreed, nodding. "I don't think I got *any* wrong."

Emily squinted at them both, but before she could say anything, Robbie grinned and said, "Easiest test ever. Did you say you got a couple *wrong*, Em?"

Fenton chimed in. "Heck, even I aced that one. And that was without Hal's help. No need for me to beat Robbie up this time."

Robbie, about half Fenton's weight but a few inches taller, offered an extravagantly hostile stare that included bared teeth. "Oh yeah? You and whose army, Bridges?"

"Don't push me, beanpole," Fenton snarled back, the faintest of smiles on his face. "I could take you any day. I could wrap my tail a hundred times around your puny frame and squeeze until your eyes pop out. Your brain would pop out as well, *if* you had one."

"That tail of yours," Robbie said, jabbing a bony finger into Fenton's shoulder, "is really, really handy for swinging you around in circles."

Hal could barely suppress a grin. How things had changed. Fenton was still the class bully, only now he was just kidding around. Even Dewey made insulting remarks about the big boy from time to time, and Fenton took it all in good cheer. At least, most of the time.

"You didn't really find that test easy, did you?" Emily asked, frowning.

Abigail patted her affectionately on the shoulder. "There, there, don't worry, I'm sure Mrs. Hunter will still think of you as her number one student even if everyone gets higher marks than you." She smiled at the red-haired boy, who was staring off into space. "How about you, Thomas? How'd you do?"

Since he'd been out of school for the past six years, living off the forest, Mrs. Hunter was working him at a lower grade level and had given him a far more basic set of questions. "Seems pointless to me," Thomas muttered. "I already know everything I need to know."

"Well," Emily immediately argued, "you never can tell when—"

There was a distant crash from across the rooftops, followed by a yell. All nine children looked in that direction but saw nothing over the high stone walls that surrounded the squat school building.

"I hate not being there to help," Robbie said wistfully. "The village needs rebuilding! I wish I could just skip school and work all day."

"I bet the builders wish that, too," Lauren said. "You can do ten times more work than the whole team put together."

One of the gates squeaked open, and all heads turned. Miss Simone entered the courtyard, her long blond hair shining in the sunlight. Several weeks ago, when she had first shown up on the perpetually foggy island, she had seemed supremely tanned. Now that the children were getting used to the harsh sunlight and had stopped using sunblock, their pale skins were darkening to the same shade. They had a long way to go to match the rest of the villagers' weather-beaten faces and arms, but they were beginning to fit in.

"Morning, Miss Simone!" Emily called cheerily.

"Morning, children," she replied, smiling as she approached. It had been a while since they'd seen her last, and Hal found himself entranced once again. He couldn't put his finger on it, but it seemed as though she glowed, somehow radiating an aura of beauty that affected all she passed in the street. At first, Hal and his friends had assumed that since she was one of the leaders of the village, all the sideways glances and lengthy gazes she received were out of simple respect. But no other member of the council attracted the same sort of attention; they were a collection of older men and women who mingled easily with the crowds. Even the fact that Miss Simone was a shapeshifter failed to explain the effect she had on people; men and boys alike watched her slack-jawed, while women tended to look on with a mixture of envy and jealousy. Darcy had often commented, quite openly, that she wished she looked like Miss Simone, while Emily, Lauren and Abigail were a little more close-mouthed—at least while Hal and the other boys were around.

"Quit staring," Abigail whispered in Hal's ear. She nudged him sharply, and he jumped.

"Are you on recess?" Miss Simone asked, looking toward the school. "I was hoping to speak with you all this morning . . . unless you're doing something really important?"

"We just finished a test," Emily said. "I think we're supposed to be studying geography next. Does Mrs. Hunter know you're coming?"

Abigail stepped in front of Emily. "Emily means that we'd *love* for you to take over and give Mrs. Hunter a break. Poor thing's overworked."

Miss Simone frowned. "Emily's overworked?"

"Mrs. Hunter is," Abigail clarified. "I'm sure she wouldn't mind if you popped in for a while."

Miss Simone nodded. "I'll go and talk to her."

She headed for the side door, her long silky cloak flowing easily in the still morning air.

When she disappeared inside, Fenton sighed heavily. "I swear she gets more gorgeous every day."

"Why isn't she married?" Robbie demanded, sounding almost angry.

Darcy lowered her voice. "I asked her that once. At first, she said it wouldn't be fitting for someone in her position to date anyone in the village."

Abigail snorted. "Doesn't stop anyone else on the council. They're *all* old and married, aren't they?"

"Anyway," Darcy went on, "after some prompting, she said that she had eyes for one man only, and he's not here."

There was a long silence as everyone digested this. Darcy looked around expectantly, and Hal suspected she already knew who the man was. After a while, Lauren whispered, "It's Charlie, isn't it?"

Darcy nodded. "Her childhood friend."

"Shh, she's coming," Emily said urgently.

Miss Simone approached again. "Mrs. Hunter wants to continue with class as normal." When everyone groaned, she held up her hands. "She's right. I can't just come barging in whenever I feel like it. But we can still have our chat. What are you doing after school?"

"I have to go to work," Robbie said, sounding torn. It was no secret that he enjoyed helping the builders but was clearly as intrigued as the rest of them about the 'little chat' Miss Simone proposed.

"Of course you do," she said, nodding. "And I don't want to interfere with that, either. You end around mid-afternoon, don't you?"

The builders started at dawn and worked until the sun was at its hottest, which irritated Robbie no end since that only gave him about three hours after school.

"All right," Miss Simone said, "let's all meet wherever and whenever the workers finish up today. As soon as Robbie's free, I want to show you around the laboratory."

* * *

When class ended at midday, Robbie tore out of the room with a happy grin on his face, yelling "Bye!" over his shoulder.

"Nerd," Fenton muttered.

"What's nerdish about wanting to rebuild the village?" Hal argued. "He's an ogre. Nobody is better suited to haul stone blocks around than our Robbie."

"Nothing nerdish about the job," Fenton agreed. "I'm just saying he's a nerd, that's all. Always was, always will be."

After a noisy round of "goodbyes," the children peeled off in different directions, most heading home for lunch. Emily, Lauren and Darcy filed out of the gate and then, once in the street, linked arms and went off with their heads together. Fenton and Dewey exchanged a few words before splitting. Thomas strolled away on his own.

Hal and Abigail watched him go, then joined the busy streets that cut through the market area.

"I wonder how Thomas is doing," Abigail wondered aloud.

"Why don't you ask him?" Hal said.

Abigail scowled. "Why don't *you*? Honestly, don't you boys look out for each other? If Thomas were a girl, I'd be checking with him, making sure he's fitting in okay at home, that sort of thing."

"If Thomas were a girl, I'd be wondering why his parents named her Thomas."

"Oh, you're very funny," Abigail said, rolling her eyes. "Seriously, aren't you curious? He's had a tough life. He fell off a cliff, for goodness' sake, and we all thought he was dead. He spent six years growing up in a forest living with savage beasts. Now he's back home, sharing his parents with two adopted younger sisters. How do you think he feels about that?"

Hal shrugged. "I've asked him a few times. He just says he's fine. Look, boys aren't like girls; they don't cry and whine about everything. They just—"

Abigail rounded on him. "*Cry and whine?*"

"Oh, I didn't mean you," Hal said hastily, stepping away from her before she could hit him. "You're not like normal girls. I mean, you *are*, but—"

"Look out!" Abigail exclaimed, yanking him by the shirt.

A man with a wheelbarrow hurried past, sweating profusely, missing Hal by inches. The man was carting a pile of rounded glowing rocks, each about the size of a head but slightly elongated. Most of what was grown, baked, roasted, weaved or built in the village was traded on a daily basis, but geo-rocks were free for whoever needed them, delivered upon request when old ones fizzled out. Energy in the home, Miss Simone and the council had decreed long ago, should not be a luxury but a necessity, the same way that medicine was freely available to whoever needed it.

That said, nothing was completely free in a thriving community; the miners who brought in the rocks had to be paid for their work, so they were paid by the council who, in turn, recuperated their costs via taxes. The children had learned all about this stuff, and far more, in class during the past couple of weeks. Only occasional tidbits were interesting to Hal, though; the rest went in one ear and out the other . . .

He and Abigail had come to a stop in the middle of the street, and she still had a tight hold of his shirt. When he returned his attention to her, she was staring at him, her nose inches from his, eyes narrowed.

"Do you think I cry and whine?" she murmured.

Hal shook his head. "No, I was just saying that—"

"Do you still like me?"

The question threw him. "What? Of course I do! What do you—"

"Then how come you've never tried to kiss me?"

The world seemed to slow to a grinding halt around them. Hal swore that villagers were turning to peer at them, conversations dying as they tuned in to Abigail's question. It was probably all in his imagination, but he felt distinctly uncomfortable all the same.

She continued to peer at him, and he found he could see his own reflection in her deep brown eyes even though she squinted in the bright sunlight. He was so close he could count the light freckles across her nose and cheeks.

"Uh . . ." he said.

Her frown deepened. "Well?"

"It's just . . . well, I mean . . ."

Abigail released him suddenly and cast her eyes down. Then she grinned. "Had you going, didn't I? You should see your face right now." She gave him a hard shove on the shoulder. "Come on, I'm starving. Are we eating at yours or mine today?"

They set off again, and on the surface everything seemed normal again. But Hal was troubled. He knew her too well; he knew she was putting on a front to hide what she was really feeling.

Why is this boyfriend-girlfriend thing so complicated? he wondered as he allowed her to take the lead.

In truth, it wasn't. He just had to pluck up the courage to kiss her. It had been weeks since she'd pecked him on the cheek in the darkness of a tunnel, and it had somehow sealed the deal; she was officially his girlfriend. But he'd not yet kissed her back. Instead, he'd wound himself up in knots thinking about it, and the more he delayed, the more it became an issue. And now he was convinced that if he kissed her anytime soon, she would just assume he was trying to make her feel better, further compounding the problem.

They ended up in Abigail's kitchen before he knew it, and she was soon busy making sandwiches for them both, chatting about something that Hal was only half listening to. Then her mom, Dr. Porter, bustled in looking harried.

"What's up, Mom?" Abigail asked, the bread knife poised.

"Oh, nothing," Dr. Porter muttered. "It's just . . . well, you know old Norm? He hurt his foot a while ago, nearly chopped his toes off with his own shovel."

Hal remembered him. He'd first met the wrinkled old man in the waiting room at Dr. Kessler's home. Since then, Abigail's mom had been treating him.

"The injury just won't heal," she fussed, pouring herself a glass of water. "Keeps getting infected, swells up and stinks badly . . . We might end up taking half his foot off at this rate. We need a *hospital*."

Abigail sawed through the huge sandwich she'd made and offered half to Hal. "We have a hospital, Mom."

"No, we don't," Dr. Porter said, shaking her head. "We have a place in the woods with poorly trained doctors using medicine from the dark ages. All my stocks are used up already."

Hal frowned. "The stuff from storage, you mean?"

Back on the island was a huge barn full of supplies, stored in preparation for an eight- or nine-year stint in solitude. It had turned into thirteen years, but the small community had managed well enough. Being shapeshifters, immune to common illnesses and able to heal quickly from wounds, much of the medicine reserved for the growing children had not been needed. Still, much of it had been used by the adults over the years, and what little was left had been transferred to the village of Carter.

"All gone," Dr. Porter said. "Except for a few samples that the scientists are trying to duplicate. Meanwhile, Simone has just sent another team to the old world. There are pharmacies all over the country stocked to the gills with the medicine we need."

"But it's all old," Abigail said, sitting at the table alongside Hal.

"Better old than nothing at all," Dr. Porter said stiffly. She pulled out a chair and sat heavily. "Simone thinks there's a better way, though."

"A better way than what?" Hal said with his mouth full.

"A better way than making a trip to the other world. Simone has an idea that will do away with the need for medicine altogether."

Hal and Abigail stopped chewing and stared at each other.

"Does this plan involve us?" Hal said suspiciously.

Dr. Porter shrugged. "I have absolutely no idea. I'm not really kept in the loop regarding Simone's ideas. Anyway, I'm too busy doctoring. All I know is that she has some bright idea that has some of the scientists excited and others clicking their tongues."

"We're supposed to be seeing her later," Abigail said. "She wants to show us something and have a chat."

Dr. Porter scowled. "No doubt you'll be off on a mission, then, to find some kind of magical plant that grows on the top of the highest mountain in some distant, dangerous land guarded by hundreds of nightmarish monsters."

"You think?" Hal said.

Immediately the doctor looked worried. "Gosh, I hope not! Although I hope Simone's serious about this idea of hers because otherwise old Norm is soon going to be called Hopalong. He's ninety-three, you know, and still planting potatoes in that field of his! He needs to quit. He already has one foot in the grave; he can't afford to lose the other."

For some reason, this set her off laughing hysterically.

Chapter Four
The Science Laboratory

The damage to the village was extensive. After threading their way through the ebbing market, Hal and Abigail turned onto a street that was virtually empty. The only people who bothered to walk this way now either lived in these parts, were on the reconstruction work force, or simply had a hankering to see how things were going.

The narrow street curved gently, stone-walled thatched cottages at both sides. A woman was sweeping her front step; the village was dry and dusty at the best of times, but here the air was filled with a haze that coated everything in sight. The noise was terrific, too—the clattering of pulleys and chains, the resounding *clacks* of old wooden frames being tossed onto scrap heaps, the *tink-tink* of small masonry peins, the rasping of wood being sawn, and the constant yells of tired foremen.

As Hal and Abigail rounded the curve, the street ahead opened up into an expanse of rubble over which hung a dust cloud. Roughly fifty men and twenty centaurs toiled in the heat.

It had not taken long for the angry, wounded, hundred-foot lizard to cause all this damage. It would take many months of tireless building to restore dozens of ruined homes, even with the help of the shamed centaurs and a happy ogre. The building site was long, a path of destruction that ran from the village center all the way out to the far northeastern perimeter. Cottages had either been flattened by the rampaging beast or dismantled afterward. Many thousands of stone blocks had been salvaged from the rubble, along with wooden beams, window frames, doors, and whatever else could be dug free. The rest, endless tons of dust and debris, was still being carted away to use as landfill.

Hal started coughing the moment he entered the work zone. He and Abigail followed a meandering path around piles of stone and trash. Several bonfires were smoldering; blackened furniture and unidentifiable bits of wood stuck out everywhere, and smoke rolled upward to join the dust. A few cottages within the zone stood intact, having randomly survived the rampage with nothing more than a few broken windows. A prim and proper middle-aged woman known as Fussy Felonia still lived in her home, which had remained untouched while neighboring homes had collapsed all around. When she stepped out of her front door every morning, she took a circuitous route around haphazard mounds of stone, trod gingerly over a flattened bed frame, and ducked under a low-hanging roof to get to the nearest street. Naturally, she turned up her nose at the mess and complained of the filth coating her windows.

The centaurs were hauling four-wheeled carts this way and that, some piled high with junk and others stacked neatly with salvaged stone blocks. In light of recent developments, centaurs were looked upon with disdain. Nevertheless, their tireless help in the construction zone was invaluable. So, too, was that of the goblins. Despite their constant grumbling and scowling, they were always in the thick of the building work. Even children were running around doing odd jobs here and there. Yet there was a relatively small proportion of men present. While goblins were able to postpone their daily ironwork and mechanical tinkering, farmers had no such luxury. "The farms won't tend themselves!" they had exclaimed from the outset.

Robbie's giant ogre form dominated the place, looming nearly three times the height of other workers. Normally, it was a slow two-person job to hoist stone blocks off carts and into position on newly formed cottage walls, while another applied the cement ahead of them. Robbie was much faster and able to grab stone blocks on his own; the builders had gotten into a routine of constructing two walls at the same time so that Robbie could alternate his efforts between them.

Block work was only a small part of Robbie's job. At any moment, he could be called away to move some debris or to lift a beam into place. He worked with boundless energy and enthusiasm, enjoying every minute of it, and as a result had earned the gratitude and respect of everyone on the work force. Hal had come along to watch on several occasions, had even shifted into his dragon form in an effort to lend his weight . . . but he lacked dexterity, and his tail got in the way, and there was always an air of wariness as though a dragon could never fully be trusted. They asked him to light bonfires, but he sensed this was a token request to make him feel useful. He was better off out of it.

"Dewey's still not helping, then," Abigail said, scanning the burly centaurs that traipsed this way and that.

"He's too busy writing *poetry*," Hal scoffed. He shook his head in disgust. Somehow his respect for the boy had dwindled lately.

"Now, don't be mean," Abigail chided him. "Let him write. He always was a quiet one. And you know how ashamed he is of centaurs now."

Dewey hadn't switched to his centaur form in weeks, much to Miss Simone's chagrin. "Not all centaurs are bad," she reminded him constantly, "and it's foolish to shun the entire species just because of what a few bad apples did." But it was obvious she was choking on her own words. Nobody would easily forgive the centaurs for the havoc they had wreaked on humankind.

Hal watched Robbie at work, feeling a swell of pride as the ogre leaned on a partial wall and listened to the foreman's instructions. There was certainly no sign of wariness with Robbie around; he was part of the team. "We need a few more ogres," Hal remarked. "Bet they'd have the village rebuilt in no time."

"Or the clumsy oafs would end up destroying the rest by mistake," Abigail muttered. "Are they knocking off soon, or what?"

They had to wait nearly ten minutes before they heard a long warbling horn. Men, women and children trudged away without a word, mopping their brows and dusting off their hands. When Robbie finished tipping an old roof structure onto a bonfire, Hal and Abigail wandered over and called to him.

Robbie turned his huge shaggy head and squinted at them. Then he grinned, his big blunt teeth uneven and gapped. "Huhnnn."

"Uh, yeah, whatever," Hal said under his breath, nodding and waving. He raised his voice. "Come on, we gotta go."

The transformation from ogre to human was swift. The ogre's massive hulking frame dwindled in less than a second to a lanky twelve-year-old boy with a mop of untidy brown hair. At the same time, the mysterious material that formed his belt expanded into a simple shirt and pants that were woefully baggy on his frame. His trouser legs were still knitting together a full second after his transformation was complete—not that Robbie appeared to notice.

He ambled closer, brushing off his hands, a grin plastered across his face. "I can't wait for the weekend. A couple of hours just isn't enough for me. I could keep going all day—probably all night, too, if they'd let me. I get more done than a team of five or six. I reckon they should—"

"Bravo, Robbie, *bravo!*" Abigail cried, clasping her hands together. "Gosh, I'm so awestruck and impressed, I could just about *die* right now."

"I'll help you along," Robbie said, scowling. He deliberately turned away from her and faced Hal. "Hey, remember when you and I used to avoid Abigail because she was such a nuisance?" He looked whimsical. "Good times."

Abigail linked her arm through Hal's. "And then Hal realized how much he liked me, and how much of a loser *you* were." She grinned brightly.

Robbie feigned surprise. "When you poisoned his mind and manipulated him? Is that what you think being *liked* means?"

Hal could listen to Robbie and Abigail bickering all day long. Not so long ago, there had been genuine rivalry between them, but now they just seemed to enjoy bickering for the sake of it.

Still, time was pressing on. "All right, kiddies," he said, "enough already. I see a few of the others over there."

Fenton, Darcy, Emily and Lauren were emerging from one of the streets into the work zone, stepping carefully over rubble. Almost at the same time, Dewey ambled out of the haze, brushing off his pants as if he'd been sitting. He carried a small journal and had a pencil gripped between his teeth.

"Got any new poems, Dewey?" Abigail called as the groups converged.

The boy hurriedly stuffed the journal into his waistband around his back, and covered it over with his shirt. Hal saw Fenton eyeing the obvious square bulge with temptation in his eyes.

Emily shielded her eyes against the sun. "So where's Miss Simone?"

Fenton lazily turned a stone over with his toe. "I think this is Mrs. Miggins' chimney I'm standing on."

"My feet are all dirty," Darcy complained.

They all wore enchanted clothes, which came in different shades of mottled greens and grays, some plain and others with flowery, earthy patterns. Not one set of clothes matched another, yet as a group they clearly belonged together, woven by the same hand. Shoes were included, of a sort; they were simple foot-shaped pads of malleable material that eerily came to life when stepped upon, clinging to heels and toes and stretching up around the sides. They didn't cover the tops of the feet at all, giving the impression that Hal and his friends walked around barefoot . . . and yet their tender soles were cushioned and protected against the sharpest stones. These *smart clothes*, as Hal called them, felt warm to the touch. That wasn't such a welcome enhancement on sweltering afternoons but was a blessing on cold evenings.

Lauren and Robbie asked the same question in unison: "Where's Thomas?"

Straight away, the pair glanced at each other and grinned, Robbie far more broadly than Lauren, whose cheeks reddened. Their relationship was similar to Hal's and Abigail's, which was to say awkward. Robbie liked Lauren, but she remained undecided, so they seemed to be in a perpetual state of *not really sure.*

Everyone searched the haze for a boy with bright red hair. They were all craning their necks and squinting when Miss Simone appeared from the nearest street. She swept into the clearing in her usual rapid, no-nonsense manner as if she had a million and one things to do. Which she probably did.

"This way," she called, walking straight past them. She smelled of the ocean, which had always struck Hal as pleasant but odd. He was pretty sure she didn't wear perfume and that it was just her natural aroma. It was hardly surprising considering she was a mermaid, but he hadn't noticed any such odd smells emanating from his shapeshifter friends—well, except for Robbie, who always managed to have something brown and nasty smeared on his feet, and Fenton, who still hadn't learned the art of washing his armpits.

It made Hal wonder, suddenly, if *he* smelled of anything as he went about his daily life—like, for instance, a dragon. He chewed his lip and made a mental note to ask Abigail sometime.

Thomas was waiting up ahead, his bright red hair glinting in the sunlight even through the clouds of dust. He waited while the group approached, then slipped into the procession without a word. The nine were complete.

They followed Miss Simone the length of the wasteland. More than twenty homes had been pulverized by the monster lizards that had stomped into the village, and several more had suffered enough damage to render them uninhabitable. The lizards were each a hundred feet from snout to rump and double that length with their thin tails. They hadn't just stepped on buildings with tree trunk legs; they'd dragged their entire bodies over them, street after street, demolishing everything that stood upright. That had been a couple of weeks ago, and the workers were still clearing the mess and salvaging materials to use for new homes. They had a long way to go.

Fenton appeared unaffected by the carnage caused by his alter-kind. If it had been dragons that had caused this mess, Hal would have been mortified just by association. Still, the damage would have been much, much worse if Fenton hadn't arrived atop the grandest lizard of all—the mother. The two enraged young bulls, one injured by a soldier's rocket launcher, had stopped dead in their tracks at the sight of their long-lost parent.

Toward the top end of the work zone, near the perimeter where green rolling hills loomed on the horizon, Miss Simone led the children off to one side and into a street. She walked quickly, and Hal found that his calf muscles were burning as he tried to keep in step. He focused on her silky green cloak, which flapped and undulated gently. He had wondered why she always wore it until, one day, he had seen her walking through town without it. She had attracted the unashamed stares of every man she passed. "Some things never change," she had muttered sourly. The poor woman had since returned to wearing her cloak.

They arrived at a familiar two-story building with small dust-coated windows. Despite its outward derelict appearance, Hal knew it was a hive of activity within. "We're going to send a message?" he whispered to Abigail.

Miss Simone pushed open the door and stepped inside. The children crowded in after her and, when they were all standing together in the cool, dingy hallway, she gestured into one of the rooms where two or three figures moved around in the shadows.

"You already know this building is used for communications. In here, we send and receive holographic messages. For example, I can speak directly to Charlie even though he's hundreds of miles away in Louis."

Hal had seen the equipment before. It was a complex setup of lenses and geo-rocks and marks on the floor, and a fishbowl containing some strange blue liquid, and lights that came on and somehow created a fuzzy projection of a man or woman with a tinny, warbled voice.

"You also know that we hold our council meetings upstairs," Miss Simone continued, jerking her thumb skyward. The staircase was around the back, with its own entranceway. "The other rooms here— well, they don't really matter." She waved her hand to dismiss several other doorways that lined the hall. "But that room at the end is where I started my work."

She moved up the hall, and Hal was ushered along with the crowd. Abigail's eyes were wide, her level of curiosity probably far higher than Hal's.

Miss Simone turned the doorknob and walked into the room without knocking. She gestured for her audience to enter. Hal was jostled as his friends clamored to squeeze through the narrow frame. He ended up at the back of the room, standing on tiptoes, trying to peer over shoulders.

The room seemed utterly uninteresting: just a couple of surprised men seated at desks, writing in journals. There was a large chest of drawers in the corner, a few tall cabinets along the side wall . . . All in all, absolutely nothing worth looking at. But Miss Simone was waving her hands expansively.

"This is where I first came to work. The building used to be the science laboratory, back in the days when old Bartholomew was in charge. He died several years ago, but he gave me his job long before. He seemed to think I was well suited for the task of running the science lab. I wasn't, of course; I was only interested in the work I was doing and found myself being pestered every minute of the day by others seeking permission to do this and that . . ." She smiled ruefully. "Old Bart was right. If you love your work and want to get on uninterrupted, then don't be in charge."

Nobody said anything. Hal, like his friends, sensed that she was gradually getting to a point.

"We'll go to the new laboratory in a moment, but I wanted to show you where it all started for me. And where it started for Jolie."

Hal felt a nudge and glanced sideways to find Abigail raising her eyebrows at him. He shook his head. *No, I don't know who Jolie is.*

"You left the island nearly four weeks ago," Miss Simone said, looking around and studying each of them in turn. "You hit the ground running and spent the first ten days dealing with dragons, harpies, giant lizards, and of course uncovering the mystery of the virus. Now you're back at school. No doubt you're feeling that your lives are a little . . . well, anticlimactic? Not quite what you imagined?" She smiled. "Well, if it were up to me, I'd whisk you out of school and enroll you in the science program."

"It *is* up to you," Emily piped up.

Miss Simone laughed. "I'm just part of the council, Emily. I'm not a supreme ruler with the power of veto. You need to stay in school and finish your education like everyone else. But . . ."

"But?" Abigail blurted.

"But you're shapeshifters, and you have important roles in this world. I need to take you out of school on occasion and send you on missions."

Abigail gave a sigh, and Hal could tell by the look on her face that it was one of happiness. Hal had to agree. Despite the dangers they'd all faced on Miss Simone's missions thus far, they were far more interesting than Mrs. Hunter's test papers.

"I have a new mission for you," Miss Simone said. She looked wistfully at the wall directly opposite the door where a framed painting hung. It depicted a herd of unicorns galloping across a plain.

Lauren voiced the question everyone seemed to be thinking. "We're going to ride unicorns?"

"Or are we going to *paint* unicorns?" Darcy said.

Abigail reached forward and poked Darcy in the back. "You really think a unicorn would stand by and let you dab paint all over it?"

"No, I meant—"

"Maybe it's simpler than that," Fenton interrupted loudly. "Maybe we're just going to learn to hang paintings on the wall. Did you consider *that*?"

"What are you all going on about?" Emily retorted, scowling around at everyone. "Why don't we just let Miss Simone explain?"

"Thank you, Emily," Miss Simone said quietly. She had the faintest of smiles on her lips. "No, you won't be painting unicorns, or hanging frames. I wasn't looking at the picture itself but at the wall it's hung on. There used to be a table right there, and on the table was a large tank of water. It was in that tank that I first saw Jolie in her altered form. She was just a one-year-old baby. And after she was gone, we emptied the tank and got rid of it, and I filled this wall with notes, sketches, and diagrams relating to the shapeshifter program. I sat in this very spot."

She indicated the exact position of her desk, suggesting that she simply had to turn her head to study her notes pinned to the wall.

"This was my office for years. I spent all day cooped up in this drab little room, and many evenings as well. I worked on the shapeshifter program, organized everything right here . . ."

Miss Simone seemed to be lost in memories as she turned in a circle, taking in every dark, dusty corner. The two men, both middle-aged, one with thin gray hair and the other with a mop of greasy curls, had paused to watch her, their quills poised over small ink wells.

"And what's our mission?" Abigail asked softly.

"What?" Miss Simone blinked, then shook her head. "Sorry. It's been a while since I stepped foot in here. Years ago, after we got the shapeshifter program running and then had to deal with the virus, everything settled down and we sat back and waited for you children to grow up. All was pretty quiet, and I had time to deal with politics. I requested a larger science laboratory, and that's where we're going now. Come along."

With that, she cut a path through the crowded children to the door, brushing past Hal as she went. Once again, he caught that familiar ocean scent.

Now Hal was in front of the crowd, right behind Miss Simone as she headed back down the hall to the front door. Behind him, Abigail was busy clicking her tongue and sighing noisily. "What's our *mission?*" she cried.

As infuriating as ever, Miss Simone said nothing. She swept outside and turned to head along the street. Hal and his friends hurried to keep up.

The new science laboratory was in the forest outside the village. There were a number of old barns and noisy workshops tucked away deep in the forest, most of them used or run by goblins, but it never ceased to amaze Hal when yet another building came into view, seeming to lurk behind the trees. This one was just a single story but a giant, rambling place that appeared to have been extended in a haphazard fashion. The main building was sturdy with thick log walls, surrounded by dozens of additional buildings, some with equally stout walls but others apparently built out of scrap. Every one of these buildings, large or small, was linked to the main laboratory with narrow enclosed corridors.

"The place seemed enormous at first," Miss Simone said, stopping and turning to face them all. Hal was happy to rest; the walk out of the village had been speedy and the trek through the forest mostly uphill.

He didn't like to admit it, but Miss Simone was walking his smart shoes off. "I really thought we had all the space we needed when we first moved in here. But if you put up a shelf, you soon fill it with junk, so you put up another shelf and quickly fill that with junk too. The lab has grown and grown, and we *still* don't have enough room. It's almost like it has a life of its own . . ."

She led them inside. Unlike the old building in the village, this one was clean and brightly lit, at least in the main lobby and corridors. Hal's mouth dropped open. After a lifetime on an island with no electricity, using only lanterns and candles, he had finally got to see working light bulbs here in Miss Simone's world thanks to the glowing geo-rocks, which provided clean energy straight from Mother Nature herself. In the science laboratory, light bulbs hung from every rafter and cast a brilliant white light. No doubt there were wires tucked away up there somewhere, leading to a closet full of geo-rocks.

"This way," Miss Simone said, leading them all down a wide corridor, her virtually bare feet padding on the polished boards.

"White coats," Abigail whispered as a woman appeared in a doorway, frowning at a clipboard. "This is *exactly* what I imagined back when we were on the island, before we knew what was going on."

Hal remembered it well. She had been convinced they were all going to be taken away to some brightly lit laboratory to be poked and prodded by doctors in white coats—and here they were in that exact place.

"This," Miss Simone said, gesturing into the room that the white-coated doctor had emerged from, "is where we make clothes for shapeshifters. What is it you call them, Hal?"

"Uh—smart clothes," he said as everyone turned to look at him.

Miss Simone nodded. "Well, we call them transmogrifying garments."

"Can we have a look?" Lauren asked, peering around the doorframe.

Miss Simone waved them inside. "Of course."

They filed into the small room and spread out. There was only one worker now that the white-coated woman had gone—another woman, rather tall and ugly with astoundingly thick eyebrows. It took a moment for Hal to tear his gaze away and focus on the long table stretching across the room. It was piled with bundles of material.

"Ooh, pretty," Emily said, picking up a long length of shiny green fabric. "Where does it come from?"

"The miengu," Miss Simone said. "They've never revealed where they get the silk itself from, but they certainly weave the clothes. There are caves all around their lake, many accessible only by swimming deep underwater. Some of these caves pop up inside the surrounding hills or woods, above water level and secret from the outside world. I guess it's *feasible* that the miengu breed silkworms somewhere . . ." Even as she said it, she looked doubtful. "We really don't know. The miengu are a mystery."

"That's a lot of silkworms," Robbie muttered. "I've read about it."

Miss Simone smiled. "So have I. A shirt like yours would use up a thousand silkworm cocoons. But the book I read was written in your old world, Robbie, and I'm sure you know that insects around here are much larger."

"Worms aren't insects," Fenton sneered.

Robbie rounded on him. "And silkworms aren't worms, moron. They're caterpillars—and they turn into moths. You get the silk by unraveling their cocoons. One unraveled cocoon stretches the length of *twelve football fields*, but it's so thin that it takes maybe ten lengths woven together to produce a single strand of useable silk the thickness of a hair."

Everyone was silent after his breathless outburst. Then Miss Simone patted him on the shoulder. "Very good. When you're done rebuilding the village, Robbie, I need to find you a part-time position in the biology department."

Robbie's eyes gleamed.

"As I said," Miss Simone went on, "silkworms in this world are much larger. Still, they need the right conditions to live, so I don't know where the miengu breed them. If indeed they breed them at all; it's all conjecture. In any case, none of this explains how the clothes become enchanted."

Another silence fell.

Miss Simone smiled. "There are plenty of things in this world we don't yet understand. Professor Bart came to the conclusion that there's an abundance of magic in the air we breathe, and shapeshifters transform almost as soon as they're born. In contrast, the *other* world has very little magic, and it takes eight years for a young shapeshifter to gather enough residual magic from the air to perform that first transformation."

"But you told us it was to do with the amount of *oxygen*," Abigail said.

Miss Simone nodded. "I told myself that, too. Jolie spent her first year in a room with slightly lower oxygen content, and it delayed her transformation. Of course, Old Bart argued that the hypoxicator also filtered out the magic. You could apply the same argument to the fog over the island . . ."

She sighed and held up her shiny fabric sample.

"I prefer to think there's a logical, scientific explanation for everything, but I can't explain our smart clothes, nor our shapeshifting ability. The clothes change shape as we transform, yet we don't *program* them—they just seem to do it automatically. They respond to us. It's nothing short of magical."

Hal tugged gently at his shirt, puzzled. It was soft and warm under his touch. It seemed so *ordinary*, and yet . . .

"When you meet the miengu of the lake," Miss Simone said, "you'd better keep an open mind about magic. Much of what we know of the miengu is utterly perplexing and quite beyond the realms of science as we know it."

There was a silence.

Finally, Lauren murmured, "We're . . . going to meet the miengu?"

"Some of you are, yes. That's your mission. Come with me. I want you to meet someone."

Chapter Five
Molly

The tour of the laboratory continued down a bright corridor with log walls and highly polished floorboards. Hal's gaze was again drawn to the dazzling lights hanging from the rafters. This gave him a hint of what his own world had been like before the virus, in the 'good old days' his mom often spoke of, when homes were powered by electricity. Even though Miss Simone strode along the corridor without stopping, not one of the children could resist peering around every door they passed—or at least those that stood open. Hal saw rooms filled with bizarre mechanical equipment, white-coated people hunched over tables, weird glowing objects, glass containers filled with bubbling liquids, and more. There were unsettling hums and whines coming from one room, and strange smells from another . . .

"What's all this for?" he heard one of his friends ask for the umpteenth time as they rounded a bend in the corridor. The light faded up ahead.

Miss Simone turned abruptly, forcing everyone to stop and bump into one another. "Sorry—I was distracted, thinking of something else. Did someone say something?"

Abigail repeated the question. "What's all this stuff for?"

"Oh, well," Miss Simone said airily. "Much of this section is for the research and development of medicine. We've taken quite a lot from your old world, especially in the past decade—there are plenty of abandoned pharmacies to plunder." She admitted to stealing without the slightest trace of shame. "But rather than rely on limited supplies that are past their shelf dates, we're trying to replicate drugs and medicines by using ingredients that we can easily obtain from our own world. It's a slow process, but we're getting there."

"My mom said she's short on medicine," Abigail said. "She said old Norm is going to lose his foot if it doesn't heal soon."

Miss Simone nodded. "We have a team on its way to your world now. Hopefully they'll come back with plenty of supplies."

"So they're actually going through a hole?" Hal said. "Who's going? And which hole?"

"A small group—three men, a woman, and two goblins. They tend to use the portal up at Louis, on the fourth floor of the science lab."

"The one that comes out over the lake," Abigail said, nodding.

"It's the safest and most convenient," Miss Simone agreed. "Except that we have to go so far north, of course. The alternative is using the ones on the island, and now that we've closed the one in the tunnel, that leaves two underwater. Hardly ideal, and too risky now that the soldiers are aware of the place."

She turned and gestured for them to continue following. Everyone shuffled in silence as the bright lights ended and they were plunged into shadows. At the far end of the corridor, the building ended at a large set of double doors, which stood open, allowing access to a dingy narrow passage beyond, barely wide enough to walk single file.

"We're heading into one of many lab extensions now," Miss Simone said from up ahead, calling back over her shoulder. "This one is goblin territory."

The floorboards here were rough and uneven, and squeaked noisily. There were gaps in the walls that allowed daylight to flood in—the only source of illumination, Hal realized. Oil lamps hung in places but none were lit.

The passage rose up and down, clearly following the terrain of the forest outside. It wasn't long before they reached the end and passed through a thick-framed doorway. The heavy wooden door with wrought-iron fittings stood wide open. The group emerged in a hexagonal room with several narrow doors leading to further gloomy corridors. The place was a maze!

"Through here," Miss Simone said, her voice lowered. She disappeared through a doorway to the right. Hal lost sight of her with all his friends crowding the place, and he wished he was at the front of the group instead of stuck at the back. How come that always happened? Robbie had somehow wrangled his way to the head of the crowd, and even timid Dewey was bobbing in and out near the front, small and wily. But at least Hal wasn't *last*; behind him was a thoroughly bored Thomas at the rear.

When he finally made it to the narrow doorway, he was surprised to find a sign nailed there: JANNITERS OFFISE—CLEAR OFF.

Why on earth was Miss Simone leading them *here*?

The windowless room was some twenty feet across, an odd oval shape, gloomy and musty, lit with a couple of flickering lamps that hung from the low ceiling. A couple of tables stood against the walls, stacked with bottles of colorless liquids. Chairs were tucked underneath. The powerful odor of lemon filled the room—pleasant but so strong it stung Hal's eyes. A collection of brooms, mops, and metal buckets lined one side.

Three goblins sat on the floor. Alongside them, her back to the doorway, was a woman wearing a wide-brimmed hat. The four of them were in a circle, crouching over a collection of what looked like gray clay mice on the floor. A rusty bucket stood between two of the goblins. When Miss Simone cleared her throat, one of the scowling goblins glanced up.

"Can't you see we're busy—" he started. Then his eyes widened. "Ah, sorry, ma'am. Didn't see you there. Thought it was just a bunch of nasty kids."

"Nice," Abigail murmured, appearing by Hal's side.

"How are you getting on, Molly?" Miss Simone said, giving the goblin a dismissive wave of her hand as if to indicate that his apology was unnecessary.

The woman twisted around for a brief moment, then turned away again. "Not good, Simone," she grumbled.

In the brief moment that the woman had turned their way, Hal and his friends had seen that she wore a veil over her face, under the brim of the hat. It came all the way around to her ears and hung down to her chin.

Miss Simone beckoned the children to spread out around the foursome seated on the floor. "I gave Molly your glass ball, Abigail," she said.

Abigail's eyebrows shot up.

Miss Simone smiled. "I figured it would be really wonderful if Molly could undo the effects of her gaze. No more accidental deaths, you see?"

"Didn't work, though," Molly said sourly.

She was a thin woman. As Hal circled her, he saw long black hair curling out from under her hat and bony shoulders beneath the shawl that she was wrapped in. Her hands were thin and her wrists almost skeletal. He wished he could see her face; it was odd not being able to—

Then he remembered who Molly was and understood the reason for the veil. He instinctively took a step backward and averted his gaze.

Molly chuckled. "Don't worry, my dear. I have a lifetime of experience protecting others from my curse. I won't accidentally turn you to stone unless you stumble, fall, and yank my veil down by mistake. And even then you'd need to look into my eyes."

Hal heard his friends gasp, and more than one of them backed off the way Hal had. He felt marginally better about his knee-jerk reaction . . . but was still embarrassed. "Sorry," he mumbled.

"So it didn't work?" Miss Simone asked, sounding disappointed.

Molly shook her head, and her veil bobbed from side to side. "I looked into the glass ball and saw a lot of things. A lot of memories. Some of them were good, some were painful . . . but I saw nothing I didn't know already."

She turned her head, and Hal felt sure she was looking right at him through that fuzzy white veil.

"So you're the new generation, are you?" She gave another chuckle. Hal thought it contained a hint of bitterness. "Good luck with that."

Miss Simone shook her head and rolled her eyes. "Children, poor Molly is convinced she got a raw deal. In our group we have a unicorn, a phoenix, an elf, a lycanthrope, a winged horse—"

"A mermaid," Molly interjected, pointing at Miss Simone.

"—a griffin, a goblin, a dragon . . . and a gorgon."

Molly sniffed and drew herself up straight, though remained seated. "That's me. A stone-cold killer, I am. That's my lot in life, you see—to kill."

Hal and his friends were silent as Miss Simone reached out to pat Molly on the shoulder. "Now, now, don't start that again. Are you sure you didn't see anything in the glass ball?"

"Nothing," Molly said, and lashed out with a foot, striking a large rat-sized objects. From the sound it made, a dull *clunk*, Hal recognized it as a stone ornament. And then, with horror, he realized it wasn't an ornament at all. Nor were any of the other small gray objects littering the wooden floor.

"Are those—are those real animals?" he said, pointing.

"Well, they *were*," Molly said, and laughed explosively, her veil shaking.

"Molly's been testing on rodents," Miss Simone explained, touching one of the petrified mice with her bare toes. "We hoped she'd be able to find a way to undo the damage—to return life to these statues. If so, she could have come back to the village safe in the knowledge that nobody would be at permanent risk from her gaze."

"Back to the plains for me," Molly said, sounding glum.

"Um," Hal said. A question was begging to be answered. "How come you can turn people to stone when you're not—I mean, you're human right now, so why should—why does it—"

"What my pea-brained friend is trying to say," Abigail said brightly, "is that you're in human form, not gorgon form. So why does your gaze still kill?"

Molly slowly climbed to her feet, and Hal was surprised at how tall she stood—easily six feet. She didn't wear smart clothes; instead she was garbed in a distinctly grubby white robe of some kind that came down to her ankles, beneath which her worn leather boots looked completely out of place. She pulled her heavy shawl around her shoulders.

"My gaze," she said quietly, "is so powerful that I can't switch it off. It's been this way since the day I first transformed. Simone hoped I'd be able to stare into this glass ball and figure out how to disable it—or, failing that, find a way to reverse the effects of my stonings. Ha! No such luck. I'm cursed with it day in, day out. When in human form, my looks can kill; I can turn rodents, bugs, people, even dragons into stone. As a gorgon, it's far worse; it's faster and more powerful." She paused. "Care for a demonstration?"

Hal took another step back.

One of the girls squeaked, "No!"

Fenton burst out with, "Heck, yeah!"

"Hand me one of those critters," Molly said to a goblin.

With a grunt, one of the goblins reached into the tin bucket, rummaged around, and pulled out a squirming brown mouse. Darcy visibly shuddered and muttered something as the goblin held it between a fat finger and thumb.

Molly wasted no time. She first knelt, then placed her hands on the floor and leaned close to the mouse. All three goblins squeezed their eyes shut and turned away as she started to lift the veil. The woman was dutifully facing away from Hal and his friends, but he felt an urge to tear out of the room and hide . . . only his feet seemed to have taken root.

Feeling as if he had already been turned to stone, Hal stood utterly still and watched with morbid fascination as Molly leaned close to the mouse. It was sniffing, its tiny whiskers quivering. But as Molly's face drew near, it twitched and froze. Its shiny black eyes turned gray, and then the grayness spread like a disease across its face and down its body, all the way to its toes. The tail was last; it stiffened into a curl. It had taken no more than a few seconds for it to become just another stone ornament.

As the goblin gently laid the mouse on the floor, Molly studiously replaced her veil, tugged it straight at both corners, then climbed to her feet and faced her audience. "That's my curse, children, when I'm *not* in gorgon form."

"That poor mouse!" Emily cried. "I'm not sure I like you doing that—"

"It's either that or traps, miss," one of the goblins said shortly. He pointed to a table near the wall; underneath was a mouse trap complete with a dead mouse. "They're everywhere, dirty things. Vermin. Turning 'em to stone is cleaner." He gave a derisive snort. "Or we could use poison."

"Does it . . . does it hurt, being turned to stone?" Lauren asked quietly.

"Bet it doesn't," Robbie said, patting her on the shoulder.

"Bet it *does*," Fenton argued.

Robbie sighed. "And how would *you* know, O Chubby One?"

Molly held up her hands and the argument ceased. "My gaze petrifies victims to the core the moment they look into my eyes. They never cry out. It's fast. Even faster in my gorgon form—more spectacular, you might say. Once in a while, an unfortunate soul will explode into thousands of small chunks."

"Eww," Emily said.

Abigail stepped out from behind Fenton and gave him an annoyed stare as if trying to turn *him* to stone. Hal knew why she was annoyed; Fenton had been moving around since they'd entered the room, constantly blocking the view.

"Miss Simone," Abigail said, "this is all really interesting, and it's good to meet you, Molly, but . . . what does this have to do with our mission?"

Miss Simone smiled. "I can always rely on you to get to the point, Abigail. The thing is, Molly travels a lot. She spent years with Fenton's giant lizard family, keeping track of them as they moved from place to place. She's introduced herself to many of the more reticent creatures in our land, in many cases a painstaking process."

"Took months for the dryads to show themselves to me," Molly said, moving to a chair by a table. She collapsed into it and pulled open a drawer.

"And the trolls," Miss Simone went on. "But, to stay on track, it's the miengu we're interested in. Molly's met them, too. Well, sort of. There's only so much a landwalker can do to interact with underwater folk. But Molly has made progress. She's the one who collects the offcut silk material every so often in exchange for her, uh, unique services."

Hal was about to ask exactly what that meant when Molly exclaimed and brandished a square bronze box she'd found in the drawer. "Here it is! Thought someone had stolen it for a moment there."

She got up and brought it over to Miss Simone, who took it without a word.

One of the goblins climbed to his feet, grunting and huffing as if it were a great effort. "Can we get on now? The lab don't clean itself, you know. You done with the rodents?"

Miss Simone gave a nod and began ushering the children from the room. "Come along, let's leave the goblins to clear up. Molly, come with us."

They headed back along the narrow passage to the hexagonal room, and then on to the main building. There was a tiny doorway set in the shadows that Hal hadn't noticed before, and Miss Simone ducked through it. It led into a surprisingly large but very dark room.

Miss Simone stopped and turned, the bronze box tucked under her arm. "This is a quiet zone," she whispered. "Keep your voices down."

Once everyone had crowded into the room, Miss Simone continued.

"Darcy will find this room very interesting. It's where we study and sometimes interact with dryads. Look."

A sudden square of blinding light appeared as Miss Simone opened a small hatch in the wall. Through it, Hal saw the forest.

"We found that dryads, as shy as they are, can't resist spying on us. They know we occupy this building, and they know we look out at them through this small hatch, and yet they approach without fear, sometimes peering in from no more than a foot away. Goblins and scientists alike have met face to face with dryads in this way."

Darcy pushed through to the front and peered out the hatch at the trees beyond. Then she looked around the room. "It's because there's no door. The dryads aren't afraid because they know you can't get to them easily."

"Very good, Darcy," Miss Simone said, her voice filled with satisfaction. "Yes, this place was originally a nature watch with just a simple hatch. There are some rare birds in these woods. But now we have a tentative relationship with the dryads. There are two or three regulars, one male and two female. They only show when *they* want something, though."

"Like what?" Abigail piped up.

"It varies," Miss Simone said. "They're creatures of the woods. They don't want much from us and they certainly don't *need* anything from us. But occasionally they come along and ask for pretty things—shiny trinkets, jewelry, that sort of thing."

"Even the guys?" Fenton scoffed. "Bunch of sissies."

In the darkness, Hal heard a muffled *slap* followed by an "Oomph!"

"Watch your tongue," Darcy warned. "Next time it'll *really* hurt."

"He has a point, though," a muted voice said. It was Thomas. "What do they want shiny things for?"

There was a silence. Finally, Darcy looked around. "Oh, you're asking me? Well, how should I know?"

"Perhaps you can give it some thought," Miss Simone suggested. "I'd be interested to know, too. In fact, with your help, we can hopefully find out a whole lot more about the wood nymphs and increase our trade. Their help in seeking out medicinal plants is invaluable, and sometimes they bring us concoctions in little bowls that work wonders. Maybe all the medicine we need is out there in the forest."

"So you *don't* need drugs from our world?" Hal said, confused. "I thought you said earlier that—"

"Yes, we do need drugs from your world," Miss Simone said. "We need drugs and medicine because the dryads give us so little. They have a vast knowledge of nature and keep giving us hints—like tastes of what's out there. But they leave us wanting far, far more. A little potion here and there is not much good in the long run, and they never tell us the ingredients."

"So you'd like me to work with them?" Darcy asked. "I can do that."

Miss Simone closed the hatch, and they were all plunged into darkness. "That's your job here, Darcy, starting next week after school. As far as I'm concerned, you're now running this little operation. This is why you were . . . created, if you like. Your kind can give us so much."

The tour continued in silence, and Hal could sense that his friends were digesting Miss Simone's words. Hal had already dealt with his own kind, the dragons in the north. Lauren, too, had had a run-in with the harpies and hopefully put them on the right track, at least for now. And Fenton had bridged the gap between man and beast—literally— when it came to taming the gigantic black lizards that spat glue. They'd *all* had a role to play in the few weeks they'd been in this new land, and of course Robbie was temporarily offering his ogre strength in the efforts to rebuild the village. And now it was Darcy's turn.

Clearly sensing what Hal and his friends were thinking, Miss Simone waited before speaking again. By this time, they had made it back to the brightly lit corridors of the main building where there was room to spread out.

"Medicine is important as you can imagine. We send teams across to the other world to raid old pharmacies, which solves immediate problems. We have scientists who try to replicate these drugs with the resources we have in our less-advanced world. And we have the dryads who provide us with natural but mysterious concoctions that work wonders."

She paused outside a closed door and placed her hand on the doorknob.

"But there's another resource that could become available to us, and we believe this is our only hope in certain situations. Children, this room is where patients come to die."

As Hal took a step backward, Miss Simone turned the doorknob and pushed the door open. It swung slowly, revealing a large room with twelve beds, six on each side. Seven of the beds were occupied by sleeping men. Two doctors were in the room, one seated at a table and another checking the pulse of a patient.

"Incurable disease," Miss Simone said softly. "Bad hearts, failing livers. Conditions we can't even diagnose. This is a wonderful world, children, free of the pollution and crime you find in big cities, pretty much self-sufficient while remaining clean and environmentally friendly. But technology and knowledge also has a place in our world, especially when it comes to medicine. Unless . . ."

She closed the door quietly and faced them.

"Unless we can bring Jolie back."

Abigail let out a sigh. "Finally," she murmured to Hal.

Miss Simone nodded to Molly. The taller woman tipped her hat and leaned against the wall. Her veil revealed nothing of her face, but it was clear she was looking carefully around the group.

"Jolie is one of the miengu water spirits," Molly said. "They're not really spirits; they're flesh and blood like you and I. But their skin glows underwater, and they have an ethereal quality about them. They're not very well known because they're like the dryads—not exactly sociable. Not even Simone knows much about them, and she's a mermaid."

She jerked a bony thumb at the nearby door.

"Those men are dying. There's another room next door with three women, also dying. We can't save them with medicine. I doubt even the best hospitals in the other world could save them, *if* they were still in operation. All we can do is make them more comfortable. Yet . . . it's said that the miengu have healing abilities. It's said that they can bring people back from the brink of death. Nobody really knows how much of this is true, but there are stories I can tell you on our way to the lake."

"When are we going?" Abigail asked.

"Well, we're not *all* going," Molly said. "You're the faerie, right? We'll need you—or rather, your glass ball." She pointed to the bronze box that Miss Simone carried, and Hal guessed the glass ball must be inside. "And we'll need those who can swim underwater for more than twenty minutes."

Hal and his friends glanced around, sizing each other up.

Molly nodded, her veil wobbling. "I can see you've already figured out who's coming on this mission and who's not. I'll be taking the faerie, the dragon boy, the naga, and the big black lizard, whichever four you are. The rest can sit this one out."

There were some grumbles from Lauren and Dewey. Thomas remained silent, apparently uncaring. Robbie looked strangely pleased, but when he glanced toward Lauren, Hal understood and chuckled inwardly. As long as Lauren remained behind, Robbie was happy to as well.

"Aren't *you* going, Miss Simone?" Abigail said, frowning. "I would have thought that a mermaid—"

"Of course I'm going," Miss Simone interrupted. "I was the one who took Jolie to the lake in the first place, many years ago. But Molly has been trading with them for years, and she should lead, at least initially. We need you and your glass ball, Abigail. And we need Hal, Emily and Fenton for additional, uh . . . well, just in case."

"In case?" Emily said, sounding nervous. "In case what?"

Molly and Miss Simone exchanged a glance—or at least as far as the veil would allow. It was Molly who spoke.

"In case the miengu aren't receptive to our proposal to take Jolie back."

Chapter Six
Boat Trip

School was abandoned for those recruited to fetch Jolie from the lake. While Robbie, Lauren, Darcy, Thomas and Dewey grudgingly headed to class the next morning, Hal, Abigail, Fenton and Emily had a late breakfast, explained to their parents one last time where they were going, and met at the north gate.

Hal's parents had stared at him in silence when he'd first told them of the mission, but they didn't appear overly concerned. They believed this task paled in comparison to the recent trips to the labyrinth. Perhaps distance played a part, too; the labyrinth was ten or eleven hours away in Blacknail's buggy, whereas the lake was just a quick trip west along a nearby river. The children would be back in time for dinner. So Hal's dad had shaken his head, sighed, and said simply, "Be careful."

Hal left the house the next morning with a feeling of excitement rather than trepidation. He felt sure there wouldn't be any trouble but knew if there was that the team was equipped to deal with a few bad-tempered mermaid types.

He strolled along the winding path that skirted the village. The shapeshifter families had hastened their relocation to larger, more secluded houses in the woods to make way for the homeless villagers after the lizard rampage. These houses had been built specially for the shapeshifters and their parents many years ago in anticipation of their arrival in the new world, but had stood empty longer than expected and fallen into disrepair. They were homely now, though, and Hal loved it out here in the woods—unlike his mom, who preferred to be closer to the market.

Hal usually knocked on Robbie's door on his way to school, but today he continued on around the perimeter of the village toward the north gate. This took him past Abigail's house. She stepped outside into the morning sunshine and banged the door shut behind her.

"Not even a goodbye to your mom?" Hal asked.

Abigail shook her head. "She's long gone. She's out of the house by six every morning, off to Dr. Kessler's."

"Really? So you eat breakfast on your own every morning?" When Abigail nodded, Hal pursed his lips thoughtfully. "That's kind of sad."

She linked her arm through his. "Well, next time you walk to school with Robbie, think of poor me, all alone at home . . ."

Hal immediately felt bad. Since returning to school, he and Robbie had fallen back into their old habits. It was just like old times . . . and, as before, the walk to school excluded Abigail. He saw her every day in class and they often hung out together in the afternoons, but it had never occurred to him that she might feel lonely in the mornings.

"I'll walk you to school from now on," he promised.

"You'd be going out of your way," Abigail said, shaking her head. "How about I come by *your* house? That is, if Robbie can stand the intrusion."

"Sure," Hal agreed. But in the back of his mind, he felt that Robbie would probably be annoyed.

Both Miss Simone and Molly were waiting at the north gate, leaning against the fence and enjoying the fresh morning air. Emily was there, too, bright-eyed and cheerful, perched on a large rounded boulder. There was no sign of Fenton.

"Just like him to be late," Emily said with a roll of her eyes.

Molly was dressed in shiny green smart clothes today. The simple knee-length dress was shapeless, and so was the woman. Today, without the shawl on her shoulders, she looked even more gaunt than ever, tall and gangly with knobby knees.

In contrast, Miss Simone looked dazzling. Hal wondered if Molly ever felt jealous of her old classmate. The answer was almost certainly yes; she could never reveal her face and had no hope of a normal relationship, so it must be tormenting to hang out with someone as enchanting as Miss Simone. No wonder she lived the life of a recluse, always traveling . . .

"Penny for your thoughts?" Molly said.

Hal suddenly realized she must be looking at him. It was almost impossible to tell with the veil masking her face. "Uh, sorry. Just thinking. About stuff."

"Wondering what's under this veil?"

Hal felt his face heat up. "No, not really. I just—"

Molly cackled loudly, sounding like an old witch. "Relax, boy. Although, if you want to see my face anytime, just let me know. I'll be happy to lift my veil and let you take a peek."

"Thanks," Hal mumbled.

They waited a few minutes more, chatting idly. Molly joked a lot but frequently laced her humor with jabs at herself. It was as though she couldn't stand the idea of others talking behind her back about her unfortunate lifestyle, so she forced it into the open herself. "Who'd marry *me*?" she exclaimed after bringing up the distinctly awkward subject of Miss Simone and Charlie, only to have the tables turned. "Imagine me lifting my veil at the altar, gazing into my husband's eyes, and whispering the words, 'Till death do us part.' Conversations would drag after that; I'd get nothing but a stony silence."

Under her brash, self-deprecating exterior, she was clearly a sad, desperately lonely woman. Hal wondered how many people she had accidentally killed . . . and then he shuddered and pushed the ugly thought from his head.

Fenton showed eventually. By this time, Miss Simone was chomping at the bit. "Come on, come on—we can't stand around here all day."

A little way outside the gate, a goblin waited with a couple of sturdy horses hitched to a four-wheeled cart. They all climbed aboard and got situated with Miss Simone in the driver's seat and Emily beside her. Fenton, Hal and Abigail joined Molly in the back.

Molly turned to Fenton the moment the rickety wheels starting rolling. "So you're the lizard boy? I'll put names to faces eventually. I've been looking forward to meeting you, Fenton. I've spent over a decade keeping tabs on that pair of lizard monsters. I probably know them better than anybody else—aside from you, of course."

Fenton launched into great detail about his experiences with the gigantic mother lizard and, of course, his own shapeshifting ability that allowed him to *be* one of those creatures. Molly seemed enthralled, fully turning toward him and nodding vigorously, making her wide-brimmed hat and veil wobble furiously. She had probably learned to exaggerate her head movements since she had no other way to show that she was listening.

Hal and Abigail listened for a while, then tuned them out and launched into muted conversation about the questionable relationship between Robbie and Lauren. Meanwhile, up front, Emily was going on about something to do with school, and Miss Simone seemed only half interested.

The cart trundled along a dusty trail that wound its way out of the forest, heading first north and then a little to the west. The children saw hills in the distance. The sky was clear and blue, the sun warm on their backs.

After half an hour of leisurely trotting along a narrow lane with overgrown hedges on both sides, Miss Simone pulled up next to a gate on the right leading to a paddock of long grass. Conversation dwindled. Hal watched as she jumped down, unhitched the horses, and led them through the gate. "What's she doing?" he asked Molly. "We're not here already, are we?"

Molly shook her head. "Got a little way to go yet. But this is as far as we go by cart. The horses can run around in the field until we get back. Come on."

She stood, stretched, and climbed down. Hal and the others followed her as she ambled farther along the narrow lane. Then she stepped off the trail and through the bushes. As Hal squeezed through the gap, he found himself on the bank of a river. A rowboat bobbed there, tied to a low wooden jetty.

"Oh," he said. Now he remembered Miss Simone mentioning a journey along a river.

They climbed aboard. There were three bench seats, each wide enough for two passengers. A small triangular seat was crammed into the pointed space at the bow. Molly chose a seat alongside Emily in the stern. "You boys take some oars while us girls relax and enjoy the ride," Molly ordered without a hint of shame. "Wait for Simone, though; she'll be along in a minute."

The last time Hal had rowed anything had been a raft off the coast of his old island, in thick fog, with a sea serpent lurking in the depths of the sea. He and Abigail had also used a small boat on a lake after escaping the labyrinth, but that had been self-powered.

Sitting alongside Fenton and facing backward, he grasped an oar and practiced with it, sweeping it around in the air and ignoring Abigail's feigned yawns and stretches as she got comfortable in the seat opposite. Fenton grabbed his own oar and dunked it in the water. "Piece of cake," he said.

Miss Simone arrived, clutching the familiar bronze box. She placed it carefully in the boat, then climbed aboard and sat next to Abigail. "Off we go, then. Are you boys rowing? How kind of you to offer!"

After untying from the jetty, Hal and Fenton began to row—clumsily. It took a few minutes to get the hang of keeping the oars angled just right, dipping them deep enough, and rowing in unison, all the while suffering jibes and jeers from their passengers. Even Miss Simone had a smile on her face and a gleam in her eyes. But the boys were having fun regardless.

Hal felt on top of the world. The sun was so bright that he had to squint and so hot on his neck and shoulders that he suddenly wished for a quick dip in the river. He was reminded for the umpteenth time that this was a far cry from wallowing around in fog as he'd done all his life back on the island. How things had changed in just a few weeks. He listened to the sloshing of the oars in the water, the banter between Molly and the girls, the chirping of birds in the hedges and trees, and decided that life couldn't get any better than this.

"Do you want a rest?" Molly said eventually when conversation ebbed. "You've been rowing for about three minutes, and you look pretty exhausted."

"*Three minutes?*" Hal exclaimed before he could stop himself. Everyone laughed at him. "More like three hours," he muttered.

"Actually, no more than forty-five minutes, tops," Miss Simone said.

They rested awhile, the boat drifting and bobbing. Nobody said a word, enjoying the sound of a woodpecker tapping on a tree somewhere nearby.

Then Molly said, "Fenton, how long can you hold your breath underwater?"

Fenton shrugged. "Never timed myself."

"And you, Hal?"

When Hal shook his head, Molly gave Emily a nudge. "Well, I know *you* won't have a problem. You can hold your breath for an hour or more."

Emily's mouth dropped open. "I can?"

"Snakes are cold-blooded with slow metabolisms, so have a low oxygen demand," Molly said, twisting around to face her. Emily leaned back a little as though she feared Molly's death-gaze would burn right through the veil. "About a fifth of the oxygen intake in water-dwelling snakes is absorbed directly through the skin. And did you know that water snakes typically only use their right lung? Their left lung is usually very small and non-functioning."

A smile spread across Abigail's face. "Freak," she said.

"You know," Miss Simone said seriously, "we have an awful lot to learn about the anatomies of half-creatures. Take the naga, for instance: half human, half snake. Well, the water-dwelling variety is more snake than human, basically a giant serpentine body with a human head. The land-based naga have upper human bodies that *include* arms, so are perhaps more human than snake . . . especially when you consider internal organs."

"Yes, yes," Abigail said, rolling her eyes. "I often consider internal organs."

Miss Simone ignored the sarcasm. "We have to assume that a water-dwelling naga has the internal anatomy of a large sea snake. But it makes you wonder—are they cold-blooded or warm? Humans are warm-blooded, you see."

She paused, glancing from Hal to Fenton, then back to Emily.

"All three of you shapeshift into reptilian creatures, although Hal and Fenton become fully reptilian and are therefore cold-blooded. But Emily here is a mystery. All her kind are."

Abigail frowned. "What about you, then? Being a mermaid and all . . ."

Miss Simone nodded. "Good question. I'm a cross between a warm-blooded mammal and a cold-blooded fish. Go figure."

Molly chuckled. "Science could never create such bizarre mixtures by joining random parts of animals together. There's something far more complex at work in all of us. Take centaurs, for example. Do they have two sets of hearts, lungs, and other internal organs?"

There was a silence as Hal and his friends digested that. In truth, the 'horse half' of a centaur was far more than just a half. So where exactly was Dewey's heart? In his human chest . . . or the horse's chest?

"I know what you're thinking," Molly said, amusement clear in her voice. "You're thinking that a centaur is smart, intelligent, with humanlike emotions and traits, and therefore its heart must be contained within its human chest. But if that's so, how is it big and powerful enough to pump blood around the horse half?" She sighed loudly. "Oh, the mysteries of life!"

Abigail threw up her hands. "But surely *someone* knows the answer?"

Miss Simone smiled. "As far as centaurs go, yes. Their anatomies are complex. They actually have two fairly ordinary hearts, one human and one equine, and a twin set of internal organs, yet everything is wired together in a way that defies all understanding of biology. Occasionally, two-headed animals are born, or animals with conjoined twins. Somehow nature makes them work. Centaurs are a law unto themselves where anatomy is concerned. And their human halves have no stomachs; all that kind of thing is handled by the equine half. Food literally passes right through the human torso and into the equine intestinal tract where—"

Emily squeezed her eyes shut. "I don't think I want to know."

Molly laughed. "Oh, but you *need* to know, Emily. You've spent your life learning about human bodies, and you know where your heart is, where your lungs are, where your stomach is. But in your naga form, you literally don't know your own body."

"Well, at least *I'm* pretty normal," Abigail said, winking at Hal. "I can shrink to the size of a hand, but I stay the same shape. I'm a perfectly normal, warm-blooded mammal through and through."

"With insect wings," Fenton growled. "Explain *that*, freak."

He and Hal continued rowing shortly after. They were all deep in thought. Miss Simone looked oddly satisfied, and once or twice she glanced back at Molly and winked as if she had achieved some kind of small mission. A mission to get the children thinking? If so, it had worked.

As he rowed, Hal thought about his ability to breathe fire while in his human form. This was even more screwed up than Dewey's twin hearts. He mentioned it to Miss Simone, and her eyes lit up.

"Yes, a partial transformation. I would love to see an x-ray of your chest, Hal, when you're breathing fire in human form. I wonder what kind of changes occur to make such a feat possible! And Abigail— growing wings and flying around while at full human size?" She shook her head. "Faerie wings aren't built to carry human-sized creatures. See those bugs there?"

She pointed into the water, and everyone leaned to one side to look. It took a while to figure out that she was referring to small long-legged bugs standing on the surface of the water in a small cove near the bank. The river was calm there, being so well sheltered by reeds that the water barely wobbled.

"Those are water striders," Miss Simone said. "Sometimes called pond skaters. Their legs have tiny water-resistant hairs that allow them to stand on the skin of the water. Nothing unusual there . . . but if one of those bugs were magically grown to the size of a dog, do you think it would still be able to stand on the water without breaking the surface skin?"

"No," everyone intoned together.

"Nor would it be able to stand upright on its own skinny legs," she went on. "Its mass would increase exponentially and its legs would need to be much thicker and stronger, requiring bigger muscles within its body, further altering its physical anatomy . . ." She looked around at them all, one by one. "Do you understand? You, Abigail, have faerie's wings, yet a human-sized body. I don't know for certain, but I suspect your wings are larger than a normal faerie's in proportion to your body—am I right?"

Abigail's eyebrows shot up. "Yes! That's actually true. Although not when I'm faerie-sized. Then my wings seem smaller to me."

Miss Simone nodded with satisfaction.

Fenton shook his head. "I don't get it."

Hal was glad to hear him state this so bluntly. He only partially understood it himself.

As Miss Simone struggled for a way to explain, Molly jumped in. "Think of a cube. A small cube about *so* big." She demonstrated its size with her hands spaced six inches apart. "Let's double its size with a magic wand. So now it's twice as high, twice as wide, and twice as deep. Twice the size all over. See?"

Everyone nodded.

Molly shook her head, and her veil wobbled. "No, I don't think you do. You can double the *height* of our cube by placing a second, similar cube on top. Then you can double the *width*, for which you need another two cubes, making a total of four, right? Then, to double its *depth*, you have to add another four stacked cubes—making eight in total."

Emily rolled her eyes. "Wake me up when you're done."

"So our cube has doubled its size over three dimensions, but has *eight* times the volume, and therefore eight times the weight. The same happens when you increase the size of a bug. You can make it twice the size, and it will have legs twice as long as before, and a body twice as large . . . but suddenly it's eight times heavier. Now make the bug three times the original size, or four times, or six times . . . If a bug is ten times bigger than it should be, it will be a thousand times heavier. Its poor spindly legs simply wouldn't stand the strain."

Hal's mouth fell open. "But Fenton's lizard buddies are gigantic—"

"Because they grew to that size naturally," Miss Simone said. "Their bodies *evolved* to be powerful and muscular, just like dinosaurs were millions of years ago and elephants are today. Yet large beasts are extremely heavy and slow-moving. Also, it's worth remembering that gravitational forces are proportional to volume. If you drop a ten-inch lizard from a height of ten inches, it will be absolutely fine and will skitter away. But if you drop a hundred-foot lizard from a height of a hundred feet, it will splatter into a big gory mess."

Hal found that Fenton had stopped rowing, so he paused also.

Miss Simone's eyes were gleaming with excitement as she turned to Abigail. "When you shrink down to faerie size, there has to be *dramatic* internal changes to accommodate the shift. You go from five feet tall down to a mere six inches, roughly ten times shorter. Yet your body weight starts out at, what, ninety or a hundred pounds?—and drops to probably less than a couple ounces. Ten times smaller but a *thousand* times lighter. Your metabolic rate surely must shoot up to deal with the loss of energy and heat . . ."

She trailed off, then sighed. "Keep rowing, boys."

Hal and Fenton renewed their efforts while Abigail frowned at her hands as if there were something wrong with them.

Emily sighed. "I like to think that magic is involved. It's much easier to deal with than scientific calculations."

Molly nudged her. "I've been telling Simone that for years. Don't waste time trying to figure out what would happen if Hal turned into a dragon, ate a big dragon-sized meal, and then turned back into a human again."

The oar nearly slipped from Hal's grasp. He paused in his rowing and stared at the veiled lady with suspicion. "What do you mean? *What* would happen?"

He immediately tried to remember if he had ever eaten anything while in dragon form. He concluded that he hadn't—yet.

Fenton showed concern, too. "Yeah, what would happen?"

Molly chuckled. "Sorry. I shouldn't have said anything."

Miss Simone rolled her eyes. "She's kidding. Nothing will happen. Nothing bad, anyway. Try it sometime. It's important you figure out your own bodies and understand what happens when you change back and forth."

"Yeah, but—" Fenton said.

"Keep rowing, boys," Abigail said, grinning. "Why do you keep stopping?"

"Here, why don't I give you a break?" Miss Simone said. She untied her cloak from around her neck, folded it neatly, and handed it to Molly. Hal was getting ready to switch seats with her when she tipped sideways and fell with a splash into the water. The boat rocked violently and Emily gave a small scream.

"What—" Hal exclaimed, almost dropping his oar again.

"Relax," Molly purred, shaking her head. "Just pull those oars inside before you lose them."

Miss Simone had sunk out of sight. But now her head eased out of the water with barely a ripple, her blue eyes wide open with no sign of discomfort. She slipped sideways through the water, moving smoothly and without the use of her arms. A scaly fin rose to the surface for a second, then sank again.

Hal realized this was the first time he'd seen her swimming in her mermaid form. She slid through the water without effort and reached for a rope that was tied to the bow. Then she slipped below the surface, tugging on the rope as she went. The bow dipped a little, but the boat picked up speed, waves lapping gently at the sides.

This was far quicker than rowing. Hal and Fenton glanced at each other, then threw their oars into the bottom of the boat. Since they were facing the wrong way, Hal swung himself around into Miss Simone's vacated seat next to Abigail. Fenton then had room to turn around on his own seat.

"This is cool," Abigail said.

"Wish she'd offered earlier," Hal grumbled.

They cut along the river at four or five times their previous speed. The hedges and trees continued on both sides, thick and unrelenting, crowding the river as it rounded a bend. Then the hills rose ahead, suddenly close.

"Nearly there," Molly murmured.

Sure enough, the river started to widen. Miss Simone remained a hazy blur below the water, the rope taut, although her fishtail came into view once in a while. How long had she been holding her breath? Ten or fifteen minutes?

And then they were at the lake. The overgrown banks peeled off while the boat continued directly toward the center of the huge expanse of water. There were hills all around, and Hal decided it was far more picturesque than he'd expected, especially with the bright blue sky and dazzling sunshine above. It was a little more breezy here, though in a nice way.

Finally, Miss Simone stopped towing and rose to the surface. She pulled her dripping arms over the side of the boat and hung on. Hal stared in fascination at her hair, which seemed to be drying already. The water streamed down from her scalp, running over her shoulders as though someone were pouring it from a hose. As the moisture ran free, her hair puffed up and started moving in the breeze. It was a strangely eerie spectacle.

Once again, Miss Simone seemed to read Hal's mind. "It's not magic," she said. "Simple science can explain that."

"Of course it's magic," Molly argued.

"All right, everyone," Miss Simone said. "Time for business. All of you into the water and follow either Molly or myself. We won't be able to talk, so watch for visual cues. Abigail, into the box, please."

Hal whipped his head around and watched while Abigail reached for the rectangular bronze box that Miss Simone had placed under her seat. The curious box was about six inches in length with rounded corners and an intricate clasp.

Abigail placed it carefully into Hal's hands. "Hold."

Dumbly, he watched while she struggled to open it. The lid was a tight fit, and it came free with a jerk. Inside was a magnifying glass, wedged against the sides and held in place with some kind of hardened putty. Underneath the lens, Hal saw Abigail's miniature glass ball, also fixed in place.

Almost immediately, he felt drawn into the ball's enlarged foggy interior. He stared as a swirling cloud pulsed and throbbed and . . .

"Hey, snap out of it," Abigail said, waving her hand in front of his eyes.

He blinked. "Uh, right."

Without further ado, Abigail gingerly climbed to her feet, trying not to rock the boat too much. Then the back of her shirt split apart and her wings slithered out like tendrils before snapping open. They immediately began buzzing, mere inches from Hal's face. Abigail rose off the boat's floor, lifted into the air, and abruptly shrank to the size of a hand, leaving behind a curious rush of air and a popping sound.

She dropped lightly into the bronze box and stood on the magnifying glass. Then she clambered down into a corner and slipped under the lens. She lay flat on her back, pressed against the glass ball with her knees bent and her feet against a wall, looking up at him through the lens as though she were trapped under a hard sheet of ice on a pond. She grinned and nodded.

"Close the box, stupid," Fenton said.

"What? She'll suffocate in there!"

"She'll have enough air to get where we're going," Molly assured him. "Close the box, make sure it's sealed tight, and keep hold of it."

Hal slowly closed the lid. It *was* tight. It had a fine rubber seal around the inside. He had to trust Molly and assume the box was watertight. The trouble was, it was also airtight.

He felt a huge burden of responsibility as he and the others prepared to descend into the Lake of Spirits.

Chapter Seven
The Miengu

Hal eased over the side of the boat, trying not to rock it too much. Then, with a tremendous splash, Fenton threw himself in as hard as humanly possible. The boat tossed from side to side, and Emily gave a squeal.

Molly's expression was impossible to fathom, but she gripped the sides of the boat until it became still. Then, with a wave of her hand, she urged Emily into the water.

Hal uneasily paddled with his feet and hands, aware that the bottom of the lake could be a mile down. At least the boat was nearby if he needed it. He turned to find Miss Simone. "Aren't we going to tie the boat to anything?"

Emily plunged in and disappeared with a splash.

"Tie it to what?" Miss Simone asked, gliding closer with her chin trailing in the water and her hair spread out to the sides. "It'll be fine wherever it ends up. I suggest you boys change. You, too, Emily," she added as the dark-haired girl rose to the surface. "And remember—we won't be able to communicate very well underwater, so just follow my lead."

"See ya later, doofus," Fenton murmured. He grinned, then sank out of sight. Hal caught a flash of something black and knew that his friend had transformed. Then a long, shiny, slippery tail swung into view.

Emily glanced down, her face a mask of concentration. Hal suppressed a snicker; anyone else might have assumed she was relieving herself. Then his amusement fizzled as her face grew thinner and paler. Her shoulders appeared to melt away with each lap of a wave. She smiled. "Look—no arms!"

Then she was gone, plunging deep into the water. A great scaly snake body arced up behind, then vanished with a small *plop!* sound.

Hal was about to switch to his dragon form when he froze. Molly, still in the boat, was undergoing her own transformation. Something shocking was happening under her wide-brimmed hat and veil: her hair was coming alive, her pitch-black curls thickening and moving as if—

Snakes. Molly had a head of writhing snakes. But Hal's attention was soon diverted because her skinny torso and legs were bulging under her smart clothes, becoming thick and round as a scaly serpentine body revealed itself, similar to Emily's, only dark green with thin yellow stripes. Massive coils began to unfurl within the confined space.

Hal found himself mesmerized by Molly's fearsome transformation. Her arms were as thin and bony as before, but now the skin on her upper body was turning a scaly, vivid green to match her serpent half. She reached up, whipped off her hat, and tossed it aside. Dozens of thin snakes hissed and reared as if gasping for air.

She fiddled with her veil, and Hal noticed an additional band that, until now, had been tucked under her hat, unused. Apparently, she liked her veil to hang free while on dry land . . . but, in preparation for her swim underwater, she stretched the band around the nape of her neck, firmly securing the bottom half of the veil against her face. Now there would be no chance of it floating loose.

She pulled herself over the edge of the boat. It almost tipped over with her weight, but sprang back as her long, thick coils followed her into the water.

"When you're done gawking," Miss Simone said, inches from Hal's ear, "we'll head on down. Ready?"

Hal nodded, steeled himself, and transformed. As he did so, lake water was displaced forcibly away from him, creating a moment of severe pressure on his frame. He dipped below the surface and checked himself over—four clawed feet, long club-ended tail, huge leathery wings, tough armored scales . . .

The depths of the lake were dark and murky but fairly clear near the surface. His friends were there—Fenton, swimming around in a wide circle, a ten-foot silhouette of a monster lizard with a long, thin tail; and Emily with her familiar human face and inky hair but scaly and serpentine from the neck down, undulating through the water. Miss Simone hung almost upside down, her tail fin looking enormous as it towered overhead. Her hair shone golden and bright, spread out all around.

Molly gave Hal the creeps as she shot through the water with a flick of her enormous tail. She was rather like a land-based naga, complete with arms, only she was a gorgon and her head was ablaze with tiny wriggling snakes. Hal hoped the little things could hold their breath as long as Molly herself . . .

What a strange bunch they were, he decided. A giant lizard, two snakes with human heads, one human with a fishtail, and a dragon. And the dragon carried a small bronze box in its clumsy, clawed paws.

As Miss Simone motioned for everyone to stay close, Hal checked the box carefully. There was no way of knowing if it was leaking. He wondered if Abigail would be able to force her way out if she wanted to. Could she grow in size and burst out? What if she tried but the box refused to give? And even if the box was watertight, how much air did she have?

They plunged deep into the murky depths, Molly and Miss Simone leading side by side. To Hal's left, Fenton barely flexed a muscle as he descended; to his right, Emily's body whipped back and forth.

Hal couldn't imagine how this meeting with the miengu was going to work out. Why bring Abigail at all? He understood why the box was needed: the glass ball was supposed to bring Jolie back to the world of the humans as it had done for Thomas. But why bring Abigail? And how could Jolie look at the glass ball with Abigail inside the box? If the box was opened . . .

Shaking his head, Hal blew out a puff of hot air, and the water bubbled furiously around his snout. It was a pleasant feeling, warm and tingly. He realized that the depths of the lake were pretty cold, and growing colder still as they descended. He blew more hot air and this time managed a little ball of flame. It was snuffed out instantly so was really nothing more than a flash, but still, it warmed the water and felt good as his face and shoulders passed through.

Emily was staring at him. He grinned at her—but his dragon smile was probably more of a snarling grimace and her eyes widened.

He checked his grasp on the bronze box. He couldn't shake the feeling that he was missing something. Surely Abigail realized she'd be exposed to the water when Jolie opened the box?

Still, Hal trusted Miss Simone. He'd just have to wait and see.

They were no longer descending but moving along the lakebed. It was sandy, full of pits and huge rock formations, and a jungle of reeds and delicate, slow-moving plants. Fish swam everywhere, darting out of the way as the bizarre procession approached. Oddly, it didn't seem so dark now that they were on the bottom, just a murky green haze.

Hal wondered how long he could hold his breath. He hadn't even thought about it until now; he'd plunged with the rest of them and now here he was, swimming along underwater several minutes later, feeling quite comfortable.

Emily pulled ahead. Her clothing flapped loose in places, transparent and thin as though she were shucking off a layer of soggy skin. Fenton's gathered in a band around his neck, also thin and translucent. Hal's own clothes had reformed around his neck but were looser; when friends rode on his back, they used his clothes like reins on a horse.

Miss Simone and Molly slowed, and Hal suddenly felt nervous. There was nothing to see, just more murky lakebed. Except—

They eased closer to a particularly large pit, one that fell away into pitch-blackness. It was easily thirty feet across, its perimeter and sides overgrown with swaying, undulating reeds.

Molly turned to face them, holding up her hand. Then she moved out over the pit, looking down and waiting.

Nothing happened for what seemed an age, although it was probably only half a minute. Then Molly twisted and waved to some unseen audience below. The darkness began to brighten into a white glow.

Slowly, three figures rose from the pit—two males, one female, very much like mermaids with their long, slender fishtails and human torsos, only with subtle differences. Their bare arms and faces were covered with faint scales, they had long, pointed ears, and their eyes were utterly black. They wore loose-fitting garments that began as robes around their shoulders and trailed into rags that flowed around them like slow-moving reeds.

And the miengu glowed.

Water spirits, Hal thought, awestruck. These people were like giant light bulbs, lighting up the murky depths. The hazy glow came directly from their skin—their bare arms, shoulders, and faces—and shone through their clothes.

The miengu turned to face the watching group, and Molly gestured with a series of complex hand signals. They nodded their understanding, but Hal had to wonder how these creatures normally communicated with each other.

The miengu spread out. The female remained in front while the two males circled slowly, eyeing the group with black, expressionless eyes. Molly had ceased her hand signals since nobody was watching her anymore. She waited, shrouded in darkness again now that the miengu had moved away from her.

The male on the left shifted his gaze from Fenton and approached Hal, tilting his head with what appeared to be curiosity. Despite the long, somewhat girly hair, he had an extremely high forehead, square jaw, and shoulders that seemed to be nothing but slabs of muscle. Dismissing him, the creature turned and floated past Hal, revealing several razor-sharp lines running parallel across his neck just below the ear. The lines were barely visible . . . until they all gaped open in unison.

Hal nearly jerked backward in shock before realizing they were just gills. Another way they differed from mermaids.

After the inspection was over, the miengu lazily swam back to their female companion, who had been staring at them all with a frown across her glowing face. Her black hair flowed like oil from a punctured drum. She seemed to be in charge, and the males waited by her side as she looked to Molly. Molly offered a few hand signals in return.

Then the miengu turned and dove into the pit, and darkness returned. Molly immediately followed, signaling for the others to stay close to her side. Miss Simone, in turn, made a similar gesture and plunged into the pit.

Hal, Fenton and Emily had no choice but to do as they were told. Hal glanced again at the metal box gripped in his paws and spared a thought for his own lungs, wondering how long they would hold up.

The pit was a tunnel that drilled through the earth at a slight angle and abruptly emerged into a vast cavern. They had entered the underwater miengu domain through its roof.

Gasping, Hal took everything in at once—first the dazzling illumination of what seemed to be hundreds of miengu swimming around, then their curious dome-shaped homes that appeared to be fashioned out of dark-colored stone and splashed with red. The structures were so close together that many shared walls; they looked like a mass of thick molten rock bubbles oozing up from the lakebed only cold and gray, frozen in time. All around were dull statues propped awkwardly on the sandy bed—statues of the miengu, balanced on the tips of their fishtails with arms outstretched. There was no sign of plant life in this place; apparently, it was too dark and depressing down here.

The village—if that was the right word for this underwater dwelling—was located in the very center of the cavern, with ample space all around. Numerous tunnels led through the shadowy cavern walls to unseen worlds beyond, and Hal squinted, certain that some of these openings glowed faintly.

The leader of the miengu, the scowling but strangely pretty female, led the party straight down toward the center of the village. Dozens of others, glowing softly, followed at a safe distance, eyeing them warily. Their black eyes were unblinking, their faces set. Hal decided he didn't like these people one bit.

The rounded stone building at the center was larger than the rest. Clearly it was more than just a humble abode. It was even rougher up close, made from uneven stone blocks jammed together in a haphazard fashion. The red splashes became more prominent, and some even appeared to be moving—

With a jolt, Hal realized the domed stone surfaces were covered in crabs of all shapes, sizes, and colors, predominantly red, many with vicious pincers raised as though they detected intruders from another land. They crawled sideways over the walls, in and out of gaps that Hal assumed were windows, and skittered along the rock and sand floor. They were *everywhere*. Emily visibly jerked backward and looked all set to turn around and head home, but Miss Simone grabbed her arm and shook her head.

The two male escorts waited on either side of a ridiculously low doorway while the female leader ducked inside, motioning for the visitors to follow.

Although larger than all the other domes, this one was still no more than twenty feet across and perhaps twelve high. Its door was wide but a mere four feet high, and its two windows were small and square, one to either side. It was a squeeze for Hal to get through the door. Inside, their glowing leader cast just enough illumination for them all to see the rock ceiling above. It was swarming with crabs. Some were vivid red, others pale gray with yellow patterns, and yet others a darker color with long, spindly legs.

Emily was clearly unnerved, and even Hal had a serious case of the heebie-jeebies. He imagined crabs dropping onto the back of his neck . . . but then remembered that he was a dragon and they couldn't hurt him if they tried. But poor Emily had a human head and the crabs could quite easily get tangled up in her hair . . .

He shut the thought out. Their guide was waiting for them all to cluster in the room. Suddenly, twenty feet across didn't seem very big at all as the group gathered. There seemed to be thick, undulating snake bodies everywhere, intertwined with Fenton's long, skinny tail. Poor Miss Simone was jammed between Molly's head of writhing snakes and Fenton's rear feet as he tried to navigate into a space without bumping anyone. Hal barely had room for his own tail, never mind his wings. As he backed up, he felt his wing-fingers nudge against the ceiling, felt a small nip, and realized he had attracted a crab; it came away from the ceiling as he jerked away, and a couple more floated down through the water to land on the rock floor.

Hal grew annoyed. What was *in* this room, anyway? It was completely empty, utterly devoid of anything but crabs. What was the point? And all the while Abigail was trapped in her bronze box, running out of air.

Then, as he felt an urge to belch a ball of fire, something started happening. He couldn't figure out what it was at first, and he looked all around, puzzled. There was a disturbance in the water; he felt currents lapping against his hide, saw his friends rocking gently to and fro as if buffeted by small waves. Crabs moved in a frenzy, scuttling across the shadows of the ceiling, away from the center and toward the nearest opening—either the low door or one of the two windows. Many fell in slow motion, bouncing off reptilian bodies.

There was a distinct rippling high up in the center of the room. The stonework there became blurred and indistinct. Hal looked around at his friends, seeing confusion in the way they turned their heads this way and that. Yet Molly and Miss Simone remained still and calm, looking upward. Meanwhile, their guide seemed to be in a trance with her hands widespread . . .

At last, Hal figured it out. A pocket of air was forming under the domed ceiling, right in the center at its highest point. It made no sense but there it was, growing larger, pushing the lake water downward.

He wasn't a scientist, but he knew the pocket of air could only come down as far as the tops of the windows and doorway. Beyond that, the air would escape into the cavern outside. Now he realized why the door was so low—why the tops of the door and windows were roughly level, and why the dome was so much taller than all the others. As the rippling surface descended on him, Hal found himself crouching lower.

Then he growled at himself for being so stupid. Since when did he cower away from breathable air?

He found that Molly and Miss Simone were standing tall—or as tall as they could with their aquatic lower halves. Hal straightened . . . and emerged into the impossible air pocket. Normal sound returned to his ears, clear and sharp. The stone ceiling, only feebly lit, was dripping and slimy looking, and a couple of small crabs had stayed behind, squeezed into gaps between rocks.

"Oh," he said—and his voice came out as a rumbling boom that made Miss Simone flinch and Molly's head-snakes recoil and hiss.

"You can change now, if you like," Miss Simone said. "We're going to stand here for a while and chat with the miengu. Or float, if you prefer."

Emily's white face and Fenton's lizard snout burst out of the water. "I can't believe it!" Emily exclaimed. "How did *this* happen?"

Molly laughed, and spoke in a rasping, unfamiliar voice. "*You* try getting information from these people. It's easier to get blood from a stone."

Hal had almost decided to stay exactly as he was, in dragon form, but remembered poor Abigail cooped up in the metal box. He held it aloft in huge paws, watching water pour off its bronze surface.

He switched back to his human form, seeing the tough scaly skin of his paws fade to a milky-white color and his thick clawed digits becoming smaller and thinner. The surface of the water sloshed around as his dragon body shrank. Hal found he could touch the stone floor if he stood on tiptoes. The situation improved as the water level continued to descend; in moments he was able to stand normally, the water at his shoulders.

Wasting no time, he pried the box open with ice-cold, shaking hands. The inside of the box appeared to be dry, and he breathed a sigh of relief. He peered inside and found Abigail struggling to climb out from under the magnifying glass. It was too dark to see clearly, but she didn't look very happy.

With Hal, Miss Simone, Molly, Emily and Fenton watching silently, Abigail buzzed her wings and took to the air. She flew around the darkened dome with a high-pitched whine. She had roughly eight feet of height at the center, plenty for her to stretch her wings. The water level had stopped falling because air was escaping out of the doorway and windows; the group stood in only four feet of water within a stone building under a lake. And they could breathe normally.

Molly towered out of the water in her gorgon form, swaying from side to side. Only Hal and Miss Simone had reverted to their human forms; Fenton, as was often the case, watched silently with red eyes set in the sides of his black lizard head, while Emily bobbed around in her naga form.

The glowing water spirit's black hair was slick and smooth, plastered flat on her head as though painted on. She seemed uneasy with her head and shoulders above the surface, clearly holding her breath. Fascinated, Hal stared at the delicate gills on her neck, which had collapsed like soggy tissue. "Can miengus breathe out of water?" he whispered to Miss Simone, who stood next to him.

"Miengu," she murmured. "Not miengus. Miengu is the plural."

"Well, okay, can this *miengu* breathe out of water?" Hal asked again.

Miss Simone smiled. "Jengu."

"What?"

"Jengu is the singular," Molly said. "One jengu, two or more miengu." She chortled from behind her dripping veil, which clung to her face and showed the contours of her nose and cheeks. Hal swore he saw a couple of fiery orbs behind the soggy fabric.

By this time, the jengu's mouth was moving up and down and her face contorting. Then she gasped, ragged and gurgling, and water spewed from her lungs. She coughed violently, then breathed deeply, trembling.

Then, finally, she looked at Molly and tilted her head.

Molly seemed to be listening. Moisture continued to drip from the ceiling, landing with plips and plops, and Hal became aware of Abigail buzzing around the perimeter. She flew by his ear, behind his head, and he turned to follow her. But then he felt tiny feet on the top of his head and the buzzing stopped.

"I understand that, Kamili," Molly said, bowing her head. The mass of tiny snakes quivered, apparently their way of showing humble respect. "However, this is a special occasion." She gestured toward the others. "My colleagues are involved in a shapeshifter project. They're like me, able to transform at will. And we thought it would be of mutual benefit—to the humans and to the miengu—if we reintroduced Jolie to the human world."

The jengu named Kamili reacted with surprise, the water churning as she flipped her tail fin around. Her black eyes widened and her mouth opened. "*Jolie,*" she croaked, the word sounding awkward and stilted as though her throat rarely produced sound in this way.

She frowned and leaned closer to Molly. She said nothing, but Molly seemed to answer a question anyway.

"No, no, nothing like that. That would be like forcing a human to live underwater. But we may have a way to allow her to change her form. To *shapeshift,* as she was born to do. She's forgotten, you see. She became a jengu at just a year old, as you know, too young to possess the knowledge to change back. Shapeshifters are born of two halves. They start out human but the other side constantly struggles to come through. And it usually wins. Once that happens, it's over *unless* the child is old enough to understand what's happening, old enough to will the shift back and forth. Although Jolie was lost to us many years ago, we may be able to bring her back." Molly spread her hands. "With your permission, of course."

Kamili moved backward in the water, dipping low, clearly deep in thought. She lounged there awhile, peering around at the group. Her fishtail came out of the water and hung there a few seconds, dripping. Then it sank out of sight as Kamili gestured vaguely, her head tilted again. Hal was beginning to recognize when she was asking a question or was puzzled about something—even though she seemed to be speaking directly to Molly using some form of telepathy.

"We have a box," Molly said, holding out her hand toward Hal.

He was so slow to react that Abigail stamped impatiently on his head. Sheepishly, he handed the bronze box to the gorgon.

Molly opened it. "If we show this box to Jolie—if Jolie looks inside, looks into the glass ball—then she will learn. Her shapeshifting knowledge is buried in her head somewhere, and this little faerie ball will retrieve it."

Kamili stared at the bronze box but made no effort to look inside. "Faerie?" she said hoarsely.

Both Miss Simone and Molly glanced toward Hal, or rather to Abigail perched on his head. The whine of tiny wings and a slight movement on his head told him that the faerie was airborne again. Abigail buzzed around in the air, and the jengu's mouth fell open. Finally, one of the group had impressed her!

It made sense, Hal thought. Mermaids, naga, gorgons, huge lizards, perhaps even dragons . . . most likely these were all familiar to the miengu in some form or another. But a faerie was a creature of the forest and hard even for land-dwellers to spot. This was probably the first time any of the miengu had ever seen a faerie.

Suitably intrigued, Kamili now seemed more interested in the bronze box. She sent a few more thoughts toward Molly, who returned her answers out loud, explaining again that Jolie had only to look at the glass ball for a few minutes. Either it worked or it didn't, and if it didn't, then no harm was done and the group could head home. But if it worked . . .

"Think of it," Miss Simone broke in. "Your very own intermediary between our cultures. We could learn so much about you, and you could also learn about us. But don't worry—Jolie has spent her entire life with you. She *lives* here. This is her home and nothing can change that. She would be free to come and go as she pleases. She would have the benefit of a life underwater as well as on land. The *potential*—"

Miss Simone broke off, having overwhelmed herself with excitement.

"We already have a business understanding with your people," Molly said to the jengu, her veil finally drying enough to come unstuck. "We trade often. But I believe your people and ours could truly become friends if we only knew more about each other. Perhaps you would benefit more than you know, or perhaps you won't. But . . . what have you to lose?"

The jengu was clearly seeing the positive side, and she glowed brighter and brighter as the conversation went on. It ended with an actual smile, and Kamili proved to have a very nice smile, too, even if her black eyes were cold.

"Of course," Molly said, nodding, as the jengu placed her hands together and made a silent request. "I'm always happy to trade. Now?"

Kamili gestured for the group to wait, then abruptly dove with a splash and disappeared. The illumination went with her, and the domed room was plunged into darkness.

"Well, that went well," Molly said, sounding pleased.

"It did," Miss Simone agreed. "Except for the last part."

"Ah, well . . ."

Hal felt Abigail land on his head again. "Uh, sorry, what about that last part?" he said. "The trade, you mean? What's bad about that?"

There was a curious silence that Hal found disturbing.

Then, annoyingly, Emily changed the subject. "How on earth were you *talking* to her?"

In the darkness, Molly chuckled. "Why, I simply opened my mouth and words came out."

"No, I mean, how did she talk to *you*? Were you reading her mind?"

"Not exactly," Molly said. "The miengu can project thoughts to one another. They can't read minds; they simply receive thoughts if those thoughts are loud enough. It's really no different to you or I projecting our words and another hearing them. They can even project their thoughts to two or three at a time, or an entire group if necessary, the way that we might raise our voices to be heard. Of course, nobody can eavesdrop on the miengu, so they have an advantage there."

"And they can breathe air," Hal said, amazed.

"Yes, once they've expelled the water from their underused human lungs," Miss Simone said. Although he couldn't see her face, her scientific excitement was plain as day. "It's rather fascinating that they have a backup system, and yet most of the miengu choose not to use it anymore. In the olden days, they would come up for air and sit on the rocks, looking all pretty and luring ships into danger . . . or so the stories go. My own people, the mermaids, swear they had nothing to do with those old tales—a simple case of mistaken identity, they claim. Mermaids are so much sweeter than the miengu." She snorted. "And yet I've seen the way mermaids act around small boats on lakes and rivers—like they're compelled to tip them over and cause mischief. Seems to be a trait among merfolk. Anyway, these days the miengu keep to themselves below the surface, and this ability of theirs—to breathe with their lungs—seems to be something very few of them even know how to do anymore."

There was a silence.

"And this air pocket," Emily said. "How'd she do *that*?"

Fenton gave an annoyed grunt.

Hal grinned and answered for him. "Molly already told you, Em: *nobody knows*. Why don't you ask the miengu?"

They didn't have long to wait before Kamili returned and light was restored—but only briefly. She gestured for them to follow and promptly sank out of sight again.

"Here we go, then," Molly said. "Children, you won't like this. I have to go trade. I don't want to, but must if we're to continue relations between our species. Please don't react—just keep quiet. Understood?"

An awful feeling was beginning to gnaw at Hal's stomach.

Chapter Eight
A Trade

Once Abigail had been persuaded to return to the bronze box, she crawled inside and glared at Hal as if it were all his fault. "I'm missing it all," she shouted. Although she cupped her hands around her mouth, her words still came out faint and high-pitched.

Hal grinned apologetically and closed the box.

"Ready?" Miss Simone said. "Hal, let us out of here before you change."

One by one, with Molly leading, the group ducked underwater.

The water level had risen slowly as though air had been leaking out. Hal was on tiptoes again as he watched Fenton's long black tail whipping out of sight. Alone, Hal took one last look around. He doubted he'd ever been in a more bizarre place before, and probably never would be again. In the gloom, crabs began to scuttle out of gaps in the stonework.

Hal shuddered and transformed, sending a sluice of water up the walls. He took a breath, checked his grip on the bronze box, and dove.

He had gotten cold standing around for so long, and it felt good to be moving again. He found the others outside, a procession of writhing, scaly bodies heading in a straight line over the miengu village. He glanced over his shoulder. There was no sign of anything untoward about the stone building; it looked just as dark and depressing as the others. But then a bubble squeezed out of what must be a tiny hole in the roof, the only clue that this innocuous domed cottage had a mysterious air pocket trapped under its roof.

Hal swam easily, taking in the surroundings. He discovered that the domes weren't all separate shelters as he had first assumed, but a series of structures with openings punched through, forming one large communal sanctuary. That was why they were, for the most part, so tightly packed together. He tried to peer through windows to see what the miengu might keep in their homes, but all he saw were impassive faces staring at him, glowing like ghosts.

He passed over several eerie miengu statues and wondered how they were made. He couldn't imagine these sinister creatures chipping away at rock underwater. And they were so *accurate*. He passed one whose fishtail was permanently embedded in soft sand while it leaned backward, a look of abject horror across its frozen face and its hands raised as if to fend off a violent and frightening attacker. . .

And suddenly Hal knew that it wasn't a statue at all. None of them were. A shiver swept through him as his gaze darted between this stone figure and the next, and the one after that. All were petrified into nightmarish poses of terror, some crammed into tight spots between walls and others out in the open.

He had no choice but to continue following the group, all the while wondering if Fenton and Emily had figured it out. He guessed that Emily hadn't, otherwise she wouldn't be trailing so eagerly behind Miss Simone and Molly.

Up ahead, a crowd of miengu had gathered. There were at least fifty of them bobbing around, some swimming in circles overhead and looking down like vultures, but most shoulder to shoulder in a semicircle, awaiting Hal and his friends. The crowd floated just a few feet off the lakebed, backed up against the crab-smothered walls of the village.

When Kamili arrived in the center of the semicircle, she turned and flipped her tail around, stirring up a lazy cloud of yellow sand. Molly, who was longer, darker skinned, and more fearsome than any single jengu creature, garnered wide-eyed and respectful stares as she approached. By contrast, Miss Simone seemed to attract looks of disdain. Hal, Fenton and Emily hung back.

There was an exchange of hand signals and thoughts, an obscure conversation between Molly and Kamili. Judging by the way the rest of the miengu nodded in agreement, Kamili was obviously projecting her thoughts to them as well—a public speech without uttering a word. Hal shivered again. These people were growing more eerie by the minute. Did Miss Simone really want to take one *home* with them?

He wondered if Jolie was here somewhere. Could she be one of the crowd? They all looked alike—pale skin, flowing black hair, pointed ears, scaly and oddly luminescent skin . . . and those awful shiny black eyes. Hal knew they were a strangely beautiful species, but right now they were creeping him out.

Emily looked across at him, clearly puzzled. Hal wished he could communicate with her, tell her to close her eyes and turn away, or better still head for the surface. Instead he had to save his breath—

literally—and watch grimly as a struggling jengu was pushed through the crowd.

The audience was a mass of flailing fishtails as the prisoner caught sight of Molly and tripled his efforts to escape. He didn't stand a chance with six pairs of hands gripping his arms and shoulders. He was brought to face Kamili, who turned and touched his face with surprising tenderness.

Then she snarled and displayed her fangs—the razor sharp fangs of a piranha as her mouth stretched wide.

Still the exchange was deathly silent. She seemed to be screaming at the prisoner using only the force of her mind, and the prisoner was struggling again, cowering from her fury.

Finally, all eyes turned to Molly. She eased forward and began to circle Kamili, the prisoner, and his captors, who held him still—only now they were gripping him by his long hair, the back of his neck, and his waist, keeping him still but allowing him the freedom to thrash and twist with terror. His elbows knocked heads, his desperate fingers clawed over skin, but he could not get free.

When Molly came back around to the front, she moved with surprising speed, suddenly whipping close to the prisoner and putting her veiled face inches from his. He reared back, the gills on the sides of his neck opening and closing rapidly. The crowd seemed to quiver with excitement and Hal swore he saw many of them smiling with delight.

Then there was a moment of stillness as Molly raised a hand to her veil.

In unison, every pair of eyes in the vicinity squeezed shut. Many of the miengu covered their faces, too. The prisoner's captors maintained their unrelenting grips but bowed their heads, staring hard at the sandy floor. Kamili turned away. Miss Simone glanced over her shoulder at Hal and his friends and made a gesture that clearly meant *close your eyes.*

Emily did so. She swung around, almost sobbing with horror, and tore away in a trail of bubbles. But Fenton remained still, his eyeballs glowing bright red, unable to look away.

Hal couldn't look away, either. He knew he should, but . . .

It didn't seem to matter that the prisoner had his eyes more tightly closed than anyone else present. When Molly lifted her veil, Hal caught a glimpse of her profile—hooked nose, jutting chin—and thought he saw a disturbance in the water immediately in front of her face, the lake itself curdling from the power of her gorgon death-gaze. Despite the closed eyes, the prisoner's entire face turned white in an instant, like someone had thrown a sack of flour at him. A second later his body had frozen stiff, arms outstretched, torso twisted backward, the fins of his fishtail looking fragile enough to break.

Molly replaced her veil immediately and backed away, her head bowed.

Eyes opened slowly. Kamili nodded with obvious satisfaction, then spread her hands wide and spoke wordlessly to the audience. There were many bared fangs in response, but clearly they were in fierce agreement with their leader about something. Then the crowd slowly dispersed. The show was over, and another statue had been added to the lakebed.

Hal wondered how many he'd seen. Twenty? Thirty? How often did these public executions take place? And . . . *Molly?* Unless there was another gorgon around these parts, she had been responsible for them all.

Did the woman have *any* humanity left in her?

He and Fenton watched, silent and motionless, as Molly accepted a huge armful of material from the grateful miengu. She nodded, her veil bobbing dangerously high in sluggish underwater currents. Miss Simone hastened to carry the load so that Molly could fasten her veil properly. There was enough fabric to make a dozen sets of smart clothes. The trade had taken place—a life for a pile of rags.

Hal felt sick. He turned abruptly and left, gripping the bronze box so tightly that he felt the lid buckle. He saw no sign of Emily so headed for the tiny hole in the roof of the cavern high above. She was probably on her way back to the boat, and that was where Hal was going. He'd had enough of these people. He didn't even care about Jolie anymore.

He was through the roof opening within half a minute, and daylight rippled above, welcoming him to the surface. He spotted the boat silhouetted against the brightness. When he burst from the water, the warmth of the sun felt wonderful.

Emily was sitting in the boat, having already shifted back to her human form. She was sobbing, her face buried in her hands.

Hal shifted, too, and in the process accidentally sank and swallowed a mouthful of water. He came up choking and almost tossed the bronze box into the boat in his hurry to get out of the lake, but caught himself at the last moment and placed it carefully onto a seat. Then he climbed aboard.

"She *killed* him!" Emily wailed, looking up at him with tears streaming down her red cheeks. "*Murdered* him! Why would she *do* that?"

Hal inspected the bronze box, noting that the lid was indeed slightly dented from where he'd squeezed it too hard. He tried to think of something calming to say to Emily as he carefully opened the lid. "It wasn't really a murder. More like an execution," he mumbled.

"What's the difference?" she screamed in anger, and Hal jerked backward in surprise. "She still killed him!"

The whine of Abigail's wings distracted him. She flew out of the box and around his head, then abruptly grew in size. Once back to full human height, she sat down and retracted her wings. "What's going on?" she demanded, seeing Emily's tears. "Who killed who?"

Emily pointed into the water, her hand shaking. "Molly. She turned the miengu to stone. Just lifted her veil, and *wham!*"

"She turned them to stone?" Abigail exclaimed, aghast. "*All* of them?"

"No, just one," Hal muttered.

Abigail sighed with relief. "That's all right, then. You mean a single jengu, Em. 'Miengu' is the plural. For a moment I thought—"

"It doesn't matter!" Emily shouted. "Molly *murdered* him!"

Hal quickly explained to Abigail what had happened.

"So that's what Molly trades in exchange for enchanted fabric?" she said with a distasteful look. "Nice."

Emily's hands balled into fists. She seemed about ready to explode. "Who cares about the stupid fabric? I can't believe . . . I can't *believe* one of our own could go along with that sort of thing. Do you think Miss Simone knew?"

"Of course she did," Hal said. "Look, here comes Fenton."

A shiny black snout and burning red eyes had appeared, gliding toward them on the surface of the lake. As Fenton drew closer, he shifted to his human form—a gradual process this time, with his reptilian hide fading to pale, soft flesh, his translucent band of clothing unraveling and darkening, and his long lizard body shortening into something far less suited to water. Suddenly he looked clumsy, splashing noisily the rest of the way to the boat. The red glow faded from his eyes.

He clambered aboard, frowned at Emily, and said gruffly, "What's eating *you?*"

Emily burst into fresh tears and started to explain. But Abigail had had enough. "Quit, Em. Suck it up. How about giving Molly a chance to explain what this prisoner was executed for? He probably did something really bad."

"Yeah, did you think about *that?*" Fenton said. "He might be a mass murderer for all we know."

"It doesn't matter," Emily said, wiping her eyes on her sleeve. She scowled at them all. "The point is, Molly performed the execution. How would you feel, Abi, if part of Hal's job was to roast prisoners alive? The prisoners might deserve it, but how would that make you feel about Hal?"

Abigail looked at Hal with what appeared to be an expression of real disdain. "Mm."

"I wouldn't do it," Hal protested. "No matter what the situation, I'd never execute people as part of my job. That's just . . . wrong."

"There you go, then," Emily said triumphantly.

Fenton looked ready to argue. And he did, making the point that it was very easy to sit here and be all high and mighty about it, but Molly was cursed with a death-gaze; she only had to look at a living creature and it would turn to stone, and sure, she hated it, but it probably didn't affect her as much as it once had. Emily jumped on him, saying that his argument only made her seem *worse*—a person with no remorse, to whom death was just a matter of daily routine.

"I don't like her," she whispered fiercely, looking around to make sure nobody was listening. "I liked her at first, and felt sorry for her. But now I think she's evil. And I don't want to meet Jolie, either."

"Aw, come on," Hal said. "Evil? Really? Dangerous, yes—"

Fenton snorted. "We're *all* dangerous."

They went on discussing the matter until a disturbance in the water caused them to break off and look around.

"Oh," Abigail exclaimed softly.

Dozens of heads had appeared, poking up just enough that the black eyes could peer silently at them. The miengu kept their noses and mouths submerged but moved slowly, closing in on the boat from all around.

Then Miss Simone and Molly appeared mere feet away. Without a word, Miss Simone tossed the armful of soggy fabric onto a seat and began pushing the boat toward shore. Molly came to help, and the miengu followed behind, barely causing a ripple on the surface.

"What's going on?" Hal whispered to Molly.

The gorgon was back in her human form, her veil plastered to her face. Again Hal saw her profile, but her nose and chin seemed less prominent now. "Showtime," she murmured.

When the boat bumped up against a low grassy bank, Miss Simone climbed out, her transition from mermaid to human having gone unnoticed. She pulled on the rope and the boat bumped against the bank again. Then she tied the rope around the base of a thick bush.

"Stay in the boat," she said to them. She gave a wink and half a smile, and Hal felt marginally better even though the miengu were still advancing.

Molly struggled a little less gracefully out of the water, slipping on the grass and falling to one knee. Emily looked downward at that point, barely able to conceal a satisfied, scowling grin.

"The box," Miss Simone said.

Abigail handed it to her.

The miengu had stopped advancing some thirty or forty feet out, probably where the lake became shallow. They watched, ever silent, water lapping across their noses, their pointed ears poking out, black hair plastered flat and shiny over their heads.

Miss Simone climbed back down the grassy bank and waded carefully into the water, holding the bronze box with fingertips as though it were a valuable treasure being presented to a king. "Send Jolie to me," she called out.

Some of the miengu glanced sideways, and Hal followed their collective gaze and settled on one particular individual. He narrowed his eyes. So *this* was the famous Jolie? He studied her, noting that she was clearly much younger than the others gathered here, and somehow less menacing. If anything, she looked shy, perhaps frightened. Still, she was older than Hal and his friends, probably in her mid to late teens. And . . . eerily beautiful.

Those closest to her urged her forward. She glanced at a young male, and he shook his head. But she reached out to touch his face tenderly, and he dropped his gaze in grudging acceptance. Then Jolie came forward, lying flat in the water and crawling out on her hands with her fishtail splashing behind.

As she approached the lake's edge, where the water only came up to Miss Simone's thighs, Jolie seemed to lose her courage and looked ready to turn and flee. But she received nods of encouragement all around, even from the young male, and finally she rose into a sitting position, her simple dress swirling and floating on the water, her neck and shoulders bare. Her tail fin flopped in and out of the water.

Even from a distance of twenty feet, Hal saw her gills working overtime, gasping for lake water that wasn't there anymore. He tensed, knowing that she was going to have to switch to her lungs.

Jolie trembled violently, her hands clutching her throat as she gagged. Then it happened—a terrible gurgling rush and a vomit of water. After that she coughed and coughed until no more water was left in her lungs, and then she was sucking in huge, rasping breaths of air. It took a full minute for her to compose herself, and she was still shaking when Miss Simone reached out, patted her on the shoulder, and murmured something in her ear.

But Jolie was still half a fish, Hal thought, fascinated. Could she shapeshift? Become fully human?

"Showtime," Molly murmured again from the grassy bank.

Miss Simone opened the bronze box and held it in front of Jolie's face. Jolie looked into it, frowning as though it were something to be suspicious of. After a couple of seconds of staring, her frown lifted and she moved her face closer.

"There you go," Abigail whispered. Her hand slipped into Hal's.

The seconds ticked by. The silence was eerie considering how many were present: dozens of miengu heads poking from the water, four children in a boat, and Molly on the grassy bank, all watching Miss Simone and Jolie—and not a sound to be heard except gentle waves slopping against the underside of the boat, a few buzzing insects, and a gentle breeze through a line of trees.

Jolie blinked and looked up. She seemed to be staring directly at Hal, although he might have imagined that. It was impossible to tell with those—

As he watched, the blackness started to fade from her eyes. The points of her ears shrank. One of her hands absently rose to the side of her neck as her gills closed up and faded. Then she held her hand in front of her face as the faint scaly texture of her skin smoothed and softened into pink human flesh.

"She's gorgeous!" Fenton exclaimed.

Jolie toppled sideways as the delicate fins of her fishtail melted away and human legs began to take shape . . .

Then she was rolling around in the water, apparently unable to control the useless limbs she had developed. She stared at them with a look of fascinated horror, a feeling Hal remembered all too well from when he had first taken on his dragon form. Miss Simone was talking to her, reassuring her, trying to help her sit up, but Jolie acted like she had just woken from a hundred-year sleep and was still bleary-eyed and dazed.

Molly splashed into the water to assist. Together they lifted the jengu shapeshifter by her arms until she was upright, supported on both sides. Jolie seemed unable to put any weight on her legs at all. Hal wondered if she was somehow paralyzed from the waist down.

"I guess she's not used to them," he muttered.

"Her legs?" Abigail shook her head. "I guess not. She's never walked on them before. She probably doesn't know how."

Miss Simone and Molly carried the girl from the lake. As the trio approached, Hal found himself unable to take his eyes off Jolie. She was possibly the most beautiful young woman he'd ever seen. She almost made Miss Simone look ordinary in comparison. The two of them were unusually entrancing to boys and men alike, but where Miss Simone was blond and blue-eyed, Jolie had shiny black hair and deep brown eyes. The two women were not remotely similar at first glance, although both possessed some kind of . . . aura?

Abigail nudged him sharply. "Hey. Quit staring. You too, Fenton. You're like a couple of goldfish looking for food."

Hal blinked rapidly but continued watching while Jolie was dragged up the grassy bank and deposited carefully on the ground with her back to them. He shook his head. "Man, she's . . . uh . . ."

"Ugly?" Abigail offered helpfully. "Revolting? Hideous?"

"This trip is suddenly worth it," Fenton said simply.

"Oh, for goodness' sake," Emily said, sighing. She yelled suddenly. "Miss Simone? Can we get out of this boat now?"

Miss Simone had her arm around Jolie. "Sure, come on over. Bring my cloak, would you?"

The four of them stepped out of the boat, mindful that they were still being watched in silence by twenty or thirty pairs of miengu eyes. Hal tried to shake off the feeling that their stares were burning into his back.

Molly brushed past them. "I'll go and talk to our friends," she said. "It looks like we'll be able to take Jolie home—as long as her parents allow it."

Hal hadn't even given that a thought. He watched as Molly entered the water and waded out to a pair of miengu that looked just like any other, only they were evidently the concerned parents of their adopted girl. The younger male was there, too—a protective brother or perhaps a close friend. All three seemed unhappy, but the rest of the miengu were watching silently . . . and Hal thought they looked *hungry* somehow, a feeling that filled him with unease.

Jolie sat on the grass with her legs folded to one side. Her soggy dress was raggedy at the hem. It had looked perfectly natural deep underwater, like seaweed swirling around in slow motion, but the effect was lost here on land. She looked like she'd been dragged through several hedges backward and her dress torn asunder. In contrast, her pale white skin was unblemished.

She had regained her composure. She kept glancing at her legs with an expression of worry, but did so surreptitiously, nodding and smiling as Miss Simone talked to her about living in a human village. "Only for as long as you want, understand?" Miss Simone said again. "Think of it as a field trip, a little excursion from home. You're unique, Jolie—the miengu *can* breathe air, but rarely do. They hardly venture above water, and certainly don't crawl onto land. This is your chance to do just that, and when you return, you'll have a lot of stories and experiences to share."

Jolie smiled again but said nothing. Still, Miss Simone nodded vigorously. "Yes, you certainly can, Jolie. At first you can stay with me in my house, but eventually, if you stay long enough, we can get you a place of your own. So you can come and go as you please."

The girl looked around, peering at Fenton with interest, then at Hal. The moment her gaze locked onto his, Hal felt a curious tingling down his spine. Suddenly tongue-tied, he fought for words. Nothing came.

And what's your name? she asked, her voice loud and clear in his head.

"Hal," he answered before realizing what had just happened. She *looked* human but was talking directly to him inside his head. Clearly, the distinction between her jengu and human forms was somewhat blurred if she were still able to use a form of telepathy to communicate.

Jolie smiled. *Hal. That's a funny name. I like you, Hal. I have a feeling you and I are going to have a lot of fun together.*

Her eyes narrowed for just a spilt second, and Hal was sure he caught the slightest twinkle there—the same sort of twinkle Abigail often used when she was messing with his head.

He knew then that Jolie was going to be all kinds of trouble.

Chapter Nine
Jolie

The group piled into the boat as Miss Simone remained on the bank to untie it from the bush. Fenton and Hal took their seat near the bow as before, facing the rear, on the assumption that they were going to be rowing again. Abigail sat opposite Hal, saving a space for Miss Simone, also as before. Behind her, Jolie sat with Molly, draped in Miss Simone's cloak.

Since the newcomer had inadvertently taken Emily's space, Emily squeezed into the space behind Hal and Fenton, on the tiny triangular seat in the pointed bow of the boat. She'd hardly said a word since Jolie had arrived on the scene, just pouted and scowled at anyone who looked her way. Now she was even more moody. Hal could almost feel hostility radiating from her and decided she was still simmering over the execution. Perhaps she felt that Jolie, being one of the miengu, should foot all the blame.

Either that or she was flat-out jealous of the attention Jolie was receiving.

Hal watched Jolie with more than a little interest, peering over Abigail's shoulder as he absently gripped the oars. He couldn't take his eyes off her, except when she glanced his way—then he dropped his gaze and felt his face heat up. But he was soon drawn back to her. It didn't matter that her dress was shapeless and sodden, gathered in rags around her weak, useless legs, or that her long black hair hung in messy clumps. Somehow, others in her presence faded into drabness. Molly, already thin and awkward, now seemed like a veiled scarecrow. Emily had always been plain in Hal's eyes, but now her pointed chin and squinty eyes made her look mean and ugly. And suddenly Abigail looked silly and childish with those freckles across her nose. Hal couldn't remember her having so many. Maybe once he had liked them, but now—

Abigail kicked him. "What? Why are you staring at me like that?"

"I'm not!"

"Yeah, you are," Fenton said, grinning. He nudged Hal sharply. "Bet I know what he's thinking, too."

With all eyes suddenly on him, Hal turned his attention to the miengu in the lake. They were waiting patiently, the tops of their heads poking out of the water, still and silent. "Look, are we leaving, or what?" he said shortly.

"Say your goodbyes, Jolie," Miss Simone said gently as she climbed aboard and took her seat next to Abigail.

Startled, Hal saw that even Miss Simone's enchanting aura had dimmed somewhat. He clearly remembered the first time he had seen her, when she had shown up in the classroom one Monday morning several weeks ago; she had lit up the room with her smile and icy blue eyes. Now it was Jolie that was shining, forcing even Miss Simone into the shadows.

Jolie said nothing, simply stared in silence at her miengu family and friends, who stared back with eerie black eyes. It was a strange and awkward moment until Hal remembered that she was most likely having a telepathic conversation.

While she was distracted, Miss Simone leaned across and spoke in a low voice to Hal and Abigail, gesturing for Fenton and Emily to lean in closer as well. "Just so you all know, the miengu possess an aura of enchantment even more powerful than mermaids. And it appears that Jolie's is as strong now as ever, even though she's in human form." She looked meaningfully at Hal, and then at Fenton. "You boys are probably feeling the effects already. I'm sure you think she's the most beautiful creature you've ever seen."

Hal stared hard at the floor of the boat, his face burning. Jolie *was* beautiful. She had been beautiful even in her jengu form, despite her sinister black eyes, scaly skin, and fishtail. *All* of the miengu were eerily attractive, yet they paled in comparison to Jolie. Whether it was an enchantment or natural good looks, it made no difference—she was drop-dead gorgeous.

"Just be careful," Miss Simone warned, and when Hal looked up again she had the hint of a smile on her lips. "This is new territory. We've never had one of the miengu wandering around a human village before. I'm going to need you to keep an eye on her and protect her from . . . well, all those she enchants."

"Is she doing it on purpose?" Emily whispered fiercely.

Miss Simone put a hand over her mouth, clearly trying to stifle a laugh. "No, Emily, she's not. It's just part of her natural charm. I mentioned earlier about how the miengu used to come to the surface to beguile and enchant sailors, luring them with melodic singing and dreamy visions of beauty . . . until the ship smashed onto the rocks. They're a bit like sirens."

"And what's with all those executions?" Emily asked bluntly. "There were statues *everywhere!*"

Pursing her lips, Miss Simone turned to Molly. "Care to answer that one?"

Molly gave a shrug of her thin shoulders and checked to see that Jolie was still distracted. The jengu was smiling and nodding, apparently deep in a long-distance conversation with her parents in the lake.

"Beats me," Molly said quietly. "Quite frankly, I gave up asking a long time ago. Either they have extremely tough laws, or they have an inordinate number of truly horrible criminals. Or perhaps these are sacrifices to some underwater god. Either way, they have executions at least once a month, and none of them are pleasant. The victim rarely goes quietly. The very sight of me coming along strikes fear into their hearts. As far as they're concerned, I'm quite literally Death paying a visit. And if I'm not around to offer my evil gaze when they need an execution, then they use some other ghastly method."

She leaned forward and cupped a hand to the side of her veil, dropping her voice even lower.

"Also, there are small caves all over this lake, and some are used for 'private executions'—for what nefarious purpose I can't imagine. But who am I to question the ways of an entire species?"

Emily scowled. "You don't *have* to help them, though."

Miss Simone placed a hand over Molly's and interjected. "The moment Molly stops offering her services, all contact with the miengu is broken. We can't afford that. We have to maintain a relationship. And besides, what they do to their own kind is far more horrible. Molly's method is clean and fast."

"And yet somehow they fear me more than their nasty little bag of sharp tools," Molly whispered.

Nobody said a word after that. Hal wondered for a moment why on earth Miss Simone wanted to get to know these people . . . and then remembered that they were supposed to be able to cure sickness. The miengu seemed brutal and unkind, yet they offered the gift of miraculous healing as well.

And as for Jolie . . . Was she just like all the others? Or was she more like Thomas, brought up by vicious monsters but ultimately human? If so, the benefits of befriending her could be enormous. As Hal peered at her, he found himself believing with all his heart that she was different.

Jolie was teary-eyed as she lifted a hand to wave to her family in the water. The young male blew her a kiss. Then the miengu slowly sank out of sight, leaving small ripples on the surface.

Miss Simone raised her voice. "Okay, boys—off we go, please."

Hal and Fenton commenced rowing without a word, turning the boat around and heading along the bank toward the river mouth. Hal was aware of Abigail watching him with narrowed eyes as if daring him to glance over her shoulder at Jolie. He tried his best to avoid eye contact with both of them. Luckily, at least half of his attention was needed over his shoulder to see where he was going.

Idle chatter commenced between Molly and Miss Simone. They discussed how they were going to introduce Jolie to the villagers and what they should do to divert the inevitable attention of young men. Molly jokingly suggested that the jengu wear shapeless clothing and a big floppy hat.

"Won't work," Fenton muttered.

Molly laughed and put her arm around the silent girl's cloaked shoulders. "Jolie, is there any way you can switch off your enchantment and be normal?"

Jolie looked genuinely puzzled. She sent a thought, and Molly gave another bark of laughter. "Are you serious?" she exclaimed. She shook her head and winked at the others. "Jolie thinks she's ugly enough. And I don't think she's just being modest, either." She smiled at Jolie. "Maybe we'll just wrap you in drab clothes. But I think you'll have a hard time settling in if you're hounded by every man and boy for miles. Being plain and invisible makes it much easier to move around. Trust me, I know. I've had a lifetime of it."

Hal doubted that Molly had ever been invisible. She was tall and gangly, her hat was enormous, and the veil drew curious stares, which ironically was the exact opposite of what a gorgon needed.

The journey back up the river was a little harder thanks to the current. Hal's arms rapidly grew tired after only fifteen minutes. Jolie hadn't said a word the whole time. Instead she listened intently to conversation between Molly and Miss Simone, answered privately with her mind, and smiled often at Hal. He decided he liked her. She seemed pleasant enough.

"Can you, uh . . . can you talk?" he asked her.

He feared the question was downright rude. Nevertheless, all eyes turned to Jolie, and the girl pursed her lips as if wondering the same thing. She opened her mouth, formed an 'O' shape, and then looked like she was struggling to regurgitate some undigested food. A strangled cry emerged from her lips, and her eyes widened.

"Maybe it'll take practice," Molly said, patting her on the knee. "You've never spoken a word out loud in your life. And you've never walked on land, either. You know how, but you need to exercise and practice."

Jolie looked crestfallen, and Hal immediately felt sorry for her.

"I couldn't fly at first," he said. "When I first turned into a dragon, I couldn't change back again until Abigail made me."

He caught Abigail's smirk and grinned at her. Then he nodded to the bronze box clasped in her hands.

"The glass ball you looked into? I looked into it as well. It kind of reminded me how to fly—told me what I'd been doing wrong. You don't just flap your wings up and down, see? You have to angle them correctly, twist them a little, lean a certain way . . . and it all comes naturally once you know how. Walking is easy too, once you know how to do it."

There was a silence.

"Yeah," Fenton added helpfully.

Jolie had been staring at Hal. She tilted her head and smiled, and Hal felt sure he'd been hit by a wave of happiness and gratitude. It warmed him so much that he knew, without a shadow of doubt, that Jolie was all right—maybe one of the nicest people he had ever met.

Her smooth, soft voice entered his head, surprisingly clear and loud. *That makes me feel better. Thank you, Hal.*

"Welcome," he muttered, knowing his face was burning again.

"Oh, brother," Abigail murmured, rolling her eyes.

* * *

Sometime later, they arrived back at the low jetty they'd started out from. It had been a leisurely journey, with Hal and Fenton drawing steadily on the oars the whole time. Hal's shoulders burned from the workout, but he refused to give way first. "Need a rest?" Fenton had asked frequently, to which Hal had replied, "No, I'm fine. You?" Resting, they agreed out loud, was for sissies.

Although Jolie was suitably impressed, Abigail was not. She continually poked fun by grimacing fiercely and flexing her non-existent biceps.

When they finally moored up to the jetty, Hal forced himself to remain nonchalant as he climbed out of the boat even though his shoulders and back were screaming in agony. The palms of his hands were sore, too. But what was a guy to do? Moan and whine? Cry like a baby?

Miss Simone tied up the boat, then smiled as she swept past. "Good job, boys. You'll sleep well tonight, I'm sure."

"No problem," Hal said.

"Anytime," Fenton added.

As Miss Simone slipped through the gate of the paddock to fetch the horses, Abigail, Emily and the boys headed for the cart. But Molly called them back. "A little help here?"

Hal's eyes widened at the sight of the gorgon struggling to help Jolie out of the boat. "Oh, sorry!" he said, and hurried back, Fenton hot on his heels.

"Lean on the boys," Molly said as she hoisted the girl over the side of the boat. It rocked wildly as Jolie reached out a hand for help.

Hal hesitated, but Fenton leaped in. Jolie's arm slipped over his shoulders, and he took all her weight as Molly released her grip. Then Hal stepped closer and felt a tingle as Jolie shifted half her weight to him. She was taller than both of them but surprisingly light, only half the weight he'd expected.

The threesome headed for the cart, with Jolie's feet dragging uselessly. Hal avoided Abigail's glare and dismissed Emily's look of disgust. They were simply being childish, Hal decided. The fact was, Jolie couldn't walk; she needed help.

You're a gentleman, Jolie whispered in his head. *Thank you so much.*

"No problem," Hal muttered, and then fought a pang of jealousy as Fenton mumbled something similar.

Once they were all comfortable on the cart and the horses hitched up, they began the short, trundling journey back to the village. Molly resumed her rambling one-sided conversation with Jolie—or so it seemed.

"Can't you talk to *all* of us?" Emily suddenly snapped. Everyone looked at her in surprise and she reddened. "I mean—Jolie, you can make us *all* hear your thoughts, right? If you want to? It's just that we're only hearing one side of the conversation and it's kind of confusing."

Jolie looked mortified. Her voice suddenly filled Hal's head—and presumably *all* their heads judging by the reactions of his friends.

I'm so sorry. It's going to take a while to get used to living like a human. I'll try to remember to include you all in general conversation. It's easy to forget, though, and it's a bit of a strain after a while. We miengu are more used to one-on-one chats, you see.

"What a quiet, lonely place it must seem in your world," Abigail said, frowning. There wasn't an ounce of malice in her voice; she spoke matter-of-factly as if the thought had just crossed her mind.

Emily was only half satisfied. "I think it would be better if you learned how to talk out loud."

Jolie nodded. *I'll work on it.*

After that, conversation with Jolie seemed a little more natural, although her voice seemed unusually amplified and Hal wished she would turn down the volume a few notches. It was like she was shouting into his ear.

Once in a while she'd look at him and say something more private. *You're sweet,* she'd murmur in a softer voice. *Why does Abigail keep kicking you every time you look at me?* Naturally, Hal was unable to answer such questions out loud. All he could do was shrug.

As the village wound into view ahead, Jolie's mind-speak faded. She looked apprehensive. Hal couldn't imagine what it must be like for her. She'd spent a lot of time studying the scenery with a mixture of awe and curiosity, and had picked at her sodden clothes as they dried as if alarmed by the feeling. Although she answered Molly's incessant questions about her home in the lake, she was obviously distracted, probably wishing everyone would just shut up and leave her to absorb the new world around her. Talk about sensory overload!

And now she was about to enter a village full of people.

"Nothing to be afraid of," Miss Simone said softly as she gave a flick of the reins. "But people will be curious, especially since you can't walk. So I think we'll go to my house and let you settle in before we let you loose in the village."

Jolie nodded and smiled, while Hal exchanged a glance with his friends. They'd never been to Miss Simone's house before. They knew only that she lived in the woods outside the village.

"Look!" Molly exclaimed, pointing upward, her veil wobbling excitedly.

Everyone craned their necks. The blue sky was clear at the moment except for some ominous clouds in the distance. Yet another storm was brewing. What had caught Molly's attention was a large bird. It wasn't anywhere near as big as a roc but was clearly bigger than usual, perhaps the size of a harpy. Except that harpies were dirty and half human, whereas this creature was the most colorful giant bird Hal had ever seen—scarlet and blue and yellow, with shiny golden tail feathers.

"What *is* that?" Emily asked. "It's beautiful!"

Miss Simone seemed to have forgotten the cart was still moving and was twisting around, half climbing out of her seat. Her eyes shone. "Can that be—?"

"I think it is," Molly said, sounding surprised.

"What?" Fenton demanded.

But, annoyingly, silence reigned as they followed the bird's progress through the sky. When it arrived over the village, it circled as if searching, its slender neck stretched as it peered down at the distant rooftops.

"What *is* it?" Emily said again, her pitch rising.

Miss Simone was all smiles, clearly a million miles away. "That, Abigail, is a phoenix."

"My name's Emily."

Miss Simone barely heard her. "And since they're so rare, I'm guessing it's our good friend Blair returning home. He's been away for years, searching for others of his kind."

"That's a phoenix?" Hal said. He'd heard of them, and a year or so ago had read a book called *The Phoenix and the Carpet* about a group of children and a rolled-up carpet. Inside the carpet they'd found an egg, and when the egg ended up in the fireplace by mistake, it had hatched into a phoenix. Then the phoenix had granted them wishes and transported them to different places on a flying carpet. Hal had enjoyed the story immensely, even though he normally preferred more down-to-earth adventures of survival like *Robinson Crusoe*.

Suddenly eager to get home, Miss Simone clicked her tongue and urged the horses on. "First Molly comes home, and now Blair. Not to mention Jolie, of course."

"Happy reunions," Molly agreed. "I wonder if Blair found any more of his kind. He may be the only one left in existence."

"Hold on a minute," Abigail said, frowning. "How can Blair be a phoenix shapeshifter if there are no others? Weren't we all cloned?"

Molly nodded. "All of us, yes, including me—there aren't many of my kind either, thankfully. My ugly mug is plenty enough. But Blair is different. He was cloned from a feather."

"A feather," Emily said dreamily. "Ooh, this sounds like a fairy tale!"

"A single feather," Miss Simone said, nodding, "stored in a vault and guarded by elves a long way away. They worshiped that feather. They claimed it was from the tail of a phoenix, and it certainly looked the part—long and golden, and impervious to fire." She noted the puzzled expressions. "The elves demonstrated by holding it over a fire. It burned but regenerated immediately afterward. The scientists were sure it really was from the tail of a phoenix and gently cut a piece from the end. With that they created Blair, the first phoenix anyone has laid eyes on in centuries."

"They're pretty much extinct, then," Fenton mumbled. If anyone knew how it felt to be one of a few remaining specimens, it was him.

"Maybe," Miss Simone said. "Maybe not. We'll find out soon enough."

They skirted the edge of the village, sticking to the road that ran around the outside of the fence. They attracted a little attention from a group of patrolling goblins but otherwise avoided contact with the villagers. The trail wound off into the woods and Miss Simone's house came into view.

It was much smaller than Hal had imagined. He had expected someone as important as Miss Simone to live in a mansion with servants everywhere. Instead the house was little more than a cabin tucked against a slope with pines pressing in all around. The ground out front was carpeted with shiny green needles and dry brown cones.

They climbed down from the cart. Molly offered to deal with the horses while Miss Simone led the way inside. Hal and Fenton once again helped Jolie, fully supporting her weight as her legs dangled uselessly.

Hal was surprised by what he saw inside. He might have imagined a sparse, clinical laboratory, devoid of character . . . or perhaps the sort of place a witch or eccentric professor might live, with dusty books piled up everywhere. But the place was warm and comfortable, with simple, neatly arranged furniture and carefully maintained pot plants. There was also the distinct but familiar smell of salty seawater that always seemed to follow Miss Simone.

"Come in, Jolie, come in," she said, gesturing to the small sofa in the living room. "My place is small, but there's room. Molly's staying here as well, and you can share the spare bedroom with her."

"You can take the bed," Molly told Jolie. "I'm used to roughing it. I'll be quite happy on the floor."

Hal and Fenton deposited Jolie onto the sofa, and she gripped their hands for just a moment, beaming at them with an expression of gratitude. Her voice slipped into their heads.

Thanks, boys. You're the best. Don't be strangers, okay? I need you to show me around the village.

They both mumbled that it would be a pleasure, then backed slowly away as she squirmed on the sofa and arranged cushions behind her back. Then Miss Simone moved in and blocked the view, and the spell was broken.

Hal and Fenton sighed in unison and turned away—to find Abigail standing with her arms folded, glaring at them. Emily stood behind her looking equally disgusted. Fenton growled something, shouldered past, and stomped outside, leaving Hal to wilt alone.

"What?" he said, spreading his hands.

Chapter Ten
The Phoenix

It was well into the afternoon as the group hurried into the village. Jolie had told them she'd be fine on her own for a while, but neither Miss Simone nor Molly had wanted to leave her. Then again, neither had wanted to miss out on reuniting with their old friend, Blair, and so it was decided that someone else should stay behind.

Emily flatly refused, and Abigail was as curious about Blair as the older women. Hal was torn, but Abigail grabbed his arm and dragged him out of the cabin before he could open his mouth. That left Fenton. Hal watched as Miss Simone and Molly sweet-talked him into staying behind to watch over her, and although he sighed and shrugged, he didn't seem at all put out when they bid farewell and left him on the doorstep.

"Can you trust her?" Emily asked Miss Simone with a scowl as they walked quickly along the path that led into the village.

Miss Simone hesitated before replying. "I think so."

Abigail rounded on her immediately. "You *think* so? We're leaving Fenton with someone you don't really know or trust?"

"Fenton's a big boy. And he's a pretty fearsome lizard. I'm sure he can look after himself. But just to be safe, I'll send a couple of goblins along with fresh clothes for her."

She did so at the earliest opportunity, stopping to talk to a group of goblin guards at the gate. Then she rubbed her hands together.

"Now, let's stop worrying about Jolie for a moment. The guards said the phoenix came down by the inn."

There was only one inn, and it didn't have many visitors so was usually empty. If Blair was back in town, it might seem the logical place for him to head for . . . although a big nest in a tree might do just as well. Hal chuckled at the idea of such a big bird perched on the end of a sagging branch.

"What are you smiling about?" Abigail asked, nudging him. "Thinking of Jolie again, I suppose."

"You really need to curb that jealous streak," Hal said, grinning.

Abigail snorted. "I'm not jealous. I'm disgusted at how you and the fat boy are fawning over her. You should have seen yourselves—all dreamy-eyed and slack-jawed. It's grim to watch."

"Then don't watch," Hal retorted. There was a silence between them as they trailed Molly and Miss Simone, with Emily lagging behind. "Anyway," he went on, feeling it necessary to say something nice, "she's not really my type."

Abigail snorted again. "Your *type*? So you have a *type* now? And what, exactly, is your *type*?"

"Faeries."

This time Abigail gave only a muted scoffing sound. "Faeries in general? Or is there one particular faerie you like?"

Talk about fishing, Hal thought. He played along. "There's one I know. She's twelve years old, kinda pretty . . ." A smile touched the corners of her mouth, and he pressed on with glee. "Bit of a pest, though, always running her mouth, getting on people's nerves."

"Oh," she said shortly. "For a minute there I thought you were talking about *me*. So there's another faerie, then? Where'd you meet her?" She grinned at him suddenly. "I can just see you stomping through the nearest faerie glade with your big, smelly dragon feet. You'd make an impression, for sure—in the dirt."

The way she had gestured, as if pointing to something in the distance, set Hal thinking. "*Is* there a faerie glade nearby?"

She pursed her lips. "Uh, maybe. I'm not supposed to talk about it. We faeries don't advertise our whereabouts, you know."

He didn't press her but found it intriguing that she had found a secret faerie den in the nearby woods outside the village. He also found her secrecy mildly annoying. Didn't she trust him?

They were pushing through crowds of villagers by this time, working their way along a narrow street. It seemed that word had spread and everyone had come along to see the phoenix, abandoning whatever work they were doing. There were marketers, farmers, blacksmiths, cobblers, dusty construction workers from the demolition zone, a man pushing a wheelbarrow full of glowing geo-rocks, children of all ages . . . and Hal thought he spotted Darcy's bright yellow hair in the sunlight, but the crowd was too thick and he lost sight of her a second later.

Even Miss Simone was having trouble getting through. In the end, Molly yelled ahead: "Move or I'll show you my ugly mug!"

Heads automatically ducked and hands came up to cover averted eyes, and a gap appeared in the crowd, widening to allow the shapeshifters through.

Hal caught sight of Darcy again, and he waved. By her side was Dewey and Lauren, squirming to free themselves from the mass of people. They managed to squeeze through at last.

"So tell us all about it," Darcy said, falling into step alongside Abigail. "And what have you done to make Emily so miserable?"

"Later," Abigail replied quietly. "Not supposed to say too much, if you know what I mean."

Brightly colored feathers came into sight. Molly shouldered through the crowd, Miss Simone right behind. Hal and his friends followed closely until they found themselves face to face with the phoenix, which stood in the middle of the street. Another crowd had gathered just beyond the great bird, and faces peered out of windows. Rounding the corner at the far end of the street was Robbie in his ogre form, towering over everybody. And Hal thought he glimpsed a familiar red-furred manticore before an endless sea of heads blocked his view again.

The phoenix was larger than Hal had imagined—easily six feet tall, standing in the middle of the road with talons spread wide in the dirt and massive wings held open, feathers ruffling gently in the breeze. Scarlet was the dominant color, but there were also great swaths of yellow, blue and green across its chest, not to mention distinctly golden tail feathers and a similarly golden frill around its neck.

Its head was tilted, perfectly still, and the creature stared unblinking as Miss Simone and Molly approached.

Both women peered back in silence, and a hush fell across the crowd.

It was Miss Simone who finally spoke. "Blair?"

The phoenix bowed its head, dissipating any uncertainty the crowd might have had. Even Miss Simone looked relieved.

"Just checking," she said. "It's good to see you again. Are you going to shift back or just stand there showing off?"

Molly turned her veiled face to the children. "He always was a show-off, you know."

As Lauren giggled and a few others in the crowd tittered, the phoenix straightened, gaining another few inches in height. Slowly, it spread its wings wider and wider until they stretched upward and outward in a graceful arc, long feathers fluttering. If that wasn't enough to draw gasps of admiration, the bird puffed out its chest and caused its plumage to ripple and quiver.

"All right, all right," Molly said, stepping forward. "We get it. You're gorgeous. Now quit showing off and—"

"Wait," Miss Simone said sharply, grabbing Molly's arm. "Stand back. Something's happening."

Craning his neck to see around the women, Hal saw nothing that might have caused alarm . . . but he felt it. He frowned as a faint wave of heat washed over him, warming his skin. He knew Abigail had felt it, too, by the way she lifted her hands and touched the air as if warming herself by a fireplace.

The heat grew more intense, coming in ripples through the air, radiating out from the phoenix. The villagers began to murmur.

"Back," Miss Simone called, and then again, louder: "*Back, everybody!*"

She and Molly cleared well away from the bird, urging the villagers to retreat a few more paces. The innkeeper, who had been standing on his doorstep, went inside and shut the door with a bang. Moments later, he appeared in the adjacent bay window, peering out with wide eyes.

The phoenix was beginning to smoke. Wisps floated off its outspread wings and trailed up from its chest. The heat increased, and Abigail crept behind Hal, clinging to his arm. It reminded him of the time they'd spent in the labyrinth, with all the steaming hot lava and fire-breathing dragons.

Then the tips of the bird's wings burst into flame.

Several shouts rang out, and someone yelled for a bucket of water. But, as concerning as it was, Hal knew the phoenix was just doing its thing. He didn't know why or how it worked, only that this creature was purposefully setting itself alight. There was no reason to be alarmed about its safety.

Flames sprang from all over its bristling plumage. Then it flared up with a *whumph!* sound, as though someone had set fire to a gasoline-soaked effigy. The fire was bright yellow and incredibly hot to start with, and feathers quickly blackened as the bird stretched its wings wider still, apparently basking in the ritual even though the villagers were shouting and screaming. Then the flames inexplicably turned blue and burned even more fiercely . . . and yet the heat faded, the nasty crackling sounds dying away.

Some of the panic ebbed, and the street fell silent. The spectacle had gone from ghastly and frightening to something awe-inspiring and wondrous. Despite blackening horribly behind the hazy blue glow, the phoenix seemed to be—quite literally—in its element.

Hal watched in amazement as clouds of black ash and superheated feathers fluttered free and rose into the air. As the bright blue flames began to roar, all the blackness covering the bird's body turned to dust and blew free, lifting upward and floating away, leaving what appeared to be brightly colored feathers beneath—fresh new plumage, regenerated from the magic fire.

The phoenix's rebirth ended with a bang. It was a clap of thunder that sent a shockwave along the street in both directions, sending villagers reeling. Hal heard glass tinkling somewhere, something metal falling over with a clang, a number of gasps and yells. The wave of energy made him tingle all over, prickling his scalp and sending chills down his arms and back. He looked at Abigail and found that her hair was standing outward in thin strands, charged with static electricity. All around, friends and villagers alike had funky hairdos.

Then it was over.

The fire abruptly vanished, and when Hal turned to look at the phoenix, he found instead a man dressed in smart clothes just like the ones all shapeshifters wore. He was plain-looking, just an ordinary guy with dark brown hair, a thin face, and a pointed nose. He smiled sheepishly and turned in a circle.

"Sorry about that. Hope nobody got hurt."

Molly clicked her tongue and strode forward to push the man roughly in the chest. "Was that *really* necessary? Honestly, Blair—"

"Actually it was," he said, cutting her off. He raised his voice so everyone could hear. "I wasn't just showing off, I promise. I wanted to demonstrate what happens when a phoenix regenerates. I'm a shapeshifter and can do it at will, although it takes a lot of concentration and is kind of wearing." He rubbed his eyes, and Hal decided he did look a little drawn. "But my demonstration is feeble compared to what a real phoenix can do. Especially old ones."

"Old ones?" Miss Simone repeated, frowning. "What are you saying?"

Blair stared at his hands as though it had been a while since he'd seen them. "I'm saying there's a phoenix north of here, the only other phoenix I know of. He may be the last of our kind. I call him Jacob. His real name is unintelligible to humans; it's kind of scratchy and squawky but sounds a bit like 'Jacob' if you're trying to make sense of it. Anyway, Jacob is a thousand years old."

There was a gasp of amazement all around. Miss Simone's eyes widened, and she visibly shivered with excitement.

"And?" someone in the crowd prompted.

"And," Blair went on, "he's dying."

Now a puzzled silence ensued.

"Get to the point," Molly urged. "He's dying? You mean he's going to regenerate? But that's good, right?"

Blair nodded. "It's good, yes. Jacob will be reborn, to live for another thousand years. But his regeneration will be"—he spread his hands and shook his head—"I don't know, ten, twenty, maybe even fifty times more powerful than mine. Maybe *hundreds* of times. I don't really know for sure, but Jacob has communicated to me that a phoenix regeneration is a rare and beautiful thing. Energy radiates out, purging and purifying everything in the region. The exact ramifications are unclear, but . . ."

He looked directly at Miss Simone.

"What?" she said impatiently. "Spit it out!"

Blair sighed. "This could mark the end of the shapeshifter program. The holes we use to travel from our world to the other are anomalies, defects in the natural order of things. They're like pimples of energy on the face of the Earth. When the phoenix is reborn, the holes will be purged, scrubbed from the planet. And there will be no more magic."

Miss Simone absently smoothed her frizzy hair. "You're saying the holes will close? Just like that?"

Blair shrugged. "Well, some of them anyway. The extent and range of the event is unclear. The phoenix resides about eighty miles north of here, but I understand this village is inside its purging zone. So is the miengu's lake. Even Louis is in danger. All the holes we know about in this part of the world—they'll all close for good, wiped clean."

* * *

After Blair's dramatic statement, Miss Simone snapped out of her shock and bundled him across the road to the inn, calling for the villagers to go home or go back to work. "I'll make a statement when I have more information," she said loudly, sounding annoyed.

Villagers started to drift away. Hal noticed the wheelbarrow man leaning over his collection of geo-rocks, looking mystified. Even from where Hal stood it was clear that the fiery orange glows within the rocks had dulled.

At first it seemed that Miss Simone wanted to talk alone with Blair, and she started to send the children away. But then she changed her mind and ushered them inside the building. Hal, Abigail, Emily, Darcy, Lauren, and Dewey piled in through the doorway, and Hal looked around to see Robbie and Thomas hurrying through the dispersing crowd. They'd be here shortly, he thought as he headed for the large round table where Blair had slumped.

With much scraping of chairs dragged from around the room, everyone got seated, squeezed tightly in a circle around the oak table. At the back of the room, the small, bald innkeeper stood by the wall flicking a switch on and off. His inn was one of the 'modern' types with wired lighting that was the envy of many in the village. But the overhead chandelier remained dead, so the innkeeper sighed and began to light a few candles for the darker corners of the room.

Miss Simone sat right next to Blair, and Molly stood behind him, leaning on the back of his chair. "Now," Miss Simone started—but just then Robbie and Thomas came barging in, both now in their human forms. It was enough to make Miss Simone's face darken with impatience. "Hurry, boys, sit down."

"I need a drink," Blair said, rubbing his throat. I'm parched."

Molly called to the innkeeper. "Bring Blair a drink, would you?"

"A strong one," Blair added.

Miss Simone scowled. "Not *too* strong." As the innkeeper began to clatter around behind the bar, she lowered her voice. "Now look, Blair. It's good to see you and all, but I don't appreciate the theatrics. You could have demonstrated in private instead of scaring everyone half to death. None of us have ever seen a phoenix do that before. You're the only phoenix anybody has seen in hundreds of years, and even *you* never did that before."

"New trick," he agreed. "Yeah, look, I'm sorry. I just thought . . . well, at least now everyone can say they've seen a phoenix rebirth. Pretty cool, eh?"

Miss Simone rolled her eyes.

"Shall I stone him now or later?" Molly muttered.

Blair twisted around to grin up at her. "Hey, good-looking. How's your life been these past few years?"

"Rocky," she said. "Now, what else do we need to know? The holes will close, but what else will happen? You said there'd be no more *magic?*"

Blair shrugged. At that moment the innkeeper crept closer and placed a tankard of beer on the table, and Blair sank half of it in one go. He sighed and wiped his mouth, and then began.

"I don't really know. It's hard to talk to a phoenix. Jacob seems like a wise old bird, full of knowledge about the world . . . but he doesn't communicate well. He's a loner, you see, and seems to rank himself of higher intelligence and importance than anything else on the planet, so looks down on everyone and everything. It's as if he's a self-appointed guardian of the world, tasked with a job beyond our comprehension. He's not *unfriendly* as such—quite the opposite, in fact, allowing me into his cave and sharing his food and all that. But it's like I'm beneath him, like he pities me or doesn't see me as anywhere near his equal. Maybe he's right. I take on the form of a phoenix, but I've only lived thirty-odd years, whereas Jacob—" Blair shook his head with admiration. "A thousand years. Can you imagine what it's like to live that long? What you could see in that time? What you could learn?"

"And what did *you* learn?" Miss Simone urged.

"Lots of things, but I suppose right now you want to know what's to come with this rebirth thing."

He leaned closer to Miss Simone as if about to reveal a great secret.

"We've never understood how holes came into being. They just appeared, lingered for decades or hundreds of years, and then vanished—faded away, or popped out of existence. Well, I learned how they were created."

Nobody said a word. The man had been away for years and was unaware of recent developments. He knew nothing of the centaur plot to extinguish human life, or what Dewey's centaur memories had revealed about the connection between geo-rocks and dimensional portals. Blair was blissfully unaware that his 'big news' was common knowledge in the village these days.

"Turns out," Blair went on, "that when people smash those geo-rocks open, the energy released from those rocks doesn't just blow you to bits; it dissipates and reforms somewhere else, and forms a hole between worlds. *That's* where all the holes come from, Simone."

He sat back triumphantly, awaiting the reaction.

Miss Simone sighed. "We know."

Blair frowned. "You do?"

"A lot has happened here lately. I'll explain it all in good time. But yes, we know that exploding geo-rocks cause holes. We even have a machine that explodes rocks in a controlled manner, so we can create holes right where we want them." She glanced at Hal. "At least, we *did* have a machine."

"Oh." Blair looked so disappointed that Abigail couldn't stifle her giggle. He looked at her with a puzzled expression, then glanced around at the others as if wondering why they were there.

"What else do you know?" Molly pressed, tapping him on the shoulder.

"Well, when the ancient phoenix regenerates, all those holes—all those random pockets of concentrated energy—will be swept away in one massive wave of purification." He shrugged. "Something like that. It explains what happens to other holes around the world. We all thought they just closed on their own over the years, but in fact whole bunches of them are wiped clean every thousand years by a phoenix rebirth." He rubbed his nose. "Well, probably. I'm guessing, of course."

"The geo-rocks faded, too," Hal said suddenly.

Everyone looked at him.

"I saw the wheelbarrow man outside," he explained. "He had loads of fresh new rocks before Blair did his thing, and afterward they were all dull."

Miss Simone snapped her fingers and looked across the room. "That's why the lights are out in here. Gosh, that means everyone close by has lost power to their homes—heating, ovens, hot water . . ." She clicked her tongue. "Really, Blair, you're so irresponsible. Just how far did your little demonstration reach?"

"I don't know," Blair admitted. "I've only done it a few times, and I've never been near homes before. Sorry."

"Do you think the whole village was affected?" she pressed.

Blair shrugged. "Nah. A few streets, maybe?"

Molly rapped her knuckles sharply on his head, and he winced and ducked. "You said that a phoenix is all-knowing? Old and wise? How on earth did *you* end up as one?"

In an obvious effort to change the subject, Blair pointed at Hal but looked at Miss Simone. "Pardon me for asking, but why are these kids here? Is this a class outing or something?"

Darcy, who had been silently listening to the conversation with the rest of them until now, promptly vanished. One moment she was there, the next she was gone—although when Hal squinted he could see a fuzzy outline when she shifted in her seat.

Blair drew in a breath and stared with his mouth open.

Then realization dawned. "She's a shapeshifter!" He slapped his hand down on the table. "Your project, Simone. So it finally worked out."

"It did," Miss Simone said. "Four years late, but they made it. They came across just a few weeks ago."

"Good, good," he said, smiling all around. "The one that disappeared—is she the faerie? She shrank out of sight?"

"No, I'm the faerie," Abigail said. "That was Darcy. She's a dryad."

"Ah. The wood nymph. Blending into the surroundings. Yes, I think I can see her now, if I squint hard enough." Blair screwed up his face and craned his neck, leaning forward across the table. He looked so comical that everyone laughed. "But weren't there nine of you?"

Miss Simone patted Blair's hand. "Fenton's not here right now. He's babysitting. It's a long story."

"We'll sit down over a meal tonight and explain everything in detail," Molly said. "You can regale us with tales of wonder about your phoenix buddy. But we also have a guest to take care of. Do you need to take off, Simone?"

Miss Simone considered. "No, I need to hear more about this phoenix regeneration and how it's going to affect us. Perhaps the children can go back to my house and take care of Jolie for me . . ." She nodded and turned to Hal and his friends. "Show her around as best you can. If people start staring at her and asking questions, tell them she's just visiting from another village."

"That ugly, eh?" Blair said. "Who is she?"

"She's not ugly, just plain," Molly said. Hal glanced at her in surprise. *Plain?* "Thing is, if you saw her, you'd think she was the most beautiful creature in the world. And other men would think so, too."

"Plain?" Hal repeated, unable to let that go.

Abigail nudged him. "She's not so hot. Which is why it's so hard to watch you boys fawn all over her. It's insulting, actually." She grinned. "Judging by the way you and Fenton acted earlier, I assume you see her in a different light."

Hal stared at Abigail, then Emily. Both nodded soberly.

"No way!" he exclaimed. "You're just—I mean, come *on*! I know you're jealous and all, and I know she's enchanted somehow, but even you have to admit she's drop-dead gorgeous!"

Molly burst out laughing.

Miss Simone just smiled. "What did you think of the male miengu you saw back in the lake?"

"Weird-looking," Hal muttered.

"Handsome," Abigail said.

"Yes, I have to admit they were something else," Emily said. She blushed and nudged Darcy, who had slowly become opaque during the last few minutes. "You missed out there, Darcy. You too, Lauren." She leaned close to Darcy's ear and whispered something, invoking a giggle.

Hal was amazed. "But the males were *ugly*," he said. "Well, maybe not ugly, but definitely not worth—"

Then he stopped, seeing Miss Simone's raised eyebrow. He understood. "Okay, okay, I get it. We see what we want to see. But still, Jolie's not as plain as you say. I'm not *blind*. Even taking into account what you said, she—"

Miss Simone held up her hands. "Nobody is going to argue with you, Hal. Just be warned that Jolie is not all she seems. Now, off you go. Blair and I have lots to discuss."

Chairs scraped as Hal and his friends got up to leave. As they headed for the door, Miss Simone asked Blair when Jacob's regeneration was expected to happen.

"In a few days," Blair said. "Jacob said we'd all know when it was about to happen. He said he'd send *signs*, whatever that's supposed to mean."

"And the whole region will lose its magic? Its power? Holes will close?" Molly said, shaking her head. "Closing the holes is good in some ways—it'll keep those soldiers away. But closing *all* of them in the entire region?" She froze. "Oh, my goodness! We have a team of scientists in the other world, looking for medicine. What if they get trapped there?"

Blair thumped the table. "Which is why I came. I knew you were always sending people back and forth. *Now* do you see why I did my demonstration? I had to show you what we're up against here. My little example was *nothing* compared to what's coming."

Chapter Eleven
Stories

Judging by the perplexed expressions of men and women peering out of doorways, and the number of useless dull rocks being lobbed into the streets, it was evident that Blair's demonstration had blown quite a few fuses.

"Totally dead," an old woman was saying from her doorstep as Hal and his friends wandered past. She was speaking to a small group of villagers that had collected outside her home. "It was working fine before that young man showed up and burst into flames. Now it's as dead as a doornail."

"Mine too," pronounced a neighbor, leaning out of a window. "Should have known these newfangled contraptions would break down. I'll have to go back to candles. You can always rely on candles, you know."

"Except when it's windy," a wiry, gnarled man said.

The children left them to their mutterings and headed back out of the village. "I'm dying to meet this girl," Robbie said. He nudged Hal sharply and winked.

Abigail shook her head. "Lauren, you'd better keep a close watch on your guy, or you'll lose him."

Lauren blushed. "He's not my—" Then she caught herself. "I mean, he can do whatever he wants. I don't own him."

The tense moment that passed between her and Robbie didn't go unnoticed. Darcy and Emily glanced at each other, then at Lauren, while Robbie looked away and frowned. Even Thomas and Dewey, trailing behind, seemed to notice something; they immediately started whispering to each other.

"*Awk*wa-a-rd," Abigail said loudly. "What's up, Lauren? You finally wised up and ditched ogre-boy?"

"Shut up, Abi," Robbie snapped.

Abigail barely suppressed a smile but at least had the sense to refrain from any further comments.

Hal slowed a little, nudging Robbie off the road and allowing the rest of the group to carry on along the trail that wound into the woods.

Abigail threatened to turn and wait, but Hal gave her such a warning glare that she took the hint and sauntered away.

"What's going on?" Hal asked Robbie once they were alone.

Robbie leaned against a tree and sighed heavily. "Nothing."

"Well, *something's* up," Hal insisted.

"No, I mean 'nothing' is going on—literally nothing." Robbie shrugged and tried in vain to look nonchalant about the whole thing. "It's okay. I kind of prefer being on my own anyway."

Hal's heart sank. "Yeah, well, obviously Lauren doesn't know a good thing when she sees it." He spent the next few seconds searching the recesses of his mind for the right words but realized he'd never dealt with this kind of thing before. Rejection between a girl and a boy wasn't part of his life experience; heck, he barely knew what it was like having a girlfriend in the first place, never mind being dumped by one.

He latched onto this thought and the words suddenly came tumbling out. "I'm not sure what I'm supposed to do anymore," he said, staring into the depths of the bright green woods. "It's like a game. Like Abigail expects me to do or say something but never lets on what's on her mind, and then gets all huffy for no reason, even if I don't do anything. I only just found out she wants me to walk her to school in the mornings. So she'll be joining us from now on."

Robbie snorted. "Great. That's all we need."

"Right. I mean . . . I like her and all that, but . . . do I have to hang out with her *all* the time? It's not like we're married or anything."

Robbie's eyes widened, and he visibly shuddered. "We'd better catch up," he said, gesturing along the trail. Their friends were just disappearing from sight behind the trees.

They began walking. Hal found the brief silence to be comfortable and easy, the kind of silence only old friends could enjoy—unlike the somewhat puzzling, strained pauses he sometimes experienced with Abigail.

"It's weird," Hal said. "Now that you and Lauren have broken up, it's like you and I can be proper buddies again. Like before, I mean."

"Before the girls got in the way," Robbie agreed, nodding vigorously. "Does that mean you're going to ditch Abigail as well?"

Hal stopped dead. "What? Are you nuts?"

The thought horrified him for a variety of reasons. First, he didn't have the courage to tell Abigail any such thing. Second, he couldn't bear the idea of dealing with her afterward; he imagined furious glares for several days, followed by cold bitterness, and eventually a vow of unrelenting mischief in the name of revenge. And third—

"I don't *want* to break up with her," he said. He gathered his nerve and muttered, "I like her too much."

Expecting a derisive snort, he was surprised when Robbie nodded soberly and said, "Yeah, I know."

"And you're okay with that?"

"As long as you keep her off my back."

Hal grinned. "I can't promise anything. You know how she is."

They caught up to the others just as they reached Miss Simone's cottage. Together they marched up to the front door, Abigail in the lead.

She turned the doorknob and poked her head inside. "Visitors!" she yelled.

The door jerked open suddenly, yanked out of her hand so hard it caused her to stumble. A goblin stood there, small black eyes almost engulfed in the shadow of his heavy brow.

"What you yelling for?" he growled.

"Sorry." Red-faced, Abigail marched past him without another word.

The rest of the group filed past the goblin, each giving him a polite nod and receiving nothing in return but a glare. As Hal entered the darkened cottage, he saw another goblin loitering in the corner of the living room, looking thoroughly bored.

Fenton and Jolie were sitting on the sofa. She was lounging sideways, her long black hair dangling off the cushioned arm and her legs across Fenton's lap.

"Hey," he mumbled in greeting.

Jolie gave them all a broad grin of perfect white teeth. Hal felt a tingle pass through him as she turned her smoldering gaze in his direction.

Hi, Hal, she whispered in his head.

He started, then looked around to see if anyone else had heard. She had called his name only, and it both electrified and embarrassed him.

Then again, she might have greeted everyone in a similar way, very quickly, privately saying each name in turn.

Robbie murmured, "Oh, man, she's something."

"Yeah, she's something all right," Darcy muttered from right behind Hal. But unlike Robbie, her voice was tinged with mild scorn.

"Told you," Emily whispered, a little too loudly. "Don't know why the boys are going ga-ga over her."

"But she's . . . she's *beautiful*," Thomas said in a small voice. Everyone turned to the red-haired boy. Normally he looked and acted bored, not quite at ease with village life, trying his best to give his friends and family a chance while privately yearning for the forest. Now, suddenly, his eyes were bright and his cheeks flushed.

Are you whispering about me? Jolie said loudly in Hal's head—and when everyone else jumped guiltily, he realized she was talking to them all at once.

"Can't you talk out loud yet?" Abigail asked sharply.

A look of deep sorrow fell across Jolie's face. She frowned and opened her mouth. Eventually, words croaked out. "I . . . I'm sorry. I've been practicing, but I keep forgetting."

Her voice was exactly the same as the one that normally drilled into Hal's brain, only it came from across the room, softer and far more natural. Her words were slurred and clumsy, like she was just waking from a deep sleep and her mouth was not cooperating yet. But it was a good start.

"That's better," Emily grumbled.

The goblins shuffled toward the door. "We're off, then," one said. And then they left, banging the door shut after them.

"They brought Jolie new clothes," Fenton said, gesturing to a small pile of garments on the nearby armchair. "Then they kind of hung around looking annoyed. Not sure why."

Hal shared a look with his friends, but none of them said anything. It was hard to imagine that Jolie could be dangerous in any way, yet her kind was largely unknown. For all they knew, the miengu might possess laser eyes, poisoned fingernails, and brain-melting psychic abilities.

Abigail shoved the pile of clothes aside and flopped down into the armchair. Immediately, the others found places to sit—Lauren and Darcy perched themselves on the arms of Abigail's chair, and Emily nipped behind and leaned on the back, as if the girls were sticking together as a team. Thomas and Dewey drifted closer to the sofa and lowered themselves to the floor, unable to take their eyes from Jolie. Hal and Robbie remained standing where they were.

"Fenton's been telling me all about you," Jolie said carefully, pronouncing her words slowly. She stretched and flexed her lips before continuing. "So you're just like me, able to change your shape? I have to see what you can all do. Will you show me?"

"Not in here," Robbie said immediately. He jabbed a thumb at the low ceiling. "Don't want to bust Miss Simone's roof."

Jolie laughed. It was a pleasing, musical sound that Hal wished he could listen to all day. He made a mental note to think up some funny jokes to tell her.

Oddly, Abigail and the other girls seemed to wince and frown as if listening to an out-of-tune violin. He understood that they might be seeing and hearing something a little less *enchanting*, but still, their perceptions of Jolie couldn't be all that different. There had to be another factor involved here.

They're jealous, Hal thought, not for the first time that day. *Jealous that this newcomer is stealing the limelight, that we boys can't help being struck by her. Their jealousy is clouding their vision, making them see a spiteful, rude, ugly girl. It's so unfair. Jolie's a nice girl. They need to lighten up.*

"Outside then," Jolie said, smiling. "You can show me your transformations outside in a little while. Okay?"

There were sounds of agreement, a mixture of eager exclamations and reluctant mutters.

Jolie sat up straight and, one after the other, grabbed her legs with her hands and swung them off Fenton's lap. He looked disappointed. "For now," she said, "just tell me about yourselves. Let me get to know you all." She smiled sweetly at Thomas, who was kneeling on the floor. "You start."

As if in a trance, Thomas began to talk. He never really said a whole lot at the best of times, so everyone froze and hung onto his words. Hal knew that every one of his friends was thinking the same thing—that despite their urging over the past few weeks, Thomas had remained in his shell, somewhat reclusive and moody. And now, within minutes of meeting this strange young woman, he was talking nonstop and openly about his life and even his feelings.

He started out with his early years on the island with his friends, living in a house near Black Woods, going to school every day, making the best of the perpetual fog, avoiding Fenton's teasing, and generally being a happy kid. At age six, something changed in him. His memories were fuzzy, but he remembered waking up one day and feeling an urge to forage around in the woods. His parents frowned upon exploring

Black Woods as it was easy to get lost and clothes often got torn and dirty. "Just stay in the back yard," his mom told him over and over. "The woods are out of bounds."

There was another reason the woods were forbidden. The Pattens lived in a big old house on the outskirts, fairly close to the cliff edge. They had taken over the house despite Miss Simone's suggestion to stay close together on the main road where the other families had clustered. Thomas's parents had been fairly wealthy before the shapeshifter project had begun and turned up their noses at the idea of downsizing to a small, two-bedroom place on a street. So they had found the biggest place on the island and taken it over, enjoying the woods at the back and the fields to the front, and often taking strolls along the cliff edge and enjoying the view.

On that fateful day, Thomas had given in to his urges and gone foraging around the back of the yard, peering into the woods with a new sense of wonder and longing. He'd spotted a groundhog and—as embarrassed as he was to admit it to his friends—had *wanted* it. Wanted to *eat* it.

He explained to his rapt audience that he hadn't been able to stop and reason with himself, and instead had taken off after that groundhog with an excitement he'd never experienced before, and a hunger he didn't understand.

He'd heard his mom calling but ignored her. He pounced on the groundhog and nearly had it, but it wriggled out of his grasp. His clothes got caught up in bushes, and he angrily pulled free. His vision began to blur; he remembered feeling something change deep down inside . . .

And suddenly he was a red-furred lion creature with huge claws and a massive scorpion tail that arced up over his head, oozing venom. His clothes lay in tatters on the wet grass. Unbelieving, he backed up and retraced his footprints in the mud. He saw the treads of his running shoes leading through the trees, then the discarded shoes themselves, popped open and ruined, and then large catlike prints. His own inhuman prints.

Terrified, all thoughts of eating the groundhog vanished. He began to scream, his voice sounding with a strange nasal, fluty quality, quite unlike his own. He heard his mom dashing through the woods, calling his name. He ran to her, closing the distance in seconds.

And when she saw him, she screamed long and hard. He remembered the look of horror in her eyes, the way she shook and trembled all over, her pale white skin. He turned and ran, ashamed of what he had become and desperate to stop her screaming at him that way.

He was dimly aware of her calling his name again, but ran on anyway, plunging through the trees. Then—

Jolie was leaning forward, her eyes wide and her hands to her face. "Then?"

"I ran straight off the cliff," Thomas muttered. "I saw rocks below and knew I was going to hit one. But I missed by inches."

Jolie sighed and sat back. "Thank goodness!"

"I went under," Thomas said, staring at the floor. "I swallowed some water and panicked. I tried to swim back up to the surface, but there was a current pounding me against the cliff deep underwater. I knew I was going to drown. And then, just as I thought I was getting somewhere, with my lungs bursting and the surface nearly within reach, something grabbed my ankle."

Miss Simone, Hal thought.

"It turned out to be Miss Simone," Thomas said, confirming what Hal and his friends already knew. When Jolie gasped, he hastened to explain. "She was trying to help me. She knew I was drowning and knew I'd claw her to death in a panic if she tried to help me back to the surface. So she grabbed my ankle and pulled me directly downward. She was moving so fast that I couldn't reach down and grab her. I started swallowing water again. And then, before I knew it, I was floating upward . . . and I was in a puddle."

A puddle? Jolie said, forgetting herself and speaking to them all with her mind. Her voice was so loud that Hal reeled and shook his head.

"A puddle in *this* world," Thomas said. "Miss Simone dragged me way down under the sea to a hole—a sort of portal between worlds—and then let me go, and I came up through the hole and out of a puddle. I looked up to see a load of ugly faces staring at me. They were goblins, but I was six and had never met them before. I was so scared I ran off. The forest was calling me."

"And there you stayed," Abigail said softly from the armchair.

Thomas nodded. "For six years."

He went on to explain how he had wandered for days, hunting rodents and—inexplicably—enjoying the taste of raw flesh. "I don't understand how you can resist the urge," he said almost accusingly to Hal. "When you're a dragon, don't you want to . . . you know, munch on animals? Taste hot blood while the thing is still dying?"

Hal grimaced. "No."

Shrugging, Thomas continued. He briefly explained how he had finally met others of his kind—manticores—and they had treated him with suspicion at first, somehow knowing he was not *really* one of them. He learned what he was and how he was feared and respected by humans. Although he yearned to find his mother and father, thought often of his home, and cried himself to sleep at nights, his life in the forest with others of his kind was so compelling, so complete, that he never once ventured out of the forest into the goblin outpost from which he had fled. Over time, he grew to be happy, and his friends and family became distant memories.

"Until some harpies showed up," he said, shooting a hateful glance toward Lauren as if she were somehow responsible. "I found a boar, freshly killed. I started eating, but it was drugged or something and I fell asleep. When I awoke, four harpies were standing around me. I couldn't move; I was paralyzed. They must have killed that boar and put something in it."

"But why?" Jolie asked.

Hal grew tired of standing and lowered himself to the floor, his attention fully on Thomas. He'd heard a rushed version of this story before. The goblins had suspected harpies were involved, and Thomas had later confirmed it—in a few words or less.

Thomas spread his hands. "Everyone in these parts knows about the shapeshifter program. I guess some thought it would be 'a real shame' if a vicious monster got loose on the island and killed you all."

"The harpies were encouraged by the centaur khan himself," Dewey said quietly. When everyone turned to him in surprise, he reddened and looked away. "Just something I heard."

"The harpies waited until dark," Thomas went on, "then lifted me off into the sky. I was dumped in a nest high on the mountain and still couldn't move, so I had to wait and wait with three harpies guarding me and one off somewhere on a scouting mission. Finally, that scout came back and said the coast was clear and that they should hurry."

Thomas was speaking in a low monotone by this time, subdued, as if this story marked the point at which his life changed for the worse.

"I was drowsy and couldn't figure out what was going on. They carried me down the mountain, then kind of dragged me into darkness near a machine that rattled and clanked. I remember the cave floor, the narrow tunnel, the smell of damp, musty air . . ."

"The fog-hole!" Darcy exclaimed.

Thomas nodded. "I banged my head on the ground at some point and that was that. I woke late the next day by the entrance of a cave where fog poured out. I didn't recognize the place, but it was a forest—a thick one, too, so I was relieved. But. . . something about the place was familiar. I kind of wandered around, sniffing and exploring, sure I'd been there before."

He looked toward Hal and Robbie and pondered for a moment.

"That was when I heard you guys talking. You were going on about blocking the cave entrance and dragging branches around. I felt really weird, like I was in a dream. Then I saw you through the bushes and called out to you, asked you where I was—"

"I remember that!" Robbie said. "We looked and saw your bright blue eyes and horrible red face staring at us through the bushes."

"Thanks," Thomas said dryly.

"Well, when I say 'horrible,' I don't really mean—"

Thomas held up his hand. "Anyway, you ran off, and I went after you for a bit but soon gave up. I started to realize I was in Black Woods. And all I could think was, 'How unfair!' I'd spent years forgetting my human life, and there I was, dumped back into it again."

"And you didn't think about your parents?" Jolie asked, voicing the question that was on Hal's mind.

"Thought about them, yes," Thomas muttered. "Even went looking for them. And guess what? They were nowhere to be seen. The house was empty. I went through it, spent some time clawing around my old bedroom trying to find my old toys and stuff . . . but everything was gone. I wandered around the woods trying to dig up old memories. Some of it came back. I remembered faces and a few names, friends from school. But mostly I remembered my home in the forest, in *this* world." He gestured vaguely. "I just wanted to get back here. I tried going down the fog-hole but couldn't stand all that fog—it was suffocating me, and I don't like narrow tunnels either."

"And the next part of the story," Abigail piped up, "is where Thomas tried to eat Hal and I."

Thomas bowed his head, staring at the floor.

"I got in a few good punches before that," Robbie said to Jolie. Although he had joined Hal on the floor a little while ago, he now drew himself up as straight and tall as possible. "I'm an ogre, you know. Hal and I took Abi to the woods to show her the fog-hole, and I went on ahead and came face to face with Thomas. He attacked me, tried to sting me with that giant freaky tail of his. But I—" He paused. "Uh, well, I transformed. It was the first time for me, and I didn't really know what . . . what I was doing. But I remember pounding that red-haired monster into the ground."

"You did not!" Thomas protested. "You hit me once, that was all. Then you turned and ran like a girl."

"I had to go save Hal and Abi," Robbie argued. "I thought they were in trouble. I thought you'd already stung them and they were lying on the ground, dying somewhere."

"Except you ran straight past us," Abigail said, rolling her eyes. "If you'd stopped for a moment, you could have warned us what was ahead."

Robbie glared at her. "I didn't see you." He turned back to Jolie. "I didn't. They were cowering behind a tree somewhere and I just went right on past."

"And so you went home," Abigail finished. "On your bike. With no clothes on. Leaving us to fend for ourselves."

"It wasn't *like* that!" Robbie yelled.

There was a long silence during which everyone appeared to hold their breath. Then Jolie smiled grimly. "Well, it sounds like Simone is to blame for all this. Dragging you underwater, Thomas . . . That's horrible! Didn't she search for you in the forest afterward? Didn't she bring your parents to find you?"

"Well, she said she did—"

"I think we should move on," Jolie said, dismissing him with a wave. She turned to Dewey. "How about you next?"

* * *

They talked for hours, bringing Jolie up to date with everything including Blair's return to the village. Darcy and Lauren, still perched on each side of the armchair, gradually warmed to Jolie, although Abigail and Emily remained cold. Hal found himself agreeing with everything Jolie said. She made a lot of sense, perhaps because she was a newcomer and saw everything more objectively.

Dewey told how he had first changed into a centaur while fleeing the violent storm on the island and had been chased through backyards by Miss Simone and a group of goblins. Jolie listened with wide eyes as he went on to explain the entire situation with the virus, concocted and unleashed by the centaurs in an attempt to cull the world—*both* worlds—of irresponsible humans.

"Always meddling," Jolie said, nodding. "I see their point of view. You're not to blame for any of this, Dewey. Centaurs are generally decent; it was just a few bad apples who lost their way and took things too far."

That's putting it mildly, Hal thought. But her words had a calming effect on Dewey. He smiled gratefully, evidently pleased she wasn't judging him.

"If anything," Jolie went on, frowning, "it was Simone that was at fault here. She really shouldn't have pushed the centaurs so far. She knew they were upset by the use of geo-rocks in homes, but she ignored their reasoning, calling it old-fashioned and stubborn. Just because she wants to advance technology in this world doesn't mean she has a right to. It's fine to give a little power to a home, like these magic glowing lights"—she gestured to the lamp glowing dimly on the table—"but where does it end? Maybe the centaurs had the right idea. I mean, killing everyone was going too far, obviously, but putting an end to the use of geo-rocks . . . well, maybe that would be for the best."

"Don't *you* start," Abigail said with disgust.

Jolie turned her head and shot her a glance. Abigail visibly recoiled, stiffening in her seat. Hal couldn't see the glare itself because Jolie's black hair blocked his view, tumbling in front of her face.

Then she continued in an even voice. "Perhaps this phoenix you mentioned is a timely reminder not to meddle with nature. Perhaps the phoenix, Jacob, is a messenger of Mother Nature herself, sent to put things right, to reset the world." She looked around and slowly pushed her black hair aside. "Nature is far more powerful than any of us realize. We miengu have powers you know nothing about, powers that can't be explained by science."

"Like what?" Emily asked quietly. She sounded nervous, as though she, too, had felt the effect of the glare directed at Abigail moments before.

Jolie was silent as she looked around the room. Then she lowered her voice. "We can heal sick people. We can take the sickness right out of the body. That's why your friend Molly has been visiting us for so many years, offering her services as public executioner, trying to ingratiate herself into our community in the hope that one day we'll return the favor with our healing abilities."

"I thought she was trading for clothes," Lauren said weakly.

Jolie snorted. "Initially, yes. But how many clothes do you need? No, Molly performs far more executions than you think. Whenever one of our kind transgresses, we call in Molly to turn the prisoner to stone. It's far less messy than actual death and serves as a constant, visible reminder to others."

"Doesn't work, though, does it?" Abigail muttered. "Obviously your people just keep on being naughty. What is it they do wrong, anyway? What do they do to deserve the death penalty? I can't imagine how so many can do so wrong that you have to murder—sorry, *execute* them."

The silence that followed was thick with suspense as they awaited Jolie's response. Hal half expected her to lash out with another wilting glare, and he saw that Abigail was steeling herself for the same.

But Jolie simply shook her head. "Never mind. The point is, your scientists want to use us—the miengu—to cure people of illness. That's really why I'm here. That's why they created *me*, a shapeshifter. They hope to have their very own shapeshifter jengu to call on whenever they need help."

"Sounds reasonable, though, doesn't it?" Hal said. He didn't know why, but he felt guilty just for questioning her even though his point was valid. "Is there a better reason to create a shapeshifter?"

Abigail smiled at him, clearly delighted with his question.

Then Jolie smiled, outshining Abigail by several orders of magnitude. "You're absolutely right, Hal. There *is* no better reason to create a shapeshifter. And I'm here to help. Of *course* I'll cure sick people if I can. It's tiring and I'll weaken over time, and if I take on too much at once I'll be so exhausted that I'll collapse and die before the week is out. But I'll do all I can. I'll take it easy and cure one at a time, and that way I can recuperate before moving on to the next."

She played with her hair, looking sad.

"If my hair starts falling out and I don't notice, please tell me. It'll be a sign of working myself too hard."

Darcy and Lauren gasped. In contrast, Abigail's frown deepened and Emily pursed her lips.

"We won't let that happen," Fenton said quietly. He had a determined gleam in his eye. "If Miss Simone pushes you too hard, she'll have me to deal with. I'm on your side, Jolie."

"Me too," Thomas said fiercely, and even Dewey muttered his agreement with a scowl and balled fists.

Hal glanced at Robbie. His friend was nodding silently.

Jolie smiled gratefully. "This chat has gotten a little serious, hasn't it? Why don't we all go outside? Perhaps you can show me around the village and give me a demonstration of your transformations?"

Chapter Twelve
Demonstrations

Jolie wanted to put on some fresh clothes before going out, so Fenton and Thomas picked the limp-legged young woman off the sofa while Dewey peered earnestly at the two closed bedroom doors. "Which one's Miss Simone's and which one's the spare?" he asked.

Fenton snorted. "Who cares? Just open a door, idiot!"

"But—" Dewey said, backing away with wide eyes. "We can't go wandering around Miss Simone's *bedroom*," he said, sounding mortified.

"We don't need to," Fenton argued. He and Thomas were now crowding the hallway with Jolie draped across their shoulders. "Just take a peek and figure out which is which."

"How about I use the bathroom for now?" Jolie suggested sweetly.

So they bypassed the bedrooms and headed for the open bathroom door at the end of the hall. It was a tight squeeze through the doorframe, but after Fenton and Thomas had deposited their patient and left the room, Darcy and Lauren hurried in carrying the pile of clothes the goblins had brought along. They closed the door behind them.

"Let's go outside," Abigail said.

"Good idea," Emily said. "I need some air."

The afternoon sun was beginning its descent on the horizon, and the air was heavy. The clouds had moved on; it looked like the threat of a storm had abated for the time being.

"Seriously," Abigail said, spreading her hands and looking from one boy to another, "are you really taken in by her?"

Fenton and Thomas stood tall and defiant on the matter, while Dewey seemed sheepish. "Heck, yeah," Robbie said. Then he frowned. "I mean, I'm not *taken in* by her. I *like* her. I think she's cool."

Abigail looked away. "I don't. Something bothers me about her."

"I have to agree with Abigail on this," Emily said. She looked mildly disgruntled at the idea of siding with Abigail. "I didn't like Jolie from the start, and I don't like her now."

"You're just—" Fenton began.

"I am *not* jealous!" Emily snapped. "And if you could see what Abigail and I can see, then you wouldn't be either."

Fenton raised an eyebrow. "I was just gonna say that you're still peeved with the whole execution thing and you're looking for someone to blame. You have it in for Jolie even though she's done nothing wrong herself."

"Yet," Abigail murmured.

"Well, I think she's cool," Robbie said again. After Thomas, Dewey and Fenton nodded in agreement, he turned to Hal with a quizzical look. "What about you?"

"Yes, Hal—what about you?" Abigail challenged him, folding her arms.

Hal stuck his hands into his pockets. "She's, uh . . . interesting."

Abigail snorted.

"No, but she is," he went on. "I mean, she makes sense about stuff. And if she really can cure illnesses—well, think of those sick people in the science lab. If she can make them better, then it doesn't really matter what we think of her. It doesn't matter if some of us like her and some of us don't. Heck, it wouldn't matter if she was the most obnoxious person in the world. If she can make those people better, then we need to give her a chance."

For several seconds, the only sound was the buzzing of bees in a nearby clump of bright white and yellow flowers.

Emily sighed. "Your boyfriend may be right, Abi."

"Mmm," Abigail said. She rubbed her chin and analyzed him through narrowed eyes, then spoke sideways to Emily as if he wasn't standing just three feet away. "Sometimes his head seems to be screwed on properly. I think I'll keep him. For now, at least."

Supported by Lauren and Darcy, Jolie emerged from the cottage dressed in purposefully drab rags and scruffy sandals. However, Hal glimpsed shiny green smart clothes underneath. In an effort to mute Jolie's appearance further, she consented to a suggestion to rub a little dirt on her face.

"Now you look like a poor village girl," Darcy said, pleased.

Hal didn't agree. Jolie looked exactly like what she was—an intensely beautiful young woman trying to disguise herself. He was sure that none of the men in the village would be fooled. Besides, she could hardly blend in when she was being hauled around like an invalid.

"Can we go now?" Lauren complained. "Or shall Darcy and I stand here all day holding her up?"

"She can ride on my back," Dewey said. He looked breathless all of a sudden. "I mean . . . you know, after I transform."

Jolie beamed at him. "Wonderful!"

Without further ado, Dewey took a few steps back, stared at his feet, and changed into his centaur form. The shift was instant and dramatic, and as usual there was a brief moment when he was a two-legged horse rearing up on hind legs and balancing precariously while forelegs sprouted and kicked at the front end. Then he thumped down and began to dance around in a circle.

Once Jolie had gotten over her shock, she seemed eager to climb aboard. Her legs flopped uselessly so it was almost comical to watch her being lifted and shoved into position. Once seated, she leaned forward and reached around Dewey's waist to prevent herself from sliding off. "My legs don't work," she reminded him softly. "You don't mind if I hold on to you, do you?"

"No," Dewey gasped, his face bright red.

"I can carry you next," Thomas said, "when Dewey gets tired."

Robbie clicked his tongue. "That's crazy. She'd be better off sitting on my shoulders. Less chance of being stung by a whopping big scorpion tail."

"Yeah, but ogres aren't too bright," Thomas retorted. "What if you forget she's sitting on your shoulders and you walk under a tree and knock her off?"

"Boys, boys," Abigail said, holding up her hands. "Please! I'm sure you'll *all* get a chance to carry Jolie."

Jolie seemed amused by the discussion. She looked directly at Hal the next time Dewey clip-clopped around to face his direction. "And what about you? Will you take me into the sky on your dragon back?"

Trying to ignore Abigail's glare, Hal shrugged. "Sure."

They began the tour of the village. There were a couple of hours left before the sun dipped out of sight and darkness fell, and by that time Hal figured Jolie would be exhausted. He had a lot of questions to ask her, admittedly many of them insignificant, and he tried to throw one in whenever he could during the trek through the streets.

He asked if she'd ever been human before. Of course, he already knew the answer, so his question was more of a prompt to get her talking about it. She explained that she'd never known how to transform, and Abigail immediately asked whether Jolie had even been aware she was a shapeshifter.

"Oh, yes," Jolie said, nodding. She smiled down at a heavyset man wielding a sack of potatoes. The man did a double take, and his mouth dropped open at the sight of the black-haired beauty on the back of the centaur. "My parents—well, my adoptive parents—explained everything to me when I was old enough to understand. Not that it mattered much. They told me I was special when in fact I was no different to anyone else in the lake. Until you all showed up, that is. Then I learned how to shapeshift and now I really *am* special."

"How do your people switch from gills to lungs?" Emily asked, for once losing the sharp edge to her tone.

Jolie frowned. "I can't really explain. You just kind of expel water from the lungs and start breathing. The gills close on their own."

"Have you done it often?" Abigail asked.

Jolie shrugged. "A few times. Just out of curiosity. To sit on the grass and feel the sun on my shoulders. It's kind of scary being out of water."

"Then why have lungs at all?" Abigail persisted.

"I don't know, Abigail. Ask Mother Nature." Jolie was silent for a moment, and then she sighed. "I believe my people used to spend more time above water in the old days. All those stories about us singing to sailors and bringing them too close to the rocks? I'm afraid they're true."

Emily was the first to break the stunned silence. "So the miengu really are like . . . like sirens?"

"Were," Jolie corrected her. "In the last couple hundred years we've retreated to the depths, become more reclusive. We keep to ourselves."

"But . . . *why?*" Fenton asked. "I mean—what's with the shipwrecks?"

Jolie shrugged. "Why did humans burn people at the stake for being witches hundreds of years ago? Why did they torture people in ways that seem barbaric today?" She looked at them one by one. "Yes, I know more than you think about the portals from one world to the other. My people used to cross over every day, just as you did. We learned a lot about your world. Your history is full of horrible acts of violence, much worse than in *this* world."

"Yes, but there's usually a reason for everything," Abigail said. "Why did the miengu wreck ships? What was the point? Was it just for fun?"

Jolie frowned. "Can we change the subject?"

But Abigail's volume had gone up a notch or two. "We're just trying to learn all about your people. Come on, help us out. Tell us why you—"

Jolie's head snapped around and she fixed Abigail with a long stare. Hal saw this clearly because he was walking right next to Abigail, but there was nothing particularly hostile in her expression; it was just a blank, somewhat vacant gaze that struck him as a little odd. Still, Abigail stopped dead and quickly fell behind as most of the group moved on without her.

Hal returned to where she stood in the street, inexplicably trembling and white-faced. "What's wrong, Abi?"

She swallowed. "Apparently she wanted me to change the subject."

"Yeah, I got that. But what's with the white face? You look like you saw a ghost or something."

Abigail hugged herself tight, and Hal saw goosebumps on her arms. "If looks could kill . . . I swear, Hal, there's something wrong with her. She's nasty. Her eyes just then . . . I really wish you could see her from my point of view."

Hal chuckled. "I wish you could see her from mine."

Abigail gripped his arm suddenly, her eyes wide. "Wait!"

She said nothing more, but Hal could tell she was thinking hard about something. She was staring at Hal, but her focus was miles away.

"Abi?" he prompted. "Anyone in there?"

She slowly started to smile. "I have an idea. Something that might help."

"Yes?"

Annoyingly, she started to walk away. "Come on—the others have gone off around the corner."

"Tell me what you—"

"Tomorrow, Hal," she said over her shoulder. "I'm not sure if it'll even work. I have to go make some inquiries first."

Hal knew he wouldn't get another word out of her tonight. She could be infuriating like that sometimes.

When they caught up to their friends, Jolie was being transferred from Dewey onto the back of the powerful manticore. Thomas's lion form was a little too short for passengers and Jolie's feet dangled on the ground, but he was more than capable of supporting her weight. She giggled and cooed as she gripped Thomas's thick red mane, and he took off running along the street, villagers scattering in fright.

Dewey shifted back to his human form, looking sad. Then he dug into his pocket, brought out a small book, and turned away to write in it.

"Pathetic," Emily said quietly to Hal and Abigail. She shuddered. "Look at them, making a spectacle of themselves."

She was right. Everyone had started hooting with laughter at the comical sight in the street. Manticores were normally proud, formidable creatures, but Hal couldn't help thinking Thomas was being made to look like a fool, parading around in front of bemused villagers with a giggling young woman clinging to his back and trying not to slide off.

"She's clever," Abigail murmured.

"Clever?" Hal said. "She doesn't look very clever to me right now."

"But see how all the men are smiling and clapping?"

Hal looked around, studying the expressions of villagers. He saw grown men of all ages cheering and applauding the pantomime act, following Jolie closely, while women wore begrudging smiles. A group of boys were rudely wolf-whistling, but nobody told them to stop.

"So much for muting her appearance and blending in," Abigail said, thoroughly disgusted. "She's playing the part of a silly, helpless damsel and winning hearts. I bet she'll fall off any minute now."

And Jolie did, too. Less than thirty seconds later she flopped sideways off the manticore's back and landed heavily in the dust with a muffled cry. Three men immediately rushed over, but the biggest—a giant black-bearded man—shouldered the others aside and lifted her to her feet. Jolie was unable to stand alone so hung tightly to the man, talking quickly and gesturing at her useless legs until understanding dawned on the man's face. Then he hoisted her back onto the manticore, and she thanked the man.

Having enchanted the male half of her street audience and amused the rest, she urged Thomas back to the waiting children. Darcy and Lauren applauded her, then asked if she was all right after such a rough fall. Robbie, Fenton and Dewey crowded closer, and Hal heard Robbie suggesting that it was *his* turn to carry her around.

"And you're the ogre, right?" Jolie said, beaming at him. "Yes, that would be wonderful!"

Robbie wasted no time. Seconds later, he was an ogre, three times his normal height, a brute of hair and muscle with arms so long that his knuckles brushed the ground. Jolie squealed when he picked her up in one massive paw and placed her high on his shoulders behind his head. She gripped his ears tightly while he began stomping along the street. Hal and the others had to trot along behind to keep up.

The ogre took them into the demolition zone and pointed out a few things with incoherent grumbles. Jolie sobered a little when she saw the carnage, and she asked what had happened. Darcy, Lauren and Fenton took it in turns to fill her in as they kept pace, while Thomas padded alongside in his manticore form. Emily looked thoroughly bored, hanging back and continually shaking her head.

Dewey kept glancing at his book and chewing the end of his pencil.

"More poems?" Abigail asked him.

He quickly stuffed the book into his pocket as if realizing his carelessness in letting everyone see it.

"How are they coming along?" Abigail persisted. "Are you going to let us read any sometime?"

"No!" Dewey said, wide-eyed. "There's no *way* that—"

"Maybe one day," Hal said. "When you've ironed out the wrinkles and got one finished?"

"Uh, sure," Dewey said, not looking sure at all.

Hal and Abigail grew tired of following the ogre around and found a suitable pile of rubble to sit on. It was what remained of a cottage wall, no more than a couple of feet high on one side and the shell of a home on the other. The roof had collapsed into a sorry-looking pile of splintered beams smothered with straw from the thatch.

They watched Robbie for a while, enjoying the early evening air. It was cooling off, and the moon was already visible opposite the setting sun. Abigail huddled closer to Hal and put her head on his shoulder.

"Don't lose sight of me," she murmured.

"What?"

She gestured to Jolie. "Don't go all saucer-eyed over her and forget about me. I have a bad feeling about her."

"Aw, come on," Hal said awkwardly.

"I mean it." She lifted her head and stared intensely at him. "I'm serious. I can sense when things aren't right, and she's not right. I don't trust her."

Hal sighed. "You've made that clear already. I don't know what to tell you, though. I mean . . . I just don't see anything really *bad*, you know? You talk about her like she's an evil demon, but I don't see that at all."

Abigail nodded gently. "I wonder if a photograph would work."

Hal gave that some thought before responding. "Take a picture of her? You think I'd see something different then? I doubt it. What's the difference between looking at her in person and looking at a photo?"

"Depends how her magic works," Abigail said mysteriously. "If a photo doesn't work, then there might be another way, as I mentioned earlier."

Robbie was heading back toward them, his heavy footfalls sending up plumes of dust. Jolie was gripping tufts of shaggy hair on the side of his head, but if it hurt, the ogre didn't care.

"Robbie's dad used to be a photographer," Hal said, recalling a drawer full of useless, long-dead digital cameras in the Stricklands' living room back on the island. "And he kept one of the old-style ones, with 35mm film."

Abigail nudged him. "See if you can get hold of it."

"But the film's probably no good anymore," he protested, immediately seeing the flaws. "And even if it was okay and we took pictures—how are we supposed to get them developed?"

They had no time to talk further because suddenly the group was back, bustling and noisy. Jolie was hooting with joy, and she collapsed in mirth as she was helped down to the ground by Fenton and Darcy.

"Can you make me invisible?" she asked Darcy, her eyes shining. "Is that how it works with you? Can you make things invisible when you touch them?"

Darcy shook her head. "Sorry, no. Although I carried a big slab of meat once, under my shirt, and it turned invisible because my clothes were also invisible—they somehow copy what my body does." She frowned. "As Miss Simone said, they *respond* to me."

Jolie fell silent and stared at Darcy for what seemed like ages. All conversation died and the silence stretched on.

Then Jolie grinned. "I had no idea our fabric could do that!" She arranged herself into a cross-legged position and turned to look up at

Lauren. "How about you? You're the harpy, right? Can you take passengers?"

Lauren couldn't help smiling. "For a bit," she said.

"Show me."

When Lauren transformed, it was with the same *whump!* sound that the sails on Blacknail's dirigible had made as they caught the wind during a high-altitude trip to a distant mountain weeks before. The moment her enormous fluffy white feathered wings burst into being, a strong breeze inexplicably sprang up and whorled around her, creating a cloud of dust like a miniature tornado. Her eyes blazed yellow, and she flashed them all a fanged grin. Her brown hair had turned completely white to match the mass of shaggy feathers covering her body, and her dress had magically altered itself to better fit her muscular shoulders and somewhat pinched waist. The dimpled, snub-nosed Lauren they all knew was still there . . . but heavily disguised.

"Stunning," Jolie breathed, her eyes wide.

For once, the entire group agreed with her. The novelty of shapeshifting quickly wore off when performed daily, as was the case with Robbie helping out on the construction site in his ogre form; at first the villagers had stared at him with awe, but now they barely glanced his way as he stomped past with massive timber beams on his shoulders. But it had been a couple of weeks since Hal and the others had seen Lauren shift to her harpy form.

The dust cloud dissipated. Hal had never seen her generate one during a transformation before, but he knew harpies were able to control the wind to some degree. A gang of harpies could bring low-hanging clouds together and use them to cover their approach during a raid.

"I heard harpies were ugly," Jolie said. "You're more like an angel."

"Most harpies *are* ugly," Darcy said, reaching out to stroke Lauren's pure white locks. "They're greasy, dirty, smelly, and just really nasty. Lauren is the exception. She stands out among hundreds, the only one with clean white feathers and a sunny smile."

Lauren gestured with a slender, clawed hand. "Care for a ride, ma'am?"

Without waiting for an answer, she beat her wings and launched into the air, then hovered over Jolie with her legs extended toward her and powerful talons flexing. Her bird toes were long enough to circle all the way around Jolie's upper arms. With a squeal, Jolie found herself being lifted off into the sky, gripping Lauren's thick ankles.

While most of the group cheered, Emily and Abigail stood aside looking glum. "Oh, lighten up," Hal told them. "They're just having a bit of fun."

Emily scowled. "Well, *I'm* not going to parade myself around, making a fool of myself like that."

"Lauren looks pretty cool to me. Jolie's definitely impressed."

"She's not hitching a ride on *my* back," Emily went on. "I'm not going to make an exhibition of myself. It's ridiculous! I'm not even going to bother transforming for her."

"Good for you, Em," Abigail said quietly, clapping her on the back. "I think I've had enough of this now, too. I'm off home. Coming, Hal?"

Hal was torn. Part of him wanted to show off his dragon. Of course, Jolie might already have seen him and Emily in their respective forms back at the lake; there had been a lot of miengu present, and Jolie had probably been hidden among them. Maybe that was why she had left Emily, Fenton and Hal until last.

Still, what if she wanted a ride in the sky? He was sure his broad dragon back was far more comfortable and dignified than dangling from the talons of a harpy. Besides, Lauren was clearly struggling, growing weary. Hal knew he could fly Jolie around for hours if he wanted to—

"Hey," Abigail said, poking him so hard in the arm that he winced. "Quit dreaming and walk me home."

Grumbling, Hal bade his friends goodnight and headed off with Abigail. In the darkening evening sky, Lauren soared around in one last circle and then descended below the rooftops. No doubt Jolie was already demanding to know where Hal had got to.

"Okay," Abigail said, walking quickly through the narrow streets as if afraid that Jolie would come running after them—not that she could run or even walk. "Are you and Robbie hanging out tonight? If you are, see if you can get a camera from his dad. If not, I have another plan."

"Yeah, you said. How about sharing it with me instead of being all secretive about it and making me guess?"

"I will," Abigail said. Then she grinned. "Tomorrow."

They passed Hal's old home, the small cottage that he and his parents had lived in after arriving in Miss Simone's world. It was occupied by an old couple now, and the smell of something delicious wafting out of the window made Hal pick up his pace. His stomach was rumbling long before they reached the fork in the woods outside the village. Normally, Hal and Abigail would go their separate ways at this point, but Abigail insisted he walk her home.

"On Monday morning," she said as they ducked under some low-hanging trees that drooped over the path leading to the house, "I want you to stop by and keep me company on the way to school. Okay?"

Hal shrugged. "Fine. But why?"

"Do I need a reason? How about just because it'd be nice?"

Abigail's mom, Dr. Porter, had no interest whatsoever in yard work and the place was a rambling mess of overgrown bushes and weeds with ivy crawling all over the log walls.

"See you tomorrow, then," he said, his stomach growling again.

Abigail sighed. "No doubt Jolie will hang around us all day long. I'm surprised someone her age even wants to be around us."

"She's new in town," Hal reasoned. "New to a world on dry land, for that matter. For all we know, that was her boyfriend back at the lake. She's just here on a little visit, remember? And Miss Simone appointed us as her guides."

"All right, all right," Abigail said. She turned and headed inside. "Well, bye then. I guess everyone's meeting up at Miss Simone's tomorrow, but I'll swing by your house first thing."

Hal scratched his head. "Probably better if I come by yours since we'll be headed this way—"

"Not the way we're going," Abigail said mysteriously.

There she goes again, Hal thought, *being all weird*. "Well, whatever. But not too early. I'm sleeping in."

She winked. "Okay, not too early. About five?"

"Five in the *morning*?" Hal barked a laugh. "Yeah, right."

Still chuckling, he headed off home. At five in the morning, he planned to be in the middle of a really great dream with hours of deep sleep remaining.

He ate greedily when he got home, then retired to his room to dig out his battered copy of *The Phoenix and the Carpet*. He completely forgot about asking Robbie for a camera until around eight, and then decided he couldn't be bothered to go out again. No matter; it could wait.

Eventually he drifted off to bed, looking forward to his Saturday morning sleep-in. He dreamed of a great castle occupied by knights in shining armor, and Hal was the resident dragon, only he was not a threat to the land but a revered protector. So when he had to rescue a damsel in distress—a black-haired beauty by the name of Jolie, chained high on a cliff smothered in rolling fog—it wasn't Hal she was afraid of but some unseen menace lurking just out of sight in the gloom. The sounds of crashing came to his ears as he flew in to tear the manacles from her wrists; he heard splintering, like a ship being wrecked on the rocks far below. He breathed hard on the chains, and they glowed red and melted away, leaving her arms completely unharmed. Eternally grateful, Jolie—who in his dream had no trouble walking—flung her arms around his neck and kissed him.

As he closed his eyes to relish the moment, she began tapping on something, a sharp *tap-tap-tap* that puzzled him. After a while, he grew annoyed with the relentless noise and opened his eyes to demand an explanation.

Then he woke suddenly, aware that the tapping was real. It came from his window. It was dark outside, yet Abigail's pale face was pressed against the glass. She tapped again.

"What the—" he started, sitting up.

She mouthed the words "open up," and he slid out of bed, aware that he was wearing pajama bottoms but no shirt because the nights were warm. He grabbed his smart clothes, ducked into the darkest corner away from the window, and quickly dressed, muttering under his breath. What was she *doing* here?

He unlatched the window and swung it open. She immediately gestured for him to come outside, a finger to her lips. "What's going on?" he demanded, keeping his voice low.

She raised her eyebrows. "What do you mean? Did you forget? I *told* you I was coming by at around five this morning."

Hal stared at her in disbelief. When he peered through the trees, he saw the very first signs of sunrise far to the east, a slight brightening of the sky that would eventually turn orange. It was dawn, but only just.

"Are you *kidding* me?"

Abigail could barely suppress a giggle. "Actually, I'm deadly serious. Come on. I want to show you something. Something secret."

Chapter Thirteen
Faerie Glade

Hal trailed through the woods after Abigail, glaring at her ponytail as it swung from side to side. "This had *better* be worth it," he growled.

His bed still called to him, and he glanced over his shoulder to see his house fading into the darkness. His parents were tucked up in bed, sound asleep, and here *he* was wandering around the woods at a ridiculous hour for no apparent reason. Abigail hadn't even bothered to tell him where they were going.

"It's stupid o'clock," he moaned. "It's Saturday morning! The one time of the week I get to sleep in, and you go and drag me out here—"

"It has to be early," Abigail said quietly without looking back. Hal noticed that she carried the bronze box under her arm. She suddenly veered off the path and plunged into the trees. "Something to do with the sunrise."

Hal shook his head and sighed heavily. "Riddles, riddles. Do you remember how Robbie and I used to avoid you? This is exactly the reason why."

He swore he heard Abigail giggle, but she said nothing more until they had walked for ten minutes through ever-thickening vegetation. By this time, dew had soaked into Hal's clothes and he was beginning to shiver despite the odd warming sensation provided by his enchanted shirt and pants. His toes were plastered with sticky, cold earth, and he felt sure he could feel a worm wriggling around on the top of his foot.

"Did Robbie find a camera?" she asked suddenly.

"Not yet," Hal retorted. He refrained from admitting that he hadn't even bothered to ask.

"Well, we'll see how we get on," Abigail murmured.

Hal frowned. "What do you *mean?*"

"Shh, we're here."

She slowed and held up a hand in front of Hal's face so that he was forced to stop. She put a finger to her lips, then pulled gently at his sleeve, urging him to creep forward and peer around the thick trunk of a tree.

"There," she whispered, pointing.

Hal looked but saw nothing out of the ordinary, just the dark shapes of thick bushes. He shrugged, growing more and more impatient. His bed seemed a million miles away now, and yet it continued to call from afar . . .

"A faerie glade," Abigail said quietly, close to his ear.

Hal looked again. Still he saw nothing. "Where?"

"Can't you see them buzzing around?"

It was hard to see anything at all in the darkness. But now that he knew what to look for, he had to admit he could see a number of small pale things flitting around. He hadn't paid any attention to them, thinking them to be nothing more interesting than random oversized bugs. There were probably ten or fifteen of them, just faint light smudges zipping quickly from place to place, some in circles and others in zigzags.

"That's it?" he grumbled. "You couldn't wait until daylight? What, are they nocturnal or something?"

"Actually, yes," Abigail said. "Sunrise signifies bedtime, the end of the day for them. But that's when they party."

"Oh, so we're going to crash a party?" Hal said, unable to keep the sarcasm from his voice. He rubbed his eyes. "Seriously, Abi, I wish you'd—"

"Listen to me," she whispered fiercely, gripping his wrist suddenly. "If there's any such thing as magic, *this* is when you're going to see it. Most faeries sleep during the day, except for a handful that keep watch. When the sun goes down, faeries stir and wake. The brighter the moon, the more active they are. By the end of the night, just before sunrise, they're in a partying mood. The party is wild, and they pretty much wear themselves out. By the time the morning comes, they're completely wasted and sound asleep."

She hugged the bronze box to her chest and nodded toward the silent glade some distance away. "Maybe you can't hear, but they're at their most active right now. I can hear the cheering and laughing— can't you?"

Hal shook his head, hearing absolutely nothing. Even the cicadas were quiet in this patch of forest.

Abigail looked puzzled. "Mm. Well, maybe it's just something other faeries can hear. Anyway, the point is, they all get drunk—as high as kites on their own faerie dust."

"You're kidding, right?" Hal muttered. "Faerie dust?"

"I'm kidding about the dust," she admitted, smiling. "But they *do* get drunk. This place is as giddy and merry as the inn on a Friday night."

Hal thought about the noise emanating from the inn, the yells and jeers of men who had had a little too much to drink. They always burst out onto the street at closing time and staggered off home in groups, unable to keep their voices down, usually causing dogs to bark and angry residents to yell for quiet.

"So faeries have parties," he said, shrugging. "Okay. So what?"

"Well," Abigail started. Then she trailed off and thought for a moment before continuing. "This is hard to explain. I first heard about this trick weeks ago and put it aside. Late last night, I came and spoke to the faeries as they were waking. They were bleary-eyed and kind of grumpy, but I got them to tell me how to do this . . . this *trick*. So that's why we're here. I can only do this early in the morning when magic is at its strongest."

"Abigail," Hal warned.

She touched a finger to his lips, and they both stood as still and silent as the statues at the bottom of the miengu lake.

"Just wait here," Abigail said, finally lowering her hand and releasing him. "I'm going to go join the party, but I won't be laughing and zipping around everywhere like the others. Instead, I'll be concentrating on the trick." She handed him the bronze box. "Hold on to this for me."

"Why'd you bring it?"

"I've been brushing up," she replied vaguely. "Searching the recesses of my mind to figure out how to do this thing."

"And did it work?" Hal asked.

Abigail smiled. "We'll see." She gestured to the dark, moist forest floor. "You might want to get comfortable in the dirt."

"Get comfortable in the dirt," Hal repeated slowly.

"I need you to be receptive and ready. Just lie down, get comfortable, close your eyes, that sort of thing. Go to sleep."

Grumbling, Hal waved her away. "Fine. Do whatever you need to do. I'll sit here in the dirt and wait."

"See you in a minute," Abigail said with a wink. Then she sprouted wings and, in the blink of an eye, shrank to about six inches high. The air popped as it rushed to fill the sudden vacuum she'd left behind.

She buzzed away, off to join the partying faeries in the distant glade. Something about her, either her light dress or her skin, glowed faintly in the darkness. Hal hadn't noticed the glow before. He'd seen that her enchanted dress shimmered while in faerie form but had never been aware of illumination. Perhaps it was because it was morning, just before sunrise, when the magic was in the air. "Witching hour," he muttered.

Abigail became just another pale figure in the gloom, zipping around with the others. He tried to track her movements but soon lost sight of her. There were more of them about now, perhaps thirty, whirling in tight circles.

Apart from the dancing lights, there was really nothing of interest to see or hear. Hal sighed and hunted for a dry place to sit. He couldn't help mumbling to himself, still irritated—partly because of being dragged out of bed at such a silly hour but mostly because of Abigail's annoying habit of talking in riddles and stringing him along. This 'trick' she'd hinted at had *better* be worth it.

He sat and leaned back against the rough bark of a tree, the box by his side. It was impossible to get really comfortable and he ended up wriggling almost a quarter of the way around the trunk before he found a reasonably smooth, lump-free place. Then he waited, sitting quietly in the darkness and peering up through the branches at patches of lightening sky, aware of the chill and the moistness in the air.

It was probably a good twenty minutes before his eyelids started to feel heavy. Remembering that Abigail had suggested he doze off, he encouraged the drowsiness to overcome him, resting his head on the bark and trying to clear his mind of busy, random thoughts.

That was when he heard Abigail calling, her voice soft and whispery.

His eyelids fluttered open and he frowned, listening hard. Silence greeted him, and he wondered if he'd imagined the voice. Maybe he'd fallen asleep and started dreaming.

He began to doze again.

Don't wake up, Abigail called gently. Frowning, he listened as her voice brushed close to his ear. *Relax. Think of this as a dream.*

"A dream," he mumbled. "Wait—"

Relax, she said soothingly, her voice echoing around his head. *Just keep your eyes closed and listen. Trust me, Hal.*

He fought the urge to snap his eyes open and look around, certain that she was right there with him, perhaps with others of her kind. He imagined she had brought a bunch of faeries along and they were studying him, and that was why she wanted him to stay still and calm and keep his eyes shut. Oddly, he found it quite easy to obey. He trusted her, and besides, faeries were tiny—what could they possibly do to harm him even if they wanted to?

And so he drifted, his interrupted night's sleep finally resuming where it had left off. This wasn't his comfortable bed, but if he kept still enough he found that his body and limbs lost sensation . . .

Take my hand, Abigail whispered. In his mind he saw her face swimming in and out of a hazy gray murkiness. Her hand appeared, seeming way too large as if his perspective was all out of whack. He fumbled to grasp it, wondering how he could be doing so in a dream.

When his fingers touched hers, she gripped his hand firmly and started tugging. It alarmed him because he felt a curious sensation of being pulled off balance so that he was tumbling forward onto his face. Only . . . he didn't hit the ground and instead floated above it, rising higher in his gloomy, fuzzy dream world.

And then, just as he was getting used to floating in a strange, hazy darkness, everything brightened around him and noise flooded into his head. He gasped, reeling back but finding himself inexplicably trapped in what seemed to be a small, dark cave with a single round opening at the front.

"W-what's happening?" he gasped.

It's okay, Abigail assured him, her voice louder and clearer now.

He couldn't see her anymore, but he saw plenty of other faeries. They were everywhere, laughing and dancing around a fire of blue flames, the air filled with a hazy glow, and dozens of faeries zipping maniacally overhead. Hal swore he could feel the tingling of static and, confused, looked around for a phoenix, somehow sure he'd been flung into the middle of another regeneration.

But that didn't make sense. There were faeries wherever he looked, and they seemed to be his size, perched on massive clumps of mushrooms eight feet high and running through blades of grass taller than a house. Yet Hal's perception of the forest was from an abnormally low angle, so low that his cheek must be squashed flat into the earth . . .

A wave of giddiness swept over him. "Where—how did I get here?" he stuttered. "Am I asleep?"

You're in my head, Abigail said, sounding distinctly proud of herself. *I pulled you in. Welcome to the glade.*

The noise was relentless, a cacophony of screams and shrieks, yells and shouts, shrill laughter, and annoyingly squeaky music generated by odd-looking instruments carved out of twigs and leaves. He was startled by a level of detail he had previously been unaware existed—fine hairs on the surface of bright green leaves, enormous beads of water hanging under giant flowers, the weird clumpy texture of the soil . . . and, trying in vain to rub his nonexistent eyes, Hal stared in horror as a huge earthworm wriggled past, thicker than a faerie's arm.

You're panicking, Abigail told him quietly, her voice jarring. *Just relax or you'll spring back to your own body and wake up. You're in my head, seeing what I see. Nobody can see you—they only see me.*

As if to prove the point, a male faerie suddenly buzzed into view, his face inches away—or was that mere millimeters on the faerie scale? The creature had a dazed grin on his face, clearly euphoric from whatever magic was in the air.

"Come dance," he murmured, his voice curiously muffled and distant.

He was clearly talking to Abigail, and yet he appeared to be staring directly at Hal as he loitered in her mind, seeing what she saw. There was a sideways motion as Abigail shook her head, and Hal heard her say something . . . but was unable to make out her words.

Hal tried to calm himself but felt extremely vulnerable for reasons he couldn't fathom. "What are we doing?" he said nervously. Was he speaking aloud or merely thinking the words? He had no idea.

Let's get away from the party, Abigail said clearly and loudly.

Hal knew she was merely thinking the words this time, to all intents and purposes having a private conversation with him in her head.

Abruptly, the scene changed as she zipped into the air and took off through the woods. The noise abated and now all Hal could hear was a dull buzzing and the rush of wind—again, all outside the curious glass barrier that he imagined surrounded his cave. He saw clearly ahead, but it was fuzzy around the sides of the cave opening; he saw only what she saw ahead and in her periphery. He found it frustrating and limiting not being able to turn and glance wherever he wanted; he was literally confined to the back of her head, looking out through a wall of glass. And when she blinked, the blackness closed in from above and immediately lifted again, like an impossibly fast rolling shutter on the front of a garage. It was the speed of this mechanical action that startled him; it drove home how small and insignificant he was, no bigger than a bug.

Here we are, Abigail said cheerfully.

Hal's own body came into view, and he gasped. There he was, lying in the dirt, propped awkwardly against a tree, his head lolling. The bronze box lay next to him, half buried in leaves. He was sound asleep, and yet . . . he was right here, awake, in Abigail's head. Looking down at himself, he suddenly felt a strange sense of calm, knowing that he could simply wake up and be back in his body within a second.

Abigail gave him a while longer, then turned and headed off through the woods toward the village. *Now let's go take a look at Jolie through my eyes*, she said mischievously. *Let's see if she's a drop-dead babe like you boys seem to think . . . or a hag with bad hair and gap-teeth, as I see her.*

* * *

The sky was turning orange to the east as Abigail flew out of the woods and into the village. It was still far too early to be out and about, and the streets were shrouded in darkness, seemingly deserted except for a handful of eager farmers. Abigail rounded a corner to find a couple of burly bearded men strolling toward her, whistling merrily. They didn't see her at first, as small as she was, but then they exclaimed and nodded to her.

"Morning," she said brightly. She sounded to Hal like the world was deep underwater, but probably like a tiny buzzing whine to the men.

Do you feel like you're asleep or awake? she asked Hal, this time speaking directly to him in his head.

"Awake," Hal said, confused by the question. But then he realized what she meant and considered for a moment. "I do feel rested, though. My body's asleep in the woods, so . . ."

Abigail tore around another corner. *What can you see exactly?* she asked, sounding a little uncertain, perhaps even nervous.

"I see what you see. Wherever you look."

What if I keep my head still but turn my eyes?—like this.

The world outside the cave entrance shifted only a fraction to the left.

"About the same," he said. "It's like I'm crouched in the back of your head, looking right through your eyeballs. It doesn't really matter what you're focusing on; I just kind of see everything ahead. Except when you blink or close your eyes; then it all goes dark."

Interesting, Abigail murmured. *Can you tell what I'm looking at right now?*

Hal stared ahead. The cottages sped by on either side, and the upcoming T-junction meant they'd have to make a sharp left or right turn in just a few seconds. The view was clear in the center but fuzzy at the edges. Hal could only guess as to what she was focused on. "I don't know—the red door?"

Wrong, she replied triumphantly. *I was looking at that sleepy black cat.*

Abigail whizzed around the corner to the right and then made a sharp left down an alley. *So if I said "Look at that!" in a really excited way, you wouldn't necessarily know what I was looking at, only that it's something up ahead? I'd still have to point it out with my finger?*

"I guess," Hal said. "Look, can't you fly over the rooftops instead of around all these corners? It's making me nauseous."

Really? That's a weird thought. Do you think you'd be pretend-sick in my head or actual-sick back at your body in the woods?

"Stop," Hal groaned.

Abigail giggled and soared upward. Hal swore he felt his stomach drop with the sudden upward movement but couldn't imagine how that could be.

The cottages seemed very small within seconds as Abigail circled up and around. It occurred to Hal that he could see remarkably well considering how dark the sky was. Even with the orange glow filtering through the clouds on the horizon, he still considered it to be stupid o'clock, practically the middle of the night. So how come he could see everything so clearly?

Faeries have good night vision, Abigail explained.

"What?"

I said, faeries have—

"I heard what you said," Hal said sharply. "But how did you know I was thinking about that just then?"

There was a pause, and then Abigail let out a muffled laugh. *Did I just read your mind? Seriously?*

Hal was alarmed. "Stay out of my head," he warned.

There was another squeal of laughter. *Oh, that's rich coming from someone who's in* my *head!* Then she sobered. *What color am I thinking of right now?*

"Pink," Hal guessed at random. "No, blue."

Green, actually. Well, that's good. I wouldn't want you knowing all my inner thoughts, Hal. Some things are best left unsaid.

"Tell me about it," Hal mumbled, wondering if it was possible to clear his mind and speak to her without actually thinking. Or perhaps he could keep his thoughts on track and think only about what he was discussing out loud—

That would be wise, she said.

"Quit!" he yelled.

He was sorely tempted to leave her head immediately and return to his body, but Abigail was already approaching the far side of the village where Miss Simone lived. There was the gate, where three goblins were slumped over a small round table, snoozing into bowls of roasted nuts. Their campfire was cold, and they'd left quite a mess of discarded shells.

Beyond the gate, the trail led into the woods. Abigail landed neatly on a branch at the fringe of the trees and retracted her wings. Hal had no way of seeing this but experienced a curious sensation behind him, a tickling on the back of his incorporeal neck.

Do you think Miss Simone's up yet?

"Sure, if she's crazy enough."

What about Jolie? Think she's an early riser?

"I have no idea," Hal said. "How come you're so chipper this morning? You're giving me a headache. First it was Jolie talking to me in my head with the volume turned all the way up, and now *you're* doing it. I don't know what the world's coming to with all these females getting inside my brain . . ."

Abigail giggled.

She set off again, buzzing toward Miss Simone's cottage. It soon came into view. "Now what?" Hal asked. "We're not going to peep in windows, are we?"

That would be creepy, Abigail said. *No, we'll just bang on Jolie's window and get her up.*

"You can't!" Hal said. "Anyway, we don't know which window is Jolie's!"

She pondered, then shrugged. *Only one way to find out.*

She buzzed around to the left side of the house. There she found a window with its curtains drawn. It had to be either Miss Simone's bedroom or the spare that Molly and Jolie shared. But which? Without pause, Abigail flew at the window and gave it a terrific thump. Then she did it two more times.

Get ready, Abigail said, whipping behind a tree.

It seemed like ages before there was any sign of movement. Then slender fingers snaked through a gap in the curtains. *Here she is,* Abigail hissed rather unnecessarily. But who was it? Even if this was the correct room, it might be Molly coming to the window—and she might not have her veil on! But Hal told himself she surely must have her veil on with Jolie sharing the room . . .

A pale face appeared and Hal sucked in a breath, half closing his eyes just in case it was Molly—or a furious Miss Simone.

Instead, Jolie pressed her nose to the glass and peered out, looking puzzled.

There was a long silence, during which Hal sensed Abigail holding her breath. Jolie looked all around, then stared thoughtfully at the tree over the window. For a moment, Hal thought she was staring right at them . . . but then she shook her head and disappeared inside. The heavy curtains moved back into position and Abigail let out a sigh.

I can't believe it, she murmured. *She's absolutely gorgeous.*

"I told you," Hal said triumphantly. He'd seen nothing different about Jolie whatsoever. Even with disheveled hair and sleepy eyes, she looked as beautiful as she had the day before. "Wait—what did you say?"

She's gorgeous, Abigail repeated. She sighed heavily. *I felt sure you'd see her for what she is, and instead . . . instead I saw what you boys see!*

Hal snorted. "That proves it, then. Jolie's lovely, but you see her as plain and ugly because you're jealous."

Abigail flew away from the window, and Hal could sense her disgust. She said nothing until they were out of the woods. Then

Abigail reverted to full human size and ambled slowly through the streets.

No, I don't buy it, she said finally. *I can read your mind a little, but you can't read mine. I think your thoughts are invading mine, somehow influencing the way I perceive Jolie. This experiment didn't turn out the way I expected.*

"It was interesting, though," Hal said, unable to shake his feeling of glee. Whether Abigail was ultimately right or wrong about Jolie, Hal had won this round for now. He chuckled to himself.

* * *

You have to understand, Abigail said peevishly, *we girls not only see Jolie's ugly mug but also her nasty side. You should have seen how she glared at me yesterday. Twice, actually—once in Miss Simone's house, and again outside in the street. That second glare really gave me the creeps. Her eyes just . . . well, if it were really possible to stare daggers at someone, then she did it.*

They were arriving back at Hal's body. To his alarm, he found that he'd slumped over sideways and was lying with his cheek in the dirt and his arm trapped awkwardly underneath. The position he was in looked unnatural, like he'd been knocked unconscious or murdered in the night.

"How do I get back?" he asked, suddenly nervous. "And . . . what if . . ."

You'll be fine, Abigail said. *My people have been doing this sort of thing forever. Your body is just resting.* Then she considered, tilting her head to the side. *Mind you, that's not a comfortable way to sleep, is it? I'm pretty sure you'd have woken yourself up by now if your mind wasn't elsewhere.*

Horrible thoughts sprang up. What if he'd fallen face down in a puddle? What if there had been wolves or bears or harpies sniffing around? What had he been thinking, leaving his poor body behind like this, unattended?

Getting back into his body proved easy, though. He realized that he'd been gently straining at an invisible tether, one that wanted to tug him home. It hadn't taken any effort to resist the tug, to stay put in Abigail's head and leave his body behind, but now he just needed to let go. In doing so, he found himself floating up and away. In an instant, Abigail's overbearing presence was gone and he was as light as a ghost, riding on air. He tried to focus on his murky surroundings . . . but suddenly he was coughing and struggling to sit up.

He spat dirt from his mouth and checked himself over. He'd been lying heavily on his arm, and it felt completely numb. As he shook it vigorously to get the circulation going, pins and needles began to prickle him with a vengeance. "Ow!" he exclaimed. "Oh man, I feel like I've just woken from the dead."

"But you're okay?" Abigail asked.

Detecting concern in her voice, Hal stared at her while rubbing his forearm. "Are you surprised? I thought you said this mind trick was safe?"

"Well, it is . . . but faeries usually aren't too concerned about the host."

Hal froze. "What?"

Looking sheepish, Abigail shrugged and turned to squint at the distant faerie glade. "Sounds like they're all asleep now. The sun's up." She collected the bronze box from the dirt. "Come on, let's head back."

"Hey, what do you mean about the host?" Hal demanded.

Abigail forged ahead through the woods as if trying to avoid being asked such questions. Annoyed, Hal had to wait until they back on the main path before he could walk alongside her and repeat his question.

Abigail sighed. "Well, faeries often project into the minds of people. They possess incredible amounts of knowledge about how humans think—why we do what we do, what we want, and so on. Faeries are wise but also very childish." She sounded embarrassed. "Usually, no harm is done. At dawn, a faerie will nip into someone's mind while that person is sleeping, and then kind of tag along for a while when the host wakes shortly after."

"Tag along?" he repeated. "Uninvited, you mean?"

"Uninvited, yes. The host usually isn't aware, and the faerie picks up all sorts of information while lurking at the back of the mind. It's how they were able to learn so much about the brain and how to unlock deeply buried secrets that the host isn't consciously aware of, or has forgotten. They've been doing it for thousands of years. It's how they were able to develop the little glass ball, which is an actually an enchanted drop of dew. They use it to teach their young. Faeries never invade other faeries' minds—that's an unspoken rule—so they have an artificial learning device that demonstrates the trick."

She tapped the bronze box under her arm.

"That's why they gave me the glass ball in the first place. They could see I was new to the whole faerie thing."

Hal was at a loss for words.

"While lurking in a host's brain," Abigail went on, "a faerie's physical body needs to be guarded. During the parties, some faeries stay sober and act as guardians while the rest zonk out and nip off for a ride in someone's mind. They're experts at slipping in unannounced, as long as the host is asleep."

"But . . . but I was in *your* mind," Hal finally said.

"Well, that's a *reverse* mind trick," Abigail said. "Instead of invading the host's mind, the faerie kind of kidnaps it. The host finds himself yanked out of his own head and ends up whizzing around a forest, or flying through the sky, or joining in a wild party—wherever the faerie decides to take him. The sleeping host doesn't understand and always puts it down to a bizarre dream."

Hal scowled. "Nice to know."

"I would never do it without your permission," Abigail protested.

"Yeah, yeah, okay."

Abigail's house was just ahead, and Hal realized he'd not even intended coming back all this way. He stopped and turned around. "Look, I'm tired, and I'm going back home to bed. It's still way too early to be up and about."

"You don't want a muffin? Smells like Mom's made some. She's probably gone off to work already."

"Too early," Hal repeated.

Abigail nodded meekly. "Fine. I guess I'll see you later, then."

As they parted ways, Hal thought he heard the crack of a twig in the bushes, but he saw nothing. "Hello?" he called, peering into the trees.

Nobody answered.

"Did you say something?" Abigail said.

Hal shook his head. "Nothing. See you later."

Chapter Fourteen
Picnic on the River

Hal snuck into bed the moment he got back home, intent on making up for lost sleep. It took a while to drop off, but finally he was dreaming again.

"Hal?" his mom called, knocking softly on the door.

Hal woke, blinked, then groaned and buried his face in the pillow. He heard the gentle creak of his door and knew his mom was peering through the crack. He forced himself to lie absolutely still, keeping his breathing slow and regular, his mouth open.

"Hal, Robbie's here," his mom said. She spoke again, this time to someone behind her. "Come on in. See if *you* can wake him."

Hal didn't care who had come to visit. All he cared about was *staying in bed.* It was still early, wasn't it? He could tell by the angle of the sunlight streaming through the gap in the curtains that it was no later than eight. What was Robbie doing here this early, anyway? And on a *Saturday*!

"Hey, wake up," Robbie barked, giving him a hard shove on the shoulder.

It was no use pretending. Hal blinked his eyes open, scowling up at his thin, mop-headed friend. "What?" he grumbled.

"Everyone's outside waiting for you," Robbie said. "Come on."

Hal sighed and rolled over, closing his eyes again. "Go away."

"Won't," Robbie said. He began moving around the room, picking things up and putting them back down with telltale clinks and knocks. "Hey, I remember this book: *The Phoenix and the Carpet.* Did you read it?"

Robbie rambled on about this and that, doing a full tour of the room and touching just about everything there was to touch, and finally stood once more over Hal. "Come on. What's *wrong* with you?"

Sighing, Hal rolled onto his back and glared at his friend. "What's wrong with *you*? It's Saturday morning. What's the big rush? I'm tired!"

"We're having breakfast on the river," Robbie said, rubbing his hands.

"Why?" Hal asked sleepily.

As if answering a different question altogether, Robbie started going on about the hamper they'd packed. "Fresh-baked bread rolls, ham, eggs," he said, cradling imaginary goodies in his hands and staring at them longingly. "We're gonna go on the boat along the river, just us and Jolie, and we're—"

"Who's 'us'?"

Robbie frowned. "Well, everyone except Abigail and Emily. For some reason, Emily's not interested in coming with us—said the idea of it makes her sick—and Abigail's disappeared off somewhere."

Hal shook his head and closed his eyes. "I'm not really interested either. I just want to sleep."

Robbie scoffed. "You say that now, but wait until you get one of those crispy fresh-baked rolls in your hands, stuffed with thick juicy ham." He lowered his voice and grinned. "And Jolie will be there."

Totally smitten, Hal thought, looking at his friend. It was both funny and a little silly. She was seventeen, five years older than them all. And, not to put too fine a point on it, she was way out of Robbie's league.

"I'll pass," he said.

For the first time since arriving, Robbie looked alarmed. "Uh, dude, you *can't* pass. You have to come. If you don't, then it's all off."

Puzzled, Hal sat up. "Why?"

"The picnic is Jolie's idea. And she asked for you specially. She wants to ride on the dragon today. She made it pretty clear that if you didn't come along, then she wouldn't either." His voice hardened. "So you're coming."

He looked so determined that Hal couldn't help laughing. "All right, all right. I guess I can't help being the most popular guy in the village. Go on outside and wait—I'll be there in a minute."

And so, ten minutes later, Hal had dressed, brushed his teeth, and combed his hair. "I'm outta here!" he yelled into the kitchen as he passed.

His mom winced. "Have fun. I would ask if you needed to take anything, but judging by the size of the baskets your friends are carrying, I'd say they have it covered."

Hal found his friends waiting impatiently outside, pacing around like caged animals. They grumbled and clicked their tongues when he emerged. Jolie was with them but much calmer than the others, sitting in the grass with her legs crossed, smiling serenely. Was she even prettier this morning than the previous afternoon? Hal wasn't sure, but he couldn't take his eyes off her.

"'Bout time," Fenton said. He picked up one of three huge baskets, and Hal could tell by the way he was holding it that it was pretty heavy. "I'm starving."

"Let's go before it gets dark," Lauren said, already walking off with Darcy.

Hal rolled his eyes. "It's only just eight o'clock. How come you're all up so early, anyway? A bit of notice would have been nice."

Jolie held out a hand to him. "Help me up."

Hal saw that she had brought along two thick, heavily polished wooden crutches, basically long sticks that came all the way up to her armpits, with carved T-sections on the top to put her weight on. She needed help getting off the grass, and she leaned heavily on Hal until she had positioned the crutches under her arms and got a firm grip on them. He was acutely aware of the fresh scent of her hair and the faint soapy aroma of her skin.

"Thank you," she said quietly as she shifted her weight to the crutches.

"Welcome," Hal mumbled. He suddenly noticed that Fenton, Robbie, Thomas and Dewey were staring in silence, clearly jealous.

"Okay, let's go, boys," Jolie said brightly. She nodded toward Lauren and Darcy, who were already distant figures on the forest trail.

With Fenton and Robbie carrying two heavily laden baskets, the third was left in the grass for someone to collect. Thomas glanced at it, then looked away. Dewey went to lift it, but Hal waved him off. "Thanks," Dewey muttered. "I carried it here, but it was doing my shoulder in."

That was hardly surprising, Hal thought; it weighed a ton!

The walk along the trail was surprisingly fast as Jolie seemed to have mastered the crutches quickly and was able to put at least a little weight on her feet. Still, her knuckles were white where she gripped the sticks.

"Why don't you ride on Dewey's back?" Hal suggested.

"Or mine," Thomas quickly chipped in.

Jolie said nothing for a moment, then looked sheepish. "I don't want to be a nuisance. I'm trying to make my own way around."

There was a clamor as all four boys spoke in unison, telling her it was really no trouble and she shouldn't worry about asking for help when needed. "It's not your fault you can't walk," Hal added. "You've spent your life swimming around underwater with a fishtail."

Jolie gratefully accepted the ride, and Dewey transformed so she could climb aboard. Without a word, she handed her crutches to Thomas, who took them as if they were treasures.

"Let's stop by Abigail's house," Hal said.

"Already did," Robbie said, clapping him smartly on the shoulder. "She's not there."

"Probably sound asleep," Hal muttered. "We'll have to bang on the door."

Nobody seemed willing to make the detour to Abigail's house, but Hal insisted. Still, despite knocking hard enough to bruise his knuckles, nobody answered the door. He knew Dr. Porter had already left for work, but he couldn't decide if Abigail was also out somewhere or just sleeping in.

Then he wondered if she was deliberately avoiding them. She probably knew Hal would be demonstrating his dragon form today.

He shook his head and sighed. "Let's go."

The previous journey to the river had been on the back of a cart pulled by horses, with Miss Simone driving. This time they walked, and Hal realized he couldn't remember the way. Luckily, Fenton did, otherwise their picnic on the river might have ended up as a picnic in the middle of nowhere.

The morning was crisp and fresh, but the sky was filled with clouds and the sun kept disappearing behind them. Some of the clouds looked ominous. Hal had heard about the changing season and how unpredictable the weather was around this time of year. Still, it amazed him how hot it still was in this world. Autumn had set in back on the island, and leaves had been turning brown and falling off trees. And that had been several weeks ago. Yet here in Miss Simone's world, the summer was only just ending. Everything seemed out of whack—bugs were bigger, flowers were brighter, even vegetables seemed unusually large . . . and now the extended summer was boiling off in a series of thunderstorms over the past few weeks. It was said that the winter would be brutal, and newcomers to the land should be prepared.

The deep-rutted cartwheel tracks finally led them to the river, and Hal recognized the paddock in which Miss Simone's horses had grazed. "We're here," Fenton announced. "It's just through that hedge there."

They found the boat tied up to the small jetty and began clambering aboard. Previously there had been six passengers on the way to the lake, and seven once they'd collected Jolie for the return journey; now there were eight of them, plus three large baskets, and there just wasn't room.

"Lauren and Darcy can walk along the bank," Fenton suggested.

The girls rounded on him. "*You* walk!" Lauren retorted. "You could do with losing a bit of weight."

Before an argument could start, Jolie interrupted smoothly. "No, wait, this is fine. How about we sit right here on the bank and have breakfast first. Then Hal can take me for a ride in the sky. We'll work out the rest later."

Without further ado, they started into the picnic. One basket contained a few large blankets, which Lauren spread out across the grass. "We need Emily for this kind of thing," Robbie muttered. "She loves organizing picnics."

"She shouldn't have stayed home," Hal said. But although he was talking about Emily, his mind was on Abigail. He couldn't help feeling guilty that she wasn't with them. Sensing his concern, Robbie nudged and winked toward Jolie, making it clear that sparks might have flown if Abigail had been here to see Hal giving the beautiful jengu a ride on his dragon back.

Hal chewed his lip. Maybe Robbie was right . . . but still, he missed her.

Fenton and Robbie began to fight over the ham rolls. Jolie grabbed one but handed it to Hal. "Here. Eat."

They were all eating silently for several minutes when Darcy frowned and stopped chewing. "Aren't you hungry?" she asked Jolie. "You haven't touched a thing. Are you all right?"

Everyone looked up. Jolie was lounging back in the grass, her head tilted back and catching a ray of sunshine through the heavy clouds. "I don't eat what you eat," she said.

Robbie was incredulous. "You don't like ham rolls?"

Jolie laughed and cracked an eye open to peer at him. "You're funny. Why would an underwater creature like me eat a ham roll? Do you think we bake bread deep under the lake? Do you think pigs run around down there?"

Clearly embarrassed, Robbie took another bite and mumbled something.

Darcy picked up a hard-boiled egg and stared at it. "So what exactly *do* the miengu eat?"

Jolie shook her head. "You wouldn't want to know. I'll grab a bite to eat in a while—when you're not looking."

Hal wondered for a moment if she had some food stashed in her light dress. But he knew that was impossible. Then it clicked. "Oh. You're going to . . . eat a fish or something?"

"Something like that," Jolie said, nodding. She clapped her hands. "How about that ride, Hal?"

Hal stuffed the rest of the roll in his mouth and looked longingly at the eggs and some gooey pastries that Dewey had just unwrapped. "Save me some," he warned. "We'll be back in a minute."

He moved away from the group and stood alone on the grassy bank, looking up at the surrounding trees. Space was a little tighter than he liked, but he was confident he could manage. Without further ado, he transformed.

Jolie was delighted. She might have seen him in his dragon form before, when Hal had been swimming around in the lake, but he wasn't sure. In any case, her eyes were bright and she was grinning broadly. As Hal turned slowly, careful not to whack anyone with his club-ended tail, Jolie ordered the boys to help her aboard. Fenton and Thomas rushed to do so, hoisting her up onto Hal's broad reptilian back as she exclaimed in wonder.

The jealous look was back on the faces of Fenton and Thomas, and even Robbie had stopped chewing for a moment. Dewey simply cast his eyes down, crestfallen.

"This is *amazing*," Jolie gushed. She patted Hal's neck gently. "Are these your clothes? They're like reins! How adorable! Should I hold on to these or just wrap my arms around your neck? Oh, you're so big and strong, Hal—I can't believe I'm getting to ride a dragon. My fiancé will be so envious. You won't drop me, will you?"

Hal had been gently moving his wings, ready to launch, but he froze at the mention of a fiancé. "You're getting *married?*" he asked, startled. But his words tumbled out as a series of grunts and growls, so the meaning was completely lost on Jolie as she went on gushing about how tough his scaly hide was and how impressive his wings were. Hal remembered the young male jengu in the lake who had shaken his head and asked her not to leave. Not her brother, then, nor a friend or neighbor, but her *future husband*. He could tell that all his friends had heard the announcement because they were staring open-mouthed at her.

"Let's go," Jolie said, patting him again. She flung her arms tightly around his neck and pressed her cheek against his. Sadly, his armored skin desensitized him somewhat.

He flapped his wings, sprang into the air, and sailed upward with powerful beats of his wings that sent the picnic blankets billowing. Clearing the tips of trees with inches to spare, he laughed at the sound of Jolie squealing in his left ear and soared toward one of the few cloudless patches of blue sky.

"This is fantastic!" Jolie screamed. "But terrifying!"

Hal wanted to tell her that he'd catch her if she fell, even if it meant grabbing hold of her in his jaws or snatching her up in his paws. All he could do was grunt, but she wasn't listening anyway—she was too busy whooping and laughing as he climbed higher and higher.

He circled and then dove, knowing that he was impressing her beyond her wildest imagination. He felt good. This must be far better than riding on the back of a boring old centaur or clinging to the red fur of a manticore. And it was surely a far better way to travel than being yanked into the air with a harpy's talons digging into the shoulders! Of all the creatures he could have been—an ogre, a harpy, a nameless black lizard—Hal reckoned he'd gotten the best deal. He also had to *deal* with dragons, and in that sense he faced the most danger . . . but those situations were rare, and for the rest of the time Hal could enjoy being the most awesome, formidable shapeshifter in the village.

He rose into the sky again, determined to give Jolie an unforgettable experience. How often did a creature from the bottom of a lake get to fly above the clouds? Again he headed for the clear patch of blue, feeling his ears pop a little as he went. Jolie had already commented about that, and Hal could almost sense her shaking her head vigorously.

Still ascending, he chose his moment carefully and simply stopped flapping. Seconds later came her reaction. "Oh, my," Jolie said softly.

The silence high in the sky never ceased to amaze Hal. Whenever he soared straight upward and then stilled his wings, naturally his ascent slowed until he began to fall again. But there was a special moment just before he began to fall when everything seemed to freeze—a moment when he felt utterly weightless and there was absolute silence all around. It lasted just a second or two, and this was when Jolie's awed reaction came. After that, he began the rapid descent to earth with the wind rushing past his ears.

Before he lost too much height, he checked his descent, looped around, and began climbing again. This time he went even higher, blasting through the low-hanging cloud cover into clear blue sky and dazzling sunlight, and upward even farther until they were looking down on fluffy white mountain ranges.

By this time, Jolie had gone quiet. Whether she was speechless with wonder or simply petrified with fright, it was impossible to tell.

There came a point when Hal began to tire. The air was thinner this high up, and although he was beating his wings twice as fast, he was still slowing in his ascent. "This is about as high as we can go," he grumbled, knowing Jolie couldn't understand him. But she seemed to understand anyway and patted his neck as he relaxed and began to circle around. His circles grew larger and larger, and he angled his leathery wings, allowing them to catch the currents of air to slow his speed until he had almost leveled out. "It's like riding a bike up and down hills," he said. "You coast down one hill, roll up the next . . ."

"I don't know what you're saying," Jolie said, speaking for the first time in a while, "but this is the most amazing experience of my life. It makes my lake seem so . . . so *small*, all of a sudden." She added wistfully, "My people live such limited lives."

Hal wished for less cloud cover. If it were a clearer day, he knew they'd be able to see the curve of the Earth in the distance. But, through the clouds, all they saw was a small patch of green land far below.

Just to spice up the flight a little, Hal dove into the nearest cloud mountain and everything went gray. Jolie laughed, clearly delighted. Then, after what seemed an age, they burst out of the bottom and saw the entire expanse of land spread out in all directions. The horizon all around was a little curved even from this lower altitude, but not spectacularly so.

Hal began a long, hard dive. Grinning to himself, he planned to scare the living daylights out of Jolie. She had already begun to scream, although he still detected laughter and excitement. That would soon change.

The ground was rushing closer. In the distance, far to the west, he saw a vast mirror of lake where Jolie lived, and from there he traced the thin river east through the trees. Finally, he spotted the boat, almost completely hidden. He aimed toward it, judging his distance carefully. He was dropping fast and he knew it would take some precise angling of his wings to come out of the dive at exactly the right moment. He wanted to skim over the treetops and give the impression that he was out of control.

He chuckled to himself. Jolie was screeching, right on cue. But then something happened. She seemed to slip sideways, and he suddenly felt pressure on his right wing as she clung tightly to it, holding on for dear life. *Uh, okay, game over*, he thought.

When he tried to angle his wings and come out of the dive early, he realized he couldn't. She was hampering his movement, and only his left wing was giving him lift. This caused him to begin tumbling, a sort of midair tailspin that sent waves of panic through his body. "Let go!" he yelled back at her. "You need to let go or—"

It was no good trying to explain. He fought to control his descent, trying in vain to rise out of the dive but spinning faster as he angled his only useful wing. He tried beating both, finding it surprisingly difficult; it seemed that he had a lot of downward muscle power, yet hardly any strength on the uplift. And she was pressed down on his wing, clinging to it like a sailor might cling to the mast of a ship in a storm. He could fling her off, perhaps, and then catch her . . . but in the heat of the moment, with the ground and the trees rushing up to pulverize him, he felt only panic and terror, the sort of panic he might feel if he cycled down a steep hill only to realize it ended at a cliff.

His heart pounding, he let out a desperate cry and writhed in the air, the final instinctive actions of an animal about to die. He shook Jolie loose without a care, took control of his wings, and came out of the spin. He felt the treetops brush his underside as he tore over them at a colossal speed.

It was only when he had slowed and was beginning to circle around, firmly in control of his wings, that he gave poor Jolie a thought. She was still there, clinging to his neck once more, absolutely silent. Hal had wanted to give her a fright, but not this kind. He was acutely aware of how close they'd come to plunging to their deaths in the trees.

She said nothing as, with his heart pounding, he returned to the river bank. The awkward descent and landing through the treetops barely registered on his mind after the panic he'd experienced in the air. Being out of control like that, his wing hampered at a crucial moment in the dive, had been nothing short of terrifying.

"What happened?" Darcy yelled as Hal thumped down onto the grass. His friends came running, the picnic forgotten.

Hal couldn't speak to them while in his dragon form, and Jolie still clung to his back. So he waited until she had been helped down onto the grass before reverting to his human form. Then he stood there shuffling his feet and looking on nervously while his friends fussed over Jolie.

She was white-faced and wide-eyed but otherwise all right. She smiled and clutched her hands to her chest. "That. Was. *Amazing*," she enunciated. "But scary. I thought we were going to die." She grinned at Hal. "Are you all right? I think you were more frightened than I was."

"That's because I knew we *were* actually going to die," Hal said. "You had hold of my wing at the worst possible moment. I couldn't come out of the dive."

Jolie looked sheepish. "Sorry. I started sliding off and . . ." She placed a hand over her heart and closed her eyes, a dreamy look on her face. "That was easily the best experience of my life."

"What, nearly dying?" Robbie said, scowling at Hal as if it were all his fault. "Maybe you should stick to the ground, Jolie. It's safer down here."

"Thomas, where are my crutches?" Jolie said, grinning broadly. "Oh, never mind. Help me up."

Again, Thomas and Fenton rushed in to help her to her feet and stood there with Jolie hanging off their shoulders while she gushed about the flight. Hal, feeling relieved yet mildly embarrassed, wandered over to the abandoned picnic baskets and began searching for some of those gooey pastries.

To his disgust, there was only half of one left, and there were ants the size of his thumb crawling all over it.

Chapter Fifteen
Jolie's Prank

Despite the invasion of ants in the picnic baskets the moment they had been left unattended, everyone was well and truly full by mid-morning—except for Hal, who had picked through the sorry remains of the pastry with a feeling of terrible regret. "What a waste," he kept saying.

"Well, *eat* it if you really want it," Lauren told him, growing annoyed. "It was just a few ants, and they're gone now. Quit moaning and eat it. Come on, guys, pack up—I want to go for a boat ride."

Hal contented himself with a couple of hard-boiled eggs and shamelessly lazed around while a few of the others packed up the picnic baskets and crammed them under the seats of the boat. Fenton and Robbie took up rowing positions, glancing toward the bank where Jolie was riding on Thomas's manticore back. Eager to catch up, the rest of the group piled into the boat and fought over the remaining seats, causing the boat to wobble violently.

While the rowers were getting synchronized, Jolie was giggling incessantly as Thomas veered wildly back and forth.

"Sometimes she irritates me," Darcy muttered. "All this gushing and giggling . . . The girly act gets on my nerves."

"She's cool," Fenton said firmly. "Hal almost killed her, and she didn't say a bad word about him. She acts like nothing happened."

"It wasn't my fault," Hal protested. He flicked a bit of eggshell at Fenton and glared at him. "She grabbed hold of my *wing*. At the worst possible time. I've never felt so helpless."

About half an hour into the slow journey upstream, Lauren frowned and pointed back along the river. "What's that?"

Everyone craned their necks to look.

"I don't see anything," Robbie said.

Lauren sighed. "It's gone again. I think someone's watching us."

"In the trees?" Darcy said, squinting.

"No, in the water. I just saw the top of a head poking out."

Everyone looked twice as hard but saw nothing untoward.

"Could it be one of the miengu?" Hal said.

"I think so," Lauren said, nodding.

They all stared in silence. Then, slowly, a head rose from the water.

"It *is* one of the miengu," Hal whispered. "It's spying on us."

"Should we let Jolie know?" Darcy wondered aloud.

They agreed that they should. The watcher was absolutely still and silent, its black eyes staring in their direction. It gave Hal the creeps. "Jolie!" he called.

Jolie was busy ruffling Thomas's thick red mane and giggling. She glanced their way, a questioning look on her face. When she saw where Hal and his friends were pointing, she squinted and searched the river—then broke into a delighted grin. "Ooh, Thomas, give me a ride over there, would you?"

Thomas obliged and looked thoroughly disappointed when Jolie carefully climbed off his back and slipped into the calm river. She swam smoothly toward the waiting jengu. Then, as one, they sank below the surface.

"Well!" Lauren said.

"I wonder if that's her fiancé," Darcy said with a smile. "He's a bit clingy, isn't he?"

Jolie was gone for ten minutes or so. When she finally reappeared, she was chewing on the remaining half of a large fish. She swam to the river bank and tossed the fish away as she clambered out. Dripping wet, she called for Thomas and he happily ran to collect her.

"Sorry about that," Jolie said, looking flushed. "My betrothed just wanted to make sure I was safe. The poor thing's been hanging around this river since I left, waiting for me to return. I sent him home. Now, where were we?"

She resumed her place on Thomas' back and the manticore trotted happily away along the bank. Fenton and Robbie resumed rowing.

"Emily should be here," Darcy said after a while, trailing her hand in the water. "This is the nicest picnic ever. We should do this more often."

"We used to have a lot of picnics," Lauren agreed. "Remember, back on the island? Emily always arranged them." She laughed. "She'd get so flustered when things didn't go perfectly to plan."

They all chuckled, thinking of Emily's furious red face and her clenched fists when someone forgot a can opener or a knife to cut cheese with. She nearly always ended up bringing all the essentials herself, but the problem was that *everything* was essential to her and she just couldn't manage it all on her own.

"I think she stayed home because she doesn't like Jolie," Darcy said quietly. "I mean, she *really* doesn't like her. I wish I knew why. Jolie can be irritating, but she's okay most of the time."

"She's great," Fenton said.

Darcy groaned. "Someone slap his face for me."

Fenton grinned. "You're just jealous, Blondie."

Thomas and Jolie had spotted something. They were hunched in the grass, peering through the hedge into a field beyond. Curious, Fenton and Robbie stopped rowing and the boat drifted to a halt, then gradually began to drift back the other way, following the current. In the end, they steered toward the bank so they could throw a line and tie off to the thick roots of a bush.

By this time, Jolie had struggled up onto her crutches and through the bushes, leaving Thomas hiding.

"What's going on?" Hal called.

Thomas turned and scowled, then mouthed the word, "Quiet!"

Overcome with curiosity, everyone scampered out of the boat and through the long grass to where Thomas was loitering. Through the bushes they saw Jolie, hobbling across the field. A couple of young boys were in the field. They had their backs to her, trying to fix a bright orange kite.

Jolie called to them, and they jumped, startled. They looked about nine or ten years old. As she smiled and continued hobbling toward them, their faces went slack and the kite dropped to the ground, forgotten.

"Her spell works on them, too," Lauren said with a sigh. "Look at them. They're already in love."

"What's she doing?" Hal asked. He prodded Thomas in the side and couldn't help noticing how the manticore's scorpion tail rose a foot or two, arcing across his back with its ball of quills quivering. "What's going on?"

"Watch," Thomas said, a smile on his face. "It's gonna be great."

Jolie spoke to the boys for several minutes and ended up sitting in the grass with them, helping to fix their broken kite. All three were smiling and laughing, and Hal couldn't fathom what Jolie had in store.

Then Thomas edged forward into the hedge. "It's time," he whispered.

"Time for *what?*" Robbie asked.

Thomas grinned sideways at him, then glanced at Hal. "Remember that day in Black Woods, back on the island? When I first bumped into you two? I scared you so bad you ran for miles without stopping."

Realization dawned, and Hal reached out to grab a tuft of Thomas's mane. "If you're planning what I think you're planning—"

"Here we go," Thomas said, and before anyone could stop him, he let out a bloodcurdling roar and tore through the hedge. Jolie and the two boys swung around to see a vicious manticore bearing down on them at full speed, claws flashing and enormous scorpion tail jiggling overhead.

The boys screamed in unison and turned to run. But Jolie, from where she sat, grabbed them both and clung tight. "Don't leave me!" she screamed.

This made the situation worse. The boys were panic-stricken and struggling so violently to get loose that Jolie was jostled from side to side. Her terrified expression dissolved into laughter, but she masked the sound by coughing and wailing, all the while clinging to the boys as Thomas rapidly approached.

He was on them in seconds. He pounced and knocked them all flat with heavy paws, then stood over them, snapping and roaring.

"What's he *doing?*" Darcy gasped.

"Playing," Hal said grimly. He struggled through the hedge and tore across the field to put an end to the game before the boys died of fright.

They were moaning now, utterly petrified and completely unaware that Jolie was simply playacting. She was hardly even trying now, just lying there with her eyes closed, muttering and gripping each of the boys' hands.

Thomas's ball of quills was quivering violently. "Stop!" Hal yelled as he got closer. "Thomas, *enough!*"

One of the boys rolled suddenly, breaking free. He scrambled to his feet and ran, not looking back, screaming all the way across the field. The other boy had gone quiet, and a wet patch had spread across his pants.

Hal arrived and punched Thomas hard on the shoulder under his thick mane. "Quit it, you idiot!" He turned to Jolie, who was staring up at him with a dreamy look on her face as if she were half asleep. "Jolie, let him go."

"Spoilsport," Jolie mumbled.

The second boy suddenly found his hand free, and he snatched it away and stared at it in disbelief.

"You poor thing!" Darcy exclaimed as she came running up. She knelt by the stricken boy. "It's okay. These idiots were just messing with you—"

The boy leaped to his feet, gave one last look around, and tore away. Unlike his friend, who was still screaming in the distance, this boy ran silently.

Jolie began to laugh, and Thomas joined in. "Oh my goodness!" she said between gasps. "Did you ever hear boys screaming that hard before? Thomas, you were great! Truly terrifying. You almost scared *me*."

Darcy slowly stood. Hal glanced over his shoulder to find Fenton, Robbie, Dewey and Lauren with puzzled, shocked expressions.

"Man," Fenton said, "even I wouldn't have done that to a couple of little kids. That was callous."

"It was an *awful* trick to play," Lauren exclaimed. "What got into you?"

"It was just a joke," Jolie said, wiping her eyes. She giggled again, then cleared her throat. "Aw, come on, guys. You have to admit it was funny."

"It wasn't a bit funny," Hal retorted. Right now, he didn't like Jolie at all and was disgusted with Thomas for going along with the idea. "And those kids are from the village. They're going to tell on you, Thomas. On all of us. How many people hang around with manticores? Everyone's gonna know it was you, Thomas, and we're *all* going to be in trouble for terrorizing those kids."

"Hal, calm down—" Jolie said.

"Shut up!" Hal yelled, anger bubbling up.

Jolie flinched, her eyes widening. All traces of mirth drained from her face. There was a long silence, during which Thomas slowly sank into the grass like a scolded dog.

Darcy pointed directly at Jolie and spoke sternly. "You went too far, Jolie. That was nasty and mean. It's one thing to play a trick like that on adults, but those poor boys might be traumatized for life! Don't do that again."

Jolie remained silent as Lauren chimed in with much of the same. Fenton grunted his agreement.

Then Hal turned abruptly. "Let's go back to the boat. I think we'd better call it a day. I reckon we'll have some angry parents to face when we get back."

He trudged across the field and glanced over his shoulder when he was nearly back at the hedge. His friends followed with expressions of disgust and disappointment on their faces. Behind them, some distance away, Thomas was still sitting with Jolie in the grass.

* * *

As Hal had feared, there was a stirring in the village as he and his friends returned home. He caught several nasty glares directed at him, but most of the anger was aimed at Thomas. Although back in his red-haired human form, the boy was unmistakable as the resident manticore.

"Had fun, did we?" an old farmer sneered as the group passed.

"Here comes the big brave monster," a large round-faced woman said loudly to her friend. "I hear manticores eat children just for fun."

Hal was mortified, and he knew his friends were, too. If Thomas was affected, he hid it well—if anything, *too* well, for he came across nonchalant and uncaring. At least Jolie looked suitably sorry as she hobbled along on crutches.

As more insults were thrown their way, Hal rounded on Thomas. "You better find those kids and apologize," he hissed. "Until then, I'm staying away from you. I don't like the glares I'm getting from angry farmers with pitchforks. You're bad news. You too, Jolie," he added stiffly.

With that, he stomped away, shouldering past the jostling villagers with his face down in shame.

"Wait up," Robbie called.

Hal paused just long enough for his friend to catch up. Then they continued on together. At the end of the street, they both looked back to find that Thomas and Jolie, along with their innocent friends, were now surrounded by a heaving crowd. Hal felt a pang of guilt and worry, and he slowed. He knew the anger wasn't directed at Darcy, Lauren, Dewey or Fenton, and he felt certain Jolie would be fine, but . . .

"Think Thomas'll be all right?" he said.

Robbie shrugged. "He's a manticore. Nobody's gonna mess with him, however angry they are."

"True," Hal said. Then he spotted a familiar white-coated woman rushing toward the crowd. "Look, there's Dr. Porter, coming to the rescue. Oh, that reminds me—Abigail mentioned something I think might be worth trying."

Groaning, Robbie rolled his eyes. "Go on, then, spill it. Anything Abigail mentions has to be worth hearing."

Ignoring the sarcasm, which Hal knew was just lighthearted mockery, he gestured and said, "Not here. Let's find somewhere quieter."

They had to get off the busy streets to find anywhere private enough to talk. They ended up in an alley where a goat was chewing on an old wicker chair. Hal had no idea what an old wicker chair was doing in an alleyway, nor a goat for that matter, and he didn't really care. He spent some time detailing his bizarre journey inside Abigail's head that morning, and how she'd perceived Jolie when they'd drawn her to the window, and finally of Abigail's suggestion to find a camera to take a picture of the mysterious jengu.

Robbie's mouth hung open until the end. "You were *inside her head?*" he exclaimed. He thought long and hard while Hal waited with growing impatience. "So . . . were you able to read her mind and everything?"

"No, I told you, she could read mine a little bit, but I couldn't read hers."

"That's bad news, Hal," Robbie said. "You can't let her into your head like that. You can't let her have that advantage."

Hal threw up his hands. "Look, forget about that. *Focus*, Robbie. I'm asking you about the camera. Does your dad still have it or not?"

"Well, sure. It was one of the things he insisted on bringing across from the island when we first got here. He's got a bunch of 35mm film he wants to develop one day if he can figure out how. And there's a half-used film still in the camera."

"Can you get it?" Hal asked eagerly. "Abigail reckons that if we take a picture of Jolie, we might see her without her . . . her mask on."

Robbie looked doubtful. "Mask?"

"You know, her enchantment. Some people see her as plain, while others—mainly guys—see her as, well, you know, gorgeous."

"She is," Robbie said, a smile creeping across his face.

Hal wanted to punch him on the nose. "Quit! You see? That's my point. We see her as this perfect woman, but Abigail and Emily see someone totally different, someone not anywhere near as nice. Remember, these miengu creatures were known as sirens, luring sailors onto rocks. Maybe they're still like that but in a different way."

The goat, bored with the wicker chair, came over and nuzzled up to Hal's leg. When it started sniffing his feet, he shooed it away.

"Look, I don't know what to think," he continued. "Jolie comes across nice and innocent one minute and nasty the next. Or maybe she's just really childish. I don't know. The point is, can you get the camera? We'll sneak a photo of her and then your dad can develop the film."

"Just like that," Robbie scoffed. "He needs a special darkroom, Hal. And chemicals. Developing stuff. Special paper." He paused. "Then again, he brought all that stuff with him, too, so he really just needs a darkroom. I don't know . . . I can ask, I guess."

"Do it," Hal said shortly.

"Fine," Robbie said. "Well, I'm hungry. Want lunch?"

Hal's mouth dropped open. "Lunch? Are you kidding? You ate twice as much as I did, and I don't even want to *think* about food at the moment." He waved Robbie away. "Go. I'm going to find Abigail and see what she's up to."

They split, and Hal set off toward Abigail's house. She was probably sulking in her room. She'd made it pretty clear how she felt about Jolie, and yet Hal had gone off with the jengu anyway and spent the morning showing off his dragon transformation. He felt a little awkward about that. But on the other hand, he felt that Abigail was acting childishly.

He arrived at her house ten minutes later and knocked on the door.

He waited but nobody answered. He twisted the door handle and found it unlocked. He knew that Dr. Porter normally insisted on locking up because of the medicines she kept in the house; the key was kept under a plant pot on the doorstep. So this probably meant that Abigail was in.

He poked his head inside and called. "Abi?"

Still no answer.

He called again, louder this time, but received no response. He sighed. Well, maybe she'd popped out for a walk.

He spent half an hour wandering the trails in the woods, hoping to bump into Abigail. Instead, he glimpsed one or two goblins prowling in the bushes, looking as grumpy and surly as ever. He heard the excited barking of dogs, too. Giving up on his search, Hal ambled home, watching leaves flutter down off trees as the wind picked up suddenly. He could barely see the sky through the thick canopy but sensed a storm was finally brewing after days of threatening-looking clouds.

As soon as he arrived home, his mom turned to him with an exasperated look on her face. "Hal, I've got to go out. We need a few groceries, and now it's going to rain. I *knew* I should have gone earlier."

"Uh, okay."

"And a goblin came by," she added, pulling on her coat. "He was asking for Abigail, actually. Not sure what she's done, but they're out looking for her. Anyway, see you in a bit."

She dashed out, and Hal watched her hurrying up the path with her basket banging against her hip. What had Abigail done now? He imagined all sorts of mischievous things, and it amused him to think of the goblins shuffling around trying to find her, grumbling angrily. But then he remembered Dr. Porter hurrying through the streets earlier and he frowned. "Hey, Mom!" he yelled. "What do you mean they're out looking for her?"

The wind whipped his words away so he hurried out of the house. When he caught up with his mom, she glanced at him in surprise. "Oh, Hal, thank you!"

"I—what?"

"You're a darling. I made a list, look—you can get most of it at the market, but get the bread from Darcy's mom. These villagers just don't bake it the way we're used to. Hurry, before it pours down."

She handed him the basket, patted his cheek affectionately, and hurried off back to the house.

Hal blinked a few times, then sighed. Oh well, perhaps he'd find Dr. Porter out somewhere. Or better still, Abigail herself. He read the grocery list, tucked it into his pocket, and set off at a fast pace.

A gale was whistling eerily through the trees as he left the woodland trail and entered the village. Small dust clouds were forming here and there, and damp laundry flapped madly on washing lines. Villagers were holding onto hats or skirts, leaning into the fierce wind. Hal picked up his pace, fearing the market would shut down early.

He was right. Cloths and sheets were blowing all over the place, and some of the lighter goods were strewn across the dusty street, their owners dashing around shouting orders to secure the stalls. Hoping to grab a few things anyway, Hal fumbled for the grocery list—and the wind promptly snatched it out of his hands and carried it off into the sky. Still, he'd read the list already and could recall many of the items—

"Hal!"

He turned in a circle, trying to locate the girl's voice. It was Darcy.

"Hey, I was just coming to your house," he said, hurrying toward her as she jostled with the crowd. "Does your mom have any fresh-baked bread?"

"Hal, Abigail's missing," Darcy said breathlessly. "We're all out looking. Have you seen her?"

The first drops of rain plopped heavily into the street.

"Well, I know she's missing," Hal said. "She's not at home, or—" He frowned. "*Who's* out looking?"

"Miss Simone, Molly, a bunch of goblins, me, Lauren, Emily," Darcy reeled off. "And Dr. Porter, obviously. She heard Abigail leaving the house really early this morning, before dawn, but didn't think much of it—apparently that happens quite a lot."

Hal thought of the faerie glade but kept it to himself for now. "Yes? So?"

"So Dr. Porter got up about an hour after that to go to work," Darcy went on. "She made muffins and left a couple out, still warm, expecting Abigail to be back for breakfast. That happens quite a lot, too. But Dr. Porter came home from work a little while ago, and the muffins are *still there*, untouched. It looks like Abigail hasn't been home all day, ever since she left early this morning."

Villagers continued to hurry past in all directions. Someone's hat flew over their heads and fluttered off into a vegetable garden.

Hal carefully put down his basket. "She was with me at dawn," he murmured. "Then she went home. At least, I *thought* she went home . . ."

"What?" Darcy said, tilting her head and cupping a hand behind her ear. "Did you say she was *with* you?"

Hal raised his voice over the increasing noise of wind and shouting and things falling over in the street. "She was. But then I thought she went home. We were only gone an hour, maybe a bit longer."

"When Dr. Porter got home from work, she found a bloody handprint on one of the wooden fence posts on the path."

Hal froze. "A bloody handprint," he repeated dully.

"And a small piece of smart clothes snagged on a bush," Darcy said, tears welling up. "It's like . . . it's like someone kidnapped her."

Hal closed his eyes, his voice quavering as he said, "*Kidnapped* her?"

"Something bad has happened, I just know it," Darcy moaned. "Goblins are searching the woods all around the house, but Abigail's nowhere."

Thunder rumbled loudly, and the rain began to fall in earnest, a heavy deluge that sent villagers shrieking as if it were acid. Hal and Darcy simply stood there, ignoring the rivulets that had begun to stream down their faces.

"She went home," Hal said again. "She woke me around five, before dawn. We . . . went off somewhere together." He realized how that sounded as soon as the words left his mouth. He tried to ignore the way Darcy narrowed her eyes. "She invited me in for muffins, but I went home to bed. It was nearly seven when I got back. Then you guys showed up on my lawn a little later."

Darcy frowned. "Dr. Porter left around six, after breakfast. So you're saying Abigail headed home between six and seven this morning? But she didn't make it home to eat those muffins, so she must have disappeared right after you two split—*before* she got home." She gripped Hal's arm. "We need to tell Miss Simone. It might help to know that."

They tore off along the streets in the pelting rain, their feet beginning to splash as puddles formed. The storm was right over the village, heavy gray clouds that seemed to boil and churn with anger. The lightning was blinding, and the deafening claps of thunder that followed had villagers jumping with fright as they rushed for their homes.

Hal and Darcy were drenched from head to toe by the time they reached the familiar gate at the edge of the village. "Where *is* everyone?" Darcy exclaimed breathlessly, turning in a circle and shielding her eyes against the driving rain. "This was where we were supposed to meet back. There's supposed to be someone here to coordinate the search!"

A goblin came stamping purposefully through the puddles toward them, apparently uncaring of the weather. "They moved," he said shortly, jabbing a finger along the trail where it disappeared into the woods. "Too wet."

"They're at Miss Simone's house?" Darcy urged.

When the goblin nodded curtly, Hal and Darcy took off at speed.

Until ten minutes ago, the roads had been dry and dusty. Now they were sloppy with mud, and swamps were forming along the sides. Trees swayed in the wind, twigs and small branches snapped off and flew down, and soggy leaves swirled around. The wind was terrible, but at least there was some level of shelter as Hal and Darcy hurried into the woods.

They caught up with Robbie, who was hurrying along on his own. "Heard the news?" the boy yelled. "Abigail's gone missing!"

"Of course I've heard," Hal snapped.

They said nothing more until they arrived at Miss Simone's cottage. It was half hidden behind the top of a tree that had crashed down yards from the front door. "Miss Simone!" Darcy yelled, and Hal spotted the woman standing in the doorway, shrouded in the darkness of the storm despite it being early afternoon.

Miss Simone waved them inside, then looked expectantly at Hal as he stood dripping wet in the living room. The place was crammed full of people, a sea of familiar faces and a few he didn't recognize. His friends were there, plus Molly, Blair, Dr. Porter, a number of goblins . . .

"Well?" Miss Simone prompted. "Do you know where Abigail is?"

"No," Hal said.

Although the storm raged outside, the noise was greatly subdued in the crowded cottage, and Hal heard all too clearly the sigh of disappointment.

"I saw her this morning," he hastened to explain. "Around 5 AM. We headed home around six or six-thirty."

All eyes were on him, and Hal knew everyone but Robbie was wondering the same thing. Finally, Jolie spoke up from somewhere. "What on earth were you guys doing at five in the morning?"

Hal located her lying on the sofa, partially obscured by Lauren, Fenton and Thomas, all of whom kneeled on the floor in front.

"Does it matter?" Hal said, his face reddening.

Dr. Porter threw up her hands, looking drained. "He's right, it doesn't matter. We need to keep *looking*, Simone. She might be—"

Miss Simone turned to her and placed a hand on her shoulder. "We *are* looking, even in this storm. I have a team of goblins combing the woods, hunting for more clues. They'll find her. Or the dogs will sniff her out."

Hal realized then just how bedraggled everyone was—damp clothes, matted hair, shivering with cold . . . and all involved in the search for Abigail. He was mortified. How come *he'd* been one of the last to know about this?

"What were you doing out so early?" Miss Simone asked, repeating Jolie's question a little more sternly. "It might be important."

"It's not," Hal said. "Look, it's private. Abigail might not want anyone to know, and I don't want to give it away without asking her first."

"O-ho!" Fenton snorted. "I bet I can guess what you two were up to." He turned and winked at Thomas and Dewey. "Know what I mean? We all know Hal and Abigail have a thing going, and I bet they were *smooching*—"

"Shut up, Fenton," Darcy snapped. But then she raised an eyebrow at Hal. "Is he right?"

Hal found himself taking a step backward. "No! It's nothing like— Look, it's just something Abigail wanted to show me, out in the woods."

Dr. Porter practically leaped out of the crowd and pounced on him. "In the *woods*?" Her fingers dug into Hal's arms as she peered at him, her face inches from his. He realized in that moment how similar her eyes were to her daughter's. "*What's* in the woods?"

"Nothing," Hal said, feeling miserable.

"What's the big mystery?" Darcy asked, frowning deeply.

"Hal, you need to explain what you were both doing in the woods at that hour of the morning," Miss Simone demanded, her voice low and dangerous. She had that ice-cold glare that told Hal she was close to snapping.

And when she snapped, it usually meant a few broken windows.

"You'd better start talking, young man," she warned.

Chapter Sixteen
Where is Abigail?

With Miss Simone glaring at him, Hal told the entire room all about the faerie glade in the woods. He tried to think of an alternative reason Abigail might show him the glade so early in the morning but came up short and ended up spilling the beans about the 'magic in the air,' how she had done the mind trick and taken him on a ride. He explained how they'd flown around the village, and then walked home afterward, with Hal seeing everything through her eyes while his physical body lay unattended in the woods. He left out the part about spying on Jolie, but although he avoided meeting her gaze, he couldn't help sensing that she knew he was holding something back.

What is it, Hal? she said in his head with the volume turned up loud.

He started and bumped into the goblin that stood behind him.

What are you holding back? It's something to do with me, isn't it? You and Abigail have been up to something.

"What's wrong with you, Hal?" Lauren asked, shaking her head. "I have to say, you're acting really weird."

Jolie was sitting up now, and Hal wished he could turn and run from the cottage to escape her penetrating thoughts, not to mention endless pairs of narrowed, staring eyes. But the wall of goblins behind him seemed to have expanded in the last few minutes.

"What have you done with Abigail?" Dr. Porter suddenly demanded, her eyes widening. She advanced on Hal again, trembling with fury. "You know something. What happened? Did she have an accident and you're trying to cover it up? Did you . . . did you *hurt* her?"

"It's pretty odd how he was the last one to see her," Jolie said slowly, "*and* he's the closest to her . . . and yet he was the last to go looking for her. Almost as though he didn't care."

"Yeah, where have you been?" Fenton demanded. "We've all been running around looking for her without you."

Hal opened his mouth to speak, but then Molly cut in from the back of the room. "Where was your physical body while you were inside Abigail's head?"

Everyone turned to her, clearly puzzled by her question. Then, slowly, heads swiveled and glares were aimed in Hal's direction once more.

"What do you mean?" Hal said.

He was alarmed at how squeaky his voice was becoming. He shot a look at Robbie, hoping for some support from his best friend. But even he looked puzzled and suspicious. "I was just sleeping by a tree. Why?"

Molly glanced toward Jolie, and the young woman peered back at her through black hair that had tumbled forward over her face. Even though Molly was veiled, Hal sensed that she was listening intently. She turned back to Hal and tilted her head as if deep in thought.

"Are you sure you were just sleeping?" she said at last. "Perhaps your body didn't like being separated from your mind—if indeed that actually happened." She nodded slowly, her veil wobbling. "Yes. Perhaps Abigail got this so-called mind trick wrong and somehow managed to hypnotize you instead, so you went wandering around the woods as if in a daydream, and then clobbered Abigail from behind. Then you conveniently forgot everything and woke in the woods with a blank spot in your memory. Perhaps you only *imagined* her going back home afterward."

Hal stared at her with his mouth wide open, unable to believe his ears. "Are you nuts?" he said, realizing too late that he was speaking to an elder. "You're saying I—"

He broke off, unable to voice the idea.

Jolie smiled sweetly at him from the sofa.

"Hal?" Miss Simone said. "Is that a possibility?"

He shook his head, his disbelief turning to disgust. "You really believe I'd hurt her? Seriously?"

"Not intentionally," Molly said. "But if she did some kind of mind trick on you . . . some form of hypnosis . . . well, who's to know?"

"I was with her all the time!" Hal yelled. "We went though the village and then straight back to the woods. My body was still there where I'd left it, and I remember leaving Abigail's head and returning to my own, and then we split, and she went home. That's all. I went home to bed, and then everyone showed up and told me we were going on a picnic."

He'd had enough. Fear and disbelief had been replaced with anger, and he needed to get out of the room before he blew a fireball in someone's face. He turned to the wall of goblins and tried to shoulder through, but they were as solid as stone, their small beady eyes shrouded in the shadow under their thick brows. They were ugly and scowling at the best of times, and right now looked like they wanted to bash his head in with the various heavy weapons they had tucked into their belts.

"Move," he said quietly, "or I'll do something I'll regret later."

Still they refused to budge. Hal was trembling as he turned back to Miss Simone. "I'm going to look for Abigail. Tell these goons to move."

Miss Simone blinked a few times, and her fierce expression dissolved into uncertainty. In the silence that followed, even the raging storm seemed to pause.

Hal felt something tighten in his chest, and his throat felt like it had a huge lump in it. A deep, gurgling growl bubbled up, and his shirt started to feel tight around his shoulders. He was a little startled by the almost uncontrollable urge to transform, but he remained stolid, knowing that the threat of his dragon fury being unleashed was likely to unsettle them all. They *had* to let him leave.

Sure enough, Miss Simone gave a nod over his shoulder, and Hal sensed rather than saw the goblins shuffling aside. He reined in his anger, got a grip on himself, turned, and stalked out of the cottage.

The rain almost seemed to sizzle as it struck his heated, trembling body. He hurried away, drenched again in seconds, suddenly feeling very alone.

"Where are you, Abi?" he muttered as he arrived back at the village gate. He waited there, wondering where to start his search as the storm howled around him. Now that he was out of the woods and in the open, the rain was driving so hard into his face that it took his breath away and he could barely focus. He felt both cold and hot at the same time, shivering violently but sorely tempted to throw off his shirt.

He suddenly realized what he needed to do, and he transformed. His perception changed instantly; the rain became a cool mist on his reptilian snout, and he no longer felt a need to blink every half-second—the water simply bounced off his eyeballs without bothering him. Yes, dragons were far more suited to stormy weather.

There was nobody around in the streets, but several wide-eyed faces peered at him from nearby windows. He snapped his jaws, feeling a moment of guilty pleasure as they quickly withdrew.

Then he launched into the sky.

Lightning flickered, and thunder rumbled two seconds later. The storm was moving away. Climbing higher, Hal pinpointed the storm's exact whereabouts as several blinding bolts zigzagged across the sky. He saw a flash and a puff of smoke as a distant tree was vaporized.

Eyes down, he flew over the long trail of flattened houses. He veered back to the outskirts of the village toward the woods where he lived. The expanse of bright green foliage spread all around the village to the north and far west side. Somewhere nearby, to the west, the centaur shelter sprawled amongst the trees; to the far north lay a meandering route to the village of Louis and the distant labyrinths. There were patches of open fields here and there, as well as the river that led to Jolie's lake. It was all getting to be a familiar sight to Hal . . . but it brought home how gigantic and far-flung the world was, and how impossible it would be to find Abigail if she had been spirited away somewhere.

He thought of the picnic on the river that morning. While he'd been away with his friends, showing off to Jolie, Abigail had been—what, lying injured somewhere after a fall? Locked up in someone's basement, the victim of a sadistic torturer or murderer? Kidnapped by harpies and carried off to some filthy nest? Chewed up by any number of monsters?

Hal roared with frustration. It was no use conjecturing. He had to look for clues, do something useful.

From high up, he followed the streets of the village until he identified places he recognized, then traced the route to the perimeter fence where he walked home from school every day. Finally, he spotted a rooftop and knew it was Abigail's house in the woods.

Cautiously, he dropped straight through the treetops and thumped down onto the muddy trail, creating a couple of deeply indented footprints. Remaining in dragon form, he sniffed around, cursing the storm. The rain was most likely washing away all evidence of her existence.

He smelled goblins through the trees, and eventually saw them creeping around with their eyes on the ground. Giant dogs strained on their leashes, but the goblins were too tough and solid to be jerked along against their will. The dogs might as well have been tethered to boulders.

At least they're *out looking*, Hal thought grimly, *instead of huddling together in Miss Simone's cottage accusing each other of foul play.*

After hunting around, he found the blood that Dr. Porter had come across. It was on a fence post that stood to the side of the main path near Abigail's house—a handprint in blood.

It was then he remembered hearing the crack of a twig just as he and Abigail had parted ways early that morning. The memory sent a chill through him. The kidnapper had been *right here*, hiding in the bushes. If only Hal hadn't dismissed it, had investigated instead of running off back home to bed, or walked Abigail all the way to her door . . .

He felt sick.

He stared morosely at the bloody handprint, then sniffed it and picked up its scent. Was it hers? He wasn't sure, but somehow he felt drawn to the thickest bushes beyond the fence. He leaped, flapped his wings once, and landed squarely in the dirt on the other side, squashing a couple of prickly bushes. Something in the air tickled his flaring nostrils. He was certain he'd found something and snuffled around frantically, searching the ground, pushing more bushes aside. The scent grew stronger. It definitely smelled like the bloody handprint, and he found that he was catching up with the team of goblins that were scurrying around ahead. The dogs were on the trail, too.

But surely they'd looked here already? Why hadn't they found her?

It transpired that the scent ended at a stream that bubbled down a hill. It was flowing even faster thanks to all the rain, and Hal cursed the storm again. At least fifteen goblins were scouting the area, eyes down, moving slowly as dogs stopped and sniffed now and then.

The sight of a dragon crashing up behind them caused the dogs to go wild, and the goblins swung around. Their tiny black eyes widened slightly, and their brows creased—the extent of a goblin expression. But then they recognized their resident shapeshifter and grunted at the dogs to shut up.

One of the goblins pushed through the bushes toward him. It was Blacknail.

"Scent ends," he said shortly, jabbing a finger at the stream. "Dogs had no trouble tracing it to this point, but that's the end of it. Been back and forth fifty times, all over this place, and found nothing more."

The goblin looked angry as he turned in a circle, his shoulders slumped in defeat. When he spoke again, his words chilled Hal to the bone.

"Short of combing these woods in all directions, we ain't got no chance of finding her. She's been taken, no doubt about it. By man or beast, she's been taken."

Hal started to reply but growled instead. He considered reverting to human form, and in the end decided against it; his pink-skinned body, with its feeble olfactory senses, was utterly useless in a hunt. Better to stay as a dragon.

He crashed through the woods at random, taking in the stream and the surrounding trees, sniffing the air. He doubted his nose was any better than the dogs', but he had the advantage of being taller so reared up and stretched his neck, checking the branches above. Maybe a bear or something had hoisted her up into the trees . . .

Shuddering, he shoved that thought aside.

He returned to the stream. It was deep but narrow, although apparently wide enough for the attacker to throw trackers off the scent. So he—or it—had carried or dragged Abigail from the path and through the woods . . . and deliberately stopped at the stream and waded along it for some distance before heading off into the woods again. He wondered how far the goblins had got and in which direction. Knowing Blacknail, they'd probably been up and down the stream for miles already.

There were lots of possibilities, but Hal focused on one of them, perhaps the most obvious: the attacker surely wouldn't wade too far in a stream if he was weighted down with a limp girl over his shoulder. And, taking his conjecture a little further, it would be far easier to wade *down*stream rather than up. Why fight the current?

Ignoring the fact that the attacker had probably been heading for a specific place, which could equally be upstream or down, Hal turned and began stomping down the hill with the stream, shouldering past small trees and skidding a little as the ground grew slippery. He kept his eyes down and sniffed continuously, wondering where the stream ended. It was headed in a northerly direction. The ground leveled out, but the vegetation thickened dramatically. Hal had so much trouble getting anywhere fast that he ended up stamping and splashing along the stream, finding that it came up as high as his four knees—which to a human would be more like the upper thighs. If he were Fenton, or better still Miss Simone, he reckoned he could swim quite easily along—

He stopped dead, his heart beginning to pound. A vision of a jengu had popped into his mind, peering out of the river as Hal and his friends were rowing that morning. The sinister creature had been watching them. Could there be some kind of connection?

The trouble was, Jolie was the only jengu capable of walking on land, and—somewhat ironically—she was crippled. But, as Hal stared ahead, following the path of the stream as it wound out of view amongst the trees, he started to wonder if it led all the way to the river they'd rowed along earlier that morning. *Could* it? It was headed in roughly the right direction, and there was no reason why a stream wouldn't go on for miles and miles if the terrain allowed it. It was certainly conceivable.

He thundered on, hearing the goblins behind him. They, too, had taken to splashing along the stream, even though the water most likely came up to their waists. It was gushing rapidly, brown and murky, overflowing its banks in places—but before the storm, it had probably been a steady, calm flow, trickling down from higher ground deeper in the woods to the west, brushing by the village before angling to the north. There was every possibility that the stream intersected with the larger river several miles away.

Hal turned and gave a roar.

The goblins stopped, and Blacknail frowned at him. "What's on yer mind?"

After doing his best to indicate that the goblins should keep following the stream, Hal looked skyward, wondering how best to get out of this jungle. Impatiently, he scrambled up the nearest, thickest tree, digging his claws in deep and tearing off great chunks of bark as he went. Branches snapped off and the tree swayed horribly, but Hal continued upward until he found an opening to the gray sky above. He paused and looked down, shocked at what he was doing. Was he the first dragon to ever climb a tree?

The tree gave a sharp crack when he launched. His wingtips brushed the branches of neighboring trees, but seconds later he was airborne and heading north for the river. He found it shortly afterward, surprisingly close as the crow flies; the stream flowed into it quite a way east of where the boat was moored, even farther upstream than Hal and his friends had traveled that morning.

It didn't tell him where Abigail was, though. He flew around in circles, trying to decide what to do. Keep following the river east?

He thought again about Jolie's fiancé lurking in the water, spying on them. If the creature had somehow been involved with Abigail's disappearance, then what would it have done with her after bringing her down the stream to the river? He pictured the scene in his mind, imagining the fishtailed jengu swimming along the narrow stream, allowing the current to move him along while he gripped an unconscious Abigail in his arms . . .

It was all conjecture, of course, and he still couldn't figure out how the jengu had managed to traverse the woods and clobber her over the head in the first place. The miengu were half fish and couldn't grow legs. And why bother, anyway? To what end? And how did the jengu even know about the stream or that it came out near Dr. Porter's back yard?

His mind in turmoil, Hal set off to the lake in the west. He would ask the miengu directly. He wasn't sure exactly how he was going to achieve that and doubted they'd admit to kidnapping anyway, but he'd work it out as he went along. Maybe the goblins, still following the stream to the river, would pick up the trail again soon. In the meantime, it wouldn't hurt to check out the lake.

* * *

Not long after he plunged into the lake and located the abyss that led to the miengu, he was greeted by a cluster of the eerily glowing phantoms. Hal slowed as he approached the black hole in the lakebed. Eight miengu moved in slow motion from side to side, eyeing him warily and pointing long spears at him.

Since he was unable to communicate with them, he skipped introductions and simply sped toward them, angling down into the rocky hole. Startled, the miengu had no choice but to move aside, but Hal felt the slight jab of a spear on his rear end as one of them attempted to stop him.

He descended quickly, aware that the miengu guards were now swimming alongside, shooting him terrible glares. The six males had somewhat dull, plain features, but the two females were strikingly beautiful—or were they? Hal wasn't sure anymore; maybe they were *all* plain.

He ignored them and shot through the water to the collection of squat, crab-encrusted domes that lay below. More miengu came to meet him, and Hal could tell by the way they moved that he had created some kind of emergency. He could almost hear them shouting "action stations!" and "all hands on deck!" as the vicious dragon invaded their territory.

But what could they do? There were dozens of them already, forming a solid wall of spears, but Hal was a fire-breathing dragon. Even underwater he favored his chances in a standoff with any number of fishtailed creatures brandishing spears. He experimented with a warning burst of flame. Although it was quickly extinguished and turned into a mass of steaming bubbles, the heat was intense enough to send the miengu shooting off in all directions.

He probably wouldn't be breathing any more fire, though. He needed to hold his breath. Although he didn't feel uncomfortable just yet, he instinctively knew that he had just cut down his underwater session by ten minutes.

More of the miengu appeared, carrying a massive net with hundreds of barbs. The spear-carrying creatures swam off to a safe distance, and Hal faced the new threat with a degree of scorn. The net might be effective against a myriad of enemies, but not a dragon. He allowed the miengu to swim past him on all sides, and for the net to encompass his entire body . . . and then he lashed out with his claws, ripping a hole through the middle.

The barbs were sharper than he'd imagined and caused some discomfort, penetrating his armor-plated hide and stinging badly. He fought his way through the net as quickly as he could, then shot forward toward the domed city.

The next challenge awaited him. This time it seemed that all the remaining miengu were gathering—and, shockingly, there were hundreds of them. It seemed impossible that they all lived here in these tiny stone domes . . . but then Hal saw others emerging from caves in the distant cavern walls, and he understood that the dome-dwellers formed just a small part of the miengu population. They kept on coming, slipping out of the smallest, darkest shadows and coming to join in the battle.

Hal had no way to get his message across short of scratching messages in the lakebed. Rather than allow the miengu time to gather their entire force, he forged onward toward the nearest dome. In the back of his mind, he planned to poke his head into every one of them, just in case Abigail was being held in a magical bubble of air. He started with the large dome in the center.

The miengu, clustered tightly together over their village, stared at Hal with eerie black eyes and watched him explore. He found nothing of interest, just empty gloom, and was making good progress when he started to feel sick. The nausea swept over him rapidly and his search slowed dramatically as he fought the urge to throw up. He became dizzy and his vision blurred.

Before he knew it, he was bumping erratically against stone surfaces and dislodging crabs as he careened from one building to another. He ended up sprawled in a narrow alley between two domes where, jammed in the gap, a statue stared malevolently at him. In a moment of dazed drunkenness, Hal couldn't help noticing how very ugly this petrified jengu was, its face stretched long and thin . . . but then the miengu pressed in from above, a seething mass of ghostly figures, and Hal's attention returned to the problem at hand.

The nausea was so bad now that all Hal wanted was to crawl into a ball and sob. How were they doing this to him? They were simply staring at him, concentrating their efforts, their *willpower*, making him feel sicker to the stomach than he'd ever felt before. A headache began pounding on the inside of his skull and the back of his eyeballs. His skin, as tough as it was, seemed sensitive and tingly as if he'd suffered sunburn. He felt rotten, and all he could think to do was—

He shifted back to his human form. With his smaller body, he slipped farther back into the tiniest recess between the domes. A wave of surprise swept over the miengu, and Hal's sickness eased somewhat. He wasn't sure whether to attribute this to his healing powers as a shapeshifter or to the fact that the miengu were momentarily distracted.

But *what* had he been thinking? Dragons could manage quite easily underwater on a single breath, but humans could not. Hal felt as though his lungs were about to burst. He was beginning to convulse, his chest tightening, screaming for air. He looked around in desperation, realizing he was now squeezed between two stone walls . . . and several miengu were advancing on him, reaching for him, preventing him from escaping. He couldn't even take a breath and let off another fireball . . .

A female jengu shot toward him, her black hair streaming like oil and her face inches from his. It was Kamili. Hal jerked backward, but her touch was light and gentle, the palm of her hand on his cheek. She leaned forward and opened her mouth into a small 'O' shape, and for a bizarre moment Hal thought she was going to kiss him.

Instead, a bubble formed on her lips. It grew bigger and bigger, wobbling precariously until, impossibly, it was the size of her head. As it grew, it pushed against Hal's nose and mouth, enveloping them until his entire face was inside the bubble. He began to gray out.

Breathe, the jengu whispered in his head.

Hal barely heard her. With no other choice, he took a great, sucking breath, expecting lake water to pour into his lungs. Instead, he breathed air—not very fresh, but air all the same.

Breathe, the jengu said again, louder this time.

Hal stared straight ahead. The creature's face was inside the bubble, mere inches from his. As Hal took gasping breaths, the bubble shrank rapidly and he felt the cool lake water closing in across his face. Then the jengu blew gently, long and steady, and the bubble once more expanded.

"How are you doing that?" Hal managed to stutter.

She said nothing, but continued to blow air into the bubble, which Hal greedily took into his lungs. Dimly, outside the shimmering walls of the bubble, he saw the gills in her slender neck opening and closing. Breathing in through her gills, breathing out through her mouth . . . It was nothing short of incredible.

Finally, when Hal was taking long, measured breaths and the bubble easily encompassed both their heads, her voice came to him.

Why are you here? What are you looking for?

The question was so sincerely innocent that Hal's entire purpose for being there collapsed under a ton of flawed logic. As abruptly as he'd been convinced Abigail was here somewhere, now he was equally sure she wasn't. His conviction that the miengu had taken her had been utterly wrong, or at least off target. Perhaps one particular jengu had done something to her, the one Lauren had seen in the river, but it made no sense for the entire clan to be involved.

"I'm sorry," he said, very much aware that he was at the mercy of these people. His fumbling hands found solid stone on each side where crabs wandered across his fingers. "My friend was kidnapped."

The jengu stared at him. Up close like this, lit by her own ghostly aura, her pitch-black eyes were even more unsettling, revealing absolutely no emotion. Hal saw his own face reflected as clearly as if he were looking into tiny mirrors.

What a strange thing to say. You come here, uninvited, causing concern to the entire community, and accuse us of kidnapping?

"We saw one of your people in the river, watching us," Hal said, his heart thumping. "I just thought that—"

You assumed we were involved, the jengu whispered. She thought for a long moment. *I believe you caught a glimpse of Jolie's betrothed. He's none too pleased by her absence and is rather obsessive. He's simply keeping an eye on her the best way he can from afar.*

Hal couldn't refute her simple, straightforward statement. Also, there was no way Jolie's fiancé could have left the stream and dragged himself through the woods behind Dr. Porter's house. "I'm sorry. I was just worried."

I understand. The jengu tilted her head. Then she smiled, and any lingering suspicions Hal had about these people melted away in an instant. *Go home, boy. She's not here. Look for her in your own world, not ours.*

It wasn't until Hal, in his dragon form, had been escorted to the surface of the lake that the effects of the jengu's enchanting smile wore off and his brain began working again. As he stamped out onto the grassy bank and stood alone in the light rain, he tried to recall the conversation. *She's not here,* the jengu had said. *Look for her in your own world, not ours.*

Had Hal even mentioned out loud that his kidnapped friend was a girl?

Chapter Seventeen
The Healing

By the time evening came along, the winds had died and the rain clouds had wrung themselves dry. Hal had returned to the village in a daze, flying most of the way and pausing only to drop in on Blacknail's search party to tell the tireless goblins where he'd been. Blacknail had listened intently, then continued his search by the river. He'd passed no judgment whatsoever about Hal's lake intrusion, much to his surprise and relief.

His mom had raised an inquiring eyebrow at him when he'd trudged indoors, sopping wet and trailing mud on the floor. But it wasn't the mess she was annoyed about. "Where are the groceries?" she'd demanded.

It was only then Hal had remembered the shopping list and basket. Where on earth *was* the basket anyway? He couldn't even remember where he'd left it. But after explaining what had happened to Abigail, and brushing over his expedition to the lake, his mom completely changed her tune and went rushing off to find Dr. Porter. "The poor woman," she fussed as she pulled on a coat and headed for the door. "I can only imagine what she's going through."

Hal's dad, who was home early due to the saturated fields, rubbed his bushy beard and clapped his son on the back. "She'll turn up. You wait and see."

But 'turning up' wasn't realistic at this point. He sat at the kitchen table for a while, staring at his half-eaten sandwich while his dad ate feverishly. Then he went to his room and ended up curled in a corner, his knees drawn up, feeling miserable and angry and worried all at the same time.

"I'll find you, Abi," he whispered over and over.

By nightfall, sheer determination had replaced all his other emotions. He would gather the troops, so to speak, and storm the lake. He was once again convinced Abigail was there somewhere. The miengu had taken her. He had no idea why or what they intended to do with her, but he was certain he was right. He felt it in his bones. In retrospect, he was ashamed that he had given up the search halfway through, but somehow those eerie, conniving lake people had used their power of enchantment on him. They knew something. They had Abigail prisoner somewhere.

That is, if they hadn't killed her already.

His mom returned home to inform Hal that he was to go to the science laboratory for a conference. "Now?" he asked.

"Immediately."

This suited Hal just fine. It saved him the bother of rounding everyone up himself. "But why the science lab and not the village hall?"

Mrs. Franklin shrugged. "Simone never reveals more than she needs to. But we're all going, so stop moping and put on some fresh clothes. And comb your hair. You're a mess."

He walked with his parents through the dark streets. There were puddles everywhere, and they reflected the orange glows of lamps that hung from the eaves of many homes throughout the village. If Hal had been in a better mood, he would have enjoyed the coziness of it all. Instead, he trudged right through all the puddles, accepting the bite of icy cold water around his toes as a keen reminder that Abigail might be shivering in a cave somewhere . . .

He'd given this a lot of thought. The miengu's cavern was huge, and it was pockmarked with dozens, perhaps hundreds of small caves and tunnels. No doubt some of those tunnels led to other caverns. Abigail could be anywhere, but the miengu would likely have imprisoned her in a cave above the surface, or one that had air trapped inside, whether naturally or otherwise.

Again, *if* she was still alive at all. But until her dead body turned up, Hal was one hundred percent behind the theory that she was being held prisoner.

The science laboratory was crowded with Hal's friends and all their parents, along with Miss Simone, Molly, Blair, and villagers that Hal had never met before. Each expressed concern to Dr. Porter, who stood shaking and white-faced, utterly lost. She probably would have slumped to the floor in a daze if Mrs. O'Tanner hadn't been holding her up.

Despite his earlier urge to round up the troops and look for Abigail, Hal avoided his friends. He still felt betrayed. He ignored Molly, too. Oddly, he felt only a slight annoyance at Miss Simone, perhaps because she was the Great Leader and it was her duty to get straight to the heart of the matter and ask pointed questions. Hal's friends had no such excuse. They should have been on his side, defending him, *trusting* him.

So he stood alone, or as alone as he could be within a confined space jammed with people. He saw Robbie peering at him from across the room and edged backward a little so his view was blocked by adults. More than anyone, Robbie should have been there for him.

Jolie hobbled awkwardly on her crutches, accepting help with a grateful smile. She looked genuinely concerned and upset at the situation, and Hal stared at her for ages trying to make up his mind about her.

When everyone had crammed into the science laboratory's lobby, Miss Simone called for silence. Hal edged into a position where he could see her through the mass of bodies.

"Just to update you all," she said without preamble, "Blacknail's search party found absolutely nothing beyond what they'd already found earlier." She held up a fragment of what was assumed to be Abigail's dress. "This was caught on a bush near the bloody handprint."

Dr. Porter let out a wail, and it was a minute before Miss Simone continued.

"In Blacknail's opinion, the clues left behind by the kidnapper are a little too convenient."

If there wasn't a silence before, there was now. It seemed that everyone had sucked in a breath and held it.

Miss Simone narrowed her eyes as she stared at the small, dull green piece of fabric. "Whether this is Abigail's or not, it seems odd that it was just left snagged on a bush for us to find along with a bloody handprint on a fence post. It stinks a little of a setup."

"But *why?*" Mr. Morgan demanded in his booming voice. Dewey's dad was a head taller than everyone else, a huge Welshman. It was almost comical that his son was the complete opposite, the smallest boy in Hal's class.

Miss Simone shrugged. "Perhaps Abigail ran away and is trying to make it look like she was kidnapped?"

Dr. Porter scoffed loudly. "Why on earth would Abigail do something as horrible as that?"

"To cast suspicion on the miengu," Miss Simone said. "Given the proximity of the stream leading to the river, which in turn leads to the miengu's lake, it's possible that she—or someone else—has it in for our visitor and is trying to make it look like she was abducted."

Everyone swung around to face Jolie, who looked suitably shocked and embarrassed. Hal hadn't considered that possibility, although he tended to agree with Miss Simone that the clues seemed a little too obvious. For a second, he thought of moody Emily and wondered . . . But no, surely *she* wasn't involved.

"Another theory," Miss Simone said, "is that Abigail was seriously hurt in an accident, or perhaps even murdered, and the culprit is trying to point blame in another direction—perhaps leading us on a wild goose chase away from the actual trail."

At this, heads started turning toward Hal. He stood up straight and faced everyone with a grim, defiant glare.

"Why is everyone looking at Hal?" his mom asked, clearly puzzled.

Lots of throats were cleared, and gazes dropped to the floor. Robbie managed to work his way through the crowd so he could say something.

"We're sorry, Hal," he said loudly. "I don't know what happened back at Miss Simone's house, but somehow we thought—well, there's just no way you'd have anything to do with Abigail's disappearance."

"Deliberately or otherwise," Molly added. She sighed and absently tugged at her veil. "I think I was the one that started it. I just had this idea pop into my head that you were acting strange and your story didn't add up, and perhaps—"

"Jolie kept whispering to me," Dewey piped up. Nobody could see him until his dad stepped sideways out of the way. "She told me you had guilt written all over your face," he added sheepishly.

"She told *me* that, too!" Emily blurted. "Of course, I didn't listen to her—I don't even *like* her and don't mind saying so." She shot Jolie a glare. "I don't trust you and wish you'd leave."

Her candid remark caused everyone in the room to gasp. Mrs. Stanton looked appalled. "Emily Jane Stanton! I thought I'd taught you better manners than *that*, young lady."

"I'm just being honest," she grumbled, beginning to flush.

"Shame you didn't say that back at Miss Simone's house," Hal said. But he couldn't help feeling an intense gratitude toward Emily just then. Robbie's apology, backed up by Molly's, had helped to some degree, but in a few short sentences Emily had managed to shift the suspicion over to Jolie. As numerous gazes flitted in her direction, Hal felt a great weight lifting from his shoulders.

Jolie's eyes widened. "Are you kidding? You think *I* had something to do with it? I was *with* you guys, having a picnic!"

"Not until after she disappeared," Hal said.

"Oh, come *on*," Jolie said. Her face was drained of color and she looked pitiful as she looked from Hal to his friends. It was hard not to feel sorry for her, and once more Hal's resolve crumbled around the edges. "Look, guys, if you feel that way about me—if you think I could do something as mean as you're suggesting—well, then maybe I'd better just leave."

"Suits me," Emily retorted. Her dad whispered something in her ear and she paled. "Sorry," she mumbled.

"We don't want you to go, Jolie," Fenton said, shooting daggers at Hal. "Don't listen to them. Everyone's just worried about Abigail, that's all. You're the newcomer, so you're the first person everyone's going to blame."

"Speak for yourself," Darcy snapped. "I haven't forgiven Jolie for her nasty trick on those poor boys in the field."

Hal seized the moment. "We can't trust the miengu. I think they have Abigail at the lake. I don't know if Jolie's involved or not, or her boyfriend, but I'm sure Abigail's being held prisoner at the lake."

As a babble of voices rose, Miss Simone raised her arms and called for silence again. "Please, please—let him speak." She frowned at Hal, but it wasn't displeasure, simply curiosity. "Blacknail told me all about your trip to the lake this afternoon."

More gasps. "You went to the *lake*?" Lauren squealed.

"What were you thinking, Hal?" Miss Simone went on. "Do you know how dangerous that could have been?—not to mention rude! You might have destroyed years of work trying to integrate our species."

"I didn't mention who was kidnapped, only something about my friend," Hal said firmly. "But somehow they knew I was talking about a girl. How could they know that?"

Jolie was quick to jump in with an answer. "Aside from the fact that they had a fifty-fifty chance of guessing correctly, I think they probably just sensed you were talking about a girl. The miengu are sensitive about such things, you know. They probably saw it in your eyes or heard it in your voice."

"Well . . ." Hal said, and trailed off as he realized how lame his logic was.

"But that's okay," Jolie said, bitterness evident in her voice as she moved to the center of the laboratory lobby. She winced as she moved on her crutches, clearly in some discomfort. Her feet dragged across the polished floor. "I see how it is. Look, I'm not a child. I'm seventeen and due to be married in a month. I don't need to be here. I came because I was asked—because it seemed like a good way to get to know you people." She stood there trembling. "Do you think I like being crippled in this way? I'm used to swimming freely in the water, as fit and able as any other. Yet here, I can barely get around on my own. My throat is sore from all this talking out loud. I can't stand the food you offer and have to sneak off to raid the pond, but I keep it secret in an effort not to disgust you—even though what *you* eat makes me feel sick."

Hal swore he heard a pin drop as she paused for breath.

"I don't want to be a burden or a source of worry and anxiety. If you'd rather I went home, then I'll go—happily. But . . ."

Here she seemed troubled and chewed her lip for a moment before resuming.

"My esteemed leaders were adamant that I demonstrate what we're capable of. Although it's extremely wearing, I'm prepared to do as Miss Simone asked and heal somebody. That's why we're all here, after all."

Miss Simone gave a nod, confirming that Jolie spoke the truth.

Jolie sighed. "Then let's get on with it so I can go home."

The next ten seconds were awkward. Jolie stood completely still in the center of the lobby while children and parents shuffled their feet and stared at the floor. Even Emily looked puzzled, as if wondering how she could have been so mean to Jolie when the visitor was clearly being as gracious as possible.

Hal was shaken. Perhaps he'd been wrong about her. She'd acted a little spontaneously at times, shown herself to be a little careless, even thoughtless . . . but that didn't make her a bad person. His worry for Abigail was clouding his judgment, and he didn't have a shred of evidence to prove foul play on the part of Jolie or her people.

He began to wonder if Abigail had simply tripped and banged her head after all. Maybe she'd wandered off in a daze, caught her dress on a bush, fallen into the stream, and drowned . . .

* * *

The audience was anxious. It was impossible for the entire group—nine children and their parents, plus Jolie, Molly, Miss Simone, Blair, a team of doctors and nurses, and several curious goblins—to fit into one small ward. So the doctors, under strong protest, wheeled one of the patients into the lobby.

Miss Simone made the argument that the patient was dying anyway. Shelby was fifty-six years old and had been seriously ill for months. According to the doctors, nothing could be done for her. What possible harm could this experiment do, except speed up the lady's inevitable demise?

"What's wrong with her?" Hal's dad asked in a low, quavering voice. He could deal with sick cows and put them down if necessary, but he ran a mile from anyone with a bad cough. And this woman was coughing—dry, heaving coughs that made Hal wince.

Shelby was thin and pallid, a red-headed woman who might once have been attractive. Her cheeks were sunken, and she looked exhausted.

A nurse was fussing over her, but Miss Simone waved her away. "It's hard to diagnose a disease in this world. Where I grew up, there were hospitals with all the latest equipment and doctors with extensive knowledge."

She glanced at the nearby group of doctors with a hint of disgust.

"Not so, here. We've raided the other world of text books, journals and papers, everything we can get our hands on. We continue, to this day, to study medicines in an effort to reproduce them within our means. But there are limits to what we can do here and limits to what even the most modern facilities can do in the other world."

Shelby chose that moment to cough, then mumbled an apology. Her eyes were closed but she was clearly aware of what was going on.

"We believe Shelby is suffering from Idiopathic Pulmonary Fibrosis, where her lungs are filling with fibrotic tissue that, over time, thickens and prevents the transfer of oxygen into the bloodstream. Symptoms include shortness of breath, coughing, loss of appetite, and exhaustion. She was suffering badly before she was admitted; now she's simply clinging to existence, and we're trying to make her as comfortable as possible. She knows, as well as we do, that her time is limited. Her family is here with us tonight."

Sadly, her family was small—a young man and woman, Shelby's son and daughter, neither of whom was married. They appeared grim, resolved to their mom's plight.

Jolie hobbled forward, her crutches clacking on the floor. She leaned against the gurney and stumbled when it started to move. Once Miss Simone had put the brake on, she leaned again and propped one of her crutches against the side. She turned and scanned the sea of faces.

"I need some help. Emily?"

Of all the people to ask, Emily should have been the last on her list. But perhaps that was precisely why Jolie chose her.

Emily's parents urged her forward, and she came, frowning and uncertain. She looked like she'd been chosen as a volunteer in a magic trick where the amateur magician was nervously planning to cut his assistant in two.

When Emily approached the bed, Jolie smiled at her. "I'll need you to catch me when I fall," she said.

Jolie placed her hands on Shelby's pale, limp arm. Then she closed her eyes and eased into a deep trance.

For a while, nothing happened. The lobby was silent except for the sounds of Shelby's hoarse breathing and occasional coughs. Then the patient opened her eyes and frowned. She coughed again, lifted her head, and turned to stare at Jolie. Her eyes were bloodshot and rimmed with shadow, and she swayed with the effort of holding her head off the pillow. But she stared at Jolie with an expression of great surprise.

Half a minute later, with Miss Simone and several doctors leaning forward with their mouths hanging open, Shelby quit coughing altogether. She looked like she wanted to, like she *expected* to, but no cough came, and she looked even more puzzled than before.

Jolie staggered suddenly, and Emily instinctively caught her. The remaining crutch fell with a clatter to the floor, and Jolie, heavier than Emily could manage alone, slid down to join it. Emily ended up on her knees with a barely conscious Jolie gripping her tightly.

Doctors and nurses sprang into action, and Shelby was suddenly shielded from view. The audience, until now silent, began to shuffle and murmur.

"Her breathing's regular," a doctor exclaimed, listening to the patient's chest through a stethoscope.

"How are you feeling?" Miss Simone asked over the babble of voices. "Shelby, can you hear me? How are you feeling?"

The noise died down as Shelby lifted her head from the pillow and looked around the room. She licked her lips and croaked, "I . . . I feel fine. I feel better than I have in . . . in *years*. Just tired, that's all."

The disbelief was evident in her voice as well as in her eyes. She looked around, seeking the curious girl who had somehow cured her. "It's a miracle," she exclaimed. "Praise the gods!"

The commotion after that was tremendous, and Hal found himself pushed aside as the adults crowded the doctors, seeking confirmation of the cure, looking for answers. "How is this possible?" one of the parents demanded with what sounded like indignation. "Is this a trick?"

"Are you sure she's healed?"

"Maybe it's a mind-over-matter thing?"

Miss Simone raised her voice to be heard. "I can assure you there's no trickery here, at least not from me. Shelby appears at first glance to be . . . to be *better*, but we need to run tests and check her out properly—and for that we need to get her back to her room and let these doctors do their work."

Emily had dragged the limp Jolie to one side, away from the stampede of adults. Fenton and Thomas rushed to help, and before long the boys had gathered her up and hurried her away to a quiet place. Emily, looking like she'd seen a ghost, was left to pick up the crutches and trail after them. Hal noticed that she staggered halfway along the corridor, as if woozy.

As Shelby was wheeled away, Miss Simone again called for silence. "People, please. I just wanted to say that if Shelby is somehow cured of her disease . . . then the entire purpose of bringing Jolie to our village has been successfully fulfilled." She looked around at the children one by one. "Petty squabbles *will not* be tolerated. Do you understand? This is a scientific breakthrough. Actually, it's not a *scientific* breakthrough as such, but . . . well, the point is that there are far bigger concerns at stake here than whether or not you like Jolie."

Hal spoke up. "Abigail's disappearance isn't petty."

Dr. Porter shot him a grateful smile, then put her grim face back on for Miss Simone. "As much as I find this healing business fascinating—and I really do—all I can focus on right now is finding my daughter. What's the next step, Simone? You told us not to interfere with the search, but . . . are the goblins still out looking? I can't stand

206

this waiting around, gathering together like this, while my little girl is out there, cold and alone—"

She broke off with a sob, and Mrs. O'Tanner again consoled her.

"Nobody has forgotten Abigail," Miss Simone said quietly. She stepped closer to Dr. Porter and lightly touched her arm. "I promise you we'll keep searching. The goblins are still out there, yes, but Blacknail has already rustled up a much larger party—men and women from all over the village are searching in the darkness, and if they don't find her tonight then they'll continue at dawn. Don't worry—we'll find Abigail."

Hal saw that Robbie was gesturing urgently to him. He had a curious leather bag over his shoulder. But Hal was still annoyed with his friend and was busy listening to Miss Simone.

"Unfortunately, I have other things I need to attend to," Miss Simone said with a sigh. "There's a lot going on. Tomorrow is the day of the phoenix rebirth. I'm worried that my team won't be back in time from the other world. They're still out looking for medical supplies. I sent a messenger to bring them home, but there's been no sign of any of them yet. If they don't come back tomorrow, and the phoenix rebirth closes the portals between our worlds . . . well, they'll be trapped there."

"For how long?" Fenton's dad asked.

Miss Simone shrugged. "I don't know. Until they find a hole out of range that hasn't been closed? There are no detailed records of phoenix rebirths. They're a rare occurrence. All we know is what Blair has told us."

Everyone turned toward Blair at that point. He seemed to shrivel and wilt as numerous pairs of eyes stared at him, but he cleared his throat and began to speak in a small, nervous voice.

"Tomorrow evening, at sunset. That's when Jacob, a thousand-year-old phoenix, will begin the cycle. For those of you that saw my demonstration in the street the other day, just imagine that on a much grander scale. In my demonstration, geo-rocks within a hundred-yard radius were extinguished, their energy snuffed out. And although Jacob talks in riddles half the time, on one matter he was quite clear: the portals within his range will close."

"But where *is* this Jacob?" Hal's dad asked. "If he's miles away, surely we don't have anything to worry about here?"

Blair raised an eyebrow. "Jacob is about eighty miles north of here as the crow flies. From what I understand, the effects of his rebirth will spread across the entire region, covering hundreds of miles."

Everyone gasped. "You're kidding," someone scoffed.

"Can't we, like, execute him?" Fenton said rudely.

There was a gasp, and everyone glared at him.

He scowled. "I'm just asking, that's all."

"Wouldn't make a difference," Blair said. "Even if I were to tell you where Jacob is hidden away—which I wouldn't—you cannot simply kill a thousand-year-old phoenix. You'd just bring the rebirth event forward in a much uglier fashion. A phoenix would call this a Cleansing—and ironically it affects them, too, because their rebirths are surely magical events. It's as if, over many hundreds of years, they feel a gradual build of oppressive magic across the land and eventually wipe the slate clean with a rebirth." He began to count off on his fingers. "Geo-rocks, portals between worlds, plus various other forms of energy that we know little about—and yes, I mean magic. All will be affected. For instance, these enchanted clothes we shapeshifters wear might lose their enchantment and become ordinary. Certain species that are, uh . . . enhanced with magic? . . . will be affected in subtle ways. Take the gorgons. Their gaze of death is too extraordinary to be explained by science. I'm willing to bet they won't be able to stone anybody in the future."

"Well, hallelujah!" Molly exclaimed.

"And the way dryads turn almost invisible to blend into the surroundings—surely that will be impossible in a non-magical world."

Darcy paled, but all Hal could think about at that point was Abigail's faerie glade. If Blair was right, there would be no more early-morning parties and mind-hopping antics for the little creatures.

"Jolie, too," Blair went on. He waved toward the now empty corridor where the weary young woman had been dragged away. "She just demonstrated the power of healing, but without magic . . ."

"Magic!" Mr. Morgan scoffed loudly.

There were a few murmurs, but the fact remained that nobody could explain the healing in scientific terms.

"Expect signs from Jacob," Blair warned. "As the rebirth event approaches, we may all see or experience something in the way of warning. And . . ."

He shifted uncomfortably.

"What?" someone demanded from the crowd.

"There's something else," Blair said. "We shapeshifters . . . well, I don't quite know what's going to happen to us. We might . . . *stick*."

"Stick?" Hal said, aware that Robbie had materialized by his side. "What do you mean by that?"

Blair spread his hands. "I mean that we shapeshifters might lose our ability to shift."

Chapter Eighteen
Anxiety

Hal walked in a daze along the corridor, away from the arguing adults in the lobby. He was only dimly aware of Robbie alongside, equally silent, with the leather bag over his shoulder.

"We might not be able to shapeshift anymore," Robbie said in disbelief.

Hal grimaced. "And we might *stick*."

The thought of remaining in dragon form forever was a truly terrifying prospect. Far better to stick in his human form and become like every other twelve-year-old boy . . . although he hated the idea of that, too. Shapeshifting had become a part of his life, and the idea of losing the ability . . .

"I never thought there'd be something more important than Abigail to deal with right now," Hal muttered. "I can't believe this. We've been so caught up with Jolie that we didn't even—"

Robbie stopped and grabbed his arm. "That's what I was going to tell you," he said in a fierce whisper. He fumbled with the leather bag's zipper. Inside was a black camera with shiny silver buttons and a huge lens that stuck out in front. Robbie held the camera aloft and grinned.

"You got it, then," Hal said. For some reason, taking a picture of Jolie seemed utterly insignificant in light of everything else. Still, it would only take a moment. "But can your dad get the film developed?" he asked doubtfully.

"Once I got him interested in the idea, he got all excited and started sifting around for the equipment," Robbie said. "Suddenly he has an urge to convert the broom closet into a darkroom. Mom's fed up, but she's also curious to see what's on all those old undeveloped films." He waved the camera in Hal's face. "This has twenty-one pictures on it already. Should be room for a few more."

They found Jolie in a small room containing only a single bed and a chest of drawers—some sort of rest area, perhaps for doctors on nightshift. She was flat out on the bed, looking woozy, with Fenton and Thomas perched on each side. Emily stood in the far corner, one hand to her chest and a frown on her face.

"Smile," Robbie said to Jolie, holding up the camera. Then he scowled and looked around. "Need more light in here."

Before anyone could stop him, he flipped a large switch on the wall. There was a moment's pause, and then a blinding light flared in the ceiling, a single bulb with a reflective collar that threatened to burn out their eyeballs.

As Fenton and Thomas complained loudly and swung around, Jolie moaned and Robbie clicked the camera twice. Then Emily flipped the switch off and the room was once more plunged into gloom. Jolie let out a sigh.

"Idiot," Fenton snarled at Robbie. "I'll mash your head for that."

"Try it," Robbie retorted.

"What's wrong with *you*?" Hal asked Emily.

"I feel awful," she admitted, still clutching her chest. "I'm going home."

Concerned, Hal followed her out of the room and watched her shuffle along the corridor. From the lobby ahead came a muffled babble of voices; the adults were engaged in a heated discussion.

"So what are we going to do about Abigail?" Robbie asked, appearing in the doorway behind him.

Hal said nothing for a moment, then began striding along the corridor after Emily. "I'm going to go look for her again."

"Now?" Robbie exclaimed as he hurried to catch up. "In the *dark*?"

"She would do the same for me," Hal murmured.

"Well, she has night vision," Robbie reasoned.

Hal scowled at him, suddenly remembering that he was still angry with his friend. "You don't have to come. I'll see you tomorrow."

"No, it's okay, I'm up for it. Let me get this camera back to Dad so he can start developing when he gets home, and then we'll go a-hunting." He slowed. "And, uh . . . I'm, you know, sorry and all that."

Hal glanced back at him, then stopped and turned to face him squarely. "You really thought I had something to do with Abigail going missing?"

Robbie shrugged. "No, not really. It was all Jolie's fault. She was talking to me in my head. Talking to all of us, it turns out. She was putting ideas in our heads, and I guess we sort of . . . let her convince us."

Hal remembered that Molly had said much the same thing in the lobby. "And you believed her," he said, disgusted.

"She has a way about her," Robbie said miserably.

"Yeah, yeah."

* * *

Searching for Abigail had seemed like a good idea at the time, but once Robbie had slipped the camera to his dad and the two boys had set off into the night, they were faced with the prospect of stumbling around in complete darkness.

The ground was still squelchy and, as they left the village and plunged into the woods, they quickly realized how wet the bushes and trees were, too. Their clothes grew damp and cold within minutes.

"We'll never find her in this," Robbie said, staring into the woods. "I can't even see my hands in front of my face."

Hal sighed. They'd walked partway around the village before entering the woods, hoping to explore a different area than what the goblins had searched earlier. Besides, from what Miss Simone had said, the same goblins were *still* searching even now. There was no point covering the same ground again.

"We could go down to the river," he suggested.

Robbie turned in a slow circle, squinting in the feeble moonlight. "What about the faerie glade you mentioned? Would she have gone back there?"

Hal's mouth dropped open. "I never thought of that! Yeah, let's give that a go. Come on."

There were trails darting off all over, and the main route ran all the way around the village outside the perimeter fence, meandering wildly as it went. The boys hurried along it, grateful for the regularly spaced lanterns hanging from trees or posts. They passed a goblin whose job it was to light these lanterns every night; he was ambling along and stopping every once in a while to light another. Once Hal and Robbie passed him by, they slowed to a stop. The path and woods were pitch-black from here onward.

"I think it was around here somewhere," Hal muttered, peering into the trees. "We'll never see it from the path, though. We need to kind of head into the woods and hope we come across it."

"That's great," Robbie said with a snort. "If it were me, I'd know *exactly* where to go. I never forget a route."

Robbie always had been good with directions. But he had never been to the glade, so his ogre instincts were useless in this case.

Hal snatched the nearest hanging lantern from a post. It was the kind with a fat candle inside, presently cold. He opened the little glass door and stared at the wick. Carefully, he forced a tiny belch of fire up from his throat and aimed it into the lantern. The wick caught and began to burn, and Hal closed the glass door. Even a feeble light was better than nothing when crashing around in the dark woods.

Still, they quickly grew tired and cold. Robbie had just started complaining that the hunt for the glade was 'a complete waste of time' when Hal spotted something. He grabbed Robbie's arm. "Look!"

In a clearing ahead was a small point of light, darting around above the hulking shapes of bushes. It vanished for a moment, then reappeared, zipping through the trees. It was gone again for twenty seconds or so before returning and ducking out of sight. It was way too fast and big for a firefly.

"I'm pretty certain that's a faerie," Hal whispered, hiding the lantern behind his back in case he spooked the little creature.

"Why's it glowing?" Robbie wondered aloud.

Hal shrugged. "It just is. Faeries glow in the dark."

They watched the light zip off into the trees.

Robbie couldn't let the subject go. "Does Abigail glow, too?"

"Yeah," Hal said. "At least when she's small. It has to be really dark to see the glow."

"So that's definitely the faerie glade?" Robbie asked.

Looking around, Hal decided he wasn't sure. "Come on," he said, and began to move stealthily into the clearing.

All was silent as he and Robbie shuffled closer. Hal stood on just about every dry twig imaginable and winced every time a sharp *crack!* filled the air. If the faeries hadn't heard them by now, then they must be deaf. Still, Hal saw absolutely nothing of interest and no further sign of zipping lights. He waved the lantern around and stomped on bushes, growing more impatient and less cautious as the minutes ticked by. Poor Abigail was out somewhere on this cold, damp night, alone and probably frightened to death.

"There's nothing here," Robbie said loudly, sounding disgusted and fed up.

Hal gave up any ideas of a stealthy approach. "Faeries!" he called. "I'm looking for Abigail. Is she with you?"

Naturally there was no reply.

"Abigail's my friend—a shapeshifter faerie," he tried again. "You know her. She's gone missing, and I was hoping you'd seen her? Is she here, maybe?"

Silence.

An owl hooted somewhere.

Hal sighed. "I suppose it was asking too much to come along here and talk to the faeries. They're not exactly sociable. Besides, I still think she's probably a prisoner of the miengu." He frowned. "Maybe. I just can't make up my mind about that."

"Well, let's go, then," Robbie said. After a pause, he said, "We can go to the river, if you want. Search around there for a bit?"

He thought about how far the river stretched, of the deep woods all around.

Typical, Hal thought. *Back at the lab, all I wanted to do was get outside and search. Now we're actually out searching, it all seems so pointless.*

"Let's go home," he murmured.

"Really? You're sure?"

Hal studied Robbie's wet mop of hair and sodden clothes. "Yeah. Until morning. Then I'm going out early to find her."

"And if you don't, someone else will," Robbie said, nodding. "She'll turn up, Hal. You wait and see."

Easy to say, Hal thought.

He was deeply troubled. It was bad enough that she was missing, but then there was the bloody handprint and the scrap of fabric. Whether staged or not, it pointed to foul play. And once more he felt absolutely certain that Abigail had been kidnapped by the miengu. Yet . . . there seemed to be no logical reason for them to take her.

No *logical* reason—but perhaps they didn't need to be logical. Perhaps they were just being mean.

Of course, the guilty party didn't have to be the entire clan in the lake. It could be just *one* of the miengu, a rogue with his own agenda. What if Jolie's fiancé had, for whatever personal and unfathomable reasons, captured Abigail? What would he have done with her if that were the case? Surely he wouldn't take her back to the lake and risk other miengu finding out . . .

"You coming?" Robbie asked.

Hal nodded and followed his friend through the woods until they came upon the muddy path. He kicked ideas back and forth in his mind long after he'd mumbled goodnight to Robbie and set off home.

But it was hopeless. He still had no clue where to look for Abigail.

* * *

He slept fitfully, and Abigail kept popping into his dreams from far away. He tried to latch on to the visions of her, but she was like a distant echo, bouncing around the place but always out of reach. Nothing she said was clear except the words "Let me in," which she repeated over and over.

In the end, he woke to sunlight streaming onto his face through his bedroom window because he hadn't bothered to close the curtains the previous night. Still, that was good; it meant he could get an early start on the search.

He peered outside. Steam was rising off the lawn as the morning sun got a start on drying out the land. He remembered his dreams and suddenly wondered if Abigail had been tapping on his window in the night, asking to be let in. The idea made him shake with excitement; he had to go find out. He dressed quickly, skipped breakfast, and tore out of the house.

"Is Abigail back?" he asked Dr. Porter when she finally answered the door.

She looked exhausted and disheveled, her eyes heavily shadowed. Hal knew straight away that Abigail was still missing, and his heart sank.

"They sent me home," Dr. Porter said miserably. "We were out looking last night until—oh, I don't know, three in the morning? They sent me home to sleep. I didn't think I could ever sleep, but . . ."

"You have to rest," Hal said, feeling awkward. "Look, go back to bed. I'm going off to look for her now."

Dr. Porter emerged from the shadow of the doorway and stepped out onto the stone step, blinking in the sunlight. "You're a good boy, Hal. My daughter thinks the world of you." She blinked back tears and ran a hand through her hair. "Go find her for me. Bring her home."

Troubled, Hal again found himself wandering aimlessly for hours through the woods behind Abigail's house. The goblins had searched the area countless times, and Hal didn't expect to find anything. And he didn't. She wasn't here, and combing the woods was a waste of time.

He stopped to think. It was a beautiful late morning, clear and fresh, not as humid as it had been in recent weeks. The woods were quiet, with just the warbling and chirping of birds and the occasional rustling sounds in the bushes.

Think, he told himself.

Wherever she was, it was nowhere close. He headed back to the woodland trail and stumbled across a place he found familiar—the tree that he'd positioned himself under when Abigail had taken him on a ride in her mind. He stared down at the flattened soil, remembering how he'd slumped over sideways.

Nearby, beyond the bushes in a small clearing, he recognized the faerie glade—or where the glade was hidden if you looked hard enough. He recalled the wild dawn party, the collective faerie magic . . . and a thought struck him: Could Abigail have been using her mind trick to enter his mind that morning?

His heart began to thump hard. She'd been saying "Let me in" over and over in his dream, which is what she might say if she'd been trying to enter his mind. And he'd shut her out.

Well, that wasn't strictly true. She'd been distant, nothing but an echo. It wasn't his fault that he'd been unable to respond. Still, he was appalled at the idea that he might have connected with her if only he'd listened a little harder.

He immediately wanted to go home and sleep. Maybe she'd get through to him again, and this time he'd be listening for her. But he knew he would never get back to sleep now, and besides, wasn't faerie magic strongest at dawn? Could she even contact him during the daytime?

Hal let out a cry of frustration.

With nothing to go on, he gradually made his way out of the woods and into the village, his stomach growling. The market was in full swing, but it was clear there was anxiety in the air. Hal picked up snippets of conversation as he wandered around munching on a meat pie and concluded that the forthcoming phoenix rebirth at sundown was the primary talking point.

He came across the familiar wheelbarrow man, who was sitting on a stone bench looking glum. As always, he was laden with glowing geo-rocks. Some of them were the size of soccer balls, while others were as small as fists—but all were bright and new.

"Not much point passing them out," the man grumbled. "The miners have stopped work, and everyone's just moping around." He picked up a runt of a rock and hefted it, looking thoughtful. It was curiously flattened and no bigger than his palm but shone all the more brightly. "Can't imagine life without these things now. Got half a dozen at home, I have. They heat my water and give me light. It's gonna be weird boiling water on the fire and using candles again."

"Maybe it won't be permanent," Hal said, although he had no idea why.

The man shrugged. "Guess we'll find out soon enough. Here." He suddenly tossed the rock to Hal, making him fumble to catch it. "Enjoy it while it lasts."

With a heavy sigh, the man stood and heaved his wheelbarrow into action. He set off along the street, the single wheel squeaking noisily.

Hal stared at the glowing rock in his hands, feeling its energy under his fingertips. He'd already gotten used to these things and, like the wheelbarrow man, couldn't imagine life without them. How far would the effects of the phoenix rebirth stretch, and how long would they last?

He imagined the rock dimming, the light going out, its warmth fading—and with it the ability to shapeshift, Abigail's faerie magic, Darcy's invisibility, and no doubt a hundred and one other magical losses throughout the region.

It was late afternoon. Only a few hours to sundown.

He set off to find Robbie, staring at the small geo-rock as he ambled through the streets. Instead he came across Miss Simone and hurried toward her. "Any news?" he asked.

She looked tired. "About what?"

"Abigail!" Hal said indignantly.

Miss Simone rubbed her eyes and sighed. "Sorry. It's been a long night. We've been searching, Hal, but no sign of her yet. I have other worries, too. My scouts aren't back, and nor is the messenger I sent to fetch them. I'm afraid they're going to end up stuck in that virus-ridden world." She gestured suddenly, nearly bashing a passerby in the face with the back of her hand. "Molly!"

Hal turned to see Molly shuffling along. Her slumped shoulders suggested she was just as weary as Miss Simone; even her veil seemed oddly limp. She veered toward Miss Simone and Hal. "I'm off for a nap," she said.

"Good idea," Miss Simone agreed. "Come on—we'll talk, get some sleep, and be up and ready for whatever this evening will bring."

"Suits me," Molly said. "I need to rest my ugly old bones."

Miss Simone turned back to Hal. "Don't worry. We'll find her."

But the anxiety in her eyes said otherwise.

Chapter Nineteen
Poetry

Hal tossed his geo-rock from hand to hand as he continued through the village. He passed a hazy, dusty street and heard echoing thuds, and knew the workmen were busy rebuilding homes. Despite being a Sunday, the village continued as if it were any other day of the week. He wondered if Robbie was with the builders today, offering his ogre services.

He went to find out. There were six or seven centaurs pulling four-wheeled carts loaded up with debris, and as they trundled off in clouds of dust, several more centaurs arrived on the scene for refills. The workers had cleared a lot in the past few days, and it looked like someone was already moving into a newly built home—a lady was directing two young laborers carrying a bed frame through the narrow front door.

Robbie was nowhere to be seen, which surprised Hal.

"He showed up an hour ago," a heavyset bearded man said, wiping sweat from his brow as he paused for a breather. "Said he had a few things to do today. Some girl is missing, so I heard." He peered at Hal as if recognizing him for the first time. "But you'd know all about that, I guess. One of yours, ain't she?"

Hal nodded, thanked the man, and wandered off. On his way out of the construction zone, he noticed that one of the centaurs was Fleck—not toting a cart but instead standing by idly, staring into space while men hoisted broken stones and splintered timbers onto their shoulders and staggered past.

"What are *you* doing here?" Hal asked.

Fleck woke from his daydream. "What? Oh, it's you." He frowned at the geo-rock Hal was idly juggling. "Be careful with that. If you drop it and it cracks open, it'll blow up in your face."

"Uh, right," Hal said, staring at the rock in horror. What had he been thinking? It was like walking around with a bomb! He gingerly eased it into a pocket in his pants where it slid down to warm his outer thigh.

"Won't be much good after this evening, though," Fleck said. It was hard to work out the expression on his face. Was the centaur worried? Pleased? "You know, after you destroyed my machine in the labyrinth, I've been working on a new one. Waste of time, as it turns out. This phoenix rebirth tonight will close all the holes around here far more effectively than any clumsy machine. It's quite wonderful, when you think about it."

So he's pleased, then, Hal thought as Fleck broke into a grin. "Wonderful for you, maybe," he said. "Not so great for us."

"Oh, I freely admit that this is everything my previous 'esteemed leaders' were looking for," Fleck said with a hint of scorn as he mentioned the disgraced centaur khan and a couple of close colleagues, all of whom had been removed from office and marched off. Their crimes against humanity were so terrible that the centaur council had found it impossible to think of a punishment harsh enough without resorting to torture—but rather than a quick, painless execution, the elderly khan and his aides had been put to work to deal with the very problem they had created, personally overseeing the safe destruction of the deadly mushrooms inside Whisper Mountain. Despite his failing health, the khan was ordered to descend into the seemingly bottomless pit to begin eradicating all traces of the fungus. No doubt he would end up choking to death on the yellow dust he stirred up. "A permanent division of worlds, at least in this region," Fleck went on. "Earth restored to its natural state."

"Do you think it's *really* permanent?"

Fleck shrugged and clip-clopped around in a circle as if suddenly restless. "Define permanent. We have energy in the rocks and magic in the air, so clearly previous phoenix rebirths in this region have failed to have a lasting effect. But how long before the energy and magic return, eh? Months? Years? Decades?" He flicked his tail at an annoying fly and looked toward the sky over the nearby rooftops. "There are no reliable records. But I can assure you there will be after tonight. Ho, yes!"

Hal grinned at the sudden exclamation. "Sounds like you're looking forward to it."

Fleck turned to face Hal, his eyes flashing with excitement. "This is a momentous occasion. Not *one person* alive today has seen or felt the effects of a phoenix rebirth."

"Well—"

The centaur cut him off with a dismissive gesture. "I mean, other than Blair's little performance in the street."

"It was pretty impressive," Hal said. "He knocked out the power in all the nearby streets and gave everyone a tingly feeling."

"I wasn't there," Fleck said sadly. "And I won't be there for the real thing, either. Nobody but Blair knows where the phoenix is, and he isn't telling. Says it'd be a betrayal of his kind. Pah!" The centaur looked thoroughly disgusted. "Seems to me as if Blair has forgotten he's human!"

Hal left the centaur to rant and rave about how he was missing out on an extraordinary phenomenon. He slipped away and wondered what to do with the geo-rock in his pocket. He no longer liked the idea of carrying it around.

He found himself wandering back into the village, wishing he had some way of communicating with Abigail. He thought again about taking a nap. Maybe she'd be able to get in touch with him. At this point it seemed like the only possible course of action.

As he was pondering the idea, he came across Jolie, Fenton and Thomas standing with a small crowd of maybe thirty people on the outskirts of the market. Hal had often seen a puppeteer or mime amusing passersby just here, and sometimes a clever magician astounded everyone so much that the market grounded to a halt for twenty minutes. Hal joined the crowd, wondering who was performing today.

To his utter amazement, it was Dewey.

The boy stood before them holding a small book in trembling hands. *His book of poems*, Hal realized. Only Dewey was mumbling so quietly that nobody could hear a word. "Speak up!" someone finally yelled.

After that, a few others joined in, saying that he needed to start over and raise his voice. "Can't hear you at the back," a man said gently.

"Can't hear you at the front, neither," a dirty-faced boy said rudely.

Dewey looked like he was about to give up and run away. Jolie hobbled out of the crowd on her crutches and went to stand by him. She nudged him and whispered something in his ear.

"What's going on?" Hal asked Fenton.

The big boy rolled his eyes. "Jolie's persuaded him to read some of his poetry. She stole his book earlier and read some. Dewey caught her and looked like he was about to blow his top—but then she started gushing about how *wonderful* his poems were, and how *talented* he was, and all that." The scorn in Fenton's voice was obvious.

Hal was incredulous. "And now he's reading it out loud in public?"

Thomas laughed. "Not exactly reading it out *loud*. More like whispering it under his breath. Look at him shaking!"

Hal could almost see Dewey's knees knocking under his pants. The boy's face was flushed. "I can't believe he's doing this," he murmured.

"Nor can he," Fenton snorted.

Whatever Jolie had said seemed to have worked. Dewey was nodding vigorously and seemed to have grown in determination within the last thirty seconds. Hal had to admit that Jolie had a special way about her. Nobody else could have persuaded Dewey to stand up in public, in front of maybe thirty people of all ages in the busy street, and read aloud his poetry. He had a small podium and everything, as if an impromptu stage had been set up right there in the market. Jolie had been busy!

"All right, please shush, everyone," Jolie called loudly.

Everyone immediately went quiet, and a man muttered "Sorry" for no good reason. With the noises of the market very much in the background, silence reigned, and the audience was still and expectant.

Dewey cleared his throat and began in a quiet, wavering voice. Then, encouraged by Jolie's continued presence and the silence of the crowd, began to speak louder:

"I started out as a normal boy in a world of fog,
And changed into a centaur.
Then I came to this new world with all my friends and Emily's dog,
And Fleck became my mentor.
It's hard being a centaur with four long legs,
I'm so tall I feel like I'm really high off the ground.
I can't seem to control my hoofs and keep dancing around.
One of these days I'm going to fall over with a . . . a loud sound."

At this point there was a giggle from a girl in the second row, followed by a "Shh!" and an embarrassed cough. Jolie's expression was a mask of delight, but Hal couldn't decide if she genuinely liked the poem or just enjoyed watching Dewey squirm.

"I hope this gets better," Fenton muttered as Dewey continued:

"I'm not sure what happens to my insides when I change,
It's hard to figure out.

Do I have two stomachs or one? And how many lungs?
What happens to my human legs? Do they just melt?"

Hal shuddered. His friend seemed unaware that his poem was receiving a poor reaction. At the moment, the crowd was relatively quiet, but heads were turning and grins beginning to form. *Dewey, stop,* Hal silently pleaded, *before they start throwing tomatoes.*

The next few verses were worse. Somebody in the crowd, a tall, bald man with glasses, seemed quite put out and blurted, "You have no rhythm, boy!"

"And 'horse' doesn't rhyme with 'doors'—that's cheating," the girl in the second row pointed out.

Dewey began to falter as if realizing for the first time that his work wasn't appreciated. He looked to Jolie, who seemed to be smirking now. Hal knew then that she had planned this all along; she'd read Dewey's poems, knew they were terrible, and set him up for a humiliating experience in public.

"Keep going," she mouthed. Then Dewey tilted his head, and Hal knew the girl was sending private thoughts to him. Finally, Dewey started into the next verse, although with only half the confidence he had managed to build earlier:

"And . . . and so I gallop around the fields,
With the wind in my hair.
The fastest I could run before turning into a centaur,
Was not that fast. But now I'm as fast as a hare.
So I like being a centaur and hate the idea of NOT being one,
Which is what might happen tonight.
If the phoenix closes holes and messes with stuff,
Then my future won't be as bright.
. . . Anymore," he added quietly.

The audience burst into laughter, and while some cheered good-naturedly, most snorted derisively.

Suddenly, Dewey snapped his book shut and turned to run. Hal caught one last glimpse of the boy's face and saw misery and embarrassment before he took off, ducking and weaving out of sight in the market crowd.

The laughter in the street rose for a second or two, but then died away. After that, men and women cleared their throats and wandered away.

"Oh, poor little Dewey!" Jolie said, giggling. She looked flushed as she turned to face Hal, Fenton and Thomas. "What about you guys? Got any hidden talents you'd like to share? Thomas, how about offering rides to the kids?"

Hal was about to say something cutting when someone beat him to the punch. "You're evil," Emily said, her voice slicing through the air.

She was standing across the street, holding herself at a curious angle with one hand across her chest.

"*Evil?*" Jolie repeated. She shifted on her crutches. "I think that's a bit strong, don't you? Come on, Dewey needs the feedback if he's going to—"

"I'm not talking about Dewey," Emily snapped.

Hal hurried across the street. She was pale and trembling. "What's wrong, Em? You look awful."

"I *feel* awful," she replied loudly. Then she raised her voice a few more notches. "What did you do to me, Jolie?"

Jolie's eyebrows shot up. "What do you mean?"

"Emily, you—" Hal started.

She winced and closed her eyes, then began to cough. She was trying to say something but seemed unable to stop coughing, so Hal put his arm around her and led her off along the street. He felt he needed to get her away from the source of her anger so she could calm down and get a grip on herself.

Her voice was hoarse by the time she managed to stop coughing. She trembled badly and seemed about to drop, and she gripped Hal's arm tightly. "Hal, she did something to me. I think she . . . she . . . made me sick. She healed that woman—that Shelby woman in the lab—but then I started feeling bad right afterward. I think she took the sickness out of Shelby and gave it to me."

She was down to a rasp by the time she dragged out the last sentence, and Hal was so horrified and concerned for her health that it took a moment to register what she was saying.

"Wait a minute—are you serious? Here, sit down."

He lowered her onto a low wall, feeling the pocketed geo-rock dig into his leg as he did so. By this time, they were almost out of sight of Jolie, Fenton and Thomas. The trio were laughing about something, and once again Hal was disgusted at how deeply the boys were under her spell. Didn't they care about Emily? Or even Dewey? What was *wrong* with them?

"She's evil, Hal," Emily said miserably. Tears sprang to her eyes. "She's made me sick, and she's done something to Abigail. I *know* she has. Abigail and I are the only two who see Jolie for what she is—a nasty, vindictive witch."

"Wow, steady on," Hal said. "Look—"

Emily batted him with the back of her hand. "Don't defend her! I'm telling you, she's *done something to Abigail*. Have you asked Jolie directly?"

Hal admitted that he hadn't. "This is the first time I've seen her since last night. I guess I could go and—"

Once more Emily interrupted him. "What do you mean, this is the first time you've seen her? She was at your house this morning."

Hal stared at her blankly.

"I saw her," Emily insisted. She coughed and winced. "I came to see you. I was going to talk to you about her, and about Abigail, but I was too late. I saw you from a distance, running from your house early this morning. Jolie was outside your bedroom window."

"What?" Hal exclaimed. "Outside my *bedroom window?*"

"There was no way I could catch up with you," Emily went on, her breathing harsh and ragged, "so I stopped and watched Jolie from a distance. But she saw me, smiled, and hobbled off after you on her stupid crutches."

"She came after me?"

Emily nodded. "I assumed you'd been talking to her through the bedroom window, and she'd told you something important."

Hal was silent for half a minute. "I never saw Jolie at all. I'd been dreaming about Abigail. She called to me in my dream."

"Abigail did? Are you sure that wasn't Jolie?" Emily asked, her eyes narrowed. "Whispering through the window and trying to get your attention?"

"No way!" Hal snapped. "You think I don't know the difference between Abigail and Jolie? That's why I took off in a hurry—I went to Abi's house to see if maybe she'd come home." He frowned and shook his head. "So Jolie was outside my bedroom window while I was asleep? I looked out just before I left the house and never saw her there, so she must have hidden."

Emily seemed to have forgotten her illness. "So she was *spying* on you?" she demanded. "But why?"

Hal thought long and hard about how he had hitched a ride in Abigail's head and gone to spy on Jolie. He started to wonder if the jengu had spotted them after all. He clearly remembered Abigail flying at the window and thumping hard against the glass, and then, seconds later, Jolie peering out and staring in their direction as they hid behind the tree. The jengu hadn't reacted, but it was possible she *had* seen them and simply kept her reaction hidden so she could follow them home and—

And what? Get her revenge by kidnapping Abigail? That seemed a little drastic. Besides, Hal remembered moving at a fairly quick pace through the village afterward; how on earth could Jolie have kept pace on crutches? Then again, if she'd seen Abigail outside the bedroom window, she wouldn't have *needed* to keep pace; it would have been a simple matter, even at that early hour of the morning, to ask someone for directions to Dr. Porter's house. And then there was the sound of that twig cracking as Abigail had headed home . . .

Hal shook his head. He needed to keep a tight rein on his imagination. Even if Jolie had hobbled across the village after them and located the right house, could she have managed to overpower Abigail and cart her off to a secret place miles away on her own, and *still* be back in time for a picnic?

His theory began to crumble around the edges.

Coughing, Emily struggled to her feet. "Hold on, I need to change again."

She transformed—but slowly. She acted like switching to her serpentine naga body was a painful experience. Her face was screwed up in agony, and the transformation was sporadic as if her body wasn't quite sure what it was doing, with jerky, sudden changes in random places instead of one smooth transition. Even her smart clothes seemed confused, first lengthening to accommodate her long snake torso, and then shortening as her dark reptilian skin faded back to pink momentarily, and then stretching and thinning again . . .

With a great effort, she forced herself into her naga form and stood swaying, her thick snake body writhing and her slender human arms hanging loosely at her sides. Her eyes, though still human, had taken on an odd glassy look and reminded Hal a little of Jolie.

"This is getting harder," Emily gasped. "Changing makes me feel better, especially if I change back and forth a few times. But . . . it's getting harder to change." She had a look of desperation as she leaned forward and gripped Hal's hands in her own. "Hal, when the phoenix dies tonight and is reborn in its own ashes—when shapeshifters get stuck in one form or another—*what will I do?* If transforming heals me, what will happen when I can't transform anymore?"

Hal opened and closed his mouth, flabbergasted by this turn of events. "I don't know. Look, we need to go see Miss Simone."

Emily shook her head. "She won't help," she said bitterly. "She likes Jolie. Or at least *needs* Jolie. She won't help."

Hal began to argue, saying that even Miss Simone would recognize something was off and that Emily's sickness was evidence of sinister intentions. But Emily suggested they go see Dr. Porter instead. "She's on *our* side. She's one of us, and she really doesn't trust Jolie at the moment."

Hal agreed to accompany her as she set off. Besides, Miss Simone was probably exhausted right now. Emily slithered through the streets, attracting more than a few stares. The naga were impressive and formidable, not the sort of creatures you got on the wrong side of. They were fast and powerful and could easily squeeze the life out of a large man. And they had a bite to be wary of, too. Not venomous but painful all the same.

As they hurried, Emily reverted to her human form, then back to naga. With each change she felt better and moved more easily. And each transformation was smoother than the last. By the time she had switched forms seven or eight times in succession, color was returning to her face.

Yet she remained worried. "I've been doing this all day," she explained as they reached the gate leading out of the village. "You'd think I'd heal up and be done with this sickness. And I do feel better right now. But it keeps coming back. In less than an hour from now, I'll be coughing again, you wait and see."

"Hopefully Dr. Porter can help," Hal muttered doubtfully.

"It's like I had years of sickness dumped into my system," she complained as she returned to her human form. "I swear, Jolie is evil."

As they reached a fork in the road, someone called Hal's name. Robbie was jogging along the trail from the direction of Hal's house. "I've been looking for you," he shouted. "I've got photos to look at."

Immediately interested, Hal and Emily forgot about Dr. Porter and crowded Robbie as he fumbled to open an envelope. His hands were shaking as he handed a stack of photographs to Hal. "Nabbed these from Dad as soon as he got finished developing them. He hasn't even had a good look himself."

"Have *you?*" Hal demanded.

"Oh, yes."

"And?"

Robbie tapped his finger on the stack. "Just take a look."

The photos were a little faded—hardly surprising considering their age. In the first picture, Robbie was grinning as he held up a jar containing a nondescript bug. His dad had snapped the photo some years ago back on the island, and Robbie looked comically baby-faced, a mere nine or ten years old, even skinnier than he was now.

The next three photos were of a rare community picnic in a field on the island, with everyone present—eight children and their parents. Of course, this was before Thomas had returned to them. Still, it was a remarkably memorable photograph, and even Robbie's dad was there. Hal remembered how he'd set up the camera on a tripod, fiddled with a button or switch, and then darted around to the back of the group and smiled just as the camera clicked. Looking at the picture now, he looked for all the world like he'd been standing there the whole time.

Hal shook his head. "These are fascinating, but where are the ones of Jolie? Are they in here?"

"At the back," Robbie said.

Hal clicked his tongue and pulled out the last few photos. The one on top was a picture of Hal, and he froze. It was another from the old days, but it shocked him to see his own face so close up and *young* compared to the face he saw in the mirror every morning. He didn't remember this one being taken. It was a little fuzzy, and he clearly hadn't been paying attention at the time.

The next one was much more recent, the first of two pictures of Jolie resting in that quiet laboratory room, with Fenton and Thomas leaning over her and Emily just off frame to the right. But Fenton's shoulder obscured Jolie's face.

The final photo shocked Hal to the core. He almost dropped it in horror, and Emily jerked backward with a gasp.

In this picture, Fenton and Thomas were turned toward the camera, leaning backward and looking annoyed as they squinted in the bright light from above. Emily was in the frame this time, her hands raised to shield her eyes from the glare. In the bed, Jolie was looking directly at the camera and in full view.

Only it wasn't the Jolie they knew. The young woman lying on the bed had a long, painfully thin face with sucked-in cheeks and ears that stuck out. Her forehead was high and narrow and her chin too large. Her deeply sunken eyes were oddly misaligned. Below her crooked nose, her mouth was twisted into a hideous snarl from which protruded uneven dirty teeth.

Her black hair was not as shiny and lustrous as Hal had come to know it but an oily mess plastered across the pillow. Her pale, scaly skin had a faintly translucent quality, and Hal could plainly see, in the blinding glare of the room, darker patches of something below the surface—perhaps layers of flesh and muscle. Even her hands appalled Hal—skeletal wrists and hideously blackened clawed fingers.

The photo shook in Hal's hand as he stared and stared, unable to believe what he was looking at. "She's just about the ugliest person I've ever seen," he said weakly.

"Think what she'd look like as a jengu," Robbie murmured. He jabbed a finger at the picture. "Imagine that with pointy ears, scaly skin and black eyes."

Hal shook his head in wonder. "That *can't* be her."

"Photos never lie," Robbie said.

Hal barely heard. He couldn't get over the terrible face in the picture. *This* was what they'd all gone nuts over? *This* was what they'd been escorting around the village for the last few days? How was it possible? How could they have been so blind?

"I told you," Emily whispered. She looked awful—shaking uncontrollably and tears running down her cheeks. At first she'd jerked away, then peered again, then backed off . . . and now she seemed glued to the picture, unblinking. "Pure evil. *Now* do you believe me? She did something to me—and she did something to Abigail, too."

Chapter Twenty
Disaster

The three of them hurried through the village, the afternoon sun beating down from a clear blue sky. Hal and Robbie kept pace with one another, but Emily was lagging behind, and they had to keep stopping for her.

"Go on ahead," she gasped. "This sickness has worn me out."

But Hal refused to leave her behind, and they continued together at a slower but steadier pace.

The idea of going to see Dr. Porter had completely fled their minds after seeing the photograph of Jolie. All they could think about now was showing the picture to Miss Simone. She had to know, and Jolie had to be dealt with.

Was Jolie unique because she was a shapeshifter? Or were all the miengu the same—twisted faces of evil who got a sinister pleasure out of causing mischief. The more he thought about it, the more Hal realized that Jolie had had them all fooled with her illusion of loveliness. She could do virtually anything with a pretty face and had only to bat her eyelids afterward for forgiveness. She had men and boys alike fawning over her, most women were fooled by her so-called innocence, and of course there was the neat trick of healing poor Shelby, which dashed away any shred of doubt about her angelic intentions.

They rounded a corner and almost bumped into Fenton, Thomas and Dewey. Hal cringed, knowing for sure that Jolie was with them somewhere. To his surprise, she was nowhere to be seen.

"She went off with Miss Simone and Molly for a rest," Fenton said gruffly, sounding disappointed.

Relieved, Hal nodded. "Okay. Then you're with us. It's time you woke up."

Fenton scowled. "What's that supposed to mean?" He turned his attention to Emily and looked her up and down as if she was to blame for something. "And where do you get off telling Jolie she's evil? That really upset her. She didn't show it at first, but she went all quiet after you left. I think that's why she went off with Miss Simone and Molly—to hide her tears."

Robbie burst out laughing. "Man, you're *really* smitten."

Before Fenton could say anything, Thomas strode forward and jabbed Robbie in the chest with a finger. "And you're all beat up about Lauren ditching you. No wonder you're so sick of girls."

Robbie's mouth opened and closed, but no words came out.

Fenton guffawed. "Look, Thomas, he's about to blow his lid."

"Guys," Emily warned, "we have to stick together."

"Oh, yeah?" Fenton snapped. "Why's that, exactly?" He threw up his hands and looked exasperated. "News flash: we don't live on the island anymore. We're in a new world with a lot of new people, and we don't have to stick together at all. In fact, I'm tired of seeing your dumb faces."

Now Robbie found his tongue. "Well, you just go right ahead and hang out with Jolie. See what you get when she turns on you."

"What's *that* supposed to mean?"

His face red, Robbie delved into his pocket for the envelope of photographs. "You want to know what I mean? I'll *show* you what I mean."

His hands were shaking as he pulled the photos from the envelope. Fenton glanced at them, saw a picture of Robbie holding a bug jar, and scoffed noisily. "What, you're gonna bore us to death with a slideshow?" He casually brought his hand up and smacked Robbie's from underneath, sending the photos flying through the air.

Emily gave a cry. "You *idiot!*"

Some of the photographs fluttered in a breeze, while the rest lay scattered on the ground. Hal and Robbie fell to their knees, hurriedly scooping them up while searching for the single piece of evidence against Jolie. That was the only photograph that mattered. Where *was* it . . . ?

Hal saw the ghastly face staring at him and pounced on it. He swung it around to show Fenton, but the big boy was already wandering off with Thomas. Dewey lingered, though; he clearly hadn't enjoyed the argument and had an apologetic look on his face.

His eyes fell on the photograph and narrowed. Then he frowned and peered closer. "What *is* that?"

"That," Hal said stiffly, "is Jolie."

Now Dewey's eyes widened. "No way!"

Robbie called out to Fenton and Thomas. "Don't go yet—you need to see this. Come back here!"

The boys completely ignored him.

Hal nudged Robbie. "Make him want to beat you up. You know he can't resist that."

Grinning, Robbie yelled, "Hey, fat boy! Wobble your big butt back here so I can mash your nose with my fist."

Dewey paled and began to sidle away.

Fenton stopped in his tracks. He turned slowly. His eyes were glowing bright red as he opened his mouth to reveal fangs. For a moment, he looked dangerous—but then water dribbled down his chin, and the effect was ruined.

"*What* did you say, beanpole?" he growled, stomping back toward them with fists balled. Thomas trailed behind, looking eager for a fight.

Hal raised the photo. "Robbie's just trying to get you to come back and see this. Take a good look, Fenton."

The boy refused to remove his glare from Robbie, so Hal moved the photo in front of Robbie's face. Now Fenton had no choice but to notice the photo, to look at it briefly, just for a split second . . .

And then his interest was caught, and he faltered. He stared harder, leaning forward, and finally raised his hand to pluck the photo from Hal's grasp. He brought it close to his face, his eyes still burning red.

"Don't dribble on it," Emily murmured.

Thomas was also peering at the ghastly vision in the picture, looking more puzzled than horrified. "I don't get it," he said finally. "What's the joke?"

Robbie sighed. "It's not a joke, moron."

Thomas flared up at once. "Who are you calling a moron? You need to—"

"It's Jolie," Fenton said, silencing them both. The red glow had gone from his eyes now, and he wiped his chin with one hand while holding the photograph in the other. "I swear she was right there when this was taken—I remember it clearly last night. This isn't a joke or a prank—it can't be."

He looked up and stared first at Robbie, then at Hal.

"Tell me Jolie doesn't really look like this."

Hal shrugged. "Apparently she does."

"Photos don't lie," Robbie added.

"Sure they do," Fenton murmured. "But . . ."

Emily coughed a couple of times and winced. "All right," she croaked, "*now* can we go see Miss Simone?"

"But Jolie's there at her house," Dewey pointed out.

"Well, she's no match for us," Robbie said, lifting his chin defiantly. "Let's march in there and . . . and . . ."

—*In the shadows of a west-facing cave entrance, illuminated by a shaft of brilliant afternoon sunlight, the enormous bird shuffled wearily onto a complex mass of sticks that snapped and splintered under the weight of—*

Hal blinked and shook his head. The odd flash in his head dissipated like a dream. When he looked around at his friends, he saw that they, too, were blinking, frowns plastered across their faces. Robbie had trailed off, confused, and now stood lost for words. Even the villagers in the street had paused.

Fenton cleared his throat. "Was that—did anyone else—?"

"A vision!" Dewey exclaimed. "That was a vision! Sent by the phoenix!"

A shiver stole through Hal's bones. So it had started.

"Look, there's Lauren," Robbie said, pointing.

It wasn't just Lauren but Darcy as well—the two girls had broken into a trot and were weaving past villagers. "Did you *see* that?" Darcy yelled, making an old woman jump.

The reunion was noisy at first until the girls noticed how ill Emily had become. When she started coughing, Lauren gripped her tightly and looked around for somewhere to sit. "I'm okay," Emily said hoarsely. "But can we *please* go see Miss Simone now?"

"What about?" Darcy demanded.

Once more the photograph was produced, and this time the reaction was in the form of screams that made Hal's ears hurt.

It was several more minutes before they were all ready to confront Miss Simone and Jolie. Then they headed out of the village and onto the familiar woodland trail, a strange sense of determination settling over them all. Hal could feel it, as though all their petty differences had been set aside in order to stand together against a common enemy— which was exactly the case. They couldn't have been more unified if they were marching into the labyrinth to face the emperor dragon.

"Emily thinks Jolie's done something to Abigail," Hal said, breaking the silence as they walked.

Their pace quickened.

Hal could sense anger building. They'd all been taken in by the so-called charms of a hideous creature posing as a friendly, beautiful young woman.

"Miss Simone said they were sirens," Emily said. "She said they used to lure ships onto rocks—probably swam around in the sea or sat on rocks looking all pretty and combing their hair."

"How does it work?" Fenton asked. "I mean . . . do they have to make an effort to look gorgeous, or what?"

Robbie shook his head. "Surely not. They couldn't keep it up every minute of the day just on the off chance someone was spying on them. It must be sort of like a built-in automatic feature. All the miengu have it; we see the females as kind of pretty in a sinister kind of way, and the girls see the males as handsome. They're all enchanted, even with their creepy black eyes and pointed ears."

"Plus," Hal reasoned, "this enchantment thing must work even as a baby or else Miss Simone would have seen the newborn Jolie as a hideous monster."

"Funny how Jolie's magic works even while she's in human form," Robbie said thoughtfully. "Most of the miengu have two faces—the one we see, and the hidden face we *never* see. But Jolie's a shapeshifter so has *four* faces. That's messed up. And even then we all see her differently!"

"No wonder they became reclusive," Emily said, nodding. "They've been coming across to our world and luring ships onto rocks throughout history, but had to stop showing their faces in modern times in case people like Robbie took photographs of them from deck. If the secret got out that they were all hideously ugly and evil, there was no way they'd be able to lure anyone anywhere. They had to give up their favorite pastime."

Miss Simone's cottage came into view.

"Do we each see the exact same face?" Thomas wanted to know. He looked thoroughly miserable, as if someone had stolen something valuable from him. "Or do we see a different face and just *assume* it's the same for us all?"

"I can't speak for anyone else," Emily said grimly, "but I always saw her as a hard-faced, thin-lipped person with unfriendly eyes."

"That's because you were upset by the executions," Hal said.

Fenton gave Hal a shove. "And when Jolie popped out of the lake, Abigail took one look at Hal's slack jaw and immediately felt jealous and inferior. So she saw Jolie as an ugly old bat."

Hal was so struck by this notion that they arrived at the front door before he knew it. There was a moment when they all paused, silent, on the doorstep.

"What about the rest of you?" he whispered. "How do you see Jolie?"

Darcy and Lauren shrugged at the same time. "Ordinary," Darcy said.

"Stunning," Fenton said with a sigh, to which Thomas and Dewey muttered their agreement. "What about you, short pants?"

"Not a patch on Abigail," Hal said fiercely.

Then Emily burst into the cottage.

As they all filed in after her and spread out, the first thing they saw was Jolie sitting on the sofa with her crutches perched against the cushions. She was staring right at them, suspicion written across her face.

"Hello," she said.

For a moment nobody said anything. Jolie looked exactly the same as always—pale yet flawless skin, perfect white teeth, shiny black hair that was never properly brushed but nevertheless appealing in its natural untidiness . . . and she looked harmless, even vulnerable with her limp legs at funny angles and her feet twisted inward slightly. She was the picture of innocent beauty and Hal—even knowing what he knew, with the photograph clutched between his finger and thumb and held behind his back—felt *just for a second* that maybe they were all wrong about her, that there was a simple explanation for all this, that she was just badly misunderstood, and none of this was her fault.

Heck, she couldn't help what she was. Maybe she didn't even *know* exactly what she was. There was a thought! What if her heart was in the right place and any mischief she'd caused had been accidental?

The silence told Hal that many of his friends were having similar thoughts. But then Emily coughed, and the reminder of her illness broke the spell.

Fenton pushed past Emily and stood before Jolie, glaring at her. "Where's Miss Simone?" he demanded.

Jolie stared at him, now managing to look hurt. "Asleep." She jerked a thumb over her shoulder. "Door on the left."

Fenton marched past the sofa and headed through the dining area to the short open-ended hallway at the back end of the cottage. It was shrouded in darkness. The rest of the group hurried to catch up, while Hal stayed and wagged a finger at Jolie. "Stay there," he growled.

She grinned, and suddenly Hal felt uneasy. He paused, staring at her. Her grin faded, but she held his gaze.

Over her shoulder, in the short hallway at the rear, Fenton had come to two bedroom doors. He faced the one on the left and knocked sharply. "Miss Simone?"

Hal glanced again at Jolie. "She'd better be all right in there."

"Why wouldn't she be?" Jolie said, spreading her hands. "I told you, she's sleeping. Door on the left."

Something nagged at Hal. Something important.

"Miss Simone?" Fenton called loudly.

A muffled voice came to them. "What's—who's there?"

"We need to talk to you," Fenton said. "I'm coming in."

Without waiting for a response, he turned the doorknob, pushed the door open, and plunged into darkness. Everyone else waited dutifully outside the room, shuffling their feet and looking from one to another.

Hal remained frozen before the sofa, his mind whirling. Jolie was still staring at him. Something was wrong but he couldn't—

Then there came an exclamation, a shriek of what might be mistaken for indignation at being woken unexpectedly, but was really shock, perhaps even fright. Fenton's voice came back: "What—no! NO!"

Then he gave a strangled cry.

A memory flashed into Hal's mind: Jolie peering sleepily out of the window after Abigail had rudely woken her—the window of the spare room that Jolie and Molly shared on the *left* side of the house.

The room that Fenton had just entered.

As Hal opened his mouth to shout a warning, Molly's panicked voice came from the room. "Fenton, what are you *doing* in here?"

Hal's friends in the hallway began to surge through the bedroom door, but Molly screamed at them from within. "No! Stay out! Everyone *stay out!*"

Hal knew what had happened, and it was confirmed when the door to the right-hand bedroom opened suddenly and Miss Simone stood there, disheveled and panic-stricken. She saw at once that the neighboring bedroom door was open, that the children were trying to peer into the darkness, and she flung herself forward and blocked the way, her back to the room.

She slammed the door shut and glared at them all. "What are you *doing*? You should never burst in on Molly when she's napping. She prefers not to wear her veil when she's asleep, and you could easily—" Slowly, her eyes widened and her hands crept up to her mouth. "Wh-where's Fenton?" she whispered.

With mounting horror, Hal turned his attention to Jolie. She appeared to be in a trance. He strode over to her, leaned down, and shook her roughly by the shoulders. Her eyes snapped open.

"What have you done?" he yelled.

"Me?" Jolie said, her eyes wide. "I didn't do anything."

"You said Miss Simone was in the room on the left," Hal growled, his fingers digging into her flesh. He felt angry enough to slap her across the face.

"She is," Jolie said. Then she glanced over her shoulder to where Miss Simone crowded the hallway with the wide-eyed children. "Well, I meant *my* left. Hang on—Fenton didn't go into *Molly's* room, did he?"

At that point, everyone began to squabble and shout, and both Robbie and Darcy made a lunge for Molly's door, only to be pushed roughly back by an angry Miss Simone. She stood there, barring the way, her hair bunched up at the back and her simple dress crinkled, her feet bare. She looked like a wild woman.

"Everyone shut up!" she yelled.

Voices died, and silence fell. Only then did they hear sobbing.

Miss Simone held up her hand, clearly telling everyone to stay put. Then she tapped softly on the door. "Molly?"

After a brief pause, Molly replied tearfully, "It's safe now."

Miss Simone eased the door open and peered in. Even from where he stood in the living room, Hal could see the faint orange glow of a lamp around the doorframe. "Oh, Molly," Miss Simone said plaintively.

She pushed the door wide open, and Hal at last found his feet. He hurried to join his friends, cramming with them through the doorway into the spare room. There was just one small bed by the window and Molly was sitting up in it, trembling, her hands to her veiled face.

Leaning over her, one hand outstretched, was Fenton—utterly still and lifeless, frozen in place, his face, body, and clothing the pale gray color of stone.

"He woke me," Molly whispered. "I didn't have my veil on."

Nobody said a word for what seemed like a lifetime. Then Darcy burst into tears and began to wail. Lauren quickly joined in, and then Emily, and then Dewey, and at that point Hal began to lose it, too. As a sobbing Darcy tentatively patted and touched the statue, Hal did the opposite and backed away. He bumped into Robbie and turned to find his friend standing almost as still as Fenton, his mouth open. Then Hal blundered from the room, the corners of his vision curiously foggy and a terrible rage building in his chest.

Before he knew it, he was leaning over Jolie on the sofa, shouting and screaming at her as she pressed herself back into the cushions and turned her head away. The word *"murderer!"* spilled out of his mouth numerous times, and it was only when he felt hands gripping his arms and pulling him back that he realized he'd slapped Jolie hard across the face—suddenly she was holding her cheek and cowering, and Hal's palm stung.

It was Miss Simone that was yanking him away, and she was surprisingly strong. His friends were all there around the sofa, yelling at him to hit her again, egging him on, and Emily was in her naga form rearing up over the back of the sofa and looking like she was about to sink her fangs into Jolie's neck.

"Enough!" Miss Simone yelled, and a powerful force swept across the room, knocking lanterns over, sending a sheaf of pages fluttering, and shattering several windows. It was in that brief moment of shock that the spell of fury was broken, and everyone paused, breathing hard.

Miss Simone's fingers were digging painfully into Hal's arms, but he knew better than to try and squirm free; she'd only dig deeper.

"Everyone *calm down*," Miss Simone commanded. "Hal, is it safe to release you yet?"

Hal nodded, and she slowly released him.

Jolie straightened up and nursed her cheek with a frown. She said nothing but eyed Hal cautiously, ready to flinch if he came at her again.

Hal should have felt awful for hitting her, for hitting a *girl* . . . but she was no such thing. "You're lucky I didn't burn you alive," he said shakily.

"You're off your head," Jolie murmured. "A lunatic."

"You killed Fenton!" Emily screamed from behind her. She lunged forward over the back of the sofa, a writhing mass of scaly coils as she grabbed Jolie's hair. Pandemonium reigned again, but this time Hal watched silently, strangely detached as if watching a vicious tornado tear the room apart while he stood within an indestructible glass box. He watched as Miss Simone raced around the sofa and fought with Emily to release Jolie's hair, while Darcy and Lauren reached in to pull Miss Simone away. Robbie, Thomas and Dewey made a lot of noise but otherwise stood clear, the eager spectators of a screaming catfight.

It went on like this for a full minute, and all the while Jolie squirmed and fought from the sofa, her face a mask of determination. She didn't appear to be scared, and it struck Hal that she'd been *expecting* this backlash, an inevitable consequence of her actions. Her eyes gleamed with excitement.

It was Molly that put an end to it. She drifted slowly into Hal's view from the rear bedrooms, and when she rounded the squabbling group and stood in front of the sofa, looking down at Jolie, the noise died and Emily finally quit yanking Jolie's hair.

"You sent Fenton into my room," Molly said quietly. "When I'm sleeping alone in a room, Jolie, I don't wear my veil. You *knew* that, and yet you sent him in anyway. Why?"

Jolie shrugged and began to smooth her hair, leaning forward in case Emily jumped on her again. She glared at the naga before turning back to Molly. "It was a mistake. I said Simone was in the left-hand room, but I meant the right."

She fumbled for her crutches, which had fallen to the floor in the scuffle. Everyone watched in silence as she struggled to rise up off the sofa. Once she was standing, with most of her weight on the crutches, she awkwardly turned herself around to face Miss Simone and the crowd behind the sofa.

"So Fenton's a statue?" she asked.

There were several intakes of breath, and Emily rose higher on her slender reptilian body, baring her fangs.

Jolie seemed unable to know when to stop. "Didn't you guys think Fenton was a gargoyle the first time you saw him stuck to the side of the lighthouse, with water pouring out of his mouth? I remember the story clearly. Well, now he's made of stone, just like a gargoyle. I think it's quite poetic, really." She smiled at Dewey. "You should write a poem about it, sweetie. Don't read it out loud, though, unless you want to be laughed at some more."

Mouths dropped open as she spoke. Hal could hardly believe his ears. He knew she was crazy, a really nasty piece of work under that perfect face—he understood that. But standing there insulting them, deliberately provoking them when they were about ready to rip her to shreds, was plain nuts.

And that scared Hal.

She nodded slowly. "Well, I planned to leave in the next few hours, anyway. I figured I'd have to, with this phoenix thing happening at sunset. Without magic, my enchantment will be gone. You'll all see my *real* face, and believe me when I tell you it's not pretty."

"We know," Robbie said, holding up the photograph.

Jolie glared at him. "Well, then I guess I'll just go ahead and pack my bags and be on my way."

"You don't have any bags," Molly growled.

She suddenly grabbed Jolie's arm in a vice-like grip just above the elbow, and a crutch nearly fell to the floor. Jolie struggled but was unable to pull herself free. In the end she rolled her eyes and waited.

"When the phoenix rises and magic dies," Molly continued, "it's said that I'll lose my ability to turn living flesh to stone. I'm happy about that. I *hate* my ability. I've been killing all my life, including your own people in the lake, and I'm sick of it. But you, Jolie . . . I've a good mind to turn *you* to stone right now for doing that to poor Fenton."

With her other hand she reached for her veil, slowly and deliberately, as Hal and his friends automatically recoiled and half covered their eyes.

Jolie tilted her head. "Go ahead, Molly. But know this: if you turn me to stone, you'll never find Abigail."

Once more, a silence descended in the living room as everyone stared hard at Jolie's smug expression.

Miss Simone was the first to speak. "Let her go, Molly."

When Molly finally released her grip, Jolie tossed her hair back over her forehead and grinned. "Wise move."

"What have you done with Abigail?" Hal asked, finally finding his voice. He had many questions tumbling around in his mind but this was the biggest.

"She's at the lake," Jolie said, turning to face him. "You'll never find her on your own, though. There are hundreds of caves and tunnels in and around the lake. Feel free to send an army of goblins and shapeshifters to search the place—but the minute you arrive, Abigail will be . . ."

She rolled her eyes and stuck out her tongue to mimic the expression of a dead person. Hal was fairly sure that if she'd had a hand free, she would have run a finger across her throat as well, perhaps even mimed the placement of a noose around her neck as if she were being hanged.

"Executed," she added matter-of-factly.

"Why are you *doing* this?" Lauren burst out, tears running down her cheeks. Robbie immediately reached for her but stopped short of actually placing his hands on her shoulders. "Why are you so—so *nasty?*"

"Is this some kind of revenge?" Thomas asked. "Because I can sort of understand that. You were abandoned at a young age, and so was I. All I wanted to do was hurt people, especially Miss Simone, but after a while I realized—"

"Oh, shut *up*," Jolie snapped.

Thomas froze, his face reddening.

Jolie shook her head. "You people know nothing about the miengu, and you never will. Now, take me home, and I'll give you back Abigail."

Just like that, Hal thought, amazed, as a babble of voices started up. *She seriously thinks it's that simple? She can just walk free after murdering Fenton?*

As if reading his mind, Miss Simone spoke above the noise. "Jolie, what can we do to fix this situation? What have we done to upset you?" Incredibly, she sounded pleading, desperate. "If you're mad at me for sending you to the lake all those years ago, then be mad at *me*, not everyone else. Or if this is something bigger than that, then explain it to me. Help me understand."

Jolie fidgeted on her crutches. "Why bother?"

"Because there's no need for animosity between you and I, or between your people and mine. Whatever's happening here, I'm sure we can work it out."

"Are you seriously *negotiating* with her?" Emily blurted, outraged. "Miss Simone, she made me sick!"

"What are you talking about?" Miss Simone said, sounding almost annoyed. "Please be quiet, Emily. I know you're upset—we all are—but there are much bigger things at stake here." She stepped forward and held out her hands toward Jolie. "We need you, Jolie. Your people can offer so much to the world. You can heal the sick, and that ability outweighs everything that's happened over the last couple of days. Help us understand—"

"She healed Shelby but gave the sickness to Emily," Hal said.

Miss Simone snapped her head around. "Hal, pipe down while I—" Then she stopped and blinked rapidly. "What?"

It was Lauren's turn to jump in, as Emily had started coughing again. "It's exactly as Hal just said. Look at her, Miss Simone—Emily's not faking it."

Emily shifted back to her human form, slowly and sporadically, and stood there gasping and leaning on the back of the sofa. "I can't keep changing over and over," she said in a trembling voice. "It's wearing me down. But if I don't, then the sickness makes it hard to breathe."

Miss Simone was by her side in an instant, gripping her by the shoulders and staring into her eyes. "Oh, Emily—why didn't you *say* something? If you have what Shelby has—" Horror filled her face, and she turned back to Jolie. "Is this true? Have you passed on Shelby's sickness to Emily?"

Jolie shrugged. "What, you think all that nastiness just vanishes into thin air? No, it has to go somewhere. That's why I asked Emily to stand nearby when I healed the Shelby woman." She smiled, and Hal resisted the urge to punch her as she continued smugly. "It worked, you know; I really did heal Shelby. But Emily has it now, and I have to admit I was curious to see if repeated shapeshifting would get rid of it. But apparently not. So, probably the only way to get rid of the sickness is . . ."

She stared at the ceiling for a moment, putting on an expression of deep thought. Then she beamed.

"Oh! Yes, the only way to get rid of Emily's sickness is if I take it out of her and give it to someone else. Maybe a volunteer, like an old person? Or maybe one of the other patients in your lab, Simone. Yes, there's an idea: give a terminal illness to someone who already *has* a terminal illness. Then that person will just die twice over, and everyone will be happy."

Molly lunged at her with a screech, and both she and Jolie went down in a tangle of limbs. As they tossed and rolled, all Hal could think about was the veil coming loose and half the people in the room turning into statues. He threw himself onto them at the same time as Miss Simone, and together they dragged the raging gorgon away, thankful that her veil was still in place.

For once, even Jolie looked flustered. She sat up and glared at Molly, then looked around for her crutches, which had been flung several feet beyond her reach. The chances of anyone fetching them for her were extremely remote.

Jolie gave an impatient sigh. "All right, I've had enough of all this."

She climbed nimbly to her feet and stood there unaided, bending to brush herself down while everyone gaped. Then she strode toward the door, wrenched it open, and stood waiting.

"Well, come on, then! Take me home."

Chapter Twenty-One
Return to the Lake

Despite Jolie's sudden wish to "leave this dump immediately," there were a few matters to be discussed first. A squad of goblins manacled her to a fence well away from the cottage and left her there to scream obscenities while a conference was held around Miss Simone's small dining room table. The transformation in Jolie's attitude and demeanor was startling; she was the same disheveled beauty, but her friendly smiles and wide-eyed innocence had been replaced with scowls and a shockingly spiteful tongue.

"So now we know," Miss Simone said with a curt nod.

"She's uglier than I am," Molly grumbled.

In the center of the table was Robbie's creepy photograph, which Molly had finally turned face down.

Emily, back in her human form, slumped in the third chair trying to suppress her coughing, while Lauren sat in the fourth fighting back tears. Hal, Robbie, Dewey and Thomas loitered nearby, occasionally glancing at the closed door to the spare bedroom, behind which stood a frozen Fenton. Darcy was busy sobbing on the sofa.

"It's not about how ugly she is," Miss Simone said carefully, as if wrestling with an internal guilt. "It's about the deception and how she's acted. But now we know her true face behind the enchantment—and her ugliness isn't just skin deep. She's rotten to the core."

"And I can only assume they're *all* like this," Molly said, tapping the back of the photograph. "Or something like this, anyway. Heck, maybe she's even uglier in her jengu form."

Miss Simone climbed wearily to her feet. "Let's take her home."

They all trudged outside and walked down the lane to where fifteen goblins waited in a circle around the treacherous jengu shapeshifter. Jolie was sullen now, sitting on the ground with her manacled arm elevated above her head. She rolled her eyes and got to her feet as the group approached.

"Are we off at last?" Jolie said, scowling.

"Yes," Miss Simone said stiffly. "To say I'm disappointed in you is an understatement. These goblins will escort you to the lake. Molly and a few of the children will accompany you."

"I don't want her coming," Jolie said firmly.

"Too bad, young lady," Molly snapped, taking a step toward her.

Miss Simone restrained her friend and spoke calmly. "You have no choice in this, Jolie. By your own admission, you have Abigail prisoner somewhere in or around the lake. You'll show Molly where she is and release her unharmed. But before we leave here, you'll cure Emily of her sickness."

Jolie burst out laughing. "Really?" she said after a moment. "Just like that? And who's going to accept the sickness in her place?"

"I don't care," Miss Simone growled, "as long as it's none of my people."

"You know," Jolie said, now sounding serious, "the right thing to do would be to give the sickness back to Shelby. After all, it's her disease, right?"

Hal could see that Molly was trembling with rage and wished Jolie would quit provoking her. If Molly lost her temper and whipped away that veil, then all hope of finding Abigail would be dashed.

Miss Simone shook her head firmly. "That's not going to happen. You took the disease out of her. If you can't make it simply disappear— if it really has to be transferred—then how about a wild animal? A pig, or a bird? How about a fish? For that matter, what about a mosquito? Or are there *rules* to abide by, some *reason* you can't transfer the disease into a bug?"

Her voice was dripping with sarcasm by now, and Jolie raised an eyebrow. "You really have no idea about the miengu. Yes, there are rules to how this works, but you wouldn't understand. I'll say only that a bug is out of the question and a fish is highly unlikely, as is a bird unless it's a very large one. A pig might work."

"Then a pig it is," Miss Simone said, nodding. She turned to a goblin. "Please go fetch a—"

"But not here," Jolie interrupted. She peered around the group carefully. "I can't work that kind of magic under duress. It takes a lot of concentration, and I need to be relaxed. I'm not relaxed right now."

"You'd rather string us along?" Molly suggested mockingly. "Keep us waiting until after sunset, and then announce that your magic no longer works?" Her voice hardened. "I don't think so. You fix Emily here and now—and then we'll go fetch Abigail. Once Abigail has been delivered to us *unharmed*, then we'll set you free."

Jolie shook her head ruefully. "No way. It takes me hours to recover from a healing, and if I do it now, then I'll not be fit to travel."

"You can sleep it off on the way to the lake," Hal said.

But Jolie was adamant. "I want all my faculties about me when I release Abigail to you so we can part ways on good terms and without bloodshed." She smiled at Hal. "You think I'm stupid? I'm dead the moment I hand Abigail over to you all. You'll burn me alive."

"I won't," Hal said truthfully.

She turned to Molly. "Then you'll stone me. It's a tenuous situation—"

"And whose fault is *that?*" Molly yelled.

"You're not exactly innocent in all this, Miss Evil-Eye," Jolie griped.

"Why, you little—"

Miss Simone raised her hands for silence. "Enough. Time is wasting. Molly, can I trust you to escort this monster back to the lake without glaring at her?"

"And what about afterward?" Jolie asked.

Miss Simone sighed. "What do you mean?"

"Afterward. After I return Abigail to you. After I cure Emily. What then?" Jolie looked around shiftily. "Even if you release me . . . what's to stop you from coming back later?"

"What if we gave you our word?" Miss Simone said tightly.

Jolie burst out laughing again, and kept on laughing for quite a while, exclaiming "Your *word!*" over and over as if it were the funniest thing she'd ever heard. An awful lot of furious people were itching to pounce on her, so she was either very brave or very reckless. Meanwhile, Hal thought it was rather clever the way Miss Simone had phrased her question, making Jolie think she'd made a promise without actually doing so.

Finally, Jolie wiped her eyes. "Oh, dear. Sorry. Well, if you give me your *word*, then of course I trust you completely." Then she looked thoughtful. "Funny thing is, I actually believe you. I didn't kill your friend, but you obviously blame me. You'd really let me off the hook just like that?" She looked at Hal again. "*You* were angry enough to kill me back there in the house and probably would have if you'd been allowed. You'd honestly just let me go?"

She looked so amazed that Hal immediately began to doubt himself. No, of *course* he couldn't just let her go. None of them could. She needed to be punished. And yet the awful truth was that Jolie was right: she *hadn't* killed Fenton. Molly had. In fact, one might argue that Jolie had played a very small, decidedly negligible and random role in the incident, a mere slip of the tongue with disastrous consequences. Was it enough to attribute blame to Jolie?

The hard facts said *no*, but the overall gut feeling was a resounding *yes*. Still, the first priority was to get Abigail back and cure Emily.

"Fine," Jolie said, throwing up her hands. "Let's get going, then. Take me home, and I'll release Abigail and cure Emily for you. Don't worry about the pig. There's a better option—one of our own people. I guess we won't have the pleasure of Molly's murderous glance for executions in future, especially after sunset tonight, so we'll have to find other ways to punish those who break our laws. A good dose of terminal illness is slower but will work just as well."

Hal shuddered. How had this monster come into their lives?

The party set off on the back of the same cart Hal and the others had ridden previously, drawn by the same two sturdy horses. The goblins watched them go, anger written across their faces.

"Now *those* guys are ugly," Jolie muttered.

She was sitting alone on one side of the cart, still in chains. Hal sat with Robbie on the opposite side, watching her closely. Molly was in the driver's seat, flicking the reins and yelling at the horses. Against Molly's advice, Emily rode ahead on Dewey's centaur back, her head lolling. She had told them all flat out that she couldn't stand to be around the jengu anymore.

It was getting late and the sun would be setting in the next hour or so. Molly urged the horses on, faster and faster. It had quickly become apparent that even galloping unicorns wouldn't have been fast enough for her right now.

Then, halfway to the river, they received another sign from the phoenix, a vision that stopped even the horses in their tracks.

—*The phoenix closed its eyes and released a heavy sigh that signified its end was nigh. Slowly, its massive wings began to rise and spread until they spanned the width of the cave. Sensing the danger, rodents scurried away and bats flapped chaotically to escape the approaching inferno—*

Molly flicked the reins with frustration and got the horses moving again. "Did you get that?" she called over her shoulder. She pointed to the western horizon, where the sun was beginning its descent, and spoke through gritted teeth. "The sun is going down. We're never going to make it at this rate. The rebirth is about to start. Even assuming it takes a while, we have to get in, get Abigail, and heal Emily!"

"Let's just fly," Hal said, feeling just as anxious.

Molly shook her head. "I've got news for you, Hal: you're the only one with wings. Unless you can carry us all?"

"Not a chance," Hal said. "I could carry two at most."

Molly clicked her tongue. "What good is *that?*" She sighed. "Where's Orson when he's needed?"

Hal thought of the winged horse shapeshifter. As far as he knew, Orson was away visiting others of his kind.

"And I can't let you go off with Jolie on your own," Molly complained, "so let's forget the idea and just *pick up the pace.*" She screamed these last words at the horses so loudly that even Dewey, some distance ahead, picked up speed.

After a few more minutes glancing at the sun, Molly reached a decision. "Okay, Hal, you're right. How about you take Jolie and Robbie on your back. Robbie can sit behind her to make sure she doesn't try anything. Fly as fast as you can to the lake and rescue Abigail."

Hal nodded, a sense of relief flooding over him.

"Meanwhile," Molly said, "Dewey can continue on with Emily, and I'll not be too far behind. We'll catch up with you at the lake. Rescue Abigail—and by that time we'll have caught up."

She had no choice but to halt the horses so that Hal could climb out and transform. He stomped around in an impatient circle as Jolie, her wrists still in manacles, struggled down from the cart with no help whatsoever from Robbie. Jolie climbed onto Hal's back, looking a little too pleased for his liking. "I get to ride the dragon again!" she exclaimed. "Come on, Robbie."

Molly threw Robbie the key to Jolie's padlock, and he slipped it into his pocket before climbing aboard.

"Hold on tight, Robbie," Jolie said sweetly. "Put your arms around my waist. Go ahead, I won't bite."

Hal didn't hear Robbie's comment, but he imagined his friend had mixed feelings about this. Even now, Hal had to admit that Jolie looked amazing, as disheveled as she was and despite knowing that her real face was nothing like the illusion. He'd half expected, and half hoped, that her enchantment would fade now that he knew her secret; he'd imagined that he would start seeing her the way Abigail and Emily did, as an ugly old hag. But apparently not. His glamorous vision of her was permanently fixed in his mind.

He launched into the sky and quickly caught up with Dewey, who was galloping fast along the road. Emily clung wearily to his back, seemingly asleep. Molly had already kicked the horses back into action and the cart, now much lighter, was tearing along at a breakneck pace.

Something was pressing against Hal's throat, and it took him a while to figure out what it was. Finally, he realized it was the small geo-rock, still wrapped in his smart clothes even though the material had reformed into reins. As Jolie gripped these reins, the material pulled tight against the rock. It wasn't too bad, just an odd feeling, and he could feel its pleasant warmth even through his tough scales. In a short while, it would be cold and dead like any other rock.

The flight to the river was short, and he soon began his descent. He was aware that Jolie had been jabbering away non-stop, but he'd successfully tuned her out until now. By the sounds of it, Robbie was ignoring her, too.

"You guys have been a blast," Jolie was saying. "Honestly, despite everything, I've had fun. A pity about Fenton, but never mind. I do hope Simone won't do what my people are probably doing right now— smashing all Molly's victims into tiny pieces."

Hal was immediately curious about this. Unfortunately, Robbie didn't press her on the matter.

He eyed the trees hanging over the river and stayed airborne. Dewey and Emily weren't too far behind, but Molly and her cart were nowhere to be seen.

Hal growled to himself. There wasn't time to wait around, but if he flew off to rescue Abigail without Emily in tow, he'd end up searching for the sick naga later—and if time ran out . . .

So he waited. Dewey arrived at last, bursting through bushes and teetering on the grassy bank as Emily cautiously slipped off and staggered into the water. Once she was waist-deep, she transformed— sluggishly—and began to move downstream toward the distant lake. She gave a feeble flick of her tail to Dewey, who attempted to trot alongside the bank for a while before being thwarted by dense vegetation.

Hal kept an eye on Emily's murky shape and flew in circles above the trees. "Go, girl," he growled softly as her serpentine form shot through the water. She was a tough one, he thought proudly. He'd never particularly gotten along with Emily in the past; to him she'd always seemed a little superficial and silly . . . but she'd certainly shown her mettle over the last few days.

The lake came into view ahead. The sun was sinking, and the phoenix was probably about to go up in smoke. As Hal swooped around, he wondered exactly how long it would be until the rebirth. And what would happen if it were true that certain winged creatures flew only with the help of magic? Was he, a dragon, one of those creatures? If so, he'd end up flapping his wings madly but spinning into the water. On the other hand, he was able to fly perfectly well in his old non-magic world, which suggested that the magic that helped him fly was *within* him and not *around* him . . .

"We need to get this over with," he snapped, suddenly impatient.

"What's that?" Jolie said. "Robbie, did you understand what Hal said just then? All I heard was a load of mumbo jumbo."

Hal dove toward where Emily was emerging from the river mouth and into the lake. He performed a skid on the surface of the water and then began to sink. Jolie screamed something about not being able to swim with manacles on, but Hal felt no concern whatsoever. She could breathe just fine underwater. He was more concerned about Robbie and made sure to stay afloat for his passengers while he eased through the water toward Emily.

Even for a naga, she looked pale and haggard. She had no arms in her watery form, and her thick snake body was somewhat flattened along the sides, rather like a fish, allowing for more efficient swimming as she undulated from side to side. "I'm here," she gasped. "Wait, I need to change."

She shifted forms several times, gradually shaking off the illness. After nine or ten transformations, she grinned as a little color returned to her face. "That'll keep me going for a bit longer. Shall we?"

Her meaning was clear by the way she inclined her head and glanced into the water. She was ready to head down to rescue Abigail. Hal was, too.

"Maybe we should wait for Molly," Robbie warned from his perch on Hal's broad back. "We need her glare. I know she said to go on ahead, but what if there are loads of miengu down there? I mean, I'm not scared or anything, just being realistic, you know?"

"Yeah, but—" Hal started to say in deep rumbling tones.

Then another vision slammed into his head.

—Tiny wisps of smoke began to curl from the great bird's torso. The heat emanating from the cave was already intense, and soon the pyre of dry sticks began to catch alight. The flames crackled and spread, and the phoenix gave a tremendous shiver of anticipation—

"We can't wait," Emily said quietly. "I have to be cured right now, which means we need to go get Abigail."

"She's right," Jolie said, frowning. "We might have our differences, but I don't really want everything to go wrong with Hal stuck in his dragon form. So let's just get this over with. Abigail's not far from here, and we don't even need to dive. See those rocky hills on the other side of the lake? Head for those."

Dewey arrived on the grassy bank, his face red. "Stay put!" Robbie shouted. "Tell Molly we're heading for those hills over there."

Emily plunged below the surface and set off. Hal swung himself around and splashed through the water after her, staying afloat for his passengers.

"If you try anything—" Robbie warned. From the corner of his eye, he saw Robbie holding up an unusually large, hairy fist in front of Jolie's face.

Hal followed Emily across the lake using his tail to propel him. The rocky hills were deceptively far away. By the time they got there, the deep orange sun was sinking behind the distant mountains, and the sky had taken on a distinctly dusky hue. Panic tore through Hal. The phoenix had suggested all along that the deadline was sunset, yet the rebirth had already started. What if it all happened earlier than expected? 'Sunset' was so *vague*.

Jolie suggested they ignore the low rocks and sandy shores and instead guided them around to a towering wall of rock that leaned outward over the lake. Hal hurriedly dumped his passengers and reverted to his human form, suddenly feeling vulnerable as he paddled to stay afloat. "Where is she?" he gasped. He searched for a handhold on the sheer rock face but found none. "Where's Abigail? We need to hurry!"

Jolie seemed relaxed despite her manacled wrists. Her eyes seemed to have dimmed, becoming almost but not completely black. Her skin was glowing, and a smooth sheen of barely perceptible scales glistened on her shoulders and face. "Take these chains off me," she ordered calmly.

Hal, Robbie and Emily stared at her as they all bobbed gently in the cold water. In the end, Hal nodded to Robbie. "Go ahead."

Floundering awkwardly, Robbie fished in his pocket for the key. As he did so, Hal glanced across the lake. No sign of Molly yet, but Dewey was just about visible among the background of trees, pacing back and forth.

The rattling of Robbie's key in the lock brought his attention back to Jolie. The manacles slipped off and fell with a plop into the water, and she grinned.

"Don't get any funny ideas," Robbie snarled, again holding up his fist. It was abnormally large, even bigger than before, and his wrist and forearm was twice the thickness of his upper arm. He looked like Popeye the Sailor from an old comic collection that Hal's dad had stashed away in their house on the island. All that was missing was an anchor tattoo.

"Relax," Jolie said. "Seriously. I'm with you guys on this one. I've had my fun, and now I want to go home safely to my betrothed. I can't do that unless we part on good terms. So I need you to follow me. There's a cave entrance just below the surface here. Hang on while I take this off."

Awkwardly, trying to stay afloat, she struggled to remove her raggedy dress. Hal's eyes widened and his heart began to thump—but then he caught a glimpse of shiny fabric and remembered that she wore smart clothes underneath. She grinned at him and flipped over backwards, switching into her full jengu form as she did so. Her fishtail was long and glistening.

She rose to the surface again, her eyes now completely black. "You should make it all right," she said, for once sounding genuinely interested in their welfare. "There's a short tunnel, but it's not very long. Take a deep breath, and you'll manage just fine. Swim hard and fast, and you'll pop out into an underground cavern deep inside this hill of rock."

Before anyone could protest, she ducked her head under and disappeared. A split second later, her tail fin came up and splashed them all. Then she was gone, leaving behind a smattering of bubbles on the surface.

Hal and Robbie stared doubtfully at each other, but Emily wasted no time. "I'll check it out," she said, and in the next instant had submerged.

"Come on, Molly," Hal murmured, paddling around so he could peer across the lake again. "Where *is* she? If she doesn't hurry up, she'll never know where we disappeared to."

"Leave a marker," Robbie suggested. He dipped a little too low and accidentally swallowed a mouthful of lake water. When he'd finished coughing, he gestured to the cliff face. "Maybe a sign on the wall?"

"Good idea," Hal said sourly. "Pass me the paint and brush, would you?"

"Burn it," Robbie retorted. "Make a big black mark or something."

Hal had to admit that was rather smart of his friend. He grumbled his agreement and stared up at the leaning rock wall. Then he spent a moment concentrating, willing his fire-making equipment into being deep within his throat, just as he had the previous night. He had no idea how it worked but felt the change nevertheless.

He took a deep breath and let loose. Flames roared from his throat with an intensity that surprised him. He aimed upward, moving closer to the rocky face. It took several deep breaths and carefully aimed sheets of fire, but a blackness began to spread across the smooth gray rock. He managed to make a thick vertical line, then added an arrow tip to the bottom end, effectively pointing the way down into the water. Satisfied, and feeling lightheaded from the effort, he bobbed backward in the water to admire his handiwork.

Then Emily emerged. "It's fine," she said, nodding. "You can make it."

"You're sure?" Hal said. "I mean, I can change into a dragon and hold my breath for a long time, so it's not me I'm worried about—"

Emily shook her head emphatically. "You can't. It's a *really* narrow tunnel; you'd never fit. But I can help you. Just hold on to my tail, all right?"

Hal was about to ask her what was on the other side, but Emily had already disappeared again. He and Robbie prepared themselves to dive, an unspoken feeling of dread between them.

"This is nuts," Hal muttered. Then he took a deep breath and threw himself under the surface.

Before he had time to blink his eyes open, the tip of Emily's tail curled around his wrist and guided him to take a firm hold. A few seconds later, Robbie's hands were there, too, fumbling for a grip.

Then Emily was off, pulling them along.

The cave entrance was hard to spot in the murkiness of the lake, but the naga seemed to have no trouble. She shot into it, and Hal had to duck to avoid bashing his head on the rock ceiling. Then everything was utterly black, and he held on for dear life as Emily wriggled and undulated her way along the tunnel. Hal's elbows grazed against the unseen walls, and he tucked his limbs in tightly against his body, allowing himself to be pulled along. He was aware of Robbie bumping against him also, a little farther back along the tail.

Thankfully, the journey was short. Perhaps Hal could have made it on his own if he had swum hard and fast enough, using the rocky walls to pull himself through. But he was grateful for Emily's help.

They emerged in a cavern just as Jolie had promised, and Hal looked around suspiciously. He was shocked to find several figures lurking nearby, appearing to stand waist-deep in water—but they were just statues, or rather petrified miengu. There were at least six of them, eerily silent, with the reflections and shadows of rippling lake water playing across their dull gray surfaces. Now it occurred to Hal why the faces of miengu statues were so twisted and ugly: it was because their enchantment spell wasn't working.

High overhead, rays of light shone down through numerous tiny apertures in the cavern ceiling, the only source of illumination. It was enough to see by, and Hal continued to look around as he trudged up a ledge of slanting rock until he was only knee-deep. Absently, he licked a salty taste from his lips. The cavern smelled of ocean and seaweed, extremely musty. Behind him, Robbie and Emily remained in the water, shooting glances into dark corners.

Jolie waited on a clump of smooth rocks several feet above water level. She was back in human form, her smart clothes dripping as she leaned on the far wall with her arms crossed. By her feet was a small bronze box.

It took only a second for Hal to realize the importance of the box. He remembered that Abigail had been carrying it the last time he'd seen her, early that morning when she'd shown him the faerie glade. "That's Abigail's," he whispered, his eyes widening.

Jolie nodded and touched the box gently with her foot. "She's probably really bored. You can let her out, if you like. If she hasn't suffocated already."

Realizing what she meant, Hal cried out and dashed haphazardly across the uneven slippery rock, his heart hammering. He was trembling with fear by the time he reached the other side, and he fell on his knees by the box, hardly daring to open it.

Then he saw a small twig had been inserted under the lid, propping it open to allow fresh air in. A loop of fabric was tied around the middle of the box to prevent the prisoner from pushing open the lid and escaping.

"Abigail?" Hal whispered, his shaking fingers pulling the fabric off. He opened the box. Inside, his girlfriend lay curled in a ball, a tiny figure with delicate wings, motionless.

Chapter Twenty-Two
The Cavern

"Is she okay?" Robbie yelled, his voice echoing around the cavern. "Is she in there? Is she alive?"

Hal didn't answer. He reached in and gently touched Abigail's shoulder with his finger, fearing she would be cold and stiff. But she woke immediately, and relief flooded through him in waves.

She squinted and shielded her eyes. "Hal? Is that you?"

"She's okay!" Hal called over his shoulder. He was dimly aware of Robbie and Emily sighing with relief as he turned his attention back to his faerie friend.

"So touching," Jolie said softly.

Hal glanced up to see the jengu smiling with what appeared to be genuine sympathy. "Why?" he growled. "Why did you do this? What's it all for?"

Jolie placed her hands over her heart. "It's just the way we are, Hal. We live for moments like these. It's how we survive—literally. It's the essence of our life force. It's what makes us glow."

"*What* is?" Hal yelled suddenly, jumping to his feet and advancing on her.

Jolie closed her eyes and sucked in a deep breath, smiling softly. Hal failed to understand why she was so unafraid of him. He could tear her to shreds if he wanted, or burn her alive. If anything, she seemed to be having a moment of great joy as if tasting the fresh morning air.

"*That*," she said at last, opening her eyes.

Hal threw up his hands. "That *what*?"

Behind him, Robbie and Emily were clambering out of the water and splashing up onto the rocks. Then Abigail shot out of the bronze box, her tiny wings humming a high-pitched drone.

"Anxiety," Jolie said. "Anger, frustration, anything that makes the heart pound. But most of all, *fear*. The fear of small boys being chased across a field by a manticore; poor Dewey's butterflies when he read aloud his terrible poetry; your own terror, Hal, when I deliberately held on to your wings and nearly caused you to crash land near the river.

The anger of you all when Fenton was turned into a statue. Not to mention the terrified screams of sailors."

The pitch of Abigail's buzzing changed quickly, becoming low and loud. Hal felt a draft on his wet arms and, from the corner of his eye, saw that she had grown to her full human size. She touched down, and her wings fell silent.

"That's why I was a prisoner," Abigail said, slipping a hand through Hal's arm. Her fingers dug in as she spoke. "Her miengu friends got to come along every so often and mess with my head. The first one took out the wedge, closed the lid, and said goodbye. I thought I was going to die in there."

Hal tore his gaze from Jolie and turned to Abigail as she continued. There was no time for this, he told himself. Yet he found himself hanging on her every word, his jaw tightening and his fists balling.

"I tried to get out by making myself big, but the box was too strong and I nearly—" She swallowed. "I gave up screaming after a while. I just gave up altogether. I was starting to get sleepy. Then they opened the box and air flooded in. There was a group of them, peering down at me. Before I could escape, they jammed the wedge back in and tied the box shut. They'd been there all along, listening to me screaming for my life."

Jolie closed her eyes. "I can only imagine the buzz you gave my friends."

"Oh, that was just the start," Abigail said bitterly. "After that, they held the box underwater a few times and let it flood, nearly drowning me—then jabbed a knife through the gap in the lid over and over while I scrambled around trying not to get cut—"

She broke off, and Hal could feel her shaking. Once more he felt fire burning deep down inside as he remembered what Molly had said about 'private executions.' In reality, the miengu had little or no reason to torture or kill other than to make their victims' hearts pound with terror. That was why statues littered this very cavern; Molly must have been here before, invited to a 'special event' with a limited guest list. Public executions were one thing, but this was even more sordid and depraved.

Hal knew he could open his mouth, take a breath, and roast Jolie right where she stood. Or he could grow a handful of claws rather like Robbie's oversized fist and rake it several times across her face. *That* would take the stupid smile off her face!

But even as he stood there trembling with rage, he saw that he was fueling Jolie's appetite. She was *enjoying* his rage, breathing it in. He'd never felt so angry in his life, never wanted to seriously harm anyone more than he did right now . . . and she was loving every minute of it.

—*Smoke poured thick and fast off the phoenix as intense heat radiated outward, causing moisture on the cave walls to steam and pools of water to bubble and spit. Sheets of moss covering the rock slowly blackened, and then turned white and began crumbling away—*

"Cure me," Emily demanded, shaking her head as if to clear it. With her dress dripping, she stamped forward on human legs and shoved Jolie back against the wall. She bared her fangs and hissed. "Cure me *now*."

"Wow, steady on," Jolie said, her cheeks reddening. She gave a laugh. "You know I can't do this under duress, so unhand me, please. Besides, I need to go get a subject, one of the prisoners, to transfer your illness to."

"There isn't time!" Emily yelled desperately. "Do it now! Just . . . just take it out of me and give it to a fish!"

"I swear," Robbie growled, "if you leave it too late, you're gonna suffer."

"Oh, please," Jolie said, shaking her head. "You keep on threatening me with this and that, but I know you people better than you know yourselves. You wouldn't harm me, at least not deliberately. You couldn't. Nor could Fenton, bless him—he might be a big bully to you, but he's just big and cuddly to me. Or was, anyway. Now, Molly could harm me, only she's not here, is she? I'll bet Thomas could, too; he has a touch of the wild in him, I think."

"Where *is* Molly?" Hal demanded to nobody in particular. "She must have seen my marker by now."

"She's been here before," Jolie said, nodding toward the statues that peered sightlessly from the shadows. "There are places like this all over. Of course, this particular cavern is special. Come with me up that ledge and through that big hole in the ceiling—"

"Will you get on with it!" Emily screamed, lunging forward again. Hal and Robbie pulled her away, and she collapsed against them, sobbing.

"All right, all right," Jolie said with a sigh. "I guess I've milked you all dry by now. A fish will do, although it will have to be a really big one. If it's too small, then the disease will spill out and we'll *all* catch something nasty."

She peered into the water. Then she stepped down off the ledge and waded in, sinking quickly as she strode to the center of the cavern. She began to transform, her skin taking on a familiar glow and her ears growing long and pointed. When she faced them, her eyes were black.

Hal and his friends watched her suspiciously. If she tried to escape, there would be nothing he could do to stop her; in her jengu form, she was far quicker than he underwater, and he wouldn't be able to follow her into that tunnel as a dragon. Emily could, but she was sick and might easily be overcome by the jengu, who was both older and stronger.

But what could they do other than trust her?

As Jolie sank below the surface, Hal knew with certainty that she was going to escape and never come back. He broke free of Emily and dove into the water, transforming as he went. He was a full-sized dragon when he hit the deep end of the cavern, and he plunged below the surface and made a grab for the figure that was slipping away into darkness.

He brought her up and held her aloft. She wriggled like a fish, dangling by one arm, screaming with anger. "Let me go! What are you doing? Let me GO!"

Abigail was buzzing alongside in an instant, speaking for Hal as though she knew exactly what he was thinking—as well she did. "Sorry. Can't let you just slip away. There's no time for games. You cure Emily *right here and now*, or I'll ask Hal to start scorching your tail bit by bit. It won't kill you, but it'll really, *really* hurt."

"I *want* to cure Emily, I do," Jolie said, gasping as she hung limply.

"So do it," Emily ordered, stepping forward until she was knee-deep in the water. Robbie came forward with her, supporting her by the elbow. "Take the sickness out, and *then* you can go off and find a fish. Or let's all leave right now and go fishing together. But we don't have time to mess around."

Jolie winced as Hal squeezed his paw even tighter around her wrist. Her fingers were splayed open, utterly useless to her, and apparently she had discovered that struggling made it worse because she now hung perfectly still, her long fishtail dangling in the water.

"All right," she said. "I have a better idea. Up there, through the gap in the ceiling. There are lots of huge fat birds that nest up there.

Ugly critters, they are. Let's all head up to the surface together and use one of them."

Hal liked the sound of that plan. Simply being out of the water struck him as a good idea. He swung Jolie onto the rocks and watched for a moment while she floundered there, her fishtail flopping around as she struggled to turn over and sit up. Her tail morphed fluidly into long, pale legs.

"Quit staring," Abigail admonished him quietly, still buzzing close by.

Hal blushed under his scaly cheeks and gave a grunt.

Jolie led the way up the smooth, steep rocks, far too nimble and sure-footed for a first-timer. She had clearly done this before, for she chose just the right spots to place her feet and hands. *Another lie, then,* Hal thought grimly. She had probably been human many times in the past and had always been able to walk. Everything had been a game to her from the start. A game to *all* of them—Kamili and the rest of the miengu had played along, too. Why? For a taste of fear and anger?

Emily struggled up the rocks after her, Robbie close behind. Hal waited until they were out of his way before reverting to his human form and following.

Abigail buzzed alongside. "I'm guessing Jolie's been able to walk all along, right?" she said, speaking quickly as he scrambled. "She came out of nowhere that morning in the woods, right after we split and you went off home."

"Yeah, what happened exactly?" Hal asked.

She sighed. "I was stupid. She told me outright, to my face, that she was going to kidnap me. I backed off, expecting her to hit me with a crutch. Then she yelled for Thomas to stick me with his poison quills."

"*Thomas* was involved?" Hal exclaimed.

"No," Abigail said shortly. "She just said he was, and I believed her. I didn't have time to think about it; I acted on instinct and switched to faerie form. I shrank down small, thinking I'd be an impossible target."

Hal had to admit that was pretty clever. Usually, when Thomas raised the quivering ball of quills on the end of his tail and shot them through the air, most of them missed—but enough of them struck to bring the victim down. He imagined Abigail zipping away out of reach as needles rained down . . .

"Trouble is," Abigail said quietly, "Jolie *wanted* me small. Quick as a flash, she darted forward and swatted me out of the air. I was out like a light."

Jolie laughed from higher up. "It was *so* easy. All I had to do was stuff you in that stupid bronze box, put a rock on it so you couldn't get out, and dump you on the edge of that stream near your house. It runs all the way down to the river, so I just needed to tell my wonderful husband-to-be about the little gift I'd left him. That's why I arranged a picnic on the river. You all *loved* the idea."

Hal sighed. He'd been partially correct, then: the jengu *had* swum upstream and stolen Abigail away, only she'd been inside a small box.

"The blood and bit of material were easy to plant afterwards," Jolie boasted. She turned and pulled up her sleeve, where a faint line stretched across her inner forearm. "That was just to spice things up, though. Nothing like the sight of blood spatter to get people worked up." She then showed them how a small piece of fabric was missing from the hem of her dress. Her smart clothes had previously been hidden by her raggedy outer garments.

As she continued up the smooth rocks to the top, Abigail buzzed closer to her. "And you nabbed me for two reasons," she said accusingly. "First, so your people could get their kicks out of torturing me. And second, so you could get your own kicks from all those worried people back at the village—my mom, my friends . . . and Hal."

"And I loved every minute of it," Jolie said sourly.

Abigail returned to Hal and hovered before him as he struggled around an obstacle. "I tried to contact you, but it was difficult on my own and from so far away. Did you hear me?"

Hal stopped dead. "Yes! So that *was* you! In my dreams? Yes, I heard you, but I didn't know . . . well, I didn't realize it was anything but a dream until after I'd woken."

Abigail nodded. "That's what I figured." She smiled. "It's okay. At least now I know I can do the magic."

Jolie prepared to climb out of the narrow gap to daylight but paused again. "There was a third reason to kidnap you, Abigail. You're a royal pain in the backside. That's reason enough, if you ask me. You and Emily together."

Emily gave her a shove from behind. "Get moving."

With one swift move, Jolie hauled herself up through the gap in the rock ceiling. Emily immediately followed close behind. Robbie, silent apart from ogreish grunts from time to time, climbed up after her.

Hal waved Abigail ahead. "After you."

She landed on the rock under the gap and folded her wings away. She glanced at Hal. "So . . . did you miss me?"

Hal shrugged. "Why, have you been somewhere?"

"That's my guy," Abigail said, and patted him gently on the cheek before climbing up after Robbie.

—The phoenix burst into flames. Feathers curled and blackened, and a terrible sizzling and crackling filled the cave. The phoenix quivered not with pain but with the joyful anticipation of a thousand years of life culminating in a cleansing of epic proportions. Once the flames began to flare and glow red hot, the bird raised its head and looked toward the cave ceiling, where thick black smoke rolled—

The opening was tight and the rock about four feet thick, but Hal frantically wriggled up the tunnel into daylight and fresh air, terrified that time was going to run out before Jolie performed her healing trick.

The scenery threw him. He couldn't get his bearings. The sun was to his left, which was west, and he had expected the lake to be behind him to the south, but it wasn't. Instead was a ridge of grassy hills that he didn't recall seeing before. All around were gigantic clumps of rocks and boulders, so it was difficult to see what was what. But there was no time to think about it, and he started to follow the others around the foot of a small hill to where the lake *must* be on the other side.

Jolie stumbled and landed with an *oomph!* sound in the grass. "My ankle!" she moaned. As Hal reached for her, she waved him away and gestured urgently toward Robbie and Emily, who were hurrying on ahead around the hill. "Quick—tell them to be quiet. It's vital that we grab a big fat bird. Don't let them all fly away."

Hal and Abigail quickened their pace, but then suspicion flooded Hal's mind and he grabbed Abigail's hand and stopped her. She blinked at him, confused.

Then they heard Robbie cry out.

Without hesitation, he and Abigail hurried on around the rocks. Hal glanced back over his shoulder as he went, wondering if Jolie's expression was one of genuine surprise or, as he half expected, gleeful anticipation. Somehow he knew that whatever lay around this rocky hill was not something he and his friends were going to like. She had stumbled on purpose.

And now she had vanished.

He grabbed Abigail's hand again and yanked her to a halt. "What?" she said, trying to break free. But Hal shook his head and started tugging her back the way they had come, toward the narrow tunnel they'd climbed out of.

He paused again. The sky looked different. Cloudier than before. Nothing about the landscape looked familiar. And he heard a familiar whooshing, roaring sound, enormous waves breaking on a beach somewhere . . . and the cry of seagulls . . . and the pull of a wind that hadn't been present over the lake.

With a jolt, Hal remembered the taste of salt on his lips as he'd come through the underwater tunnel . . . but then a vision filled his head once more:

—*The flames roared, and the cave was an inferno. Grass and shrubs outside the cave withered and turned to ash. Then, with an explosion of intense heat and boiling black smoke, Jacob was enveloped in a blinding white and blue light that lit up the cave for miles around. A tremendous boom shook the mountain, and a shock wave flattened trees and animals alike—*

At that moment, a blast of air charged with energy shot out of the tunnel in the ground nearby. It made his hair stand on end and the grass wilt. The geo-rock in Hal's pocket grew extremely hot, and he yelped and jumped around, trying to dislodge it. Abigail stared wide-eyed as his sodden pocket sizzled and steamed. Then he managed to pull the rock loose, and it flew through the air and came to rest in the long grass. It lay there glowing brightly for a few seconds . . . and then its light winked out.

As static curled around his fingers, Hal stared in horror at Abigail. Her dark brown hair was standing on end and her smart clothes gradually fading, losing their familiar sheen. She held up her hands in wonder, and Hal saw arcs of blue sparking between her fingers.

Something happened within Hal's body. It felt like something was dying inside, his dragon half being extinguished. He felt empty. A coldness spread over him as his smart clothes instantly lost their warmth and dulled. As he looked in horror at Abigail, he knew she'd felt the same thing, too, because she clutched her face and tears formed in her eyes. The seagulls fell silent above, and there seemed to be a lull in the wind.

—*From within the blinding glare, vivid colors took shape: blues, reds, yellows, greens, all the colors of a young phoenix reborn to the world. The roaring white and blue flames began to ebb as Jacob slowly reared up and, triumphant, spread his new wings—*

His heart thumping, Hal looked again for Jolie. She was nowhere to be seen. He dithered for a second, wondering if he should try to find her or continue on around the rocks and confirm his worst fears. In the end, Abigail made up his mind for him.

"Come on," she whispered, trembling. "I hear Emily crying."

Hal did too, now. They rounded the rocks and found her sitting in the grass, sobbing uncontrollably. Robbie was doing his best to comfort her but seemed preoccupied with the landscape.

There was no lake. Instead, the ocean stretched to the distant horizon. They were on the coast, at some random place along a cliff that went for miles in both directions. In one direction, in the far distance along the coast, loomed a vast city of skyscrapers.

"We're in our old world," Hal murmured. "We went through a hole."

"What?" Abigail gasped. "When?"

He suddenly leaped into action and shot off back the way they'd come, yelling over his shoulder. "Come on! It might still be open!"

He was aware of shouts but ignored them. He searched for the tunnel in the grass that led down into the cavern and plunged recklessly into it. He came down hard on the rocky ledge inside, then slipped and slid down the smooth rocks into the cold water below, where he gasped and floundered. Then he sank below the surface and struck out into the murky depths, feeling for the tunnel that would lead back to the lake.

It wasn't there.

There *had* been a hole, right here, somewhere in the darkness. That was why none of them had seen it on their way through—they'd been blind and rushed, so busy trying not to drown that they'd failed to notice anything strange. This hole wasn't marked on any map, and Hal was willing to bet that Molly herself had been unaware of it.

He desperately searched the wall of rock below the surface where the tunnel should be, touching nothing but smooth wall. His chest felt like it was about to burst, and panic threatened to overcome him. He should have taken a deeper breath. He could go back, calm himself down, take things a little easier . . . but he knew there was nothing to find.

Stunned, he felt the wall all over one more time. But there was no tunnel, not even a dent in the cavern wall.

Hal kicked for the surface. He came up gasping and paddled wearily until he felt rock under his feet. Then he trudged out and looked up to find Abigail waiting for him near the cavern ceiling in a shaft of light.

"It's gone," he moaned.

But she wasn't listening. She was pointing at something in the water, her eyes wide with horror.

Puzzled, he turned. At first he didn't see anything but then jumped back in alarm. Dark shapes moved below the surface, some slowly, others darting back and forth. Sharks? Big fish? Perhaps Jolie hadn't escaped after all and was down there swimming around—

Then one of the figures rose to the surface. Hal yelled and scrambled farther up the rocks, heading for where Abigail called and waved to him. The creature behind him was holding its skeletal scaly hands in front of its hideous face. The creature's glistening pale skin was sickly and bruised, and its long black hair was coming loose by the handful, leaving various bald spots all over its head. With a shudder, chest heaving, the creature began to gurgle horribly as water spewed suddenly from its throat. Then it bobbed in the water, blinking rapidly and shaking its head from side to side as if wondering how it had got there.

The miengu statues had come alive.

Another one surfaced, and then another, each as horrifying as the last. Some of them rose up and mimicked the chest-heaving process, ejecting water from their lungs and sucking in air while swaying unsteadily; others remained submerged with only the tops of their heads and their black eyes visible.

Now Hal understood Jolie's remark about her people smashing the petrified victims into small pieces. She'd known they would come back to life.

Hal scrambled the rest of the way up the smooth rocks and followed Abigail out of the cavern through the narrow aperture in the ceiling. Hal's first thought was to block the gap so the ghastly creatures couldn't follow them, and he yelled frantically at a dumbstruck, confused Robbie to go fetch some boulders.

Only Robbie couldn't transform.

This realization filled him with fear. Suddenly, Hal felt extremely weak and vulnerable. He was just a boy. *Just an ordinary boy.*

Then he got a grip. The miengu couldn't walk. They couldn't follow even if they wanted to. They were trapped down there.

Still, the place gave him the heebie-jeebies. "We need to get away from here," he said, trying to stay calm. He spotted the small geo-rock in the grass and picked it up. It was cold and lifeless. Slipping it into his pocket, he turned to Abigail and Robbie. "Where's Emily?"

Without waiting for an answer, he hurried around the clump of rocks to find her sitting perfectly still, staring out across the sea.

"I'm dying," she said softly as he approached.

"We need to go," Hal said urgently, "or we might die much sooner."

He regretted his words immediately, but they seemed to do the trick. Emily allowed him to help her up. Then Robbie was there at her other side.

With despair in their hearts, the four of them hurried along the grassy cliffs away from the rocky outcrop and toward the distant city. Hal glanced over his shoulder once or twice, expecting to find sinister shapes emerging from the underground cavern.

"There's one good thing," he panted. "If those statues came alive, then maybe Fenton did, too."

The idea of his friend waking filled him with hope and temporarily eased the weight of the problems they faced ahead.

Still, there was no escaping the fact that they were stuck in ordinary human form in a world still afflicted by a deadly virus. Although the tiny yellow mushroom spores were no longer pumping into the atmosphere, they were still floating around the world on air currents, and it would be many months before the air was safe—and even then, a fine coating of the spores lay like dust on every external surface imaginable across the planet: cars and trucks, park benches, windows, rooftops, gutters . . .

In the meantime, Hal and his friends were stuck here, heading for a deserted city no doubt populated by Crazies—those who had survived the virus but suffered terribly and gone insane with pain and grief. Or so the stories went.

"Hold on," Hal said. He and Robbie stopped and lowered Emily to the grass, where she drew up her knees and put her head down to rest.

"Instead of running blindly, we need to figure out a plan. What are we going to do?"

"What *can* we do?" Robbie said plaintively. "I can't change into an ogre. I feel different now. We're not shapeshifters anymore." He looked like he was about to burst into tears. "And we can't go home!"

"Now, hold on," Hal said, holding up his hands. "Think this through. What's the range of this phoenix rebirth event? Blair said hundreds of miles, but nobody really knows for sure. We just need to find a hole well away from the epicenter." He tried to keep the doubt from his voice as he spoke. "Blair said the phoenix was about eighty miles north. Maybe our island escaped the blast? It's worth checking, right?"

Robbie was nodding slowly. "I vote we head there. But we can't transform. What if we get in trouble?"

Hal shrugged. "You think I have all the answers? We'll just have to figure it out as we go along. Hopefully our abilities will return. Our bodies will fight back, and normality will resume."

Abigail grinned ruefully. "Or *ab*normality will resume."

"How can you laugh?" Emily groaned. She looked up at them through teary eyes, and Hal was horrified by her pale, gaunt face. She looked like a ghost. "I'm dying. Are you planning to drag me halfway across the country as well? I can't shapeshift, so I can't heal myself. I might not last more than a day or two." She hung her head again. "I'm finished."

They stood in silence. She was right—there was no way they could carry her everywhere, and she was fading fast. And yet they couldn't transform either so were unable to offer her a ride on either Hal's back or Robbie's shoulders.

"Quit moping," Abigail said sternly, giving Emily a gentle kick.

"But I—"

"Look," Abigail interrupted, "if you give up, then you're really going to be no use whatsoever, and we might as well dump you here and leave you behind. But we need you."

Emily sighed. "For what?"

"To keep us in check. You're good at organizing, Emily. So tell us what we should do first. It's getting dark. Should we start walking and keep going through the night? Or find somewhere to make camp?"

Hal could tell that Abigail had already made up her mind, but her badgering forced Emily to give the matter some thought and take her mind off dying.

The distant city was silent. The western faces of the buildings glinted in the orange sunset, but mostly they stood dark and foreboding. Was there any civilized life in the city? Right now the military would be a welcome sight, even with their ominous face masks, biosuits, weapons, and overbearing attitudes.

A thought struck Hal, and he immediately held up his hands to study them. Were they tingling? Yes, but that was probably the static in the air. Still, he felt obliged to warn the others. "I don't want to add to your misery," he said slowly, "but if we can't shapeshift, and we can't heal ourselves . . . does this mean we're vulnerable to the virus? Should we be worried about that?"

"I don't *think* so," Abigail said, frowning. "We were always immune to it."

"Well, good," Hal muttered. "One less thing to worry about."

As they stood there in silence with a cool breeze tugging at their shirts, Hal's fingertips again found the lump of useless rock in his pocket. He brought it out and stared at it. It looked like any other piece of rock.

He brought his arm back to toss the rock over the cliff. But at the last second he stopped himself, somehow unable to let it go. Flinging it into the sea would be like discarding a memento of a lost world.

With a sigh, he slipped it back into his pocket.

Epilogue

The phoenix emerged with smoking wingtips from the scorched cave. Black grass crunched underfoot.

The evening was fine and clear, and the great bird known to the humans as 'Jacob' felt as though a thousand years of increasing burden had lifted from his shoulders, burned away in a raging inferno. Now he felt invigorated.

This region of the world had been cleansed. The terrible, awful pressure had dissipated and the phoenix felt light and agile, ready for another millennium. He flexed his tingling wings and gazed with awe at the vibrant rainbow of colors across his chest.

Over the centuries, a phoenix forgot just how miraculous and wonderful a regeneration was, not only for the land but for itself. It had no sense of its original birth, yet recalled the last few rebirths over thousands of years. Rebirths were rare enough to instill trepidation in a phoenix, even fear, because it knew that its immortality might one day bow to Mother Nature. In that case, the inferno would be as painful and horrific as it is for mortals. One day in the distant future, Jacob would suffer the same terrible fate.

But not this time.

He launched into the sky, leaving behind a mountaintop of ash. The air felt good—light and balanced, no longer charged with the thick, putrid smell of magic. Even the ground, far below, had faded. At night, Jacob had grown to hate the pockets of energy pulsating below the earth, spilling into the atmosphere, poisoning life and mutating all manner of species. Now the earth's crust was cold and silent, as it should be, its energy spent. His realm had been purified.

For now, anyway.

Unfortunately, magic had a tendency to seep back into the world no matter how well cleansed it was . . .

A note to all kids and parents

Thank you so much for taking the time to read this book! You're awesome! I'd be eternally grateful if you'd leave a review and tell me what you think. Your review helps other readers like yourself find this book and enjoy it.

So I know this one left you with a cliffhanger, but never fear, the story continues to a resolution in the next book, *Roads of Madness*, in which our friends run across gangs of crazy virus survivors on the streets of an abandoned city. Oh, and Robbie attempts to drive a van. How will the shapeshifters manage without being able to transform? Will they get their magic back? Is Emily going to be okay? All will be revealed . . .

Please visit the author's website for more information and to keep up to date with the latest releases.

https://www.islandoffog.com